# THE UNPOSSESSED CITY

ALSO BY JON FASMAN

*The Geographer's Library*

# THE UNPOSSESSED CITY

## JON FASMAN

THE PENGUIN PRESS

*New York* | 2008

THE PENGUIN PRESS
Published by the Penguin Group
Penguin Group (USA) Inc., 375 Hudson Street, New York, New York 10014, U.S.A. · Penguin Group (Canada),
90 Eglinton Avenue East, Suite 700, Toronto, Ontario, Canada M4P 2Y3 (a division of Pearson Canada Inc.) ·
Penguin Books Ltd, 80 Strand, London WC2R 0RL, England · Penguin Ireland, 25 St. Stephen's Green, Dublin 2,
Ireland (a division of Penguin Books Ltd) · Penguin Books Australia Ltd, 250 Camberwell Road, Camberwell,
Victoria 3124, Australia (a division of Pearson Australia Group Pty Ltd) · Penguin Books India Pvt Ltd,
11 Community Centre, Panchsheel Park, New Delhi – 110 017, India · Penguin Group (NZ), 67 Apollo Drive,
Rosedale, North Shore 0632, New Zealand (a division of Pearson New Zealand Ltd) · Penguin Books
(South Africa) (Pty) Ltd, 24 Sturdee Avenue, Rosebank, Johannesburg 2196, South Africa

Penguin Books Ltd, Registered Offices: 80 Strand, London WC2R 0RL, England

First published in 2008 by The Penguin Press, a member of Penguin Group (USA) Inc.

Grateful acknowledgment is made for permission to reprint an excerpt from *Invisible Cities* by Italo Calvino.
Copyright © 1972 by Giulio Einaudi editore s.p.a. English translation by William Weaver copyright © 1974
by Houghton Mifflin Harcourt Publishing Company. Reprinted by permission of the publisher.

Publisher's Note
This is a work of fiction. Names, characters, places, and incidents either are the product of the author's imagination or
are used fictitiously, and any resemblance to actual persons, living or dead, business establishments, events, or locales is
entirely coincidental.

LIBRARY OF CONGRESS CATALOGING-IN-PUBLICATION DATA
Fasman, Jon.
The unpossessed city : a novel / Jon Fasman.
p. cm.
ISBN 978-1-59420-190-5
I. Title.
PS3606.A775U57 2008
813'.6—dc22
2008027002

1  3  5  7  9  10  8  6  4  2

Printed in the United States of America

DESIGNED BY NICOLE LAROCHE

*For my mother and father*

Arriving at each new city, the traveller finds again a past of his that he did not know he had: the foreignness of what you no longer possess lies in wait for you in foreign, unpossessed places.

—ITALO CALVINO, *Invisible Cities*

# THE UNPOSSESSED CITY

ICHIKOV PRISON, INGUSHETIA

WHEN THE HOSPITAL DOOR behind him clanged shut, and the gate to Wing 3 slowly began to creak open, Yegor Semyonovich Glazov wondered how high he could count. Not how high he was able to count in the abstract, of course; though he was merely a rank-and-file guard at Buryatinsky Prison and had never become an army officer, he had education enough to know you could always add one. Instead he wondered how high he would be able to count now: he wondered how many seconds were left in his life.

If he started at sixty and counted backward, would he make it to zero? To ten? To thirty? Surely he could make it to thirty, if only by running. But how could he live with himself afterward if he ran from a fight just because he was outnumbered, hated, and had only his fists when his enemies had knives, clubs, and nails? Maybe twenty, he thought. Twenty would be a good end. People would remember a guard who lived on the other side for almost half a minute.

Yegor remembered what had happened to Yevgeny, handsome Yevgeny, who prided himself on being able to get along with anybody, who told the other guards—his seniors, to a man—that the prisoners were just men like them, caught in worse circumstances. How he and whatever greasy prisoner pleased him that day would stand on either side of the bars, sharing cigarettes, joking, each trying to outdo the other's hard-case childhood stories. One day, after an especially pleasant afternoon chat, fortified by some prisoner-made "vodka" (it involved fermenting cabbage in socks), Yevgeny leaned over to clap a prisoner a manly good-bye on the shoulder. Before you could count to three, there was Yevgeny, lying on the ground crying, his guts on the wrong side of his skin, the sharpened piece of ceramic tile still in him. And that was through the bars, one-on-one. Yegor clenched his eyes shut, but the harder he tried to put it out of his mind, the more his mind became nothing but blood and Yevgeny.

YEGOR KNEW SOMETHING was wrong from the moment the foreigner arrived at the prison. In itself this was nothing new: Russians comprised a small minority of the population of this particular prison, and things being the way they were, there was always an adventuring Arab or Pakistani bent on bringing faith, on turning a nationalist fight into a religious one. But this foreigner was different. He was European, for one thing, with the sort of intense blue eyes you either have to rip out or worship. And he was escorted by a prissy official with a fancy suit and a lisping Muscovite accent. He spoke Russian like he was spitting sunflower seeds out his grandmother's window: careful, precise, one word at a time. What really bothered Yegor, though, had less to do with the foreigner than with how Yegor had acted around him.

It took him back to a freezing night in Perm: he was in his late teens, just old enough to work alongside his father, stamping out grilles and hoods at the Moskvitch factory down by the river. It was dark but not late: time for drinking with men, not eating dinner with family. That night, though, neither father nor son had a kopeck between them, and they decided they had to roll someone. Not hurt them, of course—they weren't criminals; they just needed enough change for a liter of decent vodka to split—but neither did they want to get hurt by choosing someone likely to fight back. His father, wizened little Semyon, with his grinning little slant-eyed monkey face and his nicotine-yellow sandpaper hands, pulled his son down to his size and taught him how to pick a target. First, find a Jew. We're in Perm, so there aren't any. If there isn't a Jew around, what you do is this: walk around street corners and charge through doors as fast as you can. Keep your head down and your shoulders forward; don't watch where you're going. Sooner or later, you'll bump into someone. If the person you bump into shoves you, asks you what the hell your problem is and whether you'd like him to solve it for you, apologize. Not like a girl, you understand, but like a man: quickly, losing no face. But if the person you bump into says excuse me, or asks if you're all right, you take his money. That's your sucker. Anybody who apologizes when he doesn't absolutely have to, for something he didn't even do, is not fit to be called a man. Take his money and send him home to his husband.

When the captain introduced Yegor to the foreigner and the Muscovite, the foreigner stuck his hand out like some sort of puppet on a string. Yegor seized it and started shaking—that's what men do when they meet—but the foreigner was holding out a pack of cigarettes to him. "I give you a gift," he said. His attempt at a smile made him look like he was trying to shove his skin off his skull. "From my country." Yegor said he didn't smoke; the captain said just sell the cigarettes to the prisoners and give the case to your wife; you know how it works. Then, unprompted, Yegor apologized to the foreigner. He even smiled. "Excuse me," he said, making what he hoped was an ingratiating comedian's face as he pocketed the Rothmans in their gold-plated case. "I didn't mean to crush your gift."


YEGOR DECIDED NOT TO COUNT. He decided not to open his eyes. Let them do what they wanted; he wouldn't raise a hand; he would accept his fate. He just wanted Yevgeny to get out of his head. He wanted to die thinking of his wife, his son, the dacha with the tiny stretch of crystal lake outside of Vladikavkaz, those endless summer nights, first with his father and then with his son. As soon as Yegor resigned himself to never being able to picture it again, the image came. He was at peace. The door no longer creaked; it had opened. He was ready.

IN THE WARDEN'S OFFICE, however, they had not been ready for their foreign guest: the tea had arrived too cold, with jam instead of sugar, black bread rather than pastries, and vodka rather than brandy as a corrective. All of this was a standard tea service in Russia, but Skrupshin, the blond Muscovite, knew how important it was to put foreign businessmen at ease, to make them feel, as much as practicable, that they had never left home.

After all, their guest was not a tourist; he was a professional, and Russia was not France, Italy, or Florida; nobody came here for pleasure; everyone—even Russians—would rather be elsewhere. On the other hand, it wasn't as if he could simply take his business elsewhere. What he sought was sold nowhere else. This was capitalism without competition: the kind in which Russia specialized. Skrupshin beckoned his driver over from the corner.

"What is this?" he asked, pointing to the tray and squinting at his dinner with an expression like he had just eaten something disagreeable. The two men made a study in contrasts: Skrupshin was tall and fair, with the sort of preternatural, vapid self-assurance, blow-dried hair, and iron smile associated with television anchors and American politicians. His driver was short and pudgy with tight brown curls, and given to sweating. With his ill-fitting uniform, his nervous smile, and a pallor that gave him a slightly boiled appearance, he looked every inch the low-level apparatchik, constantly trying to gauge which way the wind is blowing, certain that whichever direction it comes from will be unfavorable.

"Tea," he said, clasping his sweaty hands in front of him and giving a little bow. "You asked that I serve tea to our foreign guest."

Skrupshin rolled his eyes and gave his guest an indulgent, apologetic smile, then turned to his driver. "You have been no farther west than Moscow, so perhaps you are unaware how our guest wishes to take tea. I shall explain . . ."

"Viktor," the guest interrupted, raising a placating hand. "It's normal. Please leave the poor man alone. This is perfectly acceptable. As you say, I am a guest. And guests, as you no doubt know I believe"—he inclined his head in a show of false modesty—"must either adapt themselves to the customs of their hosts, or they must leave." They shared the honking false laughter that follows a telling but not especially funny inside joke. Skrupshin dismissed his driver with a wave of the hand, and poured the tea.

"Will you take a correction?" Skrupshin asked, holding the vodka bottle over the cup. He was relieved to see it was Russian Standard, and bore no cartoonish representations of fierce Rus tribesmen or bearded czars.

"Thank you, no," the man sniffed. "I must admit that I find your vodka rather a simple drink. I do beg you will forgive me." Skrupshin stiffened and let it pass. There is a certain look Russian officials get when dealing with foreigners—contemptuous and nervous, as though desirous of a good opinion yet adamant that doing anything to court one would be craven—that Skrupshin forced himself to suppress.

"A simple drink, perhaps, but our own. As you wish." He passed a cup of tea, no jam, without black bread, across the table. The foreigner held the cup gingerly, between his fingertips. He set it down in front of him without sipping. "Perhaps we can find some brandy hidden in the warden's desk. It would be Caucasian, though. Perhaps Armenian. Quite smooth, Armenian brandy," he said, drawing lips down and nodding, in a show of discerning expertise. "And the winner of several prestigious international prizes. No?"

"Thank you. I have no doubt it is excellent. But brandy is one of the few products left over which we Europeans can and should claim outright superiority. I must also admit I do not drink while working. I know it is considered, perhaps, rude to refuse a drink here . . ."

"Many Russians, my friend, also abstain," Skrupshin said defensively. "Do not believe every myth you hear about us."

"Ah, but national myths persist because they are true, do they not? If we can see with our own eyes, and with scientific research, that certain peoples tend to be lazy, shall we say, or inclined toward violence, or their women uncommonly fertile, why should we refrain from saying so?"

"Why indeed," said Skrupshin, raising his glass of tea in a mock toast. "Very well. When you are ready, I will call the warden and we can go inside."

LIKE MOST RUSSIAN SPACES CLAIMED—a single room in a *kommunalka*, a train compartment, a car—no matter how briefly, by a single occupant or family, the warden's office was crammed with objects in an effort to force upon it an air of domesticity: Skrupshin and the foreigner sat in overstuffed chairs littered with pillows and antimacassars. Family photographs, from old black-and-whites in gilt frames to digital printouts, cluttered the warden's desk, behind which Skrupshin's driver sat, occasionally wiping his sweaty hands on his trousers or rubbing a greasy handkerchief across his clammy, pallid bookkeeper's brow.

To climb the long iron staircase from this room to the observation chamber, which sat above the center of the four prison wings like a bird's nest over the spot an *X* marks, was to move from the tranquillity of home into the brutality of the wide world. It sat atop about twenty feet of cement, at the intersection of the two walls that bisected the prison into four wings. Its walls were steel bars; a steel mesh sphere surrounded it, but thanks to years of shots from the chamber into the prison, the mesh hung loose and gapped like an old fishnet. Four men emerged from the trapdoor into the chamber, though there were chairs for only two: Skrupshin and the foreigner sat, while the driver and warden stood.

The warden was old enough to know that when you receive a letter announcing you would be visited by an official from the Interior Ministry all the way from Moscow and his foreign guest, and you were to extend to them every courtesy, you neither asked questions nor sought any further knowledge.

Curiosity kills more Russians than smoking in this part of the world. Still, he couldn't help wondering just what they were doing here: the last government official to visit this prison at the end of the world came in 1977; the warden remembered because it was his first year, and the official—a terrified little Komsomol brat on his first assignment—threw up on himself before addressing the guards. Then there was this visit: once, to "present credentials," a week ago, and now today. What had they been doing for the past seven days? What was there to do out here besides raping and starving? Even kidnapping had declined; nobody had any money for ransom, and nobody could afford to feed the prisoners.

Then there was the sickness. This wasn't the standard Caucasian flu, and it wasn't junk sickness (heroin, meth, or booze) like most of the Russian prisoners had; this was something else. This one actually killed people. The warden himself wasn't worried, of course; he took 100 grams of pepper vodka on rising, another 200 infused with St. John's wort with lunch, and 300 pure with dinner: this would keep any illness at bay. But two of his guards had taken sick, Ikhmat and now Yegor. Replacements were due to arrive, but now they were down to a measly fifteen, including a doctor and two cooks, for 159 prisoners, all in a space built for 50. If it weren't for the sickness, the prison would have revolted days ago.

The warden yawned, leaned back against the wall, scratched the underside of his second chin, and lit a cigarette. The foreigner actually turned around to glare at him, as if he should be forbidden from smoking inside his own prison. He didn't care, not about any of it. If a city pansy and a scarecrow with fascist eyes wanted to kill a week in this hellhole, it was none of his business.

"My God," the foreigner whispered, looking at the scene beneath him. "Never have I seen . . ." He caught himself. "It really is most effective. As you promised."

"Of course," said Skrupshin jauntily, getting his confidence back. He stood up, pulled his jacket into place, and cleared his throat for the full tour. "To your left, you see Wing Four. Here introduction happened twelve hours ago. A prisoner was admitted from Wing Three. You see, in this wing, life proceeds normally, except, you will observe, most of the prisoners are wiping their noses on their shirts repeatedly. They have colds, you see: hardly unusual, given the climate, their diets, their habits, but hardly something to cause alarm. It would not even provide reason for staying home from work." He chuckled.

"In Europe it would," the foreigner said sourly. "We have lost our strength."

"Then it is fortunate indeed we met. Turn, if you will, directly behind you, and you will see Wing Three. Here, too, you see: all normal." The room—less a room, actually, than a sea of pallets, a select few with olive-drab woolen blankets, running from wall to wall, unbroken except for two narrow paths leading to four pit toilets without walls or doors—thrummed with life and hatred. "They were exposed two days ago. Even those with colds have recovered: in the world, they would be living fully, normally."

"Their restaurants, temples, mosques," the foreigner muttered dreamily, almost lovingly.

"And one more turn over this way, thank you. This is Wing Two. Exposure as before: a single prisoner was transferred five days ago. And here, you see, the situation is more serious." Most of the men below were prone on their beds, wiping away sweat, calling out for water, groaning, wracked with pain. A voice, a high and keening wail, carried above the rest, calling God's name over and over. Still, one group of men in the far corner looked healthy enough: they were sitting up, eating, creating more space for themselves by shoving the weaker ones off their beds and seizing them for themselves. And these active men, the foreigner noticed, were all as they should have been.

"And now we come to Wing One," said Skrupshin, assuming a grave and respectful air.

"The first exposure. One week ago. A single package of cigarettes did all of this. Thirty-five prisoners dead, ten still alive. All thirty-five fatalities from the majority ethnic group; six of the ten living from the minority Russian group."

"And the four?"

"Two were vaccinated. They happened to be in the doctor's office recovering from a fight when they were given the vaccine and told it was a vitamin shot. As for the other two, well, they must have had some sort of immunity. That is to be expected with this sort of thing. Nothing is perfect. After all, I'm sure you know some people who never seem to get sick."

"I do indeed. I am never ill." He gave a thin gallows smile and ran a hand over his brush-cut steel-gray hair. "No cigarettes. Little alcohol. A vegetarian diet. A rigorous program of exercise and physical fitness. I wish to live to see my judgment day complete."

"Of course."

"Out of curiosity, may I ask what happened to the guard who transmitted the first cigarettes? The one I met on the first day?"

"Ah, that is an interesting story. Volya," he called to the warden. "The file, please. Thank you. You can see him there, in Wing Three, sitting on the bed. He has removed his uniform jacket and cap, of course, but his trousers, you see, he had to keep." Skrupshin pointed to Yegor, sitting upright in his bed, his blanket pulled around his green trousers, trying to hide them from his new cell mates. "It turns out he does, on occasion, smoke. He admitted to having kept a single cigarette to taste. A foreign brand, he said. He had never tried one before."

"But isn't he . . ."

"No. You would think so, to look at him and to hear his name, would you not? Only his father. His mother, well, you can see here. Ahmadul-laeva. Kept that one secret, I suppose."

"Quite," said the foreigner, raising his eyebrows. "Well, I suppose it can't be helped. I must say I remain skeptical."

"Why?" asked Skrupshin. "Tay-Sachs disease and our Jews—Eastern European Jews. Anemia and Americans of African descent. Cystic fibrosis and northern Europeans. Alcohol processing and east Asians. Nature does it. Why can't we?" He wondered if he spoke too loudly or too quickly: he had anticipated this question, and had prepared perhaps a bit too well to answer it.

"Please," the foreigner scoffed. "You will have to do better than that."

"I can. You know I can. You wouldn't have come if you didn't think I could. If you find this tactic a bit speculative, we have others—three others—that might appeal to you."

"So you have four, in total? Precisely four?"

"Precisely four, yes."

"Selected how?"

"What do you mean?"

The foreigner gave a crisp, mirthless laugh intended to convey that the question was idiotic and that he resented being questioned at all. "I mean, why these four? How did you find them? What do they have to offer? How do I know they will not either return to Mother Russia or refuse to work for me once you have my money? You're not talking about shipping containers full of Kalashnikovs, or even a stray airplane or two. These are people, and people, as I'm sure you have had occasion to find out, are not so predictable."

"I will take your questions individually, if I may. And might I say first that I am gratified to see your reputation for cautiousness is not undeserved." Skrupshin offered the foreigner his most respectful smile, delivered with a slight bow of the head, but received the same icy stare in return. "The four scientists in question were the *zolotoya molodyozh*—

the golden youth—of the Urban Warfare Planning Commission in the mid-1970s. They were charged with developing nonconventional weapons for use against civilian populations, either to soften resistance in advance of an invasion or to quell domestic opposition in a restive territory. These are not weapons of scale, you understand—they are not designed to make a huge show of military might. They are intended, I might say, for more precise and discerning purposes, and whoever obtains their services displays an unusual . . ."

"Please spare me the salesmanship, if you don't mind. You said they 'were': if their talents are so great, why does your government no longer employ them?"

"Money. Simply that. Money. We lack resources. We lost a great deal of territory, many citizens, of course, and then that drunken buffoon started snapping pieces off the state and selling them to his friends. With less coming in, less gets produced. We're barely managing to stay afloat on our own southern border, and we need to retain brute military superiority to stop our neighbors from nipping off every little disputed chunk they want for themselves. Our more imaginative projects are luxuries we can no longer afford."

"Yes. How sad. Then why are they not working for somebody else? Why me, and why now?"

"They're restricted. We may not be able to employ them anymore, but we certainly don't want them where we can't see them, either. So they receive a small pension, comfortable apartments, and, every so often, a visit from the government. They are, of course, welcome to work at certain menial jobs should they require more income, but we're choosy. The woman who engineered today's festivities, for instance, works three days a week at a market stall in Profsoyuznaya owned by her brother-in-law. Can you imagine? A doctorate in biochemistry, a product of the planet's finest scientific education—now she sells Bulgarian shampoo and Chinese mouthwash for ten hours a day."

"So your candidates are smart and they need money. What, then?

Have they been ideologically and culturally vetted, too? How do I know this one will want to work for me?"

"Your cup, if I may." Skrupshin extended a hand. As the foreigner turned his attention to the small table and reached for his cup, Skrupshin flicked his eyes questioningly toward his driver in the corner. Certain confidences even a deputy minister needs permission to reveal. Almost imperceptibly, the driver nodded as he refilled the foreigner's cup from the samovar in the corner of the warden's office.

"These particular scientists," Skrupshin said, "all have families left in Russia. Minimal influence and minimal immigration in all cases. They will be susceptible to certain pressures. Naturally, you might wish to ensure their physical comfort as far as you can, but it will be made clear to them prior to the point of sale and release that their loved ones at home will remain under our supervision. Should you encounter any truculence—assuming, of course, that your offer prevails—simply get word to us in the usual fashion."

"Which brings me to my next question. Delivery. To what extent must I make arrangements on my own?"

Skrupshin extracted a long, thin folder from his briefcase. "Your company, I see, has an office in Hamburg and another in Rotterdam. Is this correct?"

"It is."

"I assume you contract with a shipping company."

"With several, in fact."

"Which means your company is known on the docks?"

"Not only there."

"Of course not," Skrupshin said, reassuring the foreigner of his importance. "Both cities receive goods from Kaliningrad quite regularly. We will get your chosen shipment from the Russian mainland there, and put it on a ship. All you have to do is show up there with blankets and some tea. And the balance of your payment, of course."

The foreigner looked unconvinced. He stared at Skrupshin so intently that the Russian had to fight the urge to look away. "So may I talk with her, then?"

"If you pay," said Skrupshin slowly, "you can do whatever you like with her."

"A disgusting intimation," he said, rising to his feet. "I think I have seen all I need to see here. You will have our offer within two days of my return."

"Fine. I need hardly remind you that you are not the only interested party. A commodity such as this one draws attention from all corners."


As THEY DROVE to the airstrip, the foreigner turned to look at Skrupshin suddenly, as though he had forgotten something back at the prison. "What did you tell the warden, may I ask? And the other prisoners? Surely you don't plan on keeping all of them there forever. Do you?"

"Regrettably," Skrupshin said, "there was a fire at the prison. There were no survivors."

The foreigner looked over his shoulder quizzically at the prison they were leaving, trying to square grammar with observation. He turned to Skrupshin with the same look.

"The fire," Skrupshin explained, "happened tomorrow."

# 2

ROCKVILLE, MARYLAND

SEVEN MONTHS AGO, Jim drove home with the windows open, even though it was raining, hardly a breath above freezing, and the traffic on the Rockville Pike sat bumper to bumper. He had spent the last two hours dicing pickled herring, onions, apples, and dill for tomorrow's salad. His father, Sam, who owned Vilatzer's Fine Foods and Delicatessen for the past forty years, insisted on hand-chopped herring, and since Sam spent a bloody afternoon at the periodontist's, the messy business had fallen to Jim.

Even after washing his hands and scrubbing them with lemon peels four times, the smell still lingered, if not on his hands then on his clothes, hair, and skin. He may have been a decidedly single thirty-two-year-old living in a studio apartment, working at the same job he had when he was fourteen, and driving his parents' cast-off fifteen-year-old burgundy Dodge Omni with sagging seats and a busted tape deck and a starter that sometimes sounded like marbles skittering down a washboard, but at least the Omni didn't smell of pickled fish, and he wanted to keep it that way. Since moving back home after his engagement to Serena ended almost two years ago, he had come to cling to these small moral victories.

Just past Grosvenor, at the 495 junction, an accident slowed the traffic to a crawl, then bottlenecked it into one lane. Jim gritted his teeth and pounded the steering wheel impatiently, before realizing he didn't really have anywhere to be. The only thing he had to look forward to tonight was a beer (maybe two, probably three), some music, and a book if he was feeling ambitious, whatever flickered across the screen if not.

This wasn't supposed to happen, he told himself, and not for the first time, either. When he and Serena had split up, it wasn't supposed to take his life, his future, with it. He wasn't supposed to find himself flipping through channels, alone, night after night, especially not at this age. He didn't think of himself as chronologically old, just futureless. He noticed when he read about policemen, or lawyers, or politicians, he had stopped saying to himself, "I wonder if I should do that," and started reflecting on what a shame it was that he would never have the chance to do that.

And as much as he loved his parents and their restaurant, he didn't want to be their shelf stocker, waiter, and kitchen assistant for the rest of his life. He knew he was supposed to be—*everything* was supposed to be—different. Better. Somewhere else. With someone else.

Not without worry, he had also noticed that he recently had become increasingly anxious and irritable in the late afternoon and early evening, feelings relieved only by drinking. Jim grew up hearing his teetotaling mother, Rosie, warn him about "the demon" in his family. He had cousins, even an uncle, whom he barely knew in the flesh but who existed vividly as figures in childhood cautionary tales: Edward who slept on the docks, Margie who gave up two babies and had three more without a husband by the time she was Jim's age, Francis who lost an arm on an afternoon shift at the bottling plant that followed an eight-pint lunch at Ulm's.

Every night, after the calming effects of the first beer and a half, he resolved to teetotal for a couple of weeks, get the dependence out of his system, learn how to let the day's edge fall away on its own instead of knocking it off with magic, glistening shards of the Olds Granddad and

Dominion. The next evening, though, desperate to unclench his jaw and stop his mind from whirring, he would inevitably find himself wandering over to the refrigerator, bottle opener in hand. At least, he told himself, his drinking held steady, in both time of day and quantity consumed. Besides, he rationalized, what about the French and their red wine? Didn't that apply to Americans and a nightly brace of Bud?

Past the accident at last, the traffic started to roll, and Jim calmed a bit. Just past NIH, his phone rang.

"Hello, Seamus," said a man's fluty voice in a lilting accent. "This is Jean-Yves Bienaime." Jim smiled; Jean-Yves's accent and phone manner—and the way he called Jim by his mother-given first name that everyone else not related to Rose had long ago shortened to Jim—always made him smile. Jean-Yves had been working in his father's kitchen, all the way up from dishwasher to head chef, for the last twenty years. He had known Jim for more than a quarter century, and still, every time he spoke with Jim or his parents by telephone, he announced his first and last names, as though they knew dozens of men named Jean-Yves with Haitian accents.

"Hey, Jean-Yves. Working late?"

"No, in actual fact I am just now telephoning from my house. You know that tonight—I might have told you—I will attend Sandrine's recital? You remember?"

"Of course, of course." Sandrine was his eldest daughter, a concert pianist in training, whose pictures he kept not only in his wallet, on the cash register, and on the dashboard of his car, but also sewn into the lining of every baseball cap he wore (and wore out) in the kitchen. On that night she was playing her first recital of the season—Ravel's Second Piano Concerto, Jean-Yves said teasingly, "not one of those boom-boom, bang-bang Russians"—and Jean-Yves had been talking about it for months. He had corralled the entire crew into attending: not only Jim's parents, but also his subordinate cooks, the dour and indistinguishable Pacheco brothers; Guillermo, the tattooed dishwasher who kept a razor in his boot and scared everyone other than Jean-Yves, whom he respected, and Rosie, whom he idolized; several regular lunchers from the office park across the street; and every shop owner in the strip. "Aren't my parents going?"

"Yes, certainly they will be coming. I would have asked you, you know, but a young man has better things to do on a Friday night, doesn't he?"

In fact, this one didn't, but neither did he want to admit that, so he just said, "Well, you know," and let the implication do the work.

"But Seamus, listen, why I am calling is because your father, he is not coming to the recital, because, you remember, Cephas, they don't come this morning, so they say can they come tonight. They give us a huge discount; otherwise we don't get until Monday, you know." Cephas was their main vegetable and dry goods supplier. "And so since we are open both days this weekend your father says yes, of course, come over."

"Right," Jim said, still not quite sure where Jean-Yves was heading.

"Except of course they will come now, after their other deliveries. They say they kept the best out for us, but we see, because sometimes, they . . . No, this imports nothing, I start to ramble. Nerves, you see, for Sandrine."

"No, I understand, completely. She'll do great, though. You know that, right?"

"Ah, of course she will," he declared brightly. "You know, too, that she will. But your father is there, at the store, receiving the deliveries by himself . . ."

"Oh, God . . ."

". . . and with his back, from last month, he's going to . . ."

"Stubborn old bastard."

Jean-Yves made a hissing sound. "Ah, never say this word about your own father. I know you love him, but still, some things . . ."

"I know, I know. It's just . . ."

"Yes, I know that you know. And you know that I know that you know, you know," he giggled. "He is a rock, your father, but even rocks sometimes, they can break. And I would stay to help, but this concert, Sandrine, I just have to . . ."

Jim held the phone away from his face as he sighed and saw his relaxing evening receding in his rearview mirror. He shook his head and pulled into the left lane to turn around. "Hey, absolutely. And anyway, what are you, three years younger than Dad? Is your back really any better?"

"We Haitians are very strong people," he said defensively. "If I had not to go to Sandrine tonight, I would stay and carry."

"Two stubborn old . . . All right, all right. I'm not even ten minutes away; I'm turning around right now."

"Ah, good. I am very relieved. Your father, he makes me promise not to tell your mother about the delivery because she would worry. He says he will come at intermission anyway—Sandrine is in the second half—and say he gets lost driving. This she will have no problem believing, your mother."

"None at all. Listen, enjoy the concert, don't give it another thought. Tell her break a leg."

"It is *us* who will be breaking legs. Running for her autograph after."


JIM PULLED INTO A SPACE right in front of the restaurant. Sam called their strip "the last low-rent block between D.C. and Gaithersburg," which wasn't strictly true, if only because, since he had started using that phrase, Gaithersburg—along with the rest of the outlying Maryland suburbs—had grown up, out, and shiny with new wealth. Somehow, though, as the money had trickled up the Pike from Bethesda, leaving everything glossy in its wake, Vilatzer's Fine Foods and Delicatessen and its eleven neighbors remained as they always were: single-story shops catering mostly to the immigrants and first-generation Americans living in the single-story bungalow homes near them.

Vilatzer's was the sole reminder of the area's Eastern European Jewish past, though it was now run by an Irish American (Jim's mother), with most of the cooking done by a Haitian (an acknowledged master of the blintz, Jean-Yves had become) overseeing two Hondurans and a

Salvadoran. The other stores included O'Malley the Locksmith (run by the Krastevs, a suspicious Bulgarian couple who were utterly terrified of black people, which amused Jean-Yves to no end), Amit's Stationer and Newspapers (the Balakrishnans), Woorijip Korean Goods (Chi-Hye Cho, a forbiddingly tough woman of an age both indeterminate and, to Jim's memory, unchanging), a pager and mobile-phone store (this had opened recently; a group of francophone West Africans could always be found inside, but nobody could tell which of them was the owner and which were customers), Speedy Dry Cleaning (Guanfeng and Gong Yao), a pudgy and morose dentist named Dr. Nissal whose fillings invariably fell out after about three days (how he remained in business was a frequent topic of conversation among the other shop owners), Number One Video Club (the Ghassems), Murphy's Hardware (now run by Murphy's two taciturn sons), a Foot Locker (Manny and Conchita Alvarez), a post office, and, anchoring the place, one of the last Magruder's still standing in the D.C. area. It was shabby, no question, and some developer would inevitably buy it, raze it, and put up a shiny new thicket of stores identical to those found five miles along the Pike in either direction, but it was home.

Also, at seven thirty p.m., it was not just closed but dead. The newer strip across the street offered late hours and the bland comforts of familiarity: Harris Teeter, Cold Stone Creamery, Starbucks, P.F. Chang's. It drew plenty of foot traffic, and a younger crowd: Jim could practically smell the bubble gum and hair spray from where he stood.

Through the restaurant's front window he saw his father sitting in his characteristic end-of-day pose: at the counter seat closest to the kitchen and farthest from the front door, *Post* crossword in front of him, pen in his right hand and a glass of beer—always domestic, always canned, always poured parsimoniously into a juice glass, "so it lasts longer"—by his left. He sat ramrod straight, reading glasses perched on the tip of his nose, his full head of wavy black hair brushed back from his forehead by the ever-present comb in his shirt pocket. He pursed his mouth, drummed the pen against his fleshy lower lip, and drew his thumb-thick, caterpillar eyebrows together in concentration.

"Hey, Dad." The door wasn't yet locked. The chairs in the dining area were stacked on the cleaned tables (eight Formica four-tops, each with four red Naugahyde chairs, and four booths along the side wall, also with Naugahyde seats); the salads and prepared foods were smoothed over in the glassed-in counter fridge and covered with plastic wrap; the plates, glasses, mugs, and saucers stood stacked like waiting soldiers along the counter's back wall. The only sounds were the hum of the refrigerator cases and the occasional bubble rising from two huge stock-pots that simmered overnight on the stove's back burners.

Just as Sam took a feline pride in his appearance, so everything in the restaurant departed from and returned to its proper place. Once set free from its moorings, everything had a trajectory. He and Jean-Yves shared a fanaticism about this; his son had learned over the years to respect and understand the need for order, but it wasn't in his bones.

"Jimka," Sam said quizzically, using the Russglish nickname that his parents, Russians both, had used for their oldest grandchild. "You hear this?" he asked, pointing to the radio above the stove.

"No, what's going on?"

"Prison fire in Russia. About eight hundred people died." Sam shook his head slowly, looking down at the table and idly sweeping away invis-ible crumbs. He was always a news fanatic—subscribed to three papers, had the radio or CNN on constantly at the restaurant—and sometimes Jim thought it was just to hear what was happening in Russia, just to feel relieved anew whenever he heard bad news. Sam had neither set foot in Russia nor ever really escaped Russia. "I'll say it again, Jimka: thank God we got out." He looked at him and smiled sadly. "Thank God you were born here."

"You were, too, Dad."

"Yeah, but . . . not the same." It was true, of course: no two genera-tions are ever the same; Jim was born a mile up the road to American parents, while Sam was born just three months after his parents had fled post–World War II Minsk and landed, somehow, in a one-bedroom apartment next to the railroad tracks in what was then rural Wheaton.

But Jim heard the words' frayed and forlorn edges: I started working when I was fifteen and *had* to open a restaurant, but you, son, you could have been—should have been—anything. "Anyway, what did you do, forget something? Jean-Yves just left; we're all closed up."

"No, no. I got everything of mine." Given his father's pride, Jim was reluctant to tell Sam he had come back to help—he knew that would meet with dismissal or belligerence—but he couldn't think of anything convincing. Besides, given his gloomy mood on the ride home, he needed to feel good about *something* today, and the fact was, he rationalized, Dad needed to understand he couldn't go lifting boxes down stairs at his age anymore. If it rubbed him the wrong way a bit, so be it. "I'm here for Cephas."

"Oh, I'm taking care of that." Sam laughed, waving a hand toward Jim as he turned back to the crossword. "A few cases of onions, two boxes of carrots, some lettuce, cans, bottles. Just the usuals. Nothing. Jean-Yves can give me a hand if I don't . . ."

"He's at Sandrine's concert, Dad. I'll just lug a few . . ."

"I told you, Jimmy, I got it." He raised his head and lowered his voice, erasing the expression from his face, trying to seem both reasonable and ominous. "You and your mother, you know, always worried about something. Like nothing really counts unless you wring your hands bloody over it. What do you think, I'm going to cripple myself carrying a few stalks of celery into the basement?" He ran a hand as casually as he could over his shiny hair, patting his annoyance down, and peered at Jim over the tops of his glasses. "I been doing this since before you were born, you know."

"Dad, I know. And I'm not trying to . . . I don't want to get in your way. You've been working all day . . ."

"Well, so have you. You spend as much time on your feet at this place as I ever did. Half the time I'm here these days I'm on my ass in the back office anyway."

"Dad, look, would you just let me . . ."

"No, Jimmy," he said, his voice rising. He forced a little giggle that sounded both pathetic and aggressive. "No. Look, this is *my* place, you understand? I built it and I can still run it, and . . ."

"No one's trying to take it away from you, Dad, but you spent a week last month on your back. I'm here offering to do *manual labor* on a Friday night, for Christ's sake."

"Don't tell me you have something better to do."

Jim blinked and jerked his head back as if he'd been slapped. No sooner did Sam say it than he knew he shouldn't have. He stared intently down at the counter. Jim wanted to punch this sad, self-satisfied, blinkered old man as hard as he could, over and over, until he was on the ground where he belonged, writhing, bleeding, and apologizing; he also wanted to run from the room crying. As it was, a middle path opened.

"Cephas," announced a hairy little testicle of a man at the door. "You gotta order here I take around back or maybe what you gonna want me to do with 'em?"

"I'll take them here," said Jim, not even looking at his father.

"You sign for 'em? 'Cause usually it's him back there or the red-haired lady, or sometimes that nice-talkin' *mavros*, who signs."

"Sure, he can sign," Sam said quietly. "He's my son."

Sam rose but did not move toward Jim. "Look, I didn't mean . . ."

"Don't worry about it," Jim replied quickly, unforgivingly. "Let me just get these down the back stairs and I'll get out of here."

The driver hadn't even laid the first box of onions flat on the ground before Jim grabbed it and walked as quickly and purposefully as he could to the back of the restaurant, avoiding eye contact the whole way as Sam stood shipwrecked by the kitchen—his shoulders sagging, eyes downcast, pen still dangling from his limp hand, feeling both the usual twinge in his lower back and the shame, anger, and frustration burning off his son.

It took Jim just over twenty minutes to carry the boxes down the precarious wooden staircase that led to the supply kitchen and rotate the back supplies forward. As he ran up and down the stairs, hoisted the boxes as quickly and violently as he could, he didn't once pause or look up from his task. He worked angrily, efficiently.

Sam returned to the counter and pretended to focus on his crossword. He opened a second beer. He and his son shared this silent, furious industry; at their angriest, both men were silent, purposeful, outwardly still but inwardly as taut as a guitar string. Sam felt the father's pride, cold as it was now, at seeing himself in his son's Vilatzer rage. He knew enough to stay out of his son's way.

When Jim came up the stairs for the last time, shutting off the stairway light and shutting the door with deliberate, protracted quiet behind him, Sam stood up, tried to smile, and started to raise both his arms, whether to explain or hug and simply admit defeat not even he fully knew. Jim cut him off before he even started to speak.

"I'm done, Dad. All set. I'm taking off."

"Jimmy, listen, I really didn't . . ."

"Forget it." Hearing it was bad enough; having to endure his father apologizing for saying something that, though mean, was true would have been even worse. "I don't know if I'll be in until later tomorrow. After lunch. That okay with you?"

"Sure, sure. Whenever you can." Sam licked his lips nervously and seemed on the brink of saying something else, but instead just chuckled. "You can help it, try not to get old. The other thing's worse, sure, but if you can, try to do me one better and stay thirty for a while."

"I'm thirty-two, Dad."

"You know what I mean."

"I do."

"Thanks for doing that. With the boxes and my back, you're probably right. I appreciate it."

"No charge, Dad. See you tomorrow."

THE SECOND CALL CAME as he waited at the light on Rollins Avenue to turn back onto the Rockville Pike.

"Mr. Vilatzer?" a guttural, accented voice inquired.

"Who is this?"

"Am I speaking with Jim Vilatzer?"

"First tell me who's calling."

"I dislike repeating questions, and I can only assume that if you were not Jim Vilatzer you would have made that clear. I am an associate of Predrag Sjindic."

A single current sent Jim's heart into his throat, sweat onto his palms, and his gut in motion. When the light turned green he drove straight across the pike into the parking lot of the new mall, heading for a space far from the crowds and out of sight of his family's restaurant. "What can I do for you?" he asked, forcing his voice to stay calm.

"Well, many things. We wish first to inquire into your health. You have not been seen in many weeks, and we felt some concern for you."

"I'm fine, thanks."

"Where we come from, one cannot simply disappear, or alter one's habits, without drawing concern. And if this concern is thrown back in our faces, with sarcasm, for instance, or by doubting our intentions, it can turn to suspicion, and then into anger, and in such situations, nobody is happy. Everyone gets hurt, but some more than others. Do you follow me?"

"I do."

"Predrag has wished to speak with you for some time now. He has come, at the expense of time with his family, to the Tuesday and Thursday evening games. Early, of course, but also late. According to our memory, you were last seen nearly a month ago. You had an excellent evening that night, yet you left us less than what we would consider a fair amount of your winnings. It caused us to doubt your expediency and your good intentions. It places us in the unwelcome position of standing before you with our hands out. And that, I can tell you, we have a most difficult time doing. That we will not do more than one time. That position we consider beneath us. You, Mr. Vilatzer, do you think of us as beggars? As simple foreigners? As stupid people there for your advantage?"

"No, of course not. I just haven't had . . . I haven't had a lot of luck recently."

"Luck, Mr. Vilatzer, is something that never used to concern you. Your problem, if I may be so bold as to offer a diagnosis, is greed: you started betting on sports, playing craps and blackjack—games we would have thought beneath you—and you ran out of opponents at the poker table. But all of this is what you might call water under the bridge." He paused, and Jim heard pages flip. "We have no choice, given your absence and the lack of courtesy with which you treated us when last we met, but to call in our debt. The full debt."

Jim let his head fall forward against the steering wheel. "What's the full amount?" he asked, marble-mouthed.

"Our records place you at twenty-four thousand two hundred dollars." After a long pause, the man asked, "Do you have any reason to dispute that?"

"I . . . No. No *good* reason."

"Yes, well, 'I don't wish to pay' is not, of course, a good reason. Mr. Vilatzer, we will give you two weeks to pay us what you owe us. After that time we will have to take some steps that may prove unfortunate. Do you understand?"

"I think so."

"This is not a threat, you understand. It is a question of cause and effect. You know where to find us. Two weeks. And if we hear from you sooner with some substantive progress, we may be able to discuss a gentler timetable. Nobody wishes any unpleasantness upon you, Mr. Vilatzer. Nor do we wish to seize or cause any harm to Vilatzer's Fine Foods and Delicatessen on Rollins Avenue. But the truth is we live in an unpleasant world, and there is no other world but this."

With that, he hung up, and Jim sat still, eyes shut, head braced against the steering wheel, listening to the giggles and squeals of bright futures all around him. He pounded the dashboard five times, as hard as he could, after which he still had nothing to do on a Friday night, no discernible future, and a twenty-four-thousand-dollar debt, but now his hand hurt also. A gaggle of high schoolers, having seen and heard Jim's pounding as they were walking to their car, stared at him with hovering expressions, unsure whether to run, laugh, or call the police. He stared back and they hurried away, leaving him feeling wound up, cheated out of a confrontation. Teetotaling was for better men than he.

"How much?" asked Vivek. He and Jim sat across from each other, yet again, in the comforting, seedy, beery darkness of The Rook, on Mount Pleasant just off Irving. They had known each other for almost thirty years, since the first day of kindergarten. Vivek was the immigrant boy-done-good: college, law school, a respectable job (a lawyer for the *Washington Post*), marriage to an acceptable girl (a pretty Bengali, Anjali, from a good family), and a house that he owned in the suburbs, ten minutes' drive from both sets of parents. He and Jim saw each other less than they did in their teens and twenties—work and a baby son on one side, embarrassment and shame on the other—but still, Jim knew nobody else he could call and wheedle out for a beer at such short notice.

As with any longstanding friendship, each had his own suspicions about the other, and each had his suspicions about those suspicions: Jim sometimes thought Vivek would rather spend time with like-salaried friends; Vivek sometimes thought Jim looked down on him for abandoning his family business (his father, Amit, ran the newsstand in the same strip as Vilatzer's), for marrying too soon, and for chasing the trappings of success too eagerly. Neither of them was right, of course, and when they actually saw each other both had good enough sense to let their guilt-inspired awkwardness fall away. Like most old friends, at some point they had moved from talking about recent experiences and meetings back to one lifelong conversation between them, punctuated by absences of irrelevant length but restarted easily and comfortably. Not many thirty-two-year-olds had an active quarter-century friendship; they were both only children, and each was the closest thing the other had to a brother.

Vivek (the older brother) sighed as Jim struck a match. "Nobody smokes anymore, man. People look at you funny if you do."

"Yeah? Listen, this miserable fucking day gives me a pass, okay? This one's for free. Anyway, since when did you get concerned about health?"

Vivek rubbed the shelf of his gut and shook his head. He looked like a mocha snowman, with the jowly, all-over paunchiness of the expense-account luncher. "Health's nothing. I'm talking about class." He made a smoothing movement with his right hand. Since Jim last saw him he had exchanged his digital watch for a chunky gold monstrosity that rattled and snicked when he moved his hand. His fingernails were perfectly rounded and almost shone. "Smoke when you're fifteen, eighteen, twenty-one, that's one thing; it's still cool. Smoke when you're our age you're a smoker. It's a weakness. Low-class. Kills you, sure, but that won't happen for a while. Problem is, it makes you look bad in the meantime." He chuckled, then fell back into seriousness. "Really, how much?"

"About twenty-four thousand dollars, give or take."

Vivek pressed his lips together and gave a lawyer's curt nod: either a good lawyer is never surprised, or twenty-four thousand dollars was too little money for Vivek to sweat over. "I'm guessing you wouldn't be acting like this if we were talking about credit-card money or overdue car payments."

"I wish. The Sjindic brothers. You remember? When you used to come out to College Park to visit and we'd play poker in the back room of that little wood-paneled diner, Skadarlija, thinking how cool and edgy and underground we were?"

"Yeah, sure," he said, his smile broadening—maybe a little ruefully, given his current respectability—at the memory. "You been playing with the frat boys out in College Park and you're still twenty in the hole?"

Jim laughed despite himself. Predrag and Dragan—Petey and Donny to their customers—Sjindic ran an informal full-service casino in the back room of their restaurant: poker tables, blackjack, craps, and a sports book for University of Maryland students and their friends. Because their customers were mostly students and their games low-stakes, they ran afoul of neither the Chinese, Russian, nor, increasingly, Albanian gangs who ran the more serious gambling businesses on the East Coast. Also, students scared better than working people.

"You believe that?" Jim asked. "If I'd just stayed at the tables it would have been fine. I took a beating in the basketball playoffs, I was pretty much out of commission after the Series, and I've been trying to get back up with football. No luck. Frat boys won't even sit down with me anymore; not for love, money, or begging can I get in a poker game. The Sjindics saw all of this happening, and what could they do? They called in the marker. I don't know why they let the debt get this bad."

"I do. You're not a student; they figure you have a job, maybe a home. Means you can pay more. How did they call it in? When?"

"Couple hours ago. Right before I called you." Jim told him about the phone call in the restaurant parking lot.

"So you didn't see anyone? Nobody in person, I mean?" Vivek asked.

"Nah. Haven't seen any of them in a few weeks. You know, Petey's got the same damn coat he had ten years ago? Just sits there smoking and staring ice at everyone, wearing that leather bathrobe and not saying anything. He's the guy they want out front. The one who looks good, who makes the kids feel all scared and cool at the same time. Truth is he's mad as cheese."

"Mad as what? What's that mean? That one of Rosie's?"

"Close. Ulm's. Her father's."

"Yep. Figures. Better still."

"Yeah, it has that old-country sound."

"Not to me, Babuji."

Jim smiled, blinking a tear away and lighting another cigarette. He thought of Ulm and Eithne, his mother's parents, and of his other grandparents, too, the Vilatzers, and what they would think of him now, their first real American, feckless and in debt on the near side of thirty. After they died his grandparents only grew more immanent; aging, without grandchildren, Jim's parents were growing more preoccupied with their pasts than their futures. For this, too, Jim felt immense guilt—Jewish guilt, Catholic guilt, only-child guilt, wayward-son guilt: he had them all; they were all a balloon rising slowly up his esophagus now, slithering into his tear ducts, choking off his voice and forcing him to keep his eyes on the table. Vivek courteously absented himself to the men's room.

By the time Jim swallowed everything, Vivek came waddle-striding back to the table with more Rook-appropriate drinks: two bottles of Bud Light and two shots of whatever was brown and in the well.

"You need some help? I mean, some . . ." Vivek trailed off, shrugging and grinning. "Some help. You know?"

Jim gave a sardonic little laugh that came out nastier than he intended. "Who from? You? You're in debt now what, over a hundred? Four years of college plus three of law school minus a few years of payment? And that Beemer, and a wife, and probably another kid or two soon?"

Vivek shrugged but didn't look at Jim. "Just offering. I didn't mean anything, I just . . ."

"I know. Sorry."

He waved the apology away but looked up again. "What about your family?"

"You were in my position, you'd go to yours?" Rose Vilatzer and Sunita Balakrishnan used to end their workdays with a glass of tea in the store while Sam and Amit had beers in the restaurant. The Balakrishnans instilled the same drive and terror of failure in Vivek as Jim's had in him, but with Vivek it seemed to have taken. He shook his head no.

"Hey, look," Vivek said, reaching across the table and laying a reassuring hand on Jim's forearm. "I know what you're worried about, and what these boys aren't going to do is take Sam and Rosie's place. They don't want it. They don't want their name on it; they wouldn't know what the fuck to do with it. Anyway, Rosie wouldn't let them. No way. Sam, sure, maybe, but your mom, no."

That raised a knowing smile from both of them. "Worst that happens to the restaurant is they start showing up, scaring away other customers, maybe throw a few rocks through the window. It's bad, sure, but then that draws the police, trouble, headaches. They just want to get paid, right? Right?" He waited for Jim to nod. "They don't want to hurt your family, right?" Another nod. "Or you." This time a skeptical half nod. "Or you," he repeated. "You go to the police, their operation's done. I'm guessing they're too small to have cops in their pockets. They may even pass on some information here and there. The cops stay indifferent as long as they stay quiet and helpful. They're small and safe, and smart enough to understand they need to stay small and safe. So knowing all of that, what do you want to do?"

"I don't know. I've got maybe seven thousand dollars in the bank. Maybe. I'd play for the rest, but the only game I know Petey and Donny are running. I don't want to sit down at a table where I don't know anyone in a situation like this, when I need to win so badly."

In the middle of beer number six, Jim reached the point where he could talk. "What I really want to do, you want to know the truth, is just take off. Send Petey a little more and tell him I'll get it to him eventually. Tell him I know the vig's running, I know I shouldn't have left, I understand all that, but that I just need some time and quiet. But I guess bookies aren't usually known for their compassion, right?"

"True. You send him a little and I could write him a letter."

"You? Why?"

"Look, this guy's as small-time as you say he is, maybe a letter from a lawyer'll buy you a little breathing room. Maybe it'll intimidate him a little. Someone comes at you with thumbscrews, or throws a couple of bottles through Sammy and Rose's windows, he'll know someone else knows who it was. Can't hurt, right?"

"Can't hurt. Thanks." Jim raised his bottle and tilted the neck toward Vivek while looking down at the table. The unexpected but characteristic canny decency of Vivek's offer combined with beer and self-pity almost brought Jim to tears. He fought it by talking. "I just feel like a fuck-up, you know? Like I've fucked up my life and I can't stop fucking it up. Serena, Boston, three years, and what's left? Just come crawling home to Mommy and Daddy? And I need to just . . . I need to just let everything stop for a minute, you know? Just get to someplace where I can just think about what I did and what I want to do and how I can do it. What I really want right now is just to go someplace where nobody knows me or my family or all the things I should have been, and just try to think for a while. So that I don't just head off somewhere else without a plan or a reason to go."

"Hey." Vivek reached across the table and gave Jim a reassuring shoulder-clap. "First, you know this is a lot of bullshit, right? You're not fucking anything up by working at your family business, first of all, and second, man, we're thirty-two. That's it. It's not like we're felons, or like you can't pick yourself up if you want to. Your problem is, when you get something in your craw you can't just let it go. It's why you like gambling so much: you just love beating people; you love outthinking them, being right. Now you got the idea of your own failure in those Jewboy teeth, and you just can't spit it out, even though it's just as much bullshit as the idea that winning a few hands of poker makes you better, overall, than the guy you're sitting across from. Too much stock in visible winning and losing, and not enough in the long term. Anyway, that's about it for me and the headshrinking. But let me just ask this one: you've been waiting it out here a while. Why not just a little longer? Move back home, maybe you save up money, send him a little at a time?"

"Because then I'd have to tell Sammy and Rose about it. Then I'd have to hear them tell their friends that their thirty-two-year-old son moved back home." Jim shook his head and stared down at the table. "Working at the restaurant's one thing, but heading back to my room with the Redskins pennants and old baseball trophies I just can't do, okay? And don't tell me I need to try, because I know and you know if you were in my situation you couldn't do it either."

Vivek nodded his agreement then looked at Jim intently, a doubtful expression on his face. "You really want to head off somewhere?"

Jim shrugged. "Yeah, why? There's a branch of the Balakrishnan empire in Hawaii that's looking for an overqualified stock boy?"

"Man, that's what cousins are for. Don't you remember the Bombay Buffet, in Rutledge Hill? My uncle's place where I worked through college? Brown dude like me macking Southern sorority girls smelling like a fucking tandoori drumstick? Gives me the shudders just thinking about it. Seriously, though, you really want to go somewhere different?"

Jim sighed and ran his hands down his face. The question is different when the answer matters. He couldn't think of a single reason to be anywhere, really. Departure was easy; arrival baffled him. Jim nodded.

"Look, this is just an idea, okay, and you may not want to even think about it. I know I wouldn't, but it might help. You see today's paper?"

"I guess so. Why?"

"The Metro profile? Alex Grynshtein?"

"The computer guy?" Calling Alex Grynshtein "a computer guy" was like saying Henry Ford tinkered with go-carts. Grynshtein specialized in bridge software: little bits of code that enabled constant, command-free updating, made embedding video clips into a Web site easier, linked reviews of films and concerts to ticket-purchasing sites. He had emigrated from Homel with his parents when he was eight, made his first $10 million before he left college, and now, just shy of his fortieth birthday, topped the billion mark and was busily engaged in trying to give chunks of his fortune away.

"That's him. He just plunked some money into the Nats. Has a house near Dumbarton Oaks and his wife's starting some horse charity out in Winchester."

"Okay. What about him?"

"Well, that's his wife's first charity, but he started one a few years ago back home. Or home for him, back in Moscow."

"I thought he was Belarussian," Jim said.

"Yeah, I guess."

"Moscow's in Russia. Two separate countries."

Vivek sighed and rubbed his eyes. "Look, you want me to keep going?"

"Yeah. Sorry. Didn't mean to get pedantic, but home's home."

Vivek waved the concern away. "Anyway, it's called the Memory Foundation. Does any of this sound familiar?"

"No. What did you do, memorize the article?"

"Yeah, me reading: funny, right? No, the guy who profiled him is a friend. Josh Rosen; did the March Madness pool last year. I gave him a lift home is all. He liked Grynshtein, and they just got to talking after the interview. He started the Memory Foundation a few years back because his father and both grandfathers spent some time in mental institutions. They used to . . ."

"I know. For political reasons. My great-uncle died in one."

"Oh. I'm sorry, I didn't mean to . . ."

"Don't worry. Go ahead."

"So he gave this foundation some start-up money, and I think Soros and MacArthur threw in some more. What it does is, it interviews political prisoners in Eastern Europe. While they're still alive. He wants to have the testimony on record."

"Interesting."

"Yeah, it is. But he says he's having staff trouble. The Middle East and South Asia are taking most of the professional nonprofit types away. 'Russia isn't sexy anymore,' he says. He's been relying on college students mostly, but says their Russian isn't good enough."

"Why's he hiring foreigners at all? Why aren't the Russians the ones asking the questions?"

"He's got this thing about opening up Russia to the West and the West to Russia. He's working with a local group; I can't remember the name . . ."

"Pamyat. Memorial. My grandmother talked to one of them about her brother Borya, the one who died in an institution. Every so often they'll send her something."

"That's it," said Vivek, breaking out his showman's smile. "See, you're qualified already. Know more than I do. Anyway, I think he also has a grudge against the Kremlin. Tried to start some kind of manufacturing concern over there and got chucked out. He says he wants to make sure there's a historical record of Soviet atrocities outside Russia. Just in case. You can imagine how popular this makes him and his foundation. Says that's another reason they might be having problems: visas haven't been getting renewed." Vivek drained his bottle and blew across the top. "So that's the story. Language is a problem, and the staff keeps getting told to fuck off. Now, you, you speak Russian pretty well, right? And you get told to fuck off all the time."

Jim smiled. True enough, especially today.

"And you do speak Russian well enough, right?"

Jim nodded slowly. It was rusty, but there: his father's parents spoke only Russian, and he had made Jim speak it with them when he was little, then go to Russian language classes on the weekends until he was old enough to learn how to skip them. By then, though, the damage had been done: he learned it young enough so it was imprinted.

"Come on; I've heard you and Sammy jabbering away at each other. You speak it fine. Better than my Hindi, anyway. You always were afraid to take a little credit."

"What are they going to do: just hire me because you said so?"

"Something like that. Maybe. Why? You too proud for Papa Vivek now?"

"Never. Never ever ever. Seriously, though. I don't have any experience with this kind of work."

"First of all, who cares? You're smart and you'll learn." Vivek and his lawyer's penchant for delivering arguments in lists. "Second of all, you're being paid to talk to people. Persistence, that's it. Third, I hate to bring this up, but the publisher? The one you worked for before? In . . . in Boston?"

Jim leaned across the table, smiling and making a "go-ahead" gesture with his hand. "*Boston*'s not a dirty word, you know. I have no problem with Boston. It's just a city. I lived there."

"Yeah, with . . ."

"You know, she just e-mailed me to say she's getting married. Some actor she's been with since we split. She wants to make sure I'd understand if she doesn't invite me to the wedding. Anyway, I was a researcher. Basically a fact-checker, with a few additional things thrown in. Why?"

"Same kind of stuff, I'd think. Or close enough. What do you think? Josh said he and Alex got along well; you want, I can start the phone chain going."

Jim opened his mouth, ready to laugh at the idea of just picking up and heading to Moscow with an entirely new job, new life, but no sound came out. What was so ridiculous, after all: he said he needed to get away, and he did; he spoke a reasonable amount of Russian, though at this particular point, without further practice, his ideal conversational partner would probably be a precocious ten-year-old with an intense interest in food and a detailed knowledge of the D.C. suburbs.

While he wasn't too fond of the bureaucratic exigencies that came with his job at the book publisher's, the truth was he loved the research aspect of it. He loved the act and process of discovery. He thought of it the way he did a poker game: he wanted information—whether, say, demographic shifts in the Berber population of Algeria, or whether the fat guy with the mustard-stained T-shirt across the table really held what he was representing—and the world wanted to keep it from him. Discovery was victory. Vivek caught the positive hesitation, the thoughtful narrowing of Jim's eyes.

"You want to go, I'll try to make it happen," he said, the Southern accent returning along with his salesmanship. "I mean, it won't be glamorous, but you've been an editor before; you speak the language; you're a charming motherfucker when you want to be. I mean, not like me, of course, but for a glum, stubborn little prick you can crank up the grin machine when you think it'll win you a fight or a couple hands."

"Hey, thanks. You don't know how much . . ."

Vivek waved him away. "Look, I'm just teasing, right, and you know you need to be teased a little bit. You head over there for a year, get paid a decent American salary, live on the cheap, and head home, cash in hand. I'm guessing most of your work will be cash and contract stuff, too, so you can afford to shade your taxes a little. Not like you know anyone there, right? Not like you're the type to go out to those three-hundred-dollar-a-drink clubs or whore it all away, right? And no gambling, either. Right? I'm serious. Right?"

"No gambling. Promise."

"'Cause if I do get you over there and anything happens I'll have to carry it with my folks and yours, right?"

"What, now I'm your son?"

"And listen," Vivek said, lowering his voice and leaning across the table, "just one more little bit of advice. Call it professional advice, okay?"

Jim rolled his eyes, but said nothing. Vivek loved playing the worldly-wise older brother to Jim's charming Peter Pan, and if he was going to take a handout he had to listen to what came with it. He nodded.

"Head down means head down. You're going to give me what you've got in the bank, what you can give, and I'm going to send a letter to your creditors along with a check. I'm going to put myself out for you here, okay, so Sammy and Rose won't have their legs broken or their cold cabinets split open. In return, you just do what you need to do to get the cash together and head back. I know leaving like this doesn't sit well with you, but don't sabotage yourself here. Figure out which way the current's flowing and flow with it. Don't get anything stuck in your teeth."

"Like you?"

"Hey, man." Vivek grinned and returned from hunched-over-counselor position to reclining friend, jangling his Beemer keys and rattling his gold watch on his wrist. "Just like."

THREE AWKWARD, painful weeks elapsed between Jim's decision to leave and his flight to Moscow. It took him ten days to work up the courage to tell his parents his plan. When he finally did, one night as the three of them were closing up the restaurant—Rose counting out the cash and checking the register receipts, Jim washing the dishes and scrubbing the grill, Jean-Yves rotating and restocking the walk-in, Sam sitting at the counter nursing a juice glass of beer—it went over poorly. Jim realized as he showed them his ticket—and saw the expressions on their faces move from the expectation of a joke to befuddlement to shock to, finally, resignation—that it was the one impulsive decision he had ever made in his life. It felt irrevocable and liberating, like stretching your legs after a long airplane flight.

Sam and Rose shared the risk aversion born of poor, immigrant upbringings: they owned their home outright, had negotiated the best long-term lease possible on their restaurant, and had a couple of smaller rental properties behind the train tracks off Twinbrook Parkway. They spent every Easter with Rose's sister in Baltimore, a week every summer at Rehoboth, Christmas at The Angler's Rest in Easton, and Thanksgiving with Sam's brother in Silver Spring. Boring, perhaps, but it was the kind of boredom that most of the planet's six billion inhabitants could only dream of. For both Sammy and Rose, this was it; this was why their parents had come over: a house and a business of their own, where nobody bothered you because of your accent or where you worshipped, where the law protected you and you knew what tomorrow would look like. The idea of picking up and moving to Russia (or, as Sam said, "going back") was insane, incomprehensible, lamentable.

There were tears followed by silence. There were recriminations all around. Then there were questions. Jim said he had to get out of a rut. He said he had to do something different, see the world. Vivek mentioned this job the other night, and it was an opportunity he couldn't turn down. All true explanations, to a point, but all chosen more for their blandness than for their truth. A couple of times, on the tense and teary ride to the airport, he tried to tell his parents about the Sjindic brothers and his debt, but he couldn't quite manage a way into the story. He couldn't quite tell them that he had put everything they were, everything they spent their lives building, at risk because of his own stubbornness, profligacy, and failure. The best he could do was make them promise to call Vivek if they ever needed a hand with the restaurant.

The emotional preparations for departure were so intense, so all consuming, that not until the lights dimmed in the airplane and he sat, sleepless but narcotized with whiskey and Valium, sandwiched in a middle seat in the back of the plane between a gel-haired Russian club kid with aerodynamic facial hair and a mousy Mormon missionary in a cheap sober suit and clip-on tie, did it occur to him that the plane would, in fact, disgorge him in Russia.

ONCE THERE, HOWEVER, Jim found his malaise gone almost instantly. It was a wintry, hospital-gray day just over two weeks after his arrival that did it.

Jim had not yet found a place to live. He was still staying in a hostel up in VDNKh (a hideous-looking acronym pronounced semiphonetically as "VedinHA," which stands for Exhibition of National Economic Achievements, the Soviet but still unchanged name of the nearby park), formerly used for provincial school athletic teams visiting the big city, its Khrushchevian grandeur faded and tattered: pilling red carpets, marble floors whose corners were covered in a measurable layer of green slime, rusty chandeliers holding low-wattage bulbs. The mucus-colored walls in Jim's room wept; the water ran either scalding or freezing but in either case brown.

He was on his way back to the faded imperial glory of the Friendship Youth Hostel from yet another unsuccessful apartment viewing—the owners wanted someone "more Western," they said (for which read: a northern European man in a suit, not a swarthy American with a suspicious surname in a sweater, jeans, and boots).

He started work at the Memory Foundation in three days; he had nowhere to live and was frittering away his savings. More than that, he was starting to tire of eating every meal, taking every walk, experiencing everything, alone. He had not yet grown used to the city's brutality—its pervasive grayness, its immensity and hardness—and was having one of those endless afternoons of oppressive befuddledment that strikes everyone who moves to a new city alone.

He exited the VDNKh Metro station and headed up Prospekt Mira in the four p.m. gloaming. The Gagarin space-flight monument caught the dying afternoon light and glowed above the gray buildings. It was supposed to represent a rocket soaring into space, but to Jim looked more like the protesting wing of a huge buried bird. He hadn't learned the Moscow Walk—quick, expressionless, squared shoulders, eyes straight ahead but peripheral vision fully engaged—and instead was following the obelisk's outline with his eyes, looking dreamily, curiously upward, when a meaty hand grabbed his arm and a uniformed figure planted itself in front of him.

"Good evening, Akhmed. Your documents, please?" A stumpy, smirking middle-aged officer with the bleary, shifting stare of the almost drunk saluted perfunctorily and extended his hand. He shifted his lower jaw back and forth, giving the impression not of hunger or of someone chewing gum but of some sort of malevolent energy looking for release. His younger, larger companion kept his hand quite firmly on Jim's arm.

Two days before Jim arrived (and much to Rose's worry), a Chechen suicide bomber blew himself up in a St. Petersburg Metro station. Since then Jim had seen trios and quartets rather than the expected duos of policemen in Metro stations. He had seen them shoving around sallow, exhausted-looking Central Asians in the orange jumpsuits of municipal construction workers, but this was the first time he had been stopped. As he would come to learn, the chances of his (or indeed anyone with black hair and olive or darker skin) being "randomly" stopped and searched correlated exactly with the number of days since he had last shaved. Jim was going on eight. He reached into his jacket, and, trying to be accommodating, smiled and said "Sure," in English.

The cop twisted one of Jim's arms and grabbed the other one on its way to Jim's pocket. For all of his fondness for gambling and his taste for risk, he had relatively little experience with actual violence, and found, to his surprise, two things. First, it hurt. It wasn't like watching a fight in a bar or on TV; this was happening not to other people but to him. Second, it sharpened him: after the pain came a tingling rush of temper and a bracing clarity, followed by instructions: *Stay still, stay calm, don't give them the satisfaction of seeing how much it hurts.*

"*Chirr,*" the policeman mocked. "What is *chirr?* Who is *chirr?* What is your fucking country, you blackassed pimp?"

"American!"

The cop laughed and winched Jim's arms, then shoved a knee into his back, driving him to the ground, as the older one grabbed his coat collar.

"Left pocket," Jim said, remembering, this time, to speak Russian.

The cop shoved a hand deep into Jim's jacket pocket, emerging with half a pack of Winstons and a Redskins Zippo, both of which he pocketed, staring down any challenge from Jim, and a passport in a black leather case. "An American passport," the policeman grunted, flipping it open.

He stared from Jim's picture to the Jim grimacing on the ground, then tried to scrape the picture off with a fingernail. Everyone knew that Americans were rich and blond, with straight teeth and loud voices:

this dark, hairy creature on the ground couldn't possibly be one of them—
or if he was, he wasn't the right kind. He licked his finger and rubbed it
across Jim's name. He held the passport by the spine and shook it to see
what would fall out. When nothing did, he reluctantly signaled for the
younger cop to let Jim go.

He released Jim and shoved him forward, into the standing cop,
who kicked him backward. Eventually Jim found his feet. He thrust his
hands deep into his pockets so the cops wouldn't see how much they
were shaking.

"There is a serious irregularity in your passport," the older cop said
with a smirk, tapping the passport with his thumb.

"No," Jim replied, not quite catching on. "You can see, my hotel
registered my passport. I can show you." He reached for the passport
and the younger cop grabbed his arm again.

"No, you cannot 'show' me," the older one sneered. "Tell me, please:
how long did your hotel registration say their stamp would last?"

"They did not tell me."

"And how long have you been on our territory?"

"Two weeks."

"Then I regret to inform you, hotel registrations last only one week.
You will have to come with us. This is a very serious penalty."

Jim felt rage, humiliation, helplessness—a very Russian cocktail. He
cursed himself for not memorizing the embassy's phone number, then
wondering when or even whether he would be allowed to use the phone,
he noticed that neither of the officers was moving. The younger one
released him, but they weren't leading him to their car; he wasn't in hand-
cuffs; instead they stood around, shuffling their feet like actors waiting
for their cue.

Then the proverbial other shoe dropped.

"Perhaps I could pay a fine here," Jim suggested helpfully, "and save
you the trouble of taking me to the police station."

The younger policeman, now standing companionably beside rather
than threateningly behind Jim, looked to his senior with an expression of

eagerness. The older man looked dubious, as though Jim had suggested some sort of unwelcome but regrettably essential innovation. Eventually he shrugged his acceptance; as he looked down and shook his head at the backwardness of the world, Jim caught the fleeting corner of a smile.

"The fine would be very expensive," the younger man said. "But you are an American; you can always get more money."

"How much?" Jim asked.

The older cop pursed his lips and raised his eyebrows, beginning the negotiation. "Five hundred rubles, I would say." About eighteen dollars.

Jim sighed and reached into his back pocket for his wallet. As he pulled it out, the younger cop snatched it out of his hand and grabbed all of Jim's cash: about twenty-six hundred rubles and a pair of folded fifty-dollar bills behind his driver's license.

He handed the money to his superior, then laughed and threw the wallet on the ground, kicking it off the curb and under a parked Lada.

"Five hundred rubles is the penalty. The rest is unlicensed cash." Jim started to protest but the older cop spoke over him. "Do you have withdrawal receipts? No? Then how can we know you obtained this money legally? When you find the receipts, bring them to Kutuzovsky station and ask for Ivanov. I will return your money. Until then, enjoy your stay in our country." He held the passport out to Jim. When he reached for it, the cop flung it beneath the car, next to the wallet.

THE COPS DIDN'T quite take all of Jim's money—he had eleven more fifties hidden throughout his belongings (pressed between book pages, stuffed between insoles and shoes, slipped into the pocket of his only sport jacket) as well as a dwindling three-figure sum in his checking account—but they made off with enough to hurt, financially as well as emotionally. His face burned, tingled, and he bit down on his inside lower lip hard enough to draw blood.

As he walked back to the unfriendly, old Friendship Youth Hostel, creative ways to harm the policemen ran through his mind. He imagined, as vividly as he could, the quickening sensation of fist meeting flesh, and felt such a rush that he nearly broke into a run.

Smiling through his fury, he recalled his father teasing Pip Lipstein, an irascible little regular who liked to narrate past fights at full volume, always ending it with a variation of "If he had said just one word more, I swear . . . I don't know what I would have done." His dad called Pip a true humanitarian for letting so many people escape just in the nick of time.

Jim cursed himself for giving up the money so easily, for carrying around so much money, for leaving the VDNKh station by the exit he had, for not catching the next train or the previous one, for having walked straight down Prospekt Mira instead of taking a side road, for picking the wrong side of the street, but most of all—even staring an insurmountable debt in the face, even to escape the most narrow and repetitive life imaginable—for ever deciding to come to this miserable, broken, failed, godforsaken shithole of a country.

People *die* to get out of here. Russians line up outside every Western embassy in Moscow just to get a visa. Young women in Denver and Manchester and Århus aren't setting up Web sites, hoping to be taken away by some Russian stranger forty years their senior. Canadian students aren't overstaying their visas in St. Petersburg—lovely though it might be—and scheming to bring their families over. Jim's own grandparents walked across who knows how many countries just not to have to live here. And now he had come back, and for what?

He had a return ticket upstairs; he could have just boarded a plane and gone. He would work out his problem with the Sjindic brothers somehow, but not from here.

THE HOSTEL'S IMPOSING, sarcophageal front foyer smelled like a hospital; the marble floor was streaked, and in opposite corners, on their hands and knees, working furiously and silently, were a girl who could not have been older than fifteen and a woman who could not have been younger than seventy. Whether they were grandmother and grandchild or just two people from the neighborhood who needed the work, Jim didn't know.

When he opened the door both turned, staring at him in that cool, frank, appraising manner Russians had. Seeing nothing worth looking at any further, they returned to their work, and Jim crossed the foyer. As he passed the dining room on his way to the broad concrete staircase at the back, the hotel matron charged forth, waddling after him. "Veelahtzir Dzheem! Veelahtzir Dzheem!"

She came out of the dining room at close to full speed, clutching her pink apron, her tight curls of bottle-auburn hair quivering with concern. She had taken an interest in Jim, watching him eat breakfast even as she served other guests, calling out his name at the slightest provocation, somehow contriving to station herself at the front desk whenever he arrived or left. To her he was incomprehensible: an American who spoke Russian, looked like a Chechen, and had a name that, though suspiciously *zhid* (or "Yid," as they said back home), could have been from anywhere east of Vienna. She seemed unsure whether she should adopt him, hate him, or introduce him to her daughter; but in any case she was unable to ignore him.

"Telephone call," she said, holding a slip of paper out toward Jim. "A woman, a Russian woman, from Moscow. She sounded older, maybe forty-five or fifty, and not so happy, perhaps, but not mean either, and I think she was a little bit fat, or maybe she smoked, because her breathing sounded, to me, quite labored."

Jim didn't ask how she knew any of this; he just thanked her and took the paper. Yet another real estate agent, yet another Svetlana.

"Everything fine?" she asked, her eyes wide with concern and her small hands clasped in front of her.

"Yes, fine. It's about an apartment."

"You're going home? An apartment in *Rukveel*, near your family?"

"No, no. An apartment here. I have a job here."

*"Here?"* she asked incredulously. "Here in *Moscow?* You are coming to live *here?*" She crossed her arms and shook her head slowly at Jim. Finally she exhaled her shock. "Oy."

"Oy," Jim repeated. "Oy. Exactly. Oy."

The woman's look of apprehensive worry softened. "Tea," she said firmly, as though a question had been asked to which the only correct answer is "Tea." Her worried look returned. "Tea? Do Americans drink tea?"

"No, I . . ." Jim felt her concern threatening to melt his fury, nuance his impression of Russia, and so, for that reason—because it would shatter his certainty, his superior self-definition, which was the only thing he had that he deemed worthwhile just now—he almost refused. Then he realized that Americans do drink tea, and this particular American would love a cup. "We do. Thank you. I can just . . ."

"I will bring it," she said, already bustling back into the kitchen. "Our restaurant is closed, but I know your room; I will bring it to you."

Jim went upstairs, took off his coat and shoes, and lay down on the bed. He was awakened by the sound of someone in the room, flipping through his books. He shot upright. The hotel matron was in fact moving, not perusing, Jim's books on the bedside table, and she nearly knocked her tray over in shock when Jim sat up.

"I'm sorry. Excuse me," Jim said. "I didn't mean to startle you."

"It's normal. You were sleeping. But it isn't healthy to rise so quickly." She wagged her finger reprovingly at Jim. Every Russian—especially every Russian mother—had dozens of arcane, dubious, unprovable doctrines about what was and was not healthy. Jim's grandmother believed that chocolate made neurons grow in the brain, bimonthly geomagnetic storms gave everyone on the planet headaches on the same days, women who sat on cold surfaces like concrete walls or metal benches would freeze their ovaries and have short children, and watching too much television would ruin your sense of smell.

Jim knew better than to ask where such beliefs came from, but he found himself, as the matron arranged his tray and poured his tea, re-membering his grandmother's house—the cheap, pebbled tile and daisy wallpaper in her kitchen; the orange shag carpet in her living room; the wood-paneled basement stocked with huge jars of home-canned fish and vegetables; the faded crescent moon stamped on her doorbell—with unusual clarity and sharpness of emotion.

He put it down to dreaminess or residual jet lag, when he looked down and saw, next to the tea, a steaming bowl of *guldene yoich:* chicken broth, strewn with chopped dill and redolent of onions, parsley, celery root, and rutabaga—redolent, in fact, of home. Jim looked up at the matron with wonder.

"It is good to eat in the afternoon, a little. Soup is one of the best things to eat. Not too hot," she warned, "because hot soup imbal-ances the nerves. But warm. Or perhaps you don't like soup? No, no you must . . ."

"Thank you," Jim said.

"Will you taste?" She clasped her hands before her in an oddly sup-plicative way, her left palm wrapped around her right thumb and the fingers of her right hand over her left. She looked at Jim with soft ani-mal eyes: clear, expectant, curious, and fearful.

Jim lifted a spoonful to his mouth. It acted on him like a drug, a powerful hallucinogen, a magical compound that gave flesh and imme-diacy to memory. His father made chicken soup for the restaurant from his mother's recipe, but something was lost in translation: a parsimoni-ous hand with the salt, fewer chicken feet, the addition of non-Slavic spices like coriander seeds and a clove or two, peeled rather than un-peeled onions, American pots. But this soup was the taste of home, right down to the minuscule size of the chopped dill. Not in two de-cades had he tasted anything like it, and not until it was in his mouth did he realize that he never expected to taste anything like it again, not in this world.

"It's perfect," Jim managed to croak. She pushed out her lower lip, lifted her chin, and almost smiled—the same half-grateful, half-challenging response Lyudmila Vilatzer would have given. It meant to convey, first, that she could receive no greater gratitude on earth than feeding her descendants (especially her male descendants, or, in this case, a young man both far from and returned to home); and second, she was glad to see the eater wasn't a fool—she knew how good the soup was.

He could think and feel whatever he wanted about this country. He could hate it as much as he liked. He could rail against it, plot against it, spit on its image every time he passed a map. But it remained, in some way, his, part of him; he was implicated in it. He could have flown home without a second thought if he had moved to China or Namibia or Belgium instead of Russia—to a country that seemed interesting rather than one that claimed a part of him. But here he couldn't just leave; he would never have forgiven himself.

Besides, as the soup and the matron's gesture showed, even if he had no further interest in Russia, Russia remained very interested in him.

And so, not especially gradually, once he accepted Moscow as, in some measure, his, and accepted himself as a part of it—once he stopped comparing it to home in all the wrong (read: material and comfort-based) arenas—he came to love the place. Where some might have found solace and space for contemplation on a beach or on top of a mountain, Jim found it in a city that constantly challenged its denizens to survive it unscathed. These challenges superseded mere crime, chaos, culture, or language (which for Jim proved less of a problem than he expected; he spoke relatively proficient Russian, meaning he could understand and be understood almost everywhere, though his grammar remained a little haphazard and, to most interlocutors' surprise and amusement, he spoke with the countrified Yiddish accent of his Belarussian grandparents). What it came down to, really, was finding a way to feel human in a city designed to make one feel insignificant: everything was outsized, immense, deliberately imposing, rough, gray, cold. One had to fight for warmth and color; it was, perhaps, no accident that in a country with endless winters the words for "red" and "beautiful" (*krasniy* and *krasiviy*) are almost identical. The city wore its bone-deep, achingly humane brutality proudly.

Daily life was a three-dimensional poker game, calling on all the skills of bluffing, maneuvering, brag, evasion, watchfulness, bet hedging, tactful mollifying, and constant vigilance he had learned around the table. Quotidian endeavors like shopping, commuting, and travel required a level of improvisation and thought they never did back home, and Jim found himself hooked. Part of this, of course, was the simple adventure of living abroad for the first time. Part of it was also the selfish, quasi-voyeuristic thrill that came from knowing that, however bad it got, he had a foreign passport and a ticket home in his pocket. But the truth was, he would not have felt nearly as at home in, say, Paris, or London, or Mumbai; the ruin and bluster of Moscow, the pulsing life in the apocalyptic setting, the pervasive sense of mystery and toughness underlaid with unexpected echoes of his grandparents—in the seasoning of a soup, the jaunty set of a flat woolen cap, the way grandmothers gripped their grandsons' hands too tightly—combined to produce a surprising, primal sense of a life just missed.

## 3

Vᴏʀᴏᴠ ʜᴀᴅ ʜᴀʀᴅʟʏ sᴛᴀʀᴛᴇᴅ to remove his hand from the pocket of his cashmere overcoat when the door swung open toward him. "Dr. Vorov," murmured the tuxedoed doorman. "What a pleasure to see you back again. Please." He stepped back to allow Vorov into the restaurant. "Your coat, if I may. I will set it aside in the Elite Coatroom." The bell-boy took Vorov's coat with an expression of utmost seriousness. Smiling hosts were Western; here at the Lermontov, service came with a frown and a furrowed brow of concentration and attentiveness.

"Your companion has already arrived," the bellboy said, careful, Vorov noticed, not to use his name. "He reserved the Lensky Room this afternoon. If you would be kind enough to wait for me to deposit your coat, I will show you the way."

"I know the way, thank you. Please do not trouble yourself. Up the stairs, through the library room, and all the way at the end of the back hallway."

"Of course. I should have remembered. Forgive me."

Over his shoulder, as he headed farther into the restaurant, Vorov waved the apology away. As he walked past the ornately carved wooden bar, with its imitation gas lamps and bartender with outsized sideburns, on his way to the staircase, Vorov listened for any language other than Russian. He did the same as he walked up the broad staircase, and back through the second floor's formal dining room, which was lined with shelves of leather-bound books whose pages, no doubt, remained uncut.

He heard none. Perhaps this was an anomaly—perhaps he had just come on a day when no Westerners happened to be there; perhaps he just took the wrong path through the restaurant; perhaps his hearing had started to go. Or perhaps not.

The Lermontov was a wholly Russian aspirational fantasy rather than a Russian-Western one: it appealed to a Russian idea of the imagined, perfect past in decor (the first floor was an early-century apothecary, the second a country-estate library, and the third a garden café), service (manly, serious, unsmiling, fast), and cuisine. Russian coffee shops are designed to look like Starbucks; Russian fast-food chains are as chintzy, plastic, and bright as their Western counterparts; even Chinese and Indian restaurants try to look like Chinese and Indian restaurants in the West, right down to the red-eyed lions and gold wallpaper. The Lermontov did none of that. Unlike so many Moscow restaurants, it failed to remind Westerners that they had won, so they did not feel comfortable there.

At the back of the large, deeply carpeted dining room, set into the thick wooden wall, was a door, watched over by yet another tuxedoed sentinel with nineteenth-century facial hair. As Vorov approached, the man glanced down at the lectern behind which he stood, then up again. Vorov saw the glow of a television screen in the man's glasses; the man registered Vorov's face, and, nodding subtly, he opened the door and stood aside. "The Lensky Room, Dr. Vorov. Last one, left side. You will find the door unlocked. Your companion is waiting for you."

Vorov felt other diners' eyes on his back as he walked down the long private hallway. The door shut behind him, and he heard the click of a lock. At the end of the hallway he knocked on the last door, and without waiting for an answer, he entered.

The man rose as Vorov entered. He was tall, thin, and balding, with a corona of sandy blond hair around a high, pale dome. His bland, observant, ticket taker's face took in everything while registering nothing—and in all the time Vorov had known him he could not recall anything ever provoking more than a raised eyebrow, a pleased curl of the lip, or a deflating sigh from the man. He seemed immune to surprise, happiness, anger—to any recognizable human emotion, in fact. He and Vorov got along well.

"Are you hungry?" he asked, nodding toward a small table in the corner laden with *zakuski:* pickles, cured fish, smoked meat, black and red caviar, aspics, cabbage pies, and vodka. The table at which he sat had two places laid. It was small and round; in fact, as Vorov looked around, it struck him that this must be the smallest of Pushkin's private rooms.

"Thank you, I am." Declining food—or any other offer of hospitality—offered by someone like him would be an unthinkable (and sometimes even fatal) breach of courtesy. Although Vorov was not hungry, he helped himself with a heavy hand. The man himself, Vorov noticed, had only a bottle of still water. "I seem to have picked something up on my travels," he said as he sat down. "Russian food, though—always restorative."

"Yes," the man said idly. "You were in Syunik, is that right, before coming here?"

"It is." The man had to show Vorov that he knew where he was and could trace his movements.

"And what were you doing there?"

"A microcredit scheme I engineered is due to start next year. I had to play tour guide for a few of the lenders. Belgians."

"I see. I also have an interest in Syunik."

"The pipeline?" The Armenia-Iran oil pipeline, nominally built to give the Caucasian former SSRs energy independence from Russia, but, of course, it was being built by a Russian-owned company.

"The pipeline." He nodded. "I would hate to see our interests collide."

"I would not compete with you."

"Nor could you," the man replied quickly, with a look that was perilously close to amusement. "But you being who you are—who you *now* are, I should say—you certainly could complicate things for me. Not insolubly, of course, but expensively."

"I have no interest in the pipeline, my friend." Vorov folded his hands in front of him and looked into his companion's eyes as directly as he could for as long as he could. "I am the same person I have always been." Vorov broke the stare first. For lack of anything better to do, he shoveled a piece of black bread with caviar into his mouth, and forced himself to swallow. "My address is different, but my name . . ."

"Is on a new passport. On a new office door, perhaps. On any number of distinguished lists."

"But I still . . ."

"Yes, of course. Of course. I have neither the time nor the inclination to enter an ontological debate with you. My concerns are far more material." He smiled sourly and reached a hand under the table. Vorov felt a jolt of panic. Then he remembered he was in a public place; he had been seen entering the private room and it was known who he was meeting; and if anything was going to happen, it would not happen here. Too much time on the other side, he reflected, made him too ready to believe in the most lurid possibilities on this side. The man opened a manila folder.

"We needed your assistance in Oakland last year. A matter of purchasing orders, which for someone in your position, with your expertise, would have been easy to fix. You said you could do nothing; we were forced to go outside, and pay for help. Six months ago, we had a similar problem in Long Beach. Again, we felt your citizenship and your connections would have provided a quick solution. Then we could not reach you."

"I was in Brasilia," Vorov said weakly. "At a conference."

"A conference," the man repeated dreamily. "Conference, conference, conference. Yet you weren't at any conference when you called on Mirsky in Sebastopol last August. Or when you saw Trevanian last week in Gyumri. I wonder: what did you need them for? What did you ask of them?"

"Ask? Nothing. Purely social calls. I served with Mirsky, and Trevanian I know from university. I happened to be passing through both towns, and thought it would be rude not to have a glass or two with them."

"Indeed? Purely social? Both of them said you asked about their plans this winter."

"I may have," Vorov said as smoothly as he could. He felt pinpricks of sweat on his thighs, and he hoped he wasn't smiling too much. "If I did, it was just part of a normal friendly conversation."

The man flipped the folder shut, laid his hands atop it, and stared at Vorov. "Many excuses," he said at last. "Many, many excuses. You asked us to help you get out and we helped. You made certain promises. You may have forgotten, but we have not. We do not forget." He stood up and straightened his tie. When Vorov rose as well, the man waved him back into his seat. "Stay, please. Stay and finish your food."

"What can I . . ." Vorov began.

The man dropped a folded piece of card stock onto Vorov's plate. "That amount. In four months' time. As an apology. After that, you will come when called; you will help when asked. No matter the capacity and no matter the inconvenience. Your name remains clear, as far as everyone below me is concerned. Above you need not worry about, but I have taken no steps against you yet. This country, though, is closed to you until then. All of your business here you will find suspended. Please do not embarrass yourself or place me in an uncomfortable position by trying to restart anything on your own. That amount there. Four months from today. Then all will be as it was. Enjoy your lunch. I do hope you feel better."

## 4

EVEN MOSCOW'S VITALITY HELD no remedy for the four p.m. eye flutters, especially when Jim's office was, like most Russian buildings in winter, stiflingly hot, and Jim was engaged in one of his more onerous but regular duties: proofreading a press release so he could change Larisa Bodnarenko's Russglish to English. Mostly that involved adding articles (Russian lacked them, and Larisa, the Memory Foundation's publicity director, seemed to choose hers by guesswork), pruning stray infinitives, removing rhetorical questions, and eliminating hortatory language. Larisa had an English-speaking assistant—Elsa McTeer, a Canadian college student on an internship—but thought it unseemly to ask Elsa to correct her mistakes. She believed her underling should view her with awe and terror, which she saw as equivalent to respect, and far easier to earn.

As dull as the work may have been, at least it was work: Jim was hired as an interviewer, a nonthreatening foreign face to send out into the public, but he hadn't done one since he arrived. People in the office spoke of interviews like gamblers or salesmen speak of streaks and told Jim not to worry, but every day he spent as a proofreader or filer or collator or glorified temp, really, was a day he spent feeling, again, he was getting it wrong, striking out, failing to move forward. Fortunately, the Foundation's purse strings were controlled from a distance: Jim had been hired with a one-year contract, which meant he worked for them for a year, whether or not he did, in fact, work.

As Jim redlined a "How to say more?" and a "Most historical event of world importance," he heard Larisa in her office discussing the advantages of blond pine over teak and mahogany. She was remodeling her apartment with Finnish furniture and an Italian architect, she said proudly (her husband had something to do with Siberian logging; nobody was stupid enough to ask exactly what).

The piece Jim was editing crowed over the increasing number of gulag survivors whose testimony would be preserved for posterity, thanks to the tireless and worthy efforts of the Memory Foundation. Jim had not quite mastered the art of making his work just work; it still seemed unsettling, profane even, to read a self-congratulatory press release about labor-camp survivors while listening to a conversation like this. Still, it was hardly unusual here, and it posed a particular problem of soul-steerage: cry over every tragedy and you would have no time left to do anything else. Ignore them all and you would rot from the inside.

His grandmother never talked about her brother, even when Jim asked, but he knew, somehow, that he was a violinist who died in Siberia in the 1930s. Jim's father never showed much curiosity either. Jim couldn't help but contrast this to the endless books, television shows, and lectures about the Holocaust and its survivors, or even to Amit Balakrishnan's tendency, when he had too much to drink, to talk with tear-swollen eyes about his cousins, who hounded their Muslim neighbors from their homes during Partition, just as his parents had been burned out of their home in Lahore. Why did some victims talk and some stay silent? Why were some asked to talk, listened to with silence and rapt stares, and others merited simply polite nods or statements of equivalence? How could tourists come here to buy Soviet kitsch— CCCP hockey jerseys, Lenin buttons, hammer-and-sickle fur caps— when they would never sport swastikas, or buy buttons with Hitler's picture on them? And when, where, and with whom did it end?

Jim read a story yesterday in a British newspaper about the last remaining resident of a town less than fifty miles from Moscow, which not two centuries ago had been a good-sized outpost between Moscow and Novgorod. Now the last man—an actual, real live Last Man—was tearing apart his neighbors' houses board by board and burning them for heat. Over the fires he cooked whatever animals he could trap in the forests for sustenance. Larisa decided on the mahogany.

Jim rubbed his eyes and stared out the grimy window. An old woman was trying to walk a skinny gray dog. The dog relieved itself glumly against a steel fence post, bounded through the snowdrifts in the court-yard, but when it reached the cleared sidewalks it stopped and looked plaintively at its owner. The woman tried pulling it onto the sidewalk behind her, but the dog wouldn't budge. She tried again, first inter-spersing insistent tugs with what Jim assumed were pleas, her face close to the dog's, but then started yanking and cursing. The dog was resolute.

"Chemics," said a deep, accented voice behind Jim. Vassily ran a hand through his white swept-back hair, squinted his deep-set, lunatic eyes.

"Sorry?" Jim asked, Vassily still staring out the window, running a hand through his white pompadour and frowning.

"Chemics. Chemicals, you can say. To make clear sidewalks." Vassily refused to credit Jim's Russian. When Jim addressed him in Russian, he spoke English; when Jim addressed him in English, he responded in Russian. Now he leaned his clothes-hanger frame over Jim to get closer to the window. His torso pinned Jim against the wall; his pelvis pressed against the arm of Jim's chair, worryingly close to his hand. Jim thought of pulling away but didn't want to make any sudden or potentially of-fensive moves around Vassily. "Very bad for dogs. Walk once, bad hurt." His eyes widened with something like fierce glee. "Walk twice, maybe blood." Wider still. "Again walk, no feet for dogs. Shoes, too, for people, last maybe one winter. No more."

Vassily's official title was research assistant, but his duties were in fact limited, specific, and essential. The Foundation's three interviewers, of which Jim was one, found survivors by scouring old state files, which, by an act of Parliament in the mid-1990s, were gradually being declassified. That was the law; that was the theory; the facts, of course, were more complicated and more human.

Unless you went to the State Archives with someone who was on good terms with the security guards and the archivists, as Vassily was, you were liable to find the declassification had halted, or even reversed. You might find yourself shut out of the archives for a day, a week, or as long as that guard was on duty. The guard might find you had an improper visa, which to fix required either a prolonged and expensive crawl through the labyrinthine bowels of numerous government departments or a brief but exponentially more expensive on-the-spot fine.

With a friendly enough guard, though, not only would the archives adhere to the law, but you might find the opening hours suddenly extended. Records listed as missing might suddenly turn up in one of the archivist's drawers. Vassily's job was to ensure such friendliness. There seemed to be many handshakes, many furtive walks around the block, an occasional wrapped gift or two. How he did it was a subject of much wonderment but no open debate: it happened; everyone was glad it happened; everyone wondered how it happened; but nobody ever asked him.

"Ah, guys?" asked a tremulous, high-pitched, reedy male voice. This was Dave Willow, head of the Russia branch of the Memory Foundation. Dave was a fortyish, milky, bearded academic plucked from Berkeley's history department by Alex Grynshtein himself after he read an article of Dave's in *The New Republic* about Putin's youth-group thugs, who were then intimidating avant-garde and obliquely critical theater groups. Dave had a gift for administration, but was otherwise a creature of carrel and classroom; he did none of the actual interviewing himself. He spoke a stammering, baroque, book-learned Russian that was almost entirely useless for daily communication. Cashiers, Metro token takers, and waitresses often laughed when he launched into one of his inflectionless, fifteen-clause sentences; it was like speaking to a subway clerk in Elizabethan English. He and his wife, Sara, had been in Moscow for three years, and he still spoke like he learned Russian from scholarly journals and Tolstoy.

"How's it going over here? I guess it's time to, you know, do our weekly talk kind of thing?" Many of Dave's sentences didn't end; they just trailed upward like questions in smoke. He smiled weakly at Vassily, of whom he seemed in constant terror.

"Right behind you," Jim said.

"Oh, great. Great," he said chummily, rolling his shoulders, stretching his arms over his head, and interlacing his fingers at the zenith of his reach. He and Sara were yoga devotees; he often broke into sudden stretches. Sara, in fact, had tried and failed to start an informal ashram in her apartment, but that was due to bad advertising: she had emphasized its health benefits rather than its exclusivity.

"I'll just kind of round up the rest of the crew over there. Be over in two secs."

"Sex?" Vassily whispered to Jim.

"No, thanks. I'm in training. Ten months without. You can hang wet towels from it every morning." Vassily blushed; score one for Jim.


NINE PEOPLE—THE FOUNDATION's entire staff, less Fyodor and Olga, the driver and receptionist, and Elsa, whom Larisa did not allow to come to staff meetings—filed in to Dave's already cramped office. Piles of newspapers, magazines, archival materials, and academic journals peeped out from beneath his couch and desk; hastily folded papers bulged from the pockets of his oatmeal-colored blazer; yellowing sheaves prevented the drawers of the filing cabinets along two walls from closing. The papers seemed almost to be quivering with anticipation, waiting for everyone to leave before they burst forth and smothered everything in their path.

"Okay, well, I guess we should kind of get started here. I need to take off a little early today, and I'm sorry about that, you know, but I'm supposed to have a drink with one of the mayor's guys, so . . ." The sentence died a lingering death.

"The mayor, well, you are really moving in quite high circles." Birgitta Voss seemed to show up every week to complain, harangue, and lecture. Like Jim, she was an interviewer; unlike Jim, she had actually spoken to a few dozen subjects.

Dave assured him this was normal, that Russians tend to be reluctant to dredge up history, especially in front of a foreigner, and even more especially in front of an American—they didn't want to make Russia look bad—but Birgitta rarely failed to point out flaws in Jim's interrogation technique, which, of course, she had never seen. Jim would even have forgiven her that had he found her attractive, but alas, she had a pale, sharp-featured face, flawless in its own cruel, robotic way, with beady blue eyes and a perpetual thin-lipped sneer: the sort of face you could warm to only if you provided all the warmth yourself. "What do you go to talk about?" she asked Dave.

Dave sighed and drummed his fingers on his desk. Speaking with Birgitta was the conversational equivalent of Jenga: one wrong move and she'd bury you. "Well, we're just talking about how the city's developing so quickly, and whether there might be a place for a memorial of some kind somewhere. But like I was just saying . . ."

"It is all development now," said Birgitta. "It just means they will throw out some more poor people to the streets to please their clients from the number one country of U.S.A. They come here for exploitation and need more nice hotels. I say why not have some anticapitalist spaces for all people, just places for talking and music and so on. Why does the U.S.A. not allow this even in Moscow?"

"Sorry, which clients are these?" This was Kirsten Platonova, who was the Foundation's grant writer. She had lived in Moscow for almost fifteen years, and was married to Yuri Platonov, who had carved out a space for himself on staff as someone who knew more or less everything about postwar Russian history. They were the only people in the office who Jim had seen outside work; they had invited him to their apartment not long after he started for an endless Russian evening around the table, smoke-cured and well marinated.

Birgitta and Kirsten had a perpetual running feud: Kirsten, who had lived in Moscow since 1993, when she married Yuri, took the city as it was, and loved it; Birgitta used Moscow as a megaphone with which to proclaim her own righteousness, but whined about it—the inefficiencies of the postal system, the dirtiness of the streets, the failure of its citizens to act like Germans—ceaselessly. One of the reasons Jim was so fond of Kirsten was the pleasure she took in baiting Birgitta. After asking her question she leaned back on Dave's ratty couch and raised her chin slightly, a cat watching a limping canary.

"The developers' clients, actually. Who gives the contracts and who is the architect and so on. And why make the new developments—why not make it into a gathering place for all people or a home for low-incomes in the center of the city? What about these ideas?" Her pale face flushed righteous, barricade-manning red.

"Look, I don't think Moscow quite works that way, so . . ."

"Yes, of course not, because it takes clues of behavior from U.S.A."

"Look, I hate to interrupt," Dave pleaded, grimacing ingratiatingly and holding up both hands pleadingly, "but, you know, I really do want to get this meeting done in a hurry. It's once a week, you know, just to catch up, and I think we need to . . . Jim? Want to tell us what you've been up to?"

"Just . . . just stuff around the office, I guess. Filing. Looking over past reports. Maybe going to the archive with Vassily again." Jim heard in his own voice the plaintive note that ended the sentence, the sense of incipient failure that predicted failure so well because it made it happen, a wooden thud of resignation that usually preceded an unwise bet or a bout of workmanlike drinking. He hadn't yet spoken to a single soul, despite all the scouring, the tracing, the letters and phone calls, and that, Dave assured him, was fine. He was still getting paid, working off his debt, but with nothing to win at, he couldn't help but feel like he was losing.

"Well, that's just fine, Jim, you know. It takes a while. Just stick at it, you know. Larisa's pretty happy with what you've been doing, I think. Right, Larisa? Having Jim give the releases a nice read before they go out?"

"Yes," said Larisa without the slightest trace of happiness, her solemn expression as firm and unmoving as her battleship prow of hair and her boxcar shoulders.

"Okay. Well, okay, then. Birgitta, do you . . ."

"Same thing. Still transcribing. I had a very productive talk last week about Kolyma. Six days, actually. It will be finished as soon as I can manage. Perhaps Jim can help if he is doing nothing else." Whether the smirk was real or imagined, it still made Jim bite his lip hard enough to draw blood.

"Kirsten?" Dave said, turning away quickly.

She turned down the corners of her mouth, raised her eyebrows, and shrugged. "A good grant writer learns to handle rejection. I am becoming an expert."

Dave chuckled and stood up, raising his arms to the ceiling straight through his fingertips, arching his back, and emitting a kind of equine whinny that, to judge from his facial expression, indicated a feeling of accomplishment. "Well, okay." He exhaled, slumping back down into his seat. "We're basically done, so I guess we can just sort of call it a day, kind of thing."

EVERY OFFICE HAS an unofficial second office, one with a full (and preferably inexpensive) bar, friendly but unobtrusive service, and food that, if not exactly gourmet, at least won't make a patron more than occasionally sick, provided he orders wisely. The Memory Foundation used The Chinese Pilot. It attracted a young, bohemian, studentish crowd, which meant the evening was unlikely to include thirty-dollar beers, fifty-dollar glasses of wine, gunfire, kidney punches, unwanted salacious propositions, or thumping "music" designed to inhibit conversation, stir loins, and rattle fillings. True, it had live music of profoundly variable quality, but on nights involving a few too many men in graying ponytails singing earnest lyrics over poorly strummed guitars, the bar was big enough to escape. Tonight, the red flyer on the table advertised "Shot from Guns: An Oppositional Noise Collective"—a trio that featured a beatboxer, a violist, and a woman who operated vacuum cleaners and hair dryers of various sizes. They took a table as far from the stage as possible.

The other main advantage of The Pilot was the way its lurid red lighting, uneven floor, and ferocious overheating made the patrons feel a little unsteady even before they started drinking, so that by ten p.m., when the office stalwarts—Jim, Yuri, Kirsten, and Elsa—were still at their oilcloth-topped table which was littered with the remnants of the down market Russian restaurant meal (chicken bones, meat gristle, sauce and grease smears, bread crumbs, french fry nubs, empty beer bottles, and overturned shot glasses), the slide into actual inebriation was almost unnoticeably gentle.

Yuri sat between Jim and Kirsten, a gesticulating arm around each, the vodka having warmed his customary reserve into a sort of expansive clubbiness, arguing with a lawyer's precision and an obsessive's passion that Pushkin was untranslatable, while Chekhov and Dostoyevsky were minor writers afflicted by a very contemporary malady that we can all recognize today: writing for foreigners instead of their own people, trying to appeal to the masses rather than understand an individual Russian soul.

Jim enjoyed seeing Yuri so enthused, but he wasn't following the argument; as soon as a Russian intellectual introduces the word *soul*, or starts discoursing on the superior richness of the Russian language, all one can do is agree vehemently or trade punches. Kirsten held on to her husband's hand, the booze blooms spreading from her neck up to her cheeks. Elsa, as loud and liberated when drunk as she was ordinarily reserved and prim, had fallen into conversation with a trio of shaggy Kiwi travelers at the adjacent table. When Yuri paused for breath, Jim slipped out from under his arm and under his protests to buy another round.

He sidled his way up to the bar, which was actually an airplane wing laid across old ammunition boxes. He slipped in between a pair of stringy young men in the cords and ratty sweaters of enthused humanities students and a young woman with an elegant, elvish look, half aristocratic drawing room and half forest spirit: long white-blond hair, gray eyes, an Asiatic cast to her eyes, and high cheekbones. He nodded at her, really more out of aesthetic appreciation than out of any desire to start a conversation, and she reached over to clear a half-full glass of beer out of the way, but in so doing managed to knock it off the bar and send the contents spilling down Jim's jeans.

Her hands flew up to her mouth, and she reached over the bar for a towel.

"*Izvenitye,*" she gasped. "I'm so sorry."

"*Nichevo.* Don't worry about it," Jim said, taking the towel from her and blotting the crotch of his jeans. "A few more beers and I'd have done it myself," he said in English. She looked at him curiously, deciding whether to head for the hills, but then laughed: a good sign, he thought, to make someone laugh despite her suspicion, even as he regretted introducing himself with a bodily-function joke.

"Your English is quite good," she said, with a singsong manner of speech and an accent that delighted him but that he couldn't place.

"I should hope so. So's yours."

"Oh, yes. Now I can hear it. Canadian?"

"Under no circumstances. Please. A bit to the south."

"American? Really? No . . ."

"American, really, yes. Born and raised. Why are you so surprised?"

"Because you talked a word of Russian. With the right accent. I didn't know any of you . . ."

"I know, I know. I spoke it at home. I always thought I was half Russian."

"What do you mean? You found you were something else?"

"Over here, yes. My nationality. *Yevrei, nye Ruski.*" Jew, not Russian. Soviet passports used to list the bearer's "nationality"—Russian, Jewish, Uzbek, Kalmyk, and a hundred others—right below his name, making it a legal impossibility to be a Russian Jew, for instance, or a Russian of Kyrgyz descent, or even a Russian Tatar, despite the Tatars' having been present on Russian soil since before the Kievan Rus tribesman even formed a state. The nationality line let every policeman who stopped a suspiciously thick-bearded citizen see whether he was loyal or not, and if not, whether he was bomb-on-the-subway disloyal or tentacles-around-the-world, pimp-your-blond-daughters disloyal. Although that line no longer existed on Russian passports, the mentality that put it there had not disappeared.

"What about the other half."

"What's your guess?"

"Hmmm . . . Turkish, maybe? Arabic? Italian?"

"No, the swarthy part's all Russian. The other's a little farther north. Irish. On my mother's side. What about you? Not Russian, I don't think."

"What do you think?"

"Well, what's your name?"

"Kaisa. Katerina, actually, but Kaisa is . . . You should call me Kaisa."

"Kaisa," he repeated, nodding sagely, using the same three-syllable pronunciation. "That sounds . . . isn't that . . ." The nods turned to bewildered head-shaking. "Not a clue. Never heard it before in my life."

"It's Finnish. Finland is a large country, just west of . . ."

"Now you're just making fun of me."

"I know; I'm sorry." She shot a hand out and laid it on his forearm. Without thinking he covered it with his hand.

"Forgiven. You have actually been to the United States, though? At least?"

"Never."

"Well," said Jim, wiping all traces of mirth from his face, "you should come. I'll buy you lunch."

Her smile froze and her eyes narrowed; she wasn't sure whether he was joking, drunk, or insane. Jim's eyes softened and she broke down laughing, and he knew the rest would be downhill.

"What are you doing in Moscow?"

"Well, I'm an actress. I know that sounds so . . . But I'm studying acting and film directing on a Moscow Arts Fellowship for a year."

"Are you? I don't think that's 'so' anything; I think it's wonderful. I actually was engaged to an actress, if you can believe that." Too soon to drag out the skeleton?

"Oh, no. I hope I don't remind you of a bad history."

"No, not at all. She was . . ." For a minute, the alcohol, the subject, and the extraordinary winter-morning eyes looking at him threatened to knock Jim off his conversational path. "She was . . . I don't know; she was different," he said, righting himself. "From you. I know I don't know anything about you, really, but I feel absolutely confident saying that."

"Well, I'm touched," she said, bowing her head slightly and letting her hair fall across her face. Jim brushed it delicately aside and she smiled.

"What about you? Why does an American come to Russia?"

He had nothing better to do. He's fleeing a lifetime of bad choices. He's making money from other people's tragedies. "Work. Nothing so interesting, just work."

"Ah, I see. You are here to get rich by telling them how to be just like you, only a little bit less."

"Less what?"

"Less everything. You're teaching them to be dutiful little brothers." If the tease had not been quite so sharp and accurate, Jim might have been able to keep flirting; as it was, she joked him into directness.

"I work at a place called the Memory Foundation. We interview political prisoners from across Eastern Europe and record their stories."

"For what?" she asked quietly, all traces of teasing vanished.

"Well, for history. So people will remember."

"That's it? What if people don't want to remember."

That was the one question the Memory Foundation and all the professional diggers in the world couldn't answer. In so much of the West, history's painful memories took on the melancholy-sweet cast of stories of hardship told in a warm, well-stocked home: "*Tsuris* overcome is good to tell," as Jim's father said. Not so in the East. It wasn't just that everything was too new, raw, and recent. There was something deeper: a hair-trigger defensiveness, a reluctance to too much cultural introversion, a desire to celebrate and move on rather than look back and wallow. "Well, we hope they will," he said quietly. What else could he say? "We hope someone will."

"My grandfather does not," Kaisa said quietly.

"Does not what. Was he . . ."

She nodded.

"A Finn?"

"Ukrainian. My grandmother was Finnish. He married her after the war. He was stationed in Karelia. There were no borders there. He married her and brought her home. Brought her to what he thought was home. Crazy, yes?"

Jim smiled and laid a hand on hers, but neither shook his head nor nodded.

"Crazy, they thought, because he went to an institution, then to a camp. I don't know how long. He never told me."

"He never talked about it?"

"Not to me. He has friends, I know, who were there with him. Other people who got out and live in Moscow."

Jim's ears pricked up at the present tense. "Who live? So he's still . . ."

"Oh, yes. Yes, he's healthy. He was young, very young, when he went in. He is now seventy-five, but healthy. Strong."

"But he doesn't like to talk about it?"

Kaisa made a beautifully resigned swan move with her head. "Not to me, at least. He says I'm too pretty."

"He's right."

She looked up slowly. It was an early-Renaissance face: long, mournful, placid, sylvan, and Jim was nearly lost in it when a crash startled him so much he nearly fell into her lap. Elsa apparently lost a game she was playing with the Kiwis that required all participants to rise from a seated position while balancing an empty bottle of beer on their foreheads. It crashed, and she bared her teeth and made a dragon's hiss; a shaggy, red-haired Kiwi guided her gently but with difficulty back to a seated position. "I work with them," Jim sighed. "I was actually up here buying a round of drinks, but I don't know if that's such a good idea."

"Oh, I'm sorry again; I didn't mean to keep you. I was also buying a drink for my friend over there . . ." She nodded toward an empty section of the bar by the back room, where Shot from Guns were tuning up their vacuum cleaners. "Who seems to have had an excellent night with someone from the opening band. Oh, well. I need to go, too, actually."

"Do you really?"

Celibate since moving to Moscow and for a good length of time before that, Jim would have considered tying her to the airplane wing with her own scarf even if she weren't beautiful, warm, responsive. That she was all of the above, and was also actually corporeal, actually standing in front of him smiling, actually looking at him with her quick-change, burning-blue eyes and slightly parted mouth, he could scarcely believe.

"But your friends . . ."

"Just give me one minute," Jim said, guiding her into a seat at the bar with both hands on her shoulders. "I'll bring them their drinks and come back. Look over there; you see one happy couple and one very happy single woman surrounded by admirers, then there's me; they won't miss me. Just . . . will you wait?"

"Of course," she said, smiling sweetly.

"And you'll fend off anyone who . . ."

"Yes, yes. Go on. I'll be right here."

Jim bought eight bottles of Sibirskaya Corona and all but ran them back to the table. "My God, Jim," Kirsten said, "we thought you'd gotten lost. What have . . ."

"Good for the rest of the night, I hope," Jim said, grabbing his coat and bag. He was, in fact, already lost. Jim glanced toward Kaisa at the bar; the rest of them followed his look.

"Don't forget," Elsa said, her eyes intensely and drunkenly unfocused. She beckoned him closer. When he leaned down, she grabbed his nose between her thumb and forefinger, made a noise like a duck, and promptly passed out.

5

WHEN THE MINISTER was finally lowered into the ground, his wife wailed appropriately, Metropolitan Vyacheslav swung the censer in a violent arc, and the mourners—all of whom hated, feared, and relied on but in no way mourned the minister—took stock. His wife, a rodential little creature with wispy gray hair and the archaic hardness of Russian political wives and outdated cars, collapsed in sobs against a fat, middle-aged man in an expensive suit and stoic face: the minister's son, grown rich, stupid, and gonorrheal, overseeing the family's "investments" in Zurich. Skrupshin took a deep breath. Like the rest of the male mourners, he squinted and clenched his teeth, hoping it would approximate the appearance of a man struggling with emotion, trying not to cry.

This deep in Novodevichy Cemetery, the air didn't smell like Moscow—no exhaust or diesel fumes, no cabbage pies or spilled beer. It smelled like Russia: pine, winter, and earth.

The minister's funeral had attracted hundreds, but only a select few dozen mourners followed the body to the grave. They calculated their positions. They weighed their options. They tried to measure their future in a dry eye, a hint of a satisfied smile, a too-jaunty gait. Those with stronger constitutions looked on the crowd with pity, thinking to themselves, "*I'll* be fine; the rest of them, though . . ." In others this calculation was reversed, and despite the wind and snow, they sweated.

Skrupshin fell into the first category. Ever since the tax police were disbanded and folded into the Interior Ministry, he had overseen the investigation of all financial crimes—and since Russia's tax code is so deliberately abstruse that every person and corporation in Russia is guilty of tax evasion, Skrupshin's position was among the most powerful and feared in the country. It was not an easy climb. Many decent, honorable backs had suffered stab wounds; many unfunny jokes garnered laughs; many tiny seeds had been carefully cultivated into fully bloomed poisonous rumors. Discerning what people wanted had never been difficult for Skrupshin; learning when to give it to them was the real art.

Though he remained, by Russian political standards, a young man— he was forty-two: just old enough to have been educated but not significantly employed by the Soviets—he was among the longest serving members of the Interior Ministry's aristocracy. He had outlasted three ministers and outmaneuvered all rivals. He sought no higher office; all he wanted was the spoils. That, and the thrill of the office itself. He remembered the first time he had pulled up someone's tax returns, the first time he had summoned an OMON brigade leader to his office and given him the name and address of those returns and had watched from his window as they brought Alyosha, handcuffed and bruised, into a ministry holding cell to await his transfer to Lefortovo. His last rival and his first kill.

Someday—not anytime soon, of course, but eventually—there would come a younger, hungrier Skrupshin. If he didn't want to end up like Alyosha, he had to be sure he had enough on hand in Russia and enough offshore to make sure he could escape, and land somewhere warm.

But it was not yet that time. The next minister would be chosen from among the Economic Crimes group, most of whom now walked through the dense, wooded, half-wild cemetery back to the Metropolitan's house for the requisite vodka-fueled wake.

Economic Crimes was once considered a backwater assignment: you made your career in Political; you had a nice life in Cultural (so easy to

turn an icy actress or ballerina pliant and willing with the right inter-
cepted phone number or steamed-open letter); you were left to molder
in Economic. But financial concerns had gradually taken precedence
over political ones. It didn't take much to set up a fake opposition group
or throw a few noisy students into an insane asylum. Tracing shell companies from Moscow to Tel Aviv to Liechtenstein to Amsterdam to
Bonnaire to Andorra: that took skill. Interior had become too important to return to Militsiya control.

And Skrupshin knew all of these men. Mironov, Yevtushenkevich,
and Shalyov had paid no taxes in five years. Tverdovsky, the idiot, had
wired his payment last year directly from his account in Jersey; Skrupshin (actually, Skrupshin's eager fifteen-year-old nephew) had sent a
bug along the payment's route, meaning the account could now be
emptied whenever Skrupshin saw fit. Maltsev had transferred all of his
assets into the name of his three-year-old son, who had filed no return.
He had nothing to fear from any of them. He did not seek the lime-
light or political glory; he had no desire to appear on television or
gallivant through Paris on the government's ruble, spouting the government line. All he wanted was to be left alone and in place until he
reached his number and it was time to leave, at which time he wanted
to disappear quietly. He did his job well; he showed respect; he asked
nothing outrageous.

In fact, he reflected, the only real danger now was that some presidential adviser, eager to gain his favor, would actually nominate him to
be minister. Give that job to someone who liked fame, to someone
clean enough to survive the rug sniffers and phone tappers around the
president. He would have to turn it down politely, of course, and in
such a way that his nominator would think he was simply steering
them toward a better candidate—no, he thought, not steering, but en-
abling them to suggest the proper candidate. Nobody wants to be re-
jected. All he had to do was figure out who they really wanted. How
hard could that be?

THE NEXT MORNING, Skrupshin strode through the ministry's immense dark wood front doors and into the marble lobby at precisely 8:30. Every so often a colleague tried to prove his zeal by arriving before him; every time either vodka or a quiet chat with Skrupshin dissuaded the early riser. Skrupshin arrived first: it was his habit; it was his privilege; and, especially during a transitional time like this one, he had to remind anyone visiting from the Kremlin of his place and his importance.

He held his badge and identity card up to the reader, and while he waited for the mirrored doors to open he checked his reflection—charcoal-gray suit, pressed; navy and white club tie, straight; blond hair, in place; jaw, set—and approved. *Ochin Londonskiy*, his first boss used to say: how Londonish. The reader flashed green; the doors slid open; and Skrupshin, turning his attention to the *Financial Times* he carried, strode through.

To his surprise, he barreled straight into a slab of granite in an army uniform, standing in the hallway as though he were waiting for someone.

"Excuse me," Skrupshin stammered. "I didn't . . . there isn't . . ."

"Nikolai Nikolaievitch Skrupshin," the slab croaked. It was not a question.

"That's right."

"I am General Savinkov."

Skrupshin recovered his swagger: it was just an army general. One of the security officers out front probably served under him, and had let the old man in out of pity: he was here to plead his case. "General," Skrupshin began with an understanding but supercilious half smile, "I have great respect for our fighting forces, but as you can tell, I am quite busy, so if you would . . ."

"I am the minister of the Interior."

"Impossible." Skrupshin's jackal grin broadened. The general did not move. "Nobody has been appointed yet. Minister Khilov was only buried yesterday; there hasn't been a search; nobody has asked me . . ."

"Nobody is required to ask you, Deputy Skrupshin," the general interrupted. He squared his shoulders and looked down at Skrupshin. "You have received no promotion." Each sentence emerged from his mouth as though chiseled into stone. "The president will announce my appointment on Thursday, but I am the minister from today. You can look on the computer that you use." He pronounced the word *computer* with requisite contempt, letting Skrupshin know that a military man like him had no need for such a device. "I will wait. I expect you back in front of me in five minutes." The sliding doors had opened onto a point at which three hallways met; to Skrupshin's unease, the general stood aside and allowed him to proceed down the one that led to his office.

When he hung up his jacket he thought the closet looked out of order; when he turned on his computer he had the sense that someone had rearranged the papers on his desk. He told himself it was paranoia; outwardly, he kept the set-jaw smile frozen in place, even as he read a dispatch sent over the government's internal mail system announcing that General Konstantin Yegorovitch Savinkov would be named Interior minister on Thursday. Unofficially, but with full departmental authority, he would start immediately.

Skrupshin clasped his hands on the desk in front of him and scrolled through the rest of his in-box: nothing of note. He rose, smoothed his tie, and prepared for humility. This is not a catastrophe, he told himself as he walked smoothly back toward the general. You've survived three previous ministers; you'll survive this one. Besides, that he didn't come from the Economic section might prove beneficial: he'll be out of his depth, and he'll need someone he can trust. All Skrupshin had to do was convince the general he could be trusted.

"General Savinkov," he began gravely, "allow me to extend my most sincere apologies. Had I known . . ."

"You were not required to know," the general pronounced. "I did not expect you to know. That is why I was waiting for you. Come into my rooms for a moment." He followed a respectful half step behind the general as they walked down the long, burgundy-carpeted hallway to the ministerial suite.

"Lieutenant," he barked as they sat down. A tall, somber, gray-eyed man in a neat soldier's uniform walked into the room holding a clipboard in one hand and his hat in the other. He nodded to the general; the general nodded back and pointed with a calloused sausage finger toward the corner. Skrupshin marked the junior man immediately as an intelligence officer; he had seen no more combat than Skrupshin himself. The lieutenant sat down just behind Skrupshin. The general did not introduce him. He picked up a file from his desk, glanced at the contents, then slapped it shut with a mild grunt.

"Nikolai Nikolaievitch, with new beginnings come many changes." He fell into the platitudinous, rising-falling cadence of the Russian politician. "This is natural. This is expected. Minister Khilov changed many things when he arrived. So did Stroyev before him, and Kurshansky before Stroyev. You know this. They changed things in order to make the ministry more effective, and in order to keep Russia strong." He clenched his hand into a fist. "But, of course, we don't change everything." The general raised his voice and lowered his head, as though he were suggesting something outlandish and wanted to be sure Skrupshin understood that he was not, in fact, changing everything. Skrupshin took heart. "That would not be natural. We need change, but also we need continuity. We must preserve balance. Do you agree, Nikolai Nikolaievitch?"

"Of course," Skrupshin said fervently, rising in his seat. He heard the lieutenant behind him scribbling. "Balance is important. I am proud to say that in this ministry are men of great experience, who are committed to efficiency and to the strength of our country."

"Correct," he intoned. "But you also agree on the need for change."

"Change is important, too, especially with new leadership."

"Balance and change, balance and change," the general murmured, looking up at the ceiling and exhaling. Seated, with his barrel chest and huge bug eyes, he looked like a gray frog with a crew cut. The general seemed at once unburdened at having imparted such wisdom and weighed down with the responsibility of understanding so much. "Sometimes people, too, benefit from a change, do you not agree?"

"They can," Skrupshin said cautiously. "It's possible. But sometimes . . ."

"I had certain advisers in my former position as chief of the Rear Services, for instance, who made matters of economics quite clear to me. I am a simple military man, you see," he said, with a lopsided, wolf-eyed grin that tried but failed to be self-deprecating, "and such matters often confuse me."

"With respect, Minister," Skrupshin began, shifting in his seat. The general raised a hand to silence him.

"Nikolai Nikolaievitch, I need you to think very deeply about whether you might be ready for a change. This is a personal matter. This is not for me to say." Again, he gave the same lopsided grin. "And I do not want you to tell me right now. I want you to think about what is best for you, and what would be best for the ministry."

Skrupshin nodded but said nothing. He heard the scratching of the lieutenant's pen. He understood well: Savinkov had his own people to whom he owed favors, and needed to see what they wanted, while at the same time scrutinizing Skrupshin to see if he could find a reason to dismiss him. Would the lieutenant be sitting in Skrupshin's office next month, or was he just a scribe, a functionary?

"During this time," the general continued, "you should not work too hard. I know, Nikolai Nikolaievitch, your reputation for diligence."

"I do what the ministry requires." In Skrupshin's mind this sounded noble; it came out petulant.

"Of course you do," the general said, opening his eyes wide and raising a hand as though he were about to cross himself. "Nobody suggests anything different. Everybody I've spoken with—and you should know this—superior officers, even men"—he leaned toward Skrupshin, beckoning him to lean in, too—"even men in the *Kremlin*. Very highly placed people, I might say, know this. You have an excellent reputation.

But now, what I want you to do is not work, but think. About yourself and your future, and the ministry and its future. Can you do this?"

"Of course," said Skrupshin, rising to his feet and preparing, for what it was worth, to salute.

"And while you are thinking," the general continued, beckoning the lieutenant over to the desk, "I do not want you to trouble yourself. I know that you have traveled a great deal. Don't do that now. Give your external passport and travel papers to the lieutenant." The general watched, his eyes no longer soft and his grin nowhere in sight, as Skrupshin handed his papers to the lieutenant. "Stay in Moscow, at home, and relax. No unnecessary journeys, no long hours. And no long trips in Russia, either. I'd like to see you around the office. You press yourself, I know, but this is not the time for that. Perhaps, over the next weeks, as I am getting used to the new position, we can have a few chats. About economic matters, about the ministry. I would like that. Should we say four p.m. each workday? Come down here, to my office, we'll drink like old soldiers. Don't be late, Nikolai Nikolaievitch. I'll be waiting for you, with great pleasure."

## 6

JIM AND KAISA TALKED at the bar for another three hours—long enough for both of them to switch to mineral water. Whatever else happened over the course of his life, whoever else he dated or slept with or married, he wanted to lock Kaisa up in his memory bank, unimpeded by alcohol. When her eyelids started to droop he asked if she wanted to see where he lived, and although she laughed at the club-footedness and clear intent of the invitation, she assented. Jim stood as straight as possible when he walked her to the door; he had to fight the urge to take a victory lap, or ask someone to photograph the departure for posterity.

They hailed a gypsy cab on the corner—as usual, one of those mid-1980s purple Ladas that looked like it had been crumpled, stuffed into a huge lint-filled pocket, and then shaken out briefly before driving. The driver was a chain-smoking, gold-toothed Azeri who insisted on taking "his special way" to Jim's apartment and would brook no suggestions or corrections about the route.

As they came over the hill and passed the neoclassical, colonnaded Moscow Choral Synagogue, with its gray dome and garish but well-intentioned sculpture outside, Kaisa leaned back into Jim and shut her eyes. She reached back and ran a hand down his face and chest as he shuddered.

"Where did you come from, really?" she whispered.

"You tell me," he said. "Wherever you like."

The driver coughed spastically, perhaps significantly, and hawked something out the window.

Kaisa started to sit up, but Jim held her against him. "I mean it." She took his hand and put it against her, inside her coat. "Who put you here?"

When I replay this in the future, he said to himself, she won't have had a thing to drink; she'll be stone-cold sober, and so will I. "Sammy and Rose. We chop fish for a living. We stack chairs at night and take them down in the morning. We're deeply ordinary people. We've never met anyone like you before."

"Peasants."

"You have no idea." He grazed her lips; they tasted like red wine, garlic, and human breath.

They passed the Hermitage Gardens, its frozen skating rink and heated restaurant and drinking area all enclosed with thick plastic, shut down and abandoned for the night. They crossed over the Garden Ring road, then turned left on a side street; squeezing between two rows of chaotically parked cars; wending their way among nineteenth-century "French-style" monoliths and their *optikas*, *aptekas*, and *obmen valyuti*s on the ground floor and haphazard courtyards behind arched entryways where silent cars slept and klatches of murmuring, track-suit-clad drinkers lurked in pools of light; now drawing closer to Jim's home as he drew Kaisa closer to him; looping right past a music school in front of which stood a drinks kiosk and a shuttered Uzbek melon stand; then left as they drew to an abrupt halt in front of the State Museum of Musical Instruments, across from which loomed Jim's building.

Jim ushered Kaisa out in a hurry, pressing one hundred rubles into the cabby's hand as he wished them a leering good night. He didn't let go of her hand until they were safely in Jim's apartment. By some miracle the moon had cooperated, and shone through the bedroom window. They disrobed in silver pools of light, hurried under the sheets and blankets (Jim's windows didn't quite fit in the frames), both of them hesitant and almost trembling at first but then growing more confident, here and there and here again, eventually falling asleep as they heard the first stirrings of predawn morning through the imperfect windows, Kaisa's hair nimbusing across Jim's chest as they locked hands and tried to breathe in unison.


THE MORNING REVEALED Jim's apartment less flatteringly. The sprinkling of dust on the windowsills that glinted in the moonlight now showed itself a good centimeter thick, and was joined by measurable piles starting to creep up the walls from the corners. Peeling duct tape tried to keep the wind from sneaking in around the sides of the bedroom windows; the threadbare curtain off the vast, empty living room that hid what Jim told Kaisa was a balcony revealed a boarded-up room outside with a few decades' worth of the landlady's discarded household appliances.

Jim woke up before Kaisa, parched, and went into the kitchen for a glass of water, only to find eight liter bottles in the fridge, each with a few sips of flat, formerly carbonated water. An off smell hit him when he opened the refrigerator door, but whether it came from the butter, the sausage, or the box of vegetables unidentifiable through the condensation that had collected on the inside, he couldn't tell. The bread box held a few heels of stale bread, two of them turning to mold; in the cabinet was half a box of old soda crackers, a nine-dollar jar of Skippy peanut butter, empty but for a smear around the bottom bevel, a jar of the cheapest instant coffee, and a few tea bags stolen from the office. Optimistically, breakfast for them would be slices of toasted stale bread with a tiny touch of peanut butter and a spoonful of cherry jam, but he hadn't yet checked the condition of the jam.

He snuck back into the bedroom, checked the clock (8:15, still a good two hours before he had to be at work), dressed, and snuck out to provision from the kiosk five stories down, hoping she'd stay asleep until he got back and cleaned up.

No such luck. He returned to find her sipping tea—without sugar, lemon, or milk—from one of his landlady's chipped, stained mugs. She wore nothing but the blue oxford shirt he'd worn yesterday, but had wrapped her legs in the thick, rough, exceptionally warm military blanket. Her hair and skin shone; how she managed to look so unblemished when he felt like he'd been dragged across Moscow behind a truck was a mystery—one for which he was deeply grateful.

"I'm sorry about this," he said, gesturing at the dilapidated surroundings. "You're probably used to . . ."

"I live in a double room at MGU with a Chinese engineer who can't speak Finnish, English, or Russian," she said, referring to the university that sprawled across the hills in the southern reaches of the city. "This is heaven." She stood up and kissed Jim, locking one hand behind his head and holding on to the blanket with the other.

"Breakfast?"

"Such as it is." He took out a loaf of black bread, a little plastic bag of greasy blinis, some butter, a Day-Glo red ball of ersatz Armenian Gouda, fresh sausage, jam, and two boxes of tea: one *Menkhetten*-brand black tea, complete with a silhouette of a glamorous woman draped suggestively over the Empire State Building, and one Bodrost linden flower. It was more than he'd spent on food at one time since the day he got off the plane.

"A feast." She grinned, clapping her hands together and widening her eyes. "It's like being at a restaurant. Will you cook for me while I go shower?"

"No, but I'll assemble. The shower, though . . . come with me." He took her by the hand, pulling the blanket off and prompting a shriek as she hopped ahead of him into the tub. He reached for the shirt but she demurred, claiming modesty.

"Simple living," he said, pointing at the 1950s vintage hot-water heater inexpertly grafted onto the pipes leading to the tub. This was a white metal box, about the size of an average window air-conditioner, with a prominent black knob in the center, protruding from the wall above the tub. "On the one hand, it's a cold-water flat, which means I have to do this every time I take a shower." He turned the knob, releasing a loud *hoosh* of gas—Russian appliances, Jim had noticed, had three states: off, furiously on, and broken—struck a match, stuck it into a small compartment, and stood back as the blue flame shot out of the contraption a few inches before it caught. "On the other hand, at least I never run out of hot water. Just let it run for a couple of minutes first."

After he shut the door behind him he heard the dreaded clank of metal on porcelain. He sighed and bit his lip, again embarrassed at his crumbling apartment. He tried to open the door again but Kaisa had locked it. "Don't worry about that; sometimes the faucet handles come off if you don't press them down when you turn them. Just . . . just put it on the sink; I'll fix it when you get out."

"You mean if I get out. Will anything else break on me?"

"No, you should be fine. I'm going to make breakfast."


"Sorry about all of that," Jim said, when they were seated across from each other at the kitchen table. He handed her a mug of tea and pushed the platter of food toward her. "I wish I had a nicer place, but . . ."

A sudden banging on his door made them both jump. Kaisa looked up, terrified, knocking her glass of tea to the floor and shattering it. Following the banging came an atonal drone that resolved itself into a crude approximation of "The Star-Spangled Banner." Jim rolled his eyes, smiled, and excused himself. Before he even opened the door he knew it was his neighbor, Murat.

On his second day in Moscow, Jim had earned Murat's deep affection by carrying Murat's mother's groceries from the street up to the apartment she shared with her son. The old woman was bent nearly double; her body echoed the shape of the cane that helped her walk, and she pushed in front of her a rickety metal cart stuffed almost to bursting with net bags filled with vegetables, bottles of water, packages of salted fish, loaves of black and white bread, and, at the bottom, three bloody paper-wrapped packages containing the freshly flayed heads of a cow, a goat, and a lamb. Jim, too, was returning from the kiosk at the end of the street, having just foraged for his first dinner in Moscow (black bread, herring, water, vodka), and it was raining that midwinter Moscow sort of sleety rain that seems not to fall but simply to materialize in midair and slither beneath the skin.

At the front door Jim found the old woman fumbling for her keys with a frozen, arthritic hand, and he offered to help. She looked at him with mute, steely suspicion. He widened his grin, making him look as harmless as possible, and she grew even more distrustful, maneuvering around so she stood between him and the luggage and casting a quick, pleading look up toward the window. She relented a bit, her gold-tooth smile peeking through her cloudy face, when Jim held the door open for her, then relented even more when he reached down and lifted her cart, groceries and all, up the entranceway steps and into the building.

When he got to the foot of the stairs, she made an upward sweeping motion with her hand, and he lugged the cart up the stairs, waddling heavily as he held the whole thing to his chest. This did nothing, however, to quiet the thing; the bags inside still rattled against the cart's metal bars, which rattled against one another, and the whole thing clanked against the stairs as Jim's hands began sweating and the cart started slipping. At about the fourth floor, he heard a door open above him, most likely, he judged, on his own floor, the sixth. Heavy footsteps came thudding down the stairs toward him, and he found himself face-to-face with a massive, bellowing, shaven-headed man with a thick beard and a long switchblade held menacingly toward him. Jim had the presence of mind to gently place the cart down between him and the knife rather than dropping it.

"Do you know whose bags you are stealing?" the man snarled.

The old woman, puffing mightily but advancing inexorably, like a little scarf-wrapped, dumpling-shaped locomotive, appeared a floor below them, waving her hands crazily, and repeated, "No, my dear one!

No, my darling!" When she reached the stairs she stood between Jim and the man for all of three seconds before she crumpled to the ground, exhausted, leaving Jim and the other man to grab an arm each. From the ground she explained to Murat—her son, the knife-wielder—that Jim was carrying her groceries *for* her, not stealing them *from* her. Murat eyed Jim with the same suspicion his mother had, but when Jim refused a tip, and said he was just helping a neighbor, Murat caught Jim's heavy-footed accent and asked him where he was from. When he said America, Murat's eyes lit up and he put away the knife.

The United States has no better friend than someone who's been ground under the heel of an officially anti-American tyranny. Murat believed in America as the repository of everything good, which is to say nothing so abstract as "freedom" or "justice," but fast cars, blond women, rich people, and pizza. On that first night he invited Jim in for an assault by hospitality that nearly resulted in a burst stomach and the first-ever case of twenty-four-hour cirrhosis. "I am not Russian," he boomed, shoving Jim into the seat of honor, farthest from the door, behind a mountain of flatbreads, kebabs, and salads, "but Tatar. We are commanded to treat a guest as God, especially when he comes from a country that God has made rich."

He demanded that Jim tell him everything about America, but really it was Murat who did most of the talking. He didn't want to hear, for instance, that Jim's car was ten years old; he didn't want to hear that he lived in apartments much smaller than Murat's; and when Jim said his parents ran a *stolovaya*—an ordinary restaurant for working people—rather than a much grander *restorant*, Murat flatly contradicted him. "It is proven that *stolovayas* do not exist in your America. You eat only at the *stay-eek khaus* or a *pitsa khat*." Of course, once Jim translated *hut* for him ("Like a yurt, but smaller"), Murat swore off the chain, which had several branches in Moscow, forever, leaving Jim to fear for the future of Radio Shack should it ever plan an eastward expansion.

If Murat was naïve about America, in all else he was the savviest person Jim had ever met; he knew nobody more expert at negotiating the tortuous paths of Russian law, an expertise born, of course, of a lifetime on the wrong side of that law. Jim was never sure just what Murat did for a living—he knew he sold electronic equipment, pirated CDs and DVDs, and the occasional car from an outdoor *rynok* on the north side of Belorusskaya station—but he seemed completely averse to regular hours, leaving Jim just as likely to head out to work with him on a weekday morning as to see him returning home then, too. He knew, too, that Murat had a wealth of guns because Murat had showed them to him, and had found it hilarious that this American had never fired, much less owned, even something as simple as a Sig Sauer 220 (which was, Jim had to admit, especially in the two-tone, chrome-topped model Murat favored, a beautiful machine).

If he had to guess, Jim would have made Murat a smuggler of sorts, perhaps a loan shark as well. He wasn't muscle; he lacked the simple dead-eyed thuggishness of someone like Predrag Sjindic, but, given his size, speed, and evident fearlessness, neither would Jim have ever bet against him in any sort of fight. All told, Jim liked the guy, even if he would rather not have had his company just now, but Jim had become Murat's charge and project. He would often stop by just to confirm for himself that, yes, an American was still alive in Moscow, across from him and his mother.

The singing stopped when Jim started flipping the three locks and pulling open the door. Murat filled the door frame: he was a six-foot-four-inch, two-hundred-pound Tatar, with a stubbly shaved head, a beard so full it was nearly spherical, and expressive, coal-black eyes. Usually it was the eyes that drew Jim's attention; this morning it was the knife, a curved, nasty bone-handled thing that Murat held toward Jim as he opened the door.

"Okay, Capone. Say good night." At least it wasn't "Time for fucking up of you, son" anymore. Jim always did as the situation required; he always acted scared, which prompted an explosion of booming laughter from Murat.

"Always so scared, this American. He knows in Moscow there are men with *knives*! And he knows he lives across from a *Tatar*! And he knows that Tatar men are famous for *cutting people up*!" He slipped the blade back into its casing and shoved Jim manfully back into the apartment. "Everything okay? Do you have any problems?"

"No problems at all. In fact"—Jim lowered his voice—"I'm not alone just now. I have company."

"You got lonely and stole some poor Russian's goat! I knew it." Another peal of laughter echoed down the staircase. "A girl! At last! Mother! Hey, Mother!" he called into the door of his apartment. The old woman appeared, floury but beaming, in the doorway. "At last, Dzheem found a real girl! She was worried, you know. She said it isn't normal for a man to live alone all the time. I said don't worry; he probably just takes care of his business somewhere else. But she's so happy now! Right, Mother? Aren't you, Mother?"

She waved at them beatifically and hobbled back to her stove.

"A Russian girl?"

"Finnish, actually."

"Even better! Finnish!" Another torrent of laughter crippled him. "The Mukhtandov Boys will never believe it! I live across from Capone and his Finnish girls! Listen, I know you have to go in and put on better clothes, and maybe shave and look nice." Jim looked down at his clothes and ran a hand over his face: he hadn't planned on doing any of this, actually. "I just wanted to give you a scare. You know, like friends. Also, listen: I should have a shipment of movies coming next week. You want anything, anything out now in the theaters at home or anything at all, please come tell me. I'll sell them to you at a discount."

"Yeah? What kind of discount?"

"Maybe I'll let you keep your fucking balls, now that you finally have some use for them!" With that, he disappeared into his apartment, slamming the door behind him, while his laughter was still bouncing off the linoleum floors and cinder-block walls.

# 7

THE TRAIN, AT LAST, was screeching to a halt. Vorov peered through the open door. He saw an absurdly grand stone building that still bore the occasional patch of scarlet paint amid the mold and crumbling gray. Atop the building, a square-jawed stone young man and flowing-haired stone young woman faced each other. The man held the hammer, the women the sickle; above them stone lettering screamed, "HERO CITY OF TILYANSK."

He saw not a single person on the platform, nor anyone inside the station, which had long since lost its doors. Nobody boarded the train; nobody aside from him alighted. After yearning for solitude for all sixty-seven hours he spent on the train, here it finally was: solitude such as only a provincial Russian train station at twilight can provide.

He closed his eyes and saw it all before him, saw it as clear as a dream, saw it as it was on the very first day, heard the children's band and even smelled the spilled spoiled beer and roasted sunflower seeds. He knew every brick on every building, every inch of tarmac and every railroad tie. His father and mother had built them all. He was, God help him, home.

Except for two skinny dogs that could barely even muster up the energy to look at Vorov, the station building was empty. Benches had been ripped from the floor; copper tubing had been ripped from walls; the mosaic that once covered the floor—a train speeding into the glorious future under the rapt gazes of happy peasants—had been looted, square by irrelevant square. The floor's bare plaster matched the walls' sickly yellow brick perfectly. Both were illuminated by a row of fluorescent bulbs that ran around the station's dome. They had eluded theft only because they were five stories up. A sign in front of the drawn maroon curtains in the ticket seller's window read TECHNICAL BREAK— 15 MINUTES, but was dated seven months ago. Judging by the station's smell and the blotchy stains on the floor and lower walls, it had become a favored public toilet for those caught short in the center of town.

Vorov breathed deeply through his mouth to calm himself, then shut his eyes and wrinkled his nose in disgust. Thirty years ago he swore never to come back, not here or anywhere else like it. There was no here here, anyway: Gertrude Stein said it about Oakland, across the bay from his adopted hometown, but what did she know? Had she ever seen a planned Soviet town that had outlived its empire and purpose? It was nothing plunked down in the middle of nothing because some nothing of a bureaucrat thought it was important to insulate the nothing it produced from the nothing the rest of the country produced. Towns like this make a journalist out of Beckett.

Red Army Street was eight lanes across and barely a car was on it. Immense stone monoliths lined it; they were dark. Vorov knew this illusion of civilization was only one street wide and about five streets long. Veer off in any direction and he would find first crumbling Khrushchev tower blocks, then dilapidated wooden houses, and then just vastness in every direction: trees and scrub and the occasional factory. Tilyansk was the graveyard's waiting room: immense buildings, dark and empty; the only signs of life on a Saturday night were packs of the desperate and haunted moving from apartment to kiosk to apartment until they could no longer stand up.

Tilyansk was built to house three hundred thousand people; the official population was fifty thousand, but he guessed the actual population was half of that. When the city was built—no, when Skrupshin's father ordered the city built—it was described as a scientific military research capital: a retreat from the world for the Soviet Union's finest minds. In fact it was a place for all sorts of scientific and military research best done away from people, whether for health, ethical, or military reasons. Skrupshin's father had a whole city to command, and this is what it had become. Everyone who could leave had left; everyone who stayed just rotted away a day at a time where they stood.

Across the street the inevitable gang of low-rent thugs, four of them, leaned against a kiosk. When they saw Vorov in his camel-hair overcoat and new fur hat, carrying a leather suitcase, hunger flickered in their eyes. They saw a target. As his upbringing in this hellhole made him painfully aware, Vorov was neither large nor strong. His benign, bookish, placid appearance went over well in his new home but was a liability here.

The tallest one leaned in close to his friends and said something that made them smile menacingly and look over at Vorov. They peeled themselves off the kiosk and began leisurely crossing the street. Vorov felt for the Sig in his pocket and flicked the safety off.

Just then a black late-model Mercedes S with rolling blue lights on top and on the dash rounded the corner and pulled to a stop in front of the station, between Vorov and the thugs across the street. The driver quickly stepped out of the car, laid a Heckler on the roof, and stared at the thugs—unlike Vorov he was large and looked quite adroit with the gun—until they turned around and vanished into an unlit side street. He gave a grim, satisfied smile, turned and saluted Vorov, and opened the back door.

"Home again, are we?" Skrupshin asked, smiling weakly as Vorov slid in beside him. Vorov noticed that Skrupshin, the consummate salesman with a smile almost as permanent and insincere as an American's, had reverted to his childhood role as the general's son, with that trembling, weak smile and the voice that strangled itself halfway up his chest. If Vorov slid over in his seat too quickly, he knew Skrupshin would flinch. A homecoming is only as happy as the home. "How long has it been for you?"

"Not nearly long enough," Skrupshin said. Scowling, he ran a finger down the window of the Mercedes—alas, the grime was on the outside. "You?"

"The same. What are you doing here? Officially, I mean."

"I am not here. I am on my way to Vladivostok for an economics conference. Russia, America, and the Pacific Rim. I decided to take the train because I work well on it and for sentimental reasons—I wanted to see the heart of my country again; I wanted to come here and see more than just decadent Moscow or European Petersburg." He sniffed ostentatiously, lifting his chin and puffing out his chest like a general. "I wanted to breathe the pure clean air and smell the rich black soil of the motherland." He laughed softly and returned to his normal posture.

"I presume you or one of your men can get me to Zelenogorsk by morning?"

"Of course. We can drive there now, in fact, and talk on the way." He leaned across Vorov and tapped his driver on the shoulder. The driver kicked the Mercedes into gear and they headed out of town, following the signs toward the M53 highway.

Not two streets off Red Army Street, stone monoliths gave way to dilapidated four-story blocks sent in chunks by train from a factory in Rostov. Thrown up in three days, they were supposed to house workers for the summer, as they were working on their permanent houses. But the slowdown hit, the money vanished, and instead of three months, they had lasted, somehow, for thirty years.

In truth they were more the proverbial ship—the one that is replaced, board by board, over a period of years—than their original selves. Skilled craftsmen in Tilyansk used to be able to build houses out of cast-off material: railroad ties, boards, quarried stones, cooking oil mixed with shredded wool for insulation. They didn't do that anymore because (a) little was cast off, and (b) the population was fleeing or dying by the hundreds every year. Why build something new when you can just take over an old house, or kick through a wall and expand?

"You can put me on the train, in my own compartment?" Vorov asked.

"We can."

"And ensure that nobody asks any questions?"

"It would be our pleasure, Tolya."

"Good. Then would you care to tell me what the fuck I am doing back here?"

Skrupshin made a pained expression but said nothing. As they passed under the stone archway—once topped with the same heroic figures that crowned the train station, now barren and crumbling—that marked the town's border, and turned onto the highway's access road, something thumped off the car's roof. The driver slowed and reached for his gun. They were hit again; this time a half-liter beer bottle shattered on the pavement in front of them. When the driver jammed on his brakes, Skrupshin laughed and waved him on.

"Please, Sergeant. This is how they entertain themselves here. This is who they are. You might as well shoot a cockroach for crawling across a floor. There is nothing else to do; just leave them, and let's go." He tried to be blithe, but Vorov saw the relief in his face. He felt it, too. He remembered the first time he passed under the arch when he was fifteen, on a Komsomol expedition to harvest potatoes or dig drainage ditches for yet another "town of the future" like this one, how free he felt, how he swore even as he sung "Build the Future Today" and "For Homeland, for Brotherhood" that one day he would go under and never come back. This, he supposed, was that day.

"I am paying a visit to the training academy in Krasnoyarsk," Skrupshin said, his superior smile pinned firmly back in place.

"Excuse me?"

"I had dinner with the generals and went right back to my hotel to work."

Vorov inclined his head toward the driver and looked pointedly at

Skrupshin, who put a finger to his lips, nodded, and patted the air reassuringly. "Sergeant," he called.

"Sir."

"Would you reach into the pocket on the driver's side door. I believe you'll find something in there to occupy you. Two things, actually."

The driver leaned down and withdrew an envelope. Opening it, he held up a banded packet of American hundred-dollar bills and a portable compact-disc player.

"Sergeant, would you mind recounting our activities this evening?"

"Yes, sir. I picked you up at the Krasnoyarsk airfield. I took you to the training academy, where I waited outside for three hours and twenty-four minutes. I took you to the Moskva Hotel. I took the car out to find a little companionship. I took her to a private spot in the fields, and then I returned to the hotel as well."

"Correct. I think you'll find you enjoy the music I've selected for you, too."

"Yes, sir."

When the driver put the earbuds in and pressed play, Vorov, leaning back and closing his eyes, hissed, "I hope you don't expect to be reimbursed for that."

"Counterfeit," Skrupshin whispered. "Stop worrying; he won't be our problem after tomorrow."

"So what *is* our problem? Again: what was so urgent that we had to speak here, of all places?"

"It's problems, plural, but we can get to that in a moment. As for 'here,' it's remote. We both know it."

"Too well, I think." Vorov turned away, looking out the window as Tilyansk abruptly ended, as planned, and the steppe began.

"It was mutually convenient."

"If you call five days on a train convenient."

"Then it was mutually inconvenient, Tolya." Skrupshin sighed. After a period of silence, he said, "We're finished. *It* is finished. I have been demoted."

"Not quite. Your foreign travel privileges have been suspended, and perhaps you won't be able to be quite so free with your paperwork, but you have not been demoted."

Skrupshin turned to look at him with a mixture of fury, amazement, and shame. "You arranged this?"

"Arranged? No. Knew of and could not stop. What can I tell you, Nikolai? Old men die. Even ministers; even our friends."

"And the new minister?"

"Konstatin Yegorovitch. Promoted from the general staff, former police commander of the Rostov Oblast. His wife is Georgian, and the rumor is he ran a smuggling operation across the border."

"So you know him."

"We know *of* him, but we are not yet connected. Again, what can I say? He spent his life in the south. I'm sure we have some mutual friends, but we do not yet know who they are."

"He says he wants to bring *change* to the ministry," Skrupshin groused, pronouncing *change* as though it were the foulest word he could think of.

"Of course he does. He has his own obligations to consider. He's not a white coat, if that's what you're worried about. He's no reformer; he just needs to feed his family."

"Yes, well, that means we can't feed ourselves. This means I can't just call in anyone in the army I please. Any general comes running at a summons from the minister himself; a summons from a deputy minister is only good for toilet paper."

"Is it? Have they started printing letters on better quality paper?"

"Funny. You don't seem as concerned as you should be. Was your dining companion at the Lermontov really that accommodating?"

Now Vorov sat forward and stared, but only for a moment. "No." He shrugged, settling back into the leather seat and stretching his legs out in front of him. "I have forgotten, apparently, to render unto Boris. His networks are closed to me until I sufficiently impoverish myself."

Skrupshin hissed and shook his head. His smile had hardened into something bitter, painful, skeletal. "So we have no transportation and we have no network of buyers. May I ask what is left to discuss? You will present your paper at your conference; I will work my way into the minister's good graces; and we will see each other in several years' time. Or not. But in any case, this is finished."

"Nothing is finished. For what we are selling, buyers are easy to find. Besides, what about the first one? The one who we took this afternoon."

"He goes home or he goes in the Yauza. I would prefer the latter, but of course, I will not be there. I can't be anywhere near you anywhere in civilization."

Vorov smiled equably, raising his eyebrows and turning the corners of his mouth down slightly, as though he had just received a low bid on something he was selling.

"You have a different thought?" Skrupshin asked skeptically.

"My only thought, Nikolai, is that you scare too easily. You always did. So your *krysha* died. So mine wants me dead. So now we have to meet in this miserable hellhole of a village rather than in Moscow. So we can't speak on the telephone anymore. You of all people, with a lifetime spent in one failed government and one failing, should know that we are never left with the ideal situation. We are not, the two of us, dead, nor is it likely that anything we do now can forestall our deaths if that is what our superiors have planned for us. All we can do is improvise."

"Improvise?" Skrupshin pronounced the word with disdain. "We made certain promises, not least that day in the prison. What do we tell our buyers?"

"We tell them the plans have changed. We don't tell them why; we don't ask for permission; we don't consult them; we don't cry on their shoulders. We *tell* them what to do. Have you really been in government so long that you no longer believe in authority without a stamp? For what we're selling, our buyers would cross the Urals barefoot."

"Fine. That's them. But we have kidnapped a man—an important man, who people will look for. What can we do with him now?"

"We hold him in Peredelkino for a little longer than we initially planned, that's all."

"And then what, Tolya? Then what? I cannot just order the army to chauffeur him to your doorstep. We cannot just put our guests on a train, can we?"

"Please, calm down. You need . . ."

"It is easy for you to be calm when you have a blue passport and a ticket back to California. I must live here."

"I understand that, which is why I have arranged for transport— army transport, no less—that keeps some distance between you, me, and our subjects. As you say, we cannot keep this between us anymore. I know that. But you must remember that one of the advantages of living in an empire—even a crumbling empire like this one—is that tendrils of influence still extend beyond state borders. We can still get them out; we just need to be more creative than perhaps we wanted to." Vorov paused, rubbed his chin, and smiled softly out the window. "Nikolai, do you remember Stavrin, from Komsomol?"

"Who?"

"Stavrin, our . . ."

"Yes, yes, of course. The fossil who marched us out in the middle of nowhere and left us to kill each other. I remember. I haven't thought of him in years. Why? Can he help?"

"I assume he's dead, Nikolai."

"Then I hope he went painfully."

"That's ungracious of you. He was a decorated officer, you know. Intelligence. He believed in what he did."

"How sweet."

"Do you remember Secrets? Each team had to pass two pieces of information down the proverbial line, from one boy to the next in opposite directions, while ferreting out the other team's secrets."

"I suppose. Those farm boys . . ."

"I know. A license to beat it out of a general's son. That's not what interests me. What interests me is the paradox of transmission, which I've never been able to forget."

"I have," Skrupshin sulked. He had the spoiled child's tendency to collapse. "Remind me."

"Two methods," Vorov said crisply, leaning forward like the professor that he was. "First, the black box. Write the information down, leave it in a mutually agreed-to location for Contact to retrieve. Problems: You can be followed. The drop can be discovered, either by accident or on purpose. Contact could miss it, either because you misspeak or he misunderstands. Weather. Wind. Entropy. Too many variables you don't control. Advantages: No interaction between you and Contact. No intermediaries. Minimal risk for human error.

"Second, the telephone chain. You pass the information to a third party who passes it to Contact. Problems: Another human means another potential for deception or error. The third party can be taken. Coerced. Vanished. Reprogrammed. Advantage is only if the third party is of equal or greater trustworthiness than Source and Contact and also is unknown to one of the two parties. Is that rare? Yes. Unheard of? No. Stavrin's solution, then . . ."

"The human black box," Skrupshin mumbled. "I remember. The person who carries information without knowing it."

"And without knowing for whom, or why."

"He also said it was impossible. No, sorry, no—not impossible. I remember the phrase: impractical to the point of impossibility."

"Except, of course, when it isn't."

"What does that mean?"

"Information can always mean one thing to one person and something else to someone else. Meaning is never fixed."

"So?"

Vorov sighed and shook his head. "You have no imagination, Nikolai. Even if you have no generals, we still have your ministerial seal, which can still induce soldiers to stand to attention. Especially when you back it with something spendable. Who knows: you might even make new friends."

"I don't . . ."

"I will explain, but you must remember two things. Two things will make this work. First, never underestimate the desire of Americans to 'fix' our country. If they want to be heroes, we should encourage them. Second, money solves all things. You still have people loyal to you because you paid them. In the event of wavering loyalty, you pay them more. We will recoup it ten times over at the end."

"But my generals—I'm sorry: our generals—who knows if they will even still acknowledge me once they hear of my transfer."

"All the more reason to work quickly."

Skrupshin retained his puzzled, wounded look, even as Vorov serenely leaned back in his seat and stretched his legs as far in front of him as they would go. Through the windshield the first hint of Zelenogorsk's corona of lights gleamed on the horizon. In the original plan, before he was demoted and before Vorov fucked them by keeping too much for his pool, his cars, his travel, and his books, he would have personally known everyone involved; he could even have been present with every transfer. He started to shake his head. "It will never work."

Vorov reached across the seat and slapped him playfully on the arm. "Of course it will. Did you never read your *Hamlet*? 'Assume a virtue if you have it not.' Be strong. It's already started."


MINA'S EYELIDS KEPT DROPPING: she was almost done redacting a security report; it was four p.m. and pitch-dark, that time of the afternoon when it should have been afternoon; and the United States Senate thermometer on her desk said it was 87 degrees in her office. With the window open. When the phone rang she nearly jumped out of her chair.

"Haddad, consular."

"Oh, I'm sorry," said the familiar voice. "I was just trying to reach Velez, in Economic Affairs." Mina lifted a flap on the back of the phone and pressed the green button: a brief whoosh of static, then the three all-clear chimes.

"We're secure."

"You'd better get down here. There's something you need to see."

"I was just about to . . ."

"Now. Don't dick around. Right now."

Click. Mina tapped her pen against her teeth, briefly entertained thoughts of staying put or taking her time, then put them out of her mind and took off down the hall: not running, exactly, but not getting out of anybody's way, either.

"Hey, Meen, where's the fire?" Phil Harlan, a fortyish economic analyst, came out of his office as she passed, sticking out a leg and pretending to trip her.

"Not now, not now." Over her shoulder, unable to resist, she asked, "Do people actually say that?"

"Why don't you tell me what you want me to say," he called after her, shrugging and flashing what he obviously thought was his most winning smile as he ran a hand along his slicked-back hair. She shook her head with disbelief as she turned the corner. Amazing, what guys can get away with—or think they can get away with—as they age, and the pool of single men without major defects becomes smaller. Harlan smelled of drugstore aftershave. He had shiny hair, whitened teeth, wingtips, an iron-on smile, an endless stream of shopworn quips, and he thought he was a foreign-service lothario. In fact he was a barely tolerable life-support system for a warm body and a functional (erratic, if the rumors were true, but functional) organ who every so often was pitied or used by a few lonely women a long way from home. Mina had known several of him.

She headed down a staircase, opened a door with an electronic swipe, headed down another hallway, entered a code into a keypad, waited for the snap of the latch, and walked through a reinforced steel door. At the end of the hallway, Crow was propped behind a desk, feet up and jacket slung over the back of the leather chair.

"You made good time."

"I'm sorry about that. Harlan waylaid me."

"That fucking prick. Makes me want to put a condom on each finger just to shake his hand." Mina cleared her throat and looked down. Twelve years of convent education made her blush her way through even the shortest conversation with Crow. "If he got to you then you made even better time."

"What happened?" Mina asked anxiously. She thrust both hands deep in her pockets and crossed her fingers: another holdover from the convent.

"Well, nobody else has disappeared, if that's what you're worried about. At least as far as we know, which means none of yours. But," Crow said with a flourish, sliding a magazine-sized picture across the desk to Mina, "we've been monitoring all the likelies, and we found this happened. Or happening, I suppose. Taken last night. That's Rodion Lisitsov's granddaughter on the left. And on the right . . ."

"Oh, my God," she muttered.

"You do know him, then? I'm remembering right? The guy from the New Year's party?"

"Yes."

"Do you have an ongoing relationship with him?"

Mina pointed to the granddaughter. "Does it look like I have an ongoing relationship with him?"

"Could you just answer . . ."

"No. No, I don't. We're friendly, but nothing more."

"You know we'll have to poly this, right?"

"Of course. Absolutely. Right now, if you want."

"I don't want. Not just yet. What exactly is your relationship with him?"

Crow had neither pen nor paper, but Mina knew everything she said was as good as recorded. Crow's memory—and willingness to deploy it vindictively—was becoming agency legend. "We grew up near each other. He moved here a few months ago and didn't know anybody. Dave

THE UNPOSSESSED CITY | 99

Willow, the guy he works for, who runs this foundation that studies Russian history, brought him to our New Year's party, and we play cards every few weeks."

"Cards? Just the two of you?"

"No," Mina drawled in the same irritated tone she used on her parents when they asked if she had been drinking. "The embassy poker game. We're playing this weekend, actually."

"Are you? Are you really?" Crow leaned back and thought, or at least simulated thinking. With Crow, as with any politician, you could never be quite sure. "You should see him beforehand."

"I . . . Why?"

"Why? First, because I told you to. And second, sound him out about this. So what if he has his arm around this blondie: are you actually trying to convince me he would be immune to a full-on Mina Haddad charm offensive?"

A subtle blush, just a slight flush and prickling of her ears this time, and a shuffling of feet.

"Of course he wouldn't. Find a way to meet."

"Can I use someone else?"

"Instead of you? Is that a fucking joke?"

"In addition to. For a chance meeting."

"Oh. Oh, feel free. Usual precautions, of course, but I don't have to tell you that, right? You are still you, after all."

"I am."

A knowing, slightly lascivious smile spread across Crow's face. "I know who you're going to use. I know exactly what you're going to do."

"I won't be too . . ."

"You won't be too anything, I know. The kid likes you, though. Be nice."

8

AS HE WATCHED HER get dressed, Jim reflected that not once since he woke up had he wanted Kaisa to leave: usually, after a night like this, he all but counted down the minutes until he could be alone and roll the situation around in his head for a while. This morning, however, he felt more ease and curiosity than awkwardness at the breakfast table. So, he surmised, did she, unless her beauty and the sheer surprise of her had completely impaired his judgment.

They headed out to the Metro, clasping their hands together in Jim's pocket as they crunched over the tamped-down snow and ice that covered sidewalks along the broad, exhaust-heavy Triumfalnaya stretch of the Garden Ring between Jim's apartment and the Metro station. Kaisa almost got blown off her feet when a dapper little man in a leather jacket and porkpie hat scurried through the rough-hewn wooden station door in front of them, sending it swinging with the heaviness and finality of a guillotine. The wooden escalator descended quickly enough to sweep distracted passengers off their feet, but the ride still took the better part of two minutes, plunging them deep into the world beneath Moscow.

They passed under ceiling mosaics depicting heroes of Soviet space flight, and waited for the train in a marble alcove beneath an ornate chandelier. Metro stations gleamed; they showcased the Russian genius for ornate, overstuffed coziness. The train screeched into the station and they squeezed into the front car, the previous night protecting them like a glorious secret from the dourness that prevailed among the other passengers.

At Teatralnaya he disembarked. She promised to call him later, after she had spoken to her grandfather. He leaned forward to kiss her but the commuter current carried him backward off the train.

HE EXITED THE STATION across from the Bolshoi Theatre, currently closed for "structural reforms" after it was found to be sinking into Moscow bedrock at the alarming rate of about three inches a year (left unchecked, in just a few years Putin's head would be at about the level of Khrushchev's knees). He turned around and passed along Mokhovaya, across from Red Square, whose sheer awesomeness—the riot and vibrancy of colors, the jarring contrast between the long, low Lenin mausoleum and Kazan's onion domes, the huge expanse of space, the endless Kremlin walls—never ceased to amaze him. Then he turned up Tverskaya, built wide enough to accommodate tank parades, passing an ophthalmological institute, a tanning salon topped by a neon Nefertiti, and several buildings of the nondescript, heavily guarded variety.

Jim crossed Tverskaya via the *perekhod:* an underground pedestrian passageway beneath main roads too broad, and with too much traffic, to ford aboveground. Some were lined with stalls selling phone cards, flowers, video games, beer, dry goods, bolts of fabric, irons, laundry racks, cigarettes, meat pies; others, like this one, were eerily empty, lit by weak yellow sodium lights. Occasionally you'd hear of skinheads or muggers beating someone up in one of these passages. This morning, though, he traversed a three-person gauntlet comprising an old woman selling plastic bags of shriveled beets and potatoes, a bearded beggar who mumbled prayers with his eyes shut and hands clasped, and an unconscious drunk in a greasy blue parka that reeked of urine and homemade booze. Jim emerged unscathed.

He cut through a narrow alley between a parking lot—or rather a vacant lot that had become a parking lot—and a robin's-egg-blue church.

Old women in headscarves nattered at the church doors. At the alley corner, he passed a bilious-looking old man, leather cap on his head and cigarette burning in the corner of his mouth, sitting in his Zhigouli, reading *Literaturnaya Gazeta*. He looked up when he heard Jim crunch on some broken glass. This wasn't unusual; sitting alone in cars seemed to be a hobby for some Russian men. Jim nodded at him—he was in an unshakably good mood this morning—but the man huffed, rolled his eyes, then started up his car and drove away. Who the man thought Jim—with his wool toggle coat, ratty boots, jeans, and backpack—could be was an open question; he was obviously not a Russian, nor anyone to be feared. Perhaps Jim simply disturbed the man's alone time.

The Memory Foundation occupied two apartments in an otherwise residential building. On the staircase leading from the street to the front door, a steel-toothed babushka in a floral headscarf attacked the stairs with a crude broom, little more than a bunch of twigs tied to the end of a stick. Each Sisyphean sweep diffused a cloud of pebbles, sunflower-seed husks, cigarette butts, and debris that settled on the steps above and below. As Jim ascended the stairs, steering as clear as he could of her and her project, she looked at him with repressed, beady-eyed rage. His phone rang; he paused on a step to pull it out of his pocket, and the woman's rage turned to savage glee: she finally found an infraction to punish.

"You uncultured young man!" she bellowed, loading the first word with ironic contempt. "Perhaps you believe these stairs were built just for you to flirt and gossip while honest people work, but I must inform you it is against regulations to talk on the telephone in front of the doorways to the building. You are impeding the entry of others; also, I must tell you that your filthy habit has consequences for the brain, for it has been proven . . ."

Jim turned on her and headed down the stairs, wishing her good day as she returned to her (doubtless self-appointed) duties, mumbling about foreigners as she attacked the butts and stones with newfound energy.

"*Slushayu vas,*" he said, flipping the receiver open. He loved the directness of that greeting: "I'm listening to you." It contained a challenge; it reminded the caller of the imposition and obligation entailed by his call, while also promising attention. Get on with it, the greeting implied. I'm already listening to you.

"Jim, good morning, how are you?" asked a female American voice, not waiting for an answer. "This is Mina Haddad calling. Am I catching you at a bad time?"

"No, not at all, Mina," he said, walking over to the side of the building and standing up straighter.

Even though Jim was three years older than Mina, she was one of those impeccably proper women who always made him watch his language, tuck his shirt in, and not slouch. She worked at the embassy; she and Jim had met at one of those painful, awkward home-away-from-home holiday parties embassies throw for their citizens abroad. This was on New Year's Day; Jim had gone with the Willows to watch the bowl games in a dank, funereal four-hundred-seat conference room underneath the embassy. Jim had no interest in any of the games; Mina had long legs, brains, and wide onyx eyes that always seemed to be watching and evaluating.

She had grown up just across the river, in suburban Virginia, where her Lebanese father and Turkish mother, both optometrists, had a practice together. Nothing romantic ever developed, but she and Jim got along quite well: her buttoned-up, pin-striped, grind-it-out ambition concealed a wicked sense of humor and a keenly observing eye. She seemed happy to have a friend outside the embassy world, and even happier that the friend came from home. Each seemed to like the idea of the other a little more than the actual person, but that gap grew smaller with each interaction.

"Jim, I'm calling to confirm for this Saturday evening. Are you 'in,' as they say?" Education had driven Mina's slang into irony long ago. She was an unsteady but avid poker player, and she had taken it upon herself to organize a game once every three weeks, mostly composed of embassy staff, with Jim thrown in as a reliable if token outsider.

"Of course I am. I'll hope for a better showing than last time, but I'm looking forward to it."

"Well, we'll see what we can do about getting you some better cards." Jim had to smile; at the last game he had suffered an inevitable off night, losing about two hundred dollars, mostly to the game's other nonembassy player, a smarmy, frattish securities analyst with Citibank.

"Well, thanks, Meen. Where and when?"

"I've reserved one of those private-cabin things at Neftchilar. It's an Azeri place near Krasnopresnenskaya. Do you need me to send you directions?"

"No, I'll find it. Thanks."

"What about a car? Do you want me to arrange for someone to pick you up?"

"No, no." She always offered, but a polished hollowness in her tone made it seem pro forma, not to be accepted. "Metro and tram work for me. When do we start?"

"Eight o'clock, same as always." She lowered her voice from professional to friend-level. "Are you feeling okay?"

"Me? Fine, why?"

"You just sound a little hoarse. A little tired."

"Oh, that. I had a late night last night. The body doesn't recover like it used to."

"Tell me about it," she said, with the forced, well-intentioned sympathy of the clean-living. "Anything interesting?"

"Nothing much." Jim stalled, not wanting to discuss Kaisa with Mina. He wouldn't have been able to say why, really; even if it hadn't been the morning after, he wouldn't have felt it was right. "One of those quick after-work drinks that ends up lasting until two. You know how it is."

"I do. Of course I do," she said unconvincingly. "We'll see you there at eight on Saturday, okay? I need to run; I'm about knee-deep in visa reviews."

"Get those ankle bracelets ready at the airport."

"Who said we were letting them in in the first place?"

"My mistake. I'll see you Saturday at eight."

IN THE OFFICE THAT DAY—another sign of either aging or a lack of close friends at the office—there was no ribbing Jim about his departure the previous night, no Walk of Shame, or leering innuendos. In the kitchen at lunch, Kirsten asked him if everything had ended up as well as it looked like it was going to; he said yes, and she said she was glad.

All morning he jumped whenever the office phone rang and exhaled with frustration whenever anyone else answered. He felt jittery, awkward, pathetic, but, underneath it all, grateful to have those same familiar old feelings again. When his mobile phone finally rang he withdrew it from his shirt pocket so quickly he sent it clattering across his desk. Vassily tossed it back to him with a wink. He answered as casually as he could.

"Hi, Jim. It's . . ."

"I know," he said too eagerly, clenching his eyes shut in self-recrimination. But given that clipped and musical accent, that tintinnabular voice that always seemed about to break into laughter, and most of all knowing what the face and body that housed the voice looked like, Jim was all but congratulating himself for not trying to leap through his phone to grab her. "How are you?"

She giggled. "Fine. As I was four hours ago. Nothing has changed." Jim started to speak but she cut in. "I'm sorry to interrupt. I don't want to be rude but I just snuck into the bathroom to call you. I'm supposed to be doing a scene review. I wanted to tell you I talked to Grandfather this morning, and he has agreed to speak with you. If you still want to talk to him."

"Yes. Yes, of course I do. Just tell me when and where."

"Tonight, if that's convenient?"

"Tonight is fine. I have no plans."

"No? Then you can talk to him at his work. He is a security guard at Sporting Palace."

"A security guard? At Sporting Palace? Your grandfather? How old is he?"

"You know this place?"

Jim did, of course. Housed in a former hard-currency shopping center on Arbat Street, Sporting Palace comprised two regular bars, three restaurants, a sports bar with international sports and an in-house bookie, a sushi bar with Russian chefs decked out like ninjas, an indoor driving range, a video-game room, an indoor firing range, a dance floor, and, at the back of the restaurant, a rather garish strip club with a spindly spiral staircase leading upstairs to an exceptionally expensive brothel. It catered to every foreign visitor's fantasy of the Wild East. Rumor had it that certain diplomats made it their first stop on arrival, even before checking in to their hotel; after ten o'clock every evening, the surrounding stretch of Arbat Street looked like a Mercedes and Hummer dealership.

She laughed again. "He is not so young. But big. Huge. And healthy. A hearty old Ukrainian size. You will see."

"Great. What's his name?"

"Naumenko. Naumenko, Grigory," she said, using the Russian convention of putting the first name last and pronouncing them staccato with pauses, as though each syllable were its own name. "You may ask for him, he said, at the bar, anytime after seven o'clock this evening, but before he becomes too busy at eleven o'clock."

"My favorite place to ask for anything."

"Yes, I know. I must . . ."

"Can I see you afterward? After I talk to him?"

There was a brief pause into which everything fell. Jim drew back from the edge. "If not, if you're busy, no problem. We can . . ."

"No, I would like to. Very much. It just depends on what time I can leave my rehearsal here. Can we speak after?"

"Absolutely."

"Or I can come to Sporting Palace, maybe?"

"That works, too. I'll try to get there around eight."

"Yes." He couldn't tell if she was agreeing to meet him or just processing information. "I will try."

"And I will hope."

She made an intimate little sound—somewhere between a sigh and a hum with an audible smile—that almost sent him to his knees. "Yes."

"HEY, THERE, JIMMY, you taking a brief trip away from planet Earth? Never seen you looking like that before." Dave Willow's forced, reedy bonhomie brought him out of his reverie. He had paused between Jim's and Birgitta's desks on one of his rally-the-troops strolls through the office. Without warning, he put a hand on each desk and lifted himself off the ground, extending his legs straight out in front of him and holding them still, closing his eyes and exhaling. Vassily peered over the top of *Argumenti y Fakti*, then raised it to cover his face. Jim heard the chuckles from behind the pink tabloid.

"Sorry, Dave. Just thinking. Listen, do you have a minute?"

"Sure do." He lowered himself back to the ground and rotated his arms in circles. How he kept a blazer unripped for more than a month was beyond Jim. "This a work thing or personal? Here, or . . ." He trailed off.

"Work, but let's go into your office."

Dave said that sounded good, really good, and beckoned him into the office. He waved Jim into a chair; he took the couch, kicking off his shoes, revealing his white tube socks with blue toes, and settling into a semireclining position in the corner. He never sat behind his desk; he wanted everyone to know he was not that kind of boss.

"What's on your mind, Jimmy?"

"I have an interview with a survivor tonight."

"Really? That's great. Congrats. How'd you find him? Or her," he added quickly.

"Him. He's the grandfather of a friend."

"So you need me to go over some standard questions?"

"No. No, I don't. I think I've got it."

"Well, I guess you do. Good for you."

"Thanks, Dave. Months of striking out, and one just falls into my lap. Funny how it happens, isn't it? Usually getting these old Russians to talk is like pulling teeth."

Dave puffed air out through his cheeks and mussed his mousy thatch of hair. "It happens sometimes, you know. I mean, there's never a line outside the door, but I've had a few reverse cold calls. They'll hear about what we do from someone or another, and just call up. At the beginning we put a few ads in the big papers, you know, but about a year ago, about the same time Greenpeace got in trouble for those pipeline protests, they just stopped printing the ads."

"I assume they didn't stop taking the money, though."

"No, no, you're right. They took everything we sent. Anyway, we got a few dozen people with those ads."

"A few dozen? Not bad."

Dave slapped his thighs and stood up, prompting Jim to do the same. "Don't get greedy, Jimmy. One at a time. And don't feel bad about your cold streak. Everyone has one now and again. Why don't you go ahead and think about it like this: you got yours out of the way first."

BY THE TIME JIM LEFT the office, a little before seven p.m., pillowy, cornflake-sized snow had started to fall, making his walk down Tverskaya slippery, but more enjoyable: the snow and the cold bring Moscow to life. Heat makes the city's imposing structures seem all the more oppressive; cold makes them seem safe, like points of refuge. The angular lines cast by the streetlights, the overcoats and fur hats, and the general air of purpose and seriousness made everybody look like protagonists in their own mystery novels.

His own mystery, however, had started out simply—how long would he have to stay in Moscow to make back what he owed Petey—but in just a few months, it had become more complicated: he loved it here. He felt challenged, alive, free from his past selves and his mistakes. He had worried that he might not feel at home, but he failed to see, never having lived off the East Coast before, that was the point: departures are calisthenics for the spirit.

SPORTING PALACE LOOMED over Novy Arbat Street in neon and concrete like a garish, fat old uncle in a Camaro. During Soviet times, Novy Arbat housed foreign-currency establishments open only to foreigners, and so had a certain exclusive cachet with Russians. The clubs and restaurants that occupied it now built on that cachet: they were some of the city's most expensive visible establishments (as opposed to the truly exclusive establishments that fetishized their own secrecy), catering both to tourists and to Russians who wanted to rub shoulders with foreigners.

Next to the Palace an ironic, Soviet-kitsch beer hall called Big Brother Funtime—whose concrete walls were festooned with propaganda posters—served greasy salads, watery beer in chipped mugs, and blocks of processed cheese, but they charged six dollars per beer. Tourists eager to have their preconceptions confirmed packed the place every night. Across the street, at a sushi restaurant where dishes were floated to diners on an intricate network of table-height canals, the rich teenage children of Moscow's political elite arrived in chauffeured SUVs, decked out in Prada and wielding rhinestone-studded cell phones. Jim had never been to either place. He couldn't afford the sushi, and culinary irony is worth paying for only when the food actually tastes good.

At Sporting Palace, a security guard in military fatigues and Ray-Bans frisked Jim, searched his bag, opened the door, and shoved him roughly through. Jim turned and gave him a challenging glare; the guard just laughed and pulled the door shut behind him. Jim found himself dwarfed, standing at the foot of a cavernous room larger than an airplane hangar. The room's varied activities reached him in echoes: clinking glasses and cutlery, electronic beeps and doinks, muffled pops, thumping Russkipop, and a soft wave of conversation.

All activities except the brothel took place in different corners of this single huge room with concrete walls and floor, lit by bare high-wattage bulbs dangling from the ceiling some five stories up and screwed into dangling, obviously improvised electrical outlets. It had all the aesthetic appeal of a displaced-persons camp. The hundreds of patrons milling around in various states of debauch could never come close to making the space feel anything but gloomy and underpopulated. The light gave everyone a ghoulish, hungry look, made their shadows shrink and expand as they teetered from one area to the next. Cinder-block partitions separated the various activities from one another, and uniformed security personnel, all holding submachine guns and wearing belts with pistols, Tasers, truncheons, and pepper spray, kept the patrons in line: no mean feat when some of those patrons were half-drunk and test-firing automatic rifles at the long, narrow range at the back of the room.

The barmaid, a tough-looking older woman wearing too few clothes and too much makeup, sauntered over with two menus, and asked him which he preferred, Russian or English. Jim chose English but he asked for it in Russian, figuring it was better to lower people's expectations and surpass them than it was to pretend to be a native and get called out. He ordered a beer, a pork shashlik, and pickled tomatoes.

"Watchin' your carbs, are you?" Jim turned his head to the right and saw looking amicably at him a scrawny bald man with the somber pinstripes, desperate smile, ruined teeth, and bleary eyes of the English businessman at the end of a long night.

"Something like that, I guess."

"Yeah," he agreed into his glass. "Canadian, is it?"

"Sorry?"

"Are you Canadian? I can't quite place your accent."

"No, no. American."

"I did actually think that, if you must know. But what I say is: always best to guess from the smaller country, know what I mean? Assume a Canadian's American, or a Kiwi's an Aussie, they're like as not to take offense. But reverse it, you know, and no problem. Been here long?"

"What, in Moscow? No, about five months, give or take. You?"

"Near on ten years, if you can believe that. Came over just after the collapse, when everyone was running the other way. Mind you, I think that whole crisis was a bit of a whoopsy-doodle, if you know what I mean."

"Yeah," Jim agreed, in the purposefully mild way one talks to a stranger at a bar who has not yet proven his sanity. "What do you do over here?"

"I'm a commodities analyst. Work for one of the big British banks. Bit boring, to tell you the truth, but the pay's good enough, and you can't really complain, can you?"

"I guess not."

"Long as you stay on the right side of the tax police, and keep bringing capital in so the bosses can keep taking it right back out again, you'll be right."

"The tax police? The tax *police*?" Jim had visions of nebbishy little accountants with calculators in their holsters trying to kick in a door and falling backward, hopping and clutching their feet.

The man emitted the weary chuckle experience gives to naïveté. "The tax police, my son, are the scariest blokes in town. The thing is, you see, the tax code here is so bollixed up that everyone—from the old babushka selling mushrooms and herbs in the underpass right up to the president—is guilty of something. Evasion, improper filing, what have you. The government keeps it that way on purpose: that way they can get who they like, when they like, with an excuse that smells sweet enough for anybody. And when they decide to get you, they send the tax police: big fucking OMON boys with even bigger guns, a dozen at a time in the middle of the night. Quite clever, really, when you think about it."

"So how does a big English bank like yours stay in business?"

"Who, us? Like everyone else: we pay a special tax-police tax. We're nice to everybody, and we hate every politician other than the ones we're told to like. But you didn't hear that from me."

"You've been here before?"

"What, here? This bar?"

"This very bar."

"Oh, yeah. Where else would you go, really? It has a bit of everything you might want." He nodded significantly at a pneumatic blonde walking behind Jim, then violently drained his half-full glass.

"Same way again, love, if you would," he said to the barmaid, running a bony finger across his top lip and jerking his head toward Jim. He had the bobbing motions and jangling limbs of a skittish, underfed primate. "And give another to my friend here."

"Oh, no, that's all right, I couldn't . . ."

"Go on. Your first night here, by the looks of it. Still wide-eyed, not got your sea legs. Got to make you feel welcome, haven't I?"

"Well, thanks. I appreciate it."

"It *is* your first time here, isn't it?"

"It is."

"Just here for the food, are you?" He jerked his head toward the waitress as his right arm flew up to his head to smooth the gray strands ringing his egg-shaped dome.

Jim nodded equivocally.

"Probably for the best. My wife hates it when I come here."

Jim let that one pass without comment. "Actually, I'm supposed to meet someone here, but I'm not sure what he looks like."

"Oh, yeah? Who's that, then?"

"Grigory Naumenko's his name."

"Nah. Sorry, mate. Don't know him. Mind you, a fair number of the great and the good come marching through here at one point or another," he said, swiveling around in his stool and blessing the audience with a sweeping wave of his pint glass. "Russian, is he, your man? A friendly native?"

"Yes, he is. Why?"

"Well, you're here on the right night for it. Our lot, foreigners, I should say, tend to keep their piss-ups to the weekend, don't they? So earlier in the week, say, a Tuesday like today, for instance, you find a more local crowd out here. Mind you, by local I don't mean the bloke at the vodka stand. I mean Russians with a bit of dosh to throw around. Speaking of which"—he pointed his chin toward the back of the room, where a quintet of heavily made-up young women who looked far too attractive to be sitting alone at a bar were, in fact, sitting purposefully alone, purposefully far apart from one another, looking gloomily downward as though waiting to be rescued, at a bar in the back—"I've got a bit to throw around myself. Word of advice: if you really are looking for someone, a smile and a twenty-dollar bill go a lot further than just a smile. Course you probably knew that. Cheers, then; I'm off."

JIM DID AS the Englishman suggested: he tried asking the bartender, in his best Russian, whether she knew where he could find Grigory Naumenko. She gave him a stony glare and a slow shake of the head. He then apologized, in English, for his poor Russian, and asked again, in English, this time ordering another beer, paying with a twenty-dollar bill, and insisting she keep the change. She sighed, rolling her eyes and smiling sardonically, then walked over to the far end of the bar and spoke into a walkie-talkie she pulled off the wall. She nodded conspiratorially at Jim, then began to reapply her makeup, and he fell from her attention completely.

After ten minutes Jim began to suspect he'd been played. The barmaid wouldn't look at him, even when he held up an empty glass and raised a hand. He'd noticed the outside door had opened and shut a few times without anyone entering, and he could swear that the guard gave him the fisheye each time. He was about to chalk tonight up for a loss and try again tomorrow, earlier in the evening, when he felt a huge paw on his shoulder press him back down into his stool. A bearish man in a navy-blue security guard jumpsuit lowered himself into the seat next to Jim's. He looked like a healthier and more jovial Boris Yeltsin, with good-natured piggy eyes, a spider-veined nose, and fleshy lips beneath a shock of shiny gray hair. "Grigory Borisovitch," he said, nodding curtly at Jim.

"Oh, right," Jim stammered. "I'm glad . . ." Correcting himself, he switched to Russian. "You are Grigory Naumenko?"

The man nodded.

"I'm Jim Vilatzer." He extended a hand, which the old man's enveloped completely. "Kaisa told you I would be coming?"

He nodded, his lips clenched into a line as he stared straight down at the bar and shifted in his seat. "She said you find Russian history interesting."

"I do," Jim said as cheerfully as he could, realizing as he did how foolish, naïve, and American it sounded. "I want to thank you for speaking with me." Of course, Naumenko had as yet done no such thing, and Jim retreated a half step, keeping his voice as even and accommodating as possible. "Do you want to talk to me about your past?"

He nodded again, this time more resolutely, and, laying his enormous hands flat on the bar, he turned to look at Jim directly. "Yes. Yes, I think it's time. I don't know who is interested in such stories, though."

"Well, your granddaughter, for one."

He chuckled sadly and waved his hand. "She has better things to think about. She has a much better life; she does not need me to drag her backward. To hear such things would . . ." He trailed off, working his hands against each other and breathing hard.

Jim wasn't sure what to do. Having thought of the past five months as a string of failures, he had naturally considered this evening a success, but that was before he arrived, before he realized that what he did entailed poking a huge stick into the muck of someone else's soul and memory, and stirring hard.

What right did he have to take such an interest in other people's stories? Why was it his business—Dave's business, Birgitta's business, the Foundation's business—if people who survived something he could not even begin to imagine chose to keep silent, to bury the past and move forward as best they could?

Naumenko exhaled loudly, his body sinking like a sad balloon. Jim thought he was preparing to stand up and leave; instead he made that quiet but piercing whistle that seems a special talent of the Russian male, and waved two fingers at the barmaid. "Excuse me," he said. "I find I cannot talk unless I drink."

"I'm the same way."

He looked at Jim doubtfully. "Americans don't drink," he said firmly as the barmaid brought a small carafe of vodka, two stemmed cut-glass shot glasses, and a plate of pickled garlic cloves, sausage, and black bread. "But tonight the American will drink." He poured vodka into both glasses until a token drop spilled over the edges. Somehow he managed to raise his without spilling any. Jim did the same and prepared for an extended, florid Russian toast. Instead Naumenko inclined his head slightly, gulped down his vodka, then picked up a slice of black bread and sniffed deeply. Jim knocked his back, coughing slightly.

"He cannot hold it," said Naumenko, to everyone and no one, as a smile broke through. "You said you drink? You Americans drink beer that tastes like sour water and go jogging all the time. You have lawns for playing golf, but you never drink. You must first eat something, or at least smell the food, to keep from getting too drunk too quickly." Jim took a pickled cherry tomato. "Now, one more for the American girl far from home." He smiled slyly as he poured. His reserve melted; his jollity was, apparently, alcohol-soluble, and it was seeping out. Jim was starting to like him.

"So where are you from?" Jim asked, after he knocked back the second shot.

"Tiraspol. Tee-ras-pol." Naumenko watched Jim write it down and nodded when he saw the spelling was correct. Jim reached into his bag and took out a digital voice recorder which he laid on the table. Naumenko eyed it dubiously.

"What is that?" he asked.

"It's so I can record the interview. We'll talk and I'll take notes, then afterward I'll transcribe everything we said. I'll preserve it. Do you mind being recorded?"

Naumenko removed his cap, setting it squarely on the bar in front of him, and scratched his head with a look of discomfort. He sighed deeply, grimaced, then smacked a palm on the bar.

"No. No, I don't mind. These devices can make someone like me very nervous, you understand. It means you can say that this happened or that happened and you have 'proof,' but maybe also you manipulated it. I am not saying that you do such things"—Naumenko laid a reassuring paw on Jim's forearm—"only that you could. Evidence to condemn can come from anywhere," he said, a distant look in his eyes. "From anybody, for anything."

"I can just take notes by hand if you prefer. And you can watch me to see if I get it right."

Naumenko turned down the corners of his mouth in consideration, bobbing his head to one side then the other. "No. We will make it official. Anyway, you are not the police. Correct?"

"I'm not."

"Not any kind of police. Are you?"

"No."

"American, Russian disguised as American, United Nations . . ."

"No, Grigory Borisovitch, I swear. I promise. I am an interviewer for the Memory Foundation and I am not a policeman of any kind, nor am I an agent of any government. I just want to hear your story."

Naumenko considered Jim's request, fixing him with his narrow, piggy eyes, running a hand across the fleshy ridge of his chin. Eventually he assented with a broad smile and a clap to Jim's back. "Let's go. Yes. You should hear it. Go: what would you like to hear?"

"Well, let's start with where you were born. And when."

"I was born in Tiraspol, as I said, in 1933. At that time it was a small city, but a proud one. My parents came from Transcarpathia: they were Ukrainian, but everybody was something. It was like Odessa. You understand? We had Ukrainians, Romanians, Russians, Moldovans, Jews, Turks, Poles. It was Soviet, sure, and during the Great Patriotic War it was Romanian, but it belonged to everybody. There was no such thing as a foreigner. This is what my parents told me, and this is what the Soviet Union was supposed to mean. All of us equal. Brothers. A union." He poured them another two shots of vodka and pushed the plate across to Jim.

"But Stalin . . ." Jim coaxed.

"Josef Stalin was a strong leader," Naumenko said firmly. "Perhaps too strong. But it was a difficult time, and the country made many advances because of him."

"You don't bear any ill will toward him for what he did to you?"

"What would be the point? If something happened, then it's over, and now we are a stronger and more powerful country than we would have been without it. And my troubles began after him. I did my army service in Belomorsk, at the head of the Baltic Sea canal. You know where that is? On the White Sea, in Karelia?"

Jim nodded, and reminded himself to examine a map when he got back to the office.

"I was sent there when I was sixteen, and it was just army and prisoners, prisoners and army. One group built, the other group guarded them and ran the prison, but really we were all prisoners. There was nowhere to go. Just sea and pinewoods, endless woods. I remember sometimes when we would go cut wood for fires, I would shout, 'Turn your back to the forest, and your front to me,' because if Baba Yaga's chicken-leg house existed anywhere, it would be in such a forest, in such a place."

"I know these stories. I suppose the house never appeared?" Jim joked.

"No, no," Naumenko replied with a rueful smile. "Would I have known what to do if it did? Sixteen, a city boy, surrounded by criminals? These were not politicals who worked in Belomorsk at that time; they were actual criminals. They were treated much better: better rations; occasional new clothes; twelve-hour days, not sixteen. Their guards—us—treated them with respect. This I know . . ." He trailed off, reached for the vodka carafe, and finding it empty, he lowered his head, took a deep breath, and plowed forward.

"This I know because in the political camp, in Solovetsky, I was on the other side. I was on the other side," he repeated, looking at Jim directly, as though he expected to be disbelieved, or judged, or laughed at.

"What happened? How did you end up there?"

"During my fourth summer at Belomorsk, in 1953, some of us were granted two weeks' leave, and sent to Tallinn. It was such a beautiful city, even then, after the war, you could see what it used to be." Naumenko rolled his glass between his hands while staring at a point far above—and fifty years behind—the bar.

"After all that time with nine months of ice and three months of mosquitoes, we could not imagine there were still human beings in the world. And women! Estonian women, Finnish women!" He beamed, laughing to himself at something only he knew.

"The first few days we were there," he began, speaking slowly and uncertainly as he narrowed his eyes, "we just felt dirty from our skin to our souls, like we had crawled up from the earth, or like we were creatures of . . . I don't know how to explain it." He rubbed his hand across the bar, staring down at it as though he were surprised to find it was still attached to his body.

"We just felt that we had been gone from this planet and now we came back to see that everything isn't carving rocks and building shacks and trading favors one cigarette at a time.

"The fourth day, August fourth, I will never forget. I was fishing in Lake Ulemiste—alone; the others who came with me had bought some women for the day—when I saw just the most beautiful girl I had ever seen, crying by the side of the road. I asked her what was wrong. She was scared; she saw my uniform, my Soviet uniform, and she was Finnish, and had crossed the gulf in secret to buy some food for her family. They were starving, she said, and they could see the port and knew that in the Soviet Union there must be food. Now, I couldn't stand to see a girl like that in such distress, so I used my military privileges to get her some food. Not much, of course. There wasn't much to get. Just some bread, a few eggs, milk, but I also bought two live chickens. I thought she could eat the eggs, then perhaps breed them. And because she had nothing to carry them with but her own beautiful arms, I went back to the farm with her. The border was poorly guarded; nobody on either side really had anything, and anyway we all thought then that Finland would be part of the Soviet Union in a year, maybe two. I told my buddies I had met a girl, and I would see them back at Belomorsk. And, of course, you know how it ends."

"Can you tell me?"

Naumenko shrugged heavily, smacked a palm on the bar. "One of them was Komsomol. He followed me and reported what I was doing. I was arrested for speculation. That is what they called selling something you didn't have permission to sell, or buying something on the black market. Never mind what it was, or how important or how small. Never mind that everyone did it because everyone had to. I spent three years in a Solovetsky political camp. He was promoted to *starshina*, and then upward. But I won in the end, though." He sniffed, nodded, and put his cap back on. "I won in the end. Because I am sitting here, with a job and a family and breath and life, and he was blown to pieces in Afghanistan. Now, I must . . ."

"I'm sorry; I don't want to keep you. But could you tell me a little more about the camp itself? Where it was, who else was there, what you did?"

He pressed his lips together and shook his head. "Other people can tell other stories. I can only tell you my own. It was in Solovetsky, as I told you," Naumenko said, standing up. "The White Sea islands, so close to home. Ice and mosquitoes. We did what we were told to do: we cut wood, we built bricks, and we smoked and canned fish. I was a woodcutter; I was always strong. My camp was a small one for so-called foreign prisoners. Non-Russian Soviets. Now, I must go. The man behind me is watching." With his hand below the bar, he jerked his thumb up and to the right; on the rafters Jim saw a shaven-headed man in sunglasses surveying the club with a handgun on one side of his belt and a walkie-talkie on the other.

"Can we speak again?"

"Of course." He stood up and let out a heavy sigh that ended in a short laugh and a wink. "I feel much younger for having spoken to you. You will have to wait a few weeks, as I can't afford to get a reputation for being lazy. I already have one for being old. If you want to talk to someone else sooner, find my friend Balderis. Vilis Balderis. He was in the camp when I arrived and stayed long after I was gone."

"Will he speak with me?"

Naumenko bobbed his huge slab of a head back and forth, pulling the corners of his mouth down. "Perhaps. Vilya is not very talkative. Not like me," he said with a wink. "But if you tell him you spoke with me he may."

"How do I find him?"

"He sells things." Naumenko mimed the giving and taking of money with his hands. "He has a stall at the Vernisazh, at Izmailovsky. I don't know where, but you should go early in the morning. He is a serious fellow; whenever there is work to do, he does it. He was always this way."

"Now," said Naumenko, interlacing his fingers, cracking his knuckles, and stretching his arms out in front of him. "Do you mind?" He worked his head to one side and then the other like a boxer limbering up before a fight.

Before Jim knew what he was agreeing to, Naumenko had him in a headlock—a light but firm headlock—and was leading him to the door. "I have to look like I'm working," he said quietly. "Just for the man upstairs; Nastya, behind the bar, is a friend. Perhaps struggle a little; it will make me look better. Balderis works at Izmailovsky Park, selling whatever he can find. Watch out for the table. I will tell him on my break to expect you tomorrow. You can go tomorrow? Good. Now, I know this is unconventional," he said under his breath as he kicked the front door open, "but it really has been a pleasure."

He shoved Jim past the security guard and into the biting Moscow night. "Fuck off!" he shouted. "This place is not for you!"

OUTSIDE, the winter night's air had a biting, new, faintly smoky quality, as if it had just been forged in the North Pole and Moscow got first crack at it. Jim breathed in and felt, for what seemed like the first time in years, alive. He dialed Kaisa's number and got voice mail: she was in rehearsal. Or maybe, he thought hopefully, she was on her way here: she was in the Metro. She knew he was talking to her grandfather; she knew when; why wouldn't she come to see them both?

From behind him he heard a hissing, and turned to see one of the security guards outside Sporting Palace gesturing for him to move on. When Jim didn't move fast enough the guard started to walk down the staircase toward him. Jim raised his hands in surrender and started walking away. When the guard turned around, he stopped, ducking into an arched entryway where he could watch and wait for Kaisa.

After ten minutes, he tried her phone again: nothing. After twenty his toes started to tingle: again nothing. He waited another fifteen minutes and gave up.

On the Metro ride home, Jim sat wedged between a sad-eyed teen-age goth girl who would have looked at home in any American suburb and a strong-jawed old woman who looked like she had willed herself into existence, like she had never been a child. He pressed his eyes shut, clenched his fists, took a deep breath, and brought his teeth down on his tongue hard enough to taste blood. He found, despite his best intention to honor his promise to Vivek to keep his head down and return home with neither incident nor attachment, that he wanted Kaisa at his apartment so badly he could feel her at the back of his throat, taste the need on his lips.

9

JIM WAS DRESSED and out the door by seven o'clock the next morning. The streetlights were still on; dawn wasn't even threatening to break, and the Garden Road's ten lanes of traffic were only just starting to sludge up. People's faces were still morning-shut, automatic, expressionless, their eyes staring grimly forward as they trudged along the icy gray sidewalks to the Metro. Jim held Mayakovskaya's heavy station door open for a trio of club wraiths leaving the station, presumably heading home. They were pasty-faced and leather-jacketed, drawn, wild-eyed but clearly exhausted, beautiful and life-drinking in a way that left Jim wondering if he'd ever been that young, if he ever had that much stamina.

As he touched his Metro card to the top of the automatic turnstiles, though, he had a sudden thought: there were hundreds of vendors at Izmailovsky Park. He had no idea what Balderis sold or where he sold it.

Jim let the Metro gates swing open, but remained still as they swung back shut, hard—Jim learned from experience that if you failed to hurry through the doors, or if, say, you were walking quickly enough so that your bag passed through the doors before you did, you wound up with a pair of meaty bruises from midchest to thigh on either side. He turned around and took out his phone.

At the top of the stairs he bought a cup of tea from a kiosk that was just opening. There was something so sweet, so human, so maternal about the process: the kiosk matron, a kind-eyed woman with a hesitant, sorrowful smile just past middle age filled an electric kettle from a ten-gallon container of water, plugged it in, and showed him an array of cardboard tea boxes behind her. There was no focus-group chosen music; she was not a moonlighting actress or an undiscovered genius; she wore neither a uniform nor an insincere smile. Just a kindly woman trying to earn some cash on a bitter winter morning. Jim wondered—as he often did—if this would have been his aunt or grandmother had the latter not headed west.

He sipped it at one of the stand-up tables outside her stall, watching the morning slowly groan to life, summoning an endless stream of long coats and pancake faces and the occasional hard-won nod of recognition from one commuter to another. He caught the quickest, most fleeting glimpse of a sliver of a face that reminded him, in the square jaw and the way a smile so obviously wanted to break out from beneath the stern visage, of his father, and a wrecking ball of homesickness crashed into his chest. He cadged a cigarette (a noxious brown little Prima) from the kiosk matron, smiled his thanks, and, as he had done for most of his life, waited out an emotion with tobacco. When his mind was clear and his heart was easy, he pulled out his phone.

"I'm listening to you," said Yuri curtly.

"And I'm talking to you. Yuri, it's Jim. I hope I'm not waking you."

"Hello, Dzheem," Yuri said cheerfully. He took immense pride in having become a Shakespeare completist (and Jonson, and Beckett, and Synge, and so on) without ever having learned to speak modern English. "Of course you aren't waking us. We do our real work before coming into the office."

"Real work" meant a history PhD for Kirsten, and plays for Yuri: he was working on what he called "The Brezhnev Decalogue," a series of ten plays about stagnation and calcification. Not surprisingly, he found it hard going.

The Memory Foundation supported him and Kirsten financially, but they were entirely their own: artists and thinkers in the soul-deep sense that seemed to Jim increasingly inaccessible at home, where even poets had to know how to play departmental politics. The evening he had spent at their house had revealed to him the full-throated, unironic, cozy, and slightly desperate nature of Russian fun, and he had been in affectionate awe of the two of them ever since. He knew if he called them out of the blue at seven thirty one weekday morning with a question of Moscow logistics, they would be neither surprised nor unprepared, and possibly even helpful.

"Well, I'm hoping I'll be better after I talk to you. I have a sort of strange question for you."

"Strange questions so early in the morning? You've called the right place. We answer only strange questions. What is it?"

"I need to know how to find someone at Izmailovsky Park."

A beat of silence. "How to find just anyone? You mean where can you meet someone, or how do you find something specific to buy, or something else?"

"No, no. I think it's someone who works there. Well, let's start from the assumption that it's someone who works there, I guess. That's easiest."

"The assumption that it's somebody who works there? What do you mean? Do you know the person you are going to meet?"

Jim told him about Naumenko and Balderis.

"So," Yuri said when he finished. "It seems you tapped a vein. Congratulations. You must feel relieved."

"Very."

"Yes. You were so worried before. It isn't uncommon, especially for a foreigner, to find nobody to speak with."

"So why doesn't a Russian do my job?"

"*Well,* this Russian doesn't want to. Too much work, too much prying. I prefer seeing what happens, writing down what happens, to making something happen. As for other Russians, I suppose Dave just finds it easier to approach people like him. Anyway, there's no guarantee that survivors would be any more inclined to talk to Russians. In front of foreigners we worry about making our country look bad; in front of natives we worry about making ourselves look bad. Our chosen solution: shut up and drink. Let me confer with Kirsten for a moment."

Yuri laughed ruefully as he put the phone down, but Jim kept quiet. Laughing at the foibles of one's own family, group, nation, or self was one thing; joining that derision from outside the group was piling on.

Back home, Jim would never have thought to call a playwright day-jobbing as a historical researcher to find someone who might have a stall selling Soviet kitsch at an open-air market in outer Moscow. At home he would have found the municipal organization that oversaw the market, found some public relations flak, and asked for a list of vendors: simple as that. In Russia, though, the front door was always locked, if you could even find it. He had no idea who oversaw the vendors at the park; if he did know, there was no way they would have shared any information with him, because who was he, and what was he going to use it for, and why should they help someone with obscure motives and no standing? What's more, if he did somehow manage to find Vilis Balderis, and just walked up to a stall and introduced himself, he would want to know how Jim found him, and with whose help, and why; if the answers didn't satisfy him, he'd clam up. Here everything was done through connections; all solutions were personal, because those attachments—family, friends, friends of trusted friends, relatives of friends, friends of the family—were the only links one could trust. Whether Yuri had the connections to help him was still an open question, but better to try this route than to poke around blindly by asking officials or other vendors without an introduction.

"Good news, Jim," said Yuri, picking up the phone. "At least I hope we have good news. Do you remember Anya, who was over at dinner with you last month? The composer, she spoke French with Kirsten, brown cigarettes?"

"Yes, sure. Of course. The Ellington fan."

"Exactly. Ellington and Boulez and that garbage. That's this month's list, anyway. Her brother has a stall at Izmailovsky selling instruments and music. If he doesn't know the person you're trying to find, at least he might know how to find him."

"Really? And he's there today?"

"I don't know. I need to call Anya and see."

"Look, I don't want to put you to any trouble," Jim said, very much wanting to put Yuri to just a little more trouble.

"No, of course it's no trouble. I know Anya was very interested to meet you, and I think she'd be happy to help. I'll just call her and see if her brother's working, and if he is I'll have her call him and mention your name. No trouble at all."

"Listen, Yuri, I really appreciate this. Tell Anya . . ."

"We do not believe in obligations among friends," said Yuri. "Bring wine and a lively spirit to the next dinner; that's all we ask."

Jim had to change Metro trains twice to reach Izmailovsky's Vernisazh market, in the city's eastern suburbs. He had come out here once before, after Kirsten recommended it with an eye-roll but also a smile, the way an American might recommend Las Vegas: as something to see, something to laugh at knowingly, but also, beneath the reflexive irony, something to enjoy, too. This wasn't one of those outdoor markets wedged into an old parking lot outside a Metro station; it occupied several square miles next to Peter the Great's Izmailovo estate. For tourists, it specialized in kitsch—*matrioshka* dolls depicting everything from *Survivor* contestants to American presidents, Soviet and faux-Soviet knickknacks, brass chess sets pitting Brezhnev's Kremlin against Nixon's cabinet (the pawns, of course, were grumpy little men in fur hats on the white side; fat, shirtless hayseeds in overalls on the black). Many of these items were sold by overeager hawkers shouting at the passersby amid the din of street performers wreathed in meat-scented smoke from the shashlik stands—and this was why Kirsten rolled her eyes. An intrepid shopper could also find surprisingly good original paintings, Tatar furs, intricate Central Asian pottery, indestructible old Lomo cameras, traditional Russian handicrafts, Turkmen rugs, carved Chechen daggers, and Baltic amber.

He walked north from the station, until he saw across a small patch of scrub the wooden gates at the market entrance. Much of the market—the prime real estate, anyway—was surrounded by a fake wooden fortress ringed by statues of animals and Russian mythological figures: Grandfather Frost loomed over the Snow Maiden with paternal concern; only when Jim drew close to the statues did he see that someone had carved pupils into Grandfather Frost's eyes to make him appear to be looking right down her dress.

When crowds thronged the market it was charming, but now, in the dawn light, the stallholders were just starting to set up; a handful of dusty green vans unloaded beer, meat, and onions for the food kiosks, and everyone worked in silence.

"Good morning. Your documents, please?"

This came not from the pasty-faced teenage guards flanking the market's entrance, but from a plainclothesman who looked to be around forty, and had the bored and sour imperiousness of the lifelong desk rider.

Instinctively the two guards put out their cigarettes, picked their Kalashnikovs up from the ground, stood up straight, and brushed imaginary lint from their uniforms. The plainclothesman held one hand out, palm up, to Jim and tapped it with the other, miming where the foreigner should put his passport.

"Of course," Jim said, reaching into his coat. "And may I see your documents, please? In accordance with the law?" He would never have deigned to ask the average spot checker for his documents—they were usually too inclined to violence and too sensitive to their lowly position, and hence very quick with an elbow to the jaw—but the plainclothesman appeared more confident in his authority.

The man sighed, and wearily pulled out a battered passport that identified him as Lyakov, Igor Ivanovich, a senior investigator with the Interior Ministry.

Lyakov scrutinized Jim's passport, turning each page slowly, reading each as though it were a novel. "Your OVIR stamp places you in central Moscow. That is where you live?"

"It is."

"And what business do you have out here so early? The market won't open for another hour."

"My work."

"And what work do you do for . . . let me see . . . for the Ulmera Corporation?"

Ulmera, of course, didn't exist. It was one of the new Russia's legal illegalities: to get a business visa, you had to be invited by an actual business. To be invited by an actual business, you had to show that you had some vital skill or attribute that couldn't be found in Russia: you had to have a reason to be there. So visa agencies, with offices in both Russia and the West, in accordance with the law's hypertrophied letter rather than its atrophied spirit, created shell companies like Ulmera. Its sole function was to issue letters of invitation; Jim's needed attribute was the possession, six months ago, of $250 in ready cash to exchange for a letter of invitation. Most foreigners got their visas this way. It was common practice but, as with the registration visa, it may have been just as illegal as the authorities wanted: legal enough to remain a plausible and effective source revenue, but illegal enough to provide a pretext when required.

"I actually work for the Memory Foundation," Jim said with a polished smile. "We record interviews with people who were imprisoned for political reasons in the Soviet Union."

"Imprisoned for political reasons in the Soviet Union," Lyakov parroted. "You are stirring up trouble for people." Jim took a deep breath and prepared to defend himself, but Lyakov handed his passport back. "Nonetheless, this is perfectly legal. Dangerous, perhaps"—he gave a shark's smile—"but legal."


IT WAS QUIET ENOUGH so not only did Jim jump when his cell phone rang, a few of the loaders turned and stared at him, too.

"Jim, this is Yuri calling. I couldn't reach you earlier."

"I was on the Metro. I'm actually out at Izmailovo now."

"Are you near the Vernisazh market?"

"Yes, just near."

"Ah. Perhaps I would have told you to wait a little. Anya said she is not certain whether her brother would be in this early, but you should look. She said he definitely will sell today; he has his stall Wednesday to Sunday, but maybe he will not show up until later."

"That's great, Yuri. Thank you. I don't mind waiting if he isn't here."

"She says you must enter the wooden gates and walk down the main road that sells wooden bowls and spoons until you reach a statue of a smiling bear. His music stall is just on the other side of that statue."

"Sounds easy. I'll go take a look now."

"You should mention her name. Her brother is called Sergei."


"SERGEI?" JIM ASKED HESITANTLY. He had done as instructed, walking down an aisle of stalls selling wooden kitchenware painted red, black, and gold with pastoral designs—about a dozen stalls, all of whose wares looked, to Jim's eyes, utterly indistinguishable—until he passed the cartoonish bear. Now he stood before an array of battered violins and violas, tarnished trumpets in tattered cases, the inevitable balalaikas and wooden flutes, and, on shelves along the stall's sides, hundreds of folders of sheet music. An elvish young man with a mop of brown hair, a patchy beard, sparkly gray eyes behind steel granny glasses, and entirely too much energy for this hour of the morning hailed Jim good-naturedly in return, before reigning in his ebullience and asking how Jim knew his name.

"I know your sister, Anya. We met at one of Yuri and Kirsten's dinners."

"Ah, those two!" he exclaimed, clapping his hands together as a broad grin relit his face. "Yes, Anya's taken me to a couple of those nights, too. They last, you know . . ." He puffed out some air and made a fluttery, swiveling gesture with his hand. "They really can talk. And drink. And talk, and drink, and talk, and drink. Very civilized people. Cultured, as we would say."

"Very. Your sister, too. And you, too, it looks like."

Sergei flipped the suggestion away with a diffident half nod. "Our parents were both musicians in the Leningrad State Orchestra. A conductor and the first violinist. *They* were cultured. I am just one more failing *biznisman.*" His wiry energy and indomitable smile said otherwise, though: failure was obviously alien to him, whatever his material circumstances.

*"'A merry heart doeth good like a medicine: but a broken spirit drieth the bones.' That'll be your father's testament,"* Rosie used to say, when at the end of a long day she barely had enough energy to drive home while Sam was still joking with the dishwashers in gutter Spanish as he rotated the produce in the walk-in.

"Are you looking for music? Or maybe for an instrument?" Sergei asked, straightening the sheet music and aligning the edges of the instruments with twitchy, darting movements.

"Not just now, I don't think. I'm actually looking for someone. I think he's also a vendor, but I'm not sure, and I didn't know who else to ask. Anya said you might be able to help me."

"If I can, I certainly will. As a friend of Anya's, Yuri's, and Kirsten's, I can trust you, I think. You aren't police, and you don't look like *mafiya.* You don't sound Russian, even."

"No. American."

Sergei merely raised his eyes with interest. "Welcome, then, from America. What is the name? Who are you looking for?"

"Vilis Balderis."

"Balderis. Bal-de-rees. A Latvian. There can't be many of those. I don't know him myself, but I know who does. Come."

Sergei stepped out from behind his counter and started striding away. Jim stood about a head taller, and probably had a good thirty pounds on him, but Sergei outpaced him easily.

"Are you just leaving your stall like that?" Jim asked, almost jogging to keep up.

Sergei pirouetted on his heel, walking backward just as quickly as he walked forward. He stuck two fingers in his mouth and gave a window-shattering whistle. "Grisha!" he called behind him. A stooped and sim-ian old man stepped out from the kitchenware stall across from Sergei's. "I'll be gone for maybe fifteen minutes. Watch my music, would you?"

The man waved and nodded at Jim, then hobbled back behind his counter. Sergei turned down another alley, leading Jim deeper into the market.

"Not much of a guard, is he?"

Sergei laughed. "You would never believe it, but Grisha was a boxing champion in the Soviet Navy. Of course, that was fifty years ago. Still, he can move quickly if he needs to. But really he uses shame. This is our culture. All I expect him to do is call out if he sees someone try to steal from me. Nine times out of ten—no, ninety-nine times out of one hundred—whoever it is will take off. The one exception would probably steal from me in front of my face."

"That's very trusting of you. Very optimistic."

Sergei gave another of his jerky, avian shrugs, accompanied by a smile and a shake of his shaggy hair. "I choose to stay that way. Perhaps I could be tougher, you know, more ruthless. Try to pressure the other music sellers in the market out as I've been pressured. But I choose not to live in that way."

"And the people who've tried to get you to leave . . ."

"*Ach*, them I don't worry about. We all pay protection to the same *krysha*, you know. The same roof. The same policeman. The same gang-sters. They only have muscle in their minds. They talk tough, maybe push me a few times. I smile and push back. I know if it gets serious I won't be the one who's hurt. Besides," he said with a sly wink, "I give violin lessons to the big boss's daughter. Free, of course. Here we are."

They stopped in front of an aluminum trailer parked against one of the wooden city walls. Jim noticed security cameras above the trailer's door, windows, and back entrance. Sergei knocked on the door, and it opened to reveal his opposite: a tall, barrel-chested, swarthy, unsmiling man, with a whale-fin mustache, a glint of gold on his teeth, and a smell of garlic, smoke, and coffee hanging around him like a cloud. He nodded reluctantly at Sergei.

"Hey, Sulyasha. How are things?" The man took a deep drag on an unfiltered cigarette, and kept his dead, hooded eyes steadily on Sergei. Sergei blinked rapidly, his hands in his pockets, shifting his weight from side to side. After two seconds, though, something broke, and a broad smile split the big man's face wide open.

"Seryozha, what have I always told you about keeping still? Too much music is your problem! Too much music has made your blood unsteady. Aisha loves you, though, so I suppose I must, too. What's the matter this morning?"

"The matter? Sulyasha, have I ever bothered you with . . ." Just then a soccer ball whizzed between Sergei and Jim, smacking off the front of the trailer next to Sulyasha. Two guys with Slavic hatchet-faces who looked barely old enough to shave, wearing the orange uniforms of Moscow trash collectors, had been kicking the ball around. Now they froze where they stood, their carefree smiles turning into rictuses of fear.

Sulyasha leaned down and picked up the ball, holding it out to the garbagemen with an indulgent smile. They looked at each other, each urging his companion to retrieve their ball. Neither made a move. Finally the bigger one shoved the smaller forward. He wiped his hands on his trousers, turned his chin up, and fixed his bravest look on his face.

When he was almost to the trailer, Sulyasha pulled a butterfly knife from his front pocket and stabbed the soccer ball with five little jackhammer jabs. His expression never changed; his smile even broadened when he handed the floppy hunk of black-and-white leather back to the boy. The boy hurried away from the trailer and began emptying rubbish bins as if his life depended on it—which, Jim thought, it just might have. Sulyasha spat on a handkerchief and wiped the ball's imaginary stain off his trailer.

"What did you say you needed?" he asked.

"We just want to know if someone works here," Sergei said. He still smiled, but Jim noticed he stood stock-still. "A name, and you can tell us . . ."

"Who's we? Who's this?"

"A friend of mine. An American. Not any sort of concern."

"Oh? Probably not. If he is, though, I'll certainly remember he's a friend of yours."

Sergei nodded significantly at Jim. "Vilis Balderis," Jim said.

"Balderis," he grumbled. "Not your class, Seryozha. He sells that fake Soviet shit over in the annex. If you really need to find him, you go out the back gate, then pass twelve tables on your right and eleven on your left, turn right, and pass six tables on your right and seven on your left, then turn left and he's the fourth table down on your left."

"How did you do that?" Jim asked. Sulyasha didn't answer; he didn't even look at Jim.

"Sulyasha's memory—Suleiman's, I should say; that is his given name—works in mysterious ways," Sergei said, leaning toward Jim. "He has a gift for dimensions, construction, sequence. His uncle built this fake wooden city, but he designed it." He spoke quietly enough to imply he was letting Jim in on a secret, but loudly enough so Sulyasha could hear the compliment.

"Does he play cards?"

"Only when he can win," Sulyasha said, grinning sardonically. He winked at Jim and shut the door to his trailer.

SERGEI LED JIM to the back gates, shook his hand heartily, kissed him three times in the traditional alternate-cheek manner, and headed back to his stall. Jim promised to stop by on his way out.

Outside the gates the market dwindled into second-class repetitiveness. Vendors stood behind long tables rather than stalls. Down the first aisle, all the vendors on the right sold Soviet film posters that looked suspiciously new; all the vendors on the left sold metalworks—flasks, clocks, key rings—with Soviet insignias.

Jim passed one table whose poster advertised, in English, THE AUTHENTIC GOODS OF SOVIET NAVY SHIPS. Beneath it, the vendor was gluing a red star onto a blank pewter flask. He glared darkly at Jim as he walked past. He turned right down the pirated CD and DVD aisle, then left, and he was in another Soviet surplus store.

At the fourth table on his left, a tall, wiry man with gray hair, a few days' growth of beard, and a cigarette in the corner of his mouth was arranging clocks and flasks on the table in front of him. He moved slowly, wincingly, with Sisyphean resignation and imperturbability; he carried his defeat around him like a gray cloud that would never burst into rain.

"Vilis Balderis?" Jim asked.

The man nodded. He grabbed another box, this one filled with key chains and picture frames, and started unloading.

"Do you know a Grigory Naumenko?"

He nodded again but kept his back to Jim as he laid out his Lenin, CCCP, and Red Army key chains. Jim pulled a box of Winstons from his pocket. He lit one and laid the box—open, with the cigarettes facing Balderis—on the table.

"Did he by any chance tell you I would be coming by this morning?"

Balderis turned back around and shrugged. It was a shrug of indifference, not dismissal. Jim couldn't tell if that meant Naumenko never called, or he did and Balderis didn't especially care. He reached for the cigarettes, looked questioningly at Jim, who nodded. He pulled one out of the box, sniffed it, smiled, tore the filter off, and lit it, sliding the box into his shirt pocket. He nodded for Jim to start speaking.

"I work for the Memory Foundation. It's an organization that interviews people who served time in prison camps in Eastern Europe. Have you heard of it?"

He placed the last picture frame upright against a small wooden clock with the Hotel Ukraina carved into it. Whether the clock was meant to commemorate the Stalinist-Baroque structure or whether it had actually been stolen was unclear. Balderis exhaled a plume of smoke at Jim's lapel. "I have heard of such organizations, yes."

"Can you spare a few minutes to speak with me?"

"Why?"

"Grigory Naumenko told me you spent time in the same camp."

"No. You misunderstand me. I know why you want to speak to me. I don't know why I should talk to you."

Jim had to admit, it was a good question. "Because it is important that we know what happened, from the survivors themselves. Your story will help shed light on a dark period of Russian history. We want . . ."

Balderis gave a quiet, bitter laugh. "You want, you want, you want." He shrugged again and grabbed a small folding table that was leaning against a crumbling brick pillar. "It's early," he said, yanking open the legs with a hideous creak. "I have to work. Stand and talk if you like."

"I can come back."

"Better now than later." He grabbed another box from under the first table and started unloading. Pewter bookends, this time, with Socialist-Realist etchings in red.

Jim preferred Naumenko's erratic garrulousness, although Balderis's reticence, he had to admit, felt more real, less strange. He realized this was because Balderis acted more like Jim assumed he himself would act were he a survivor, which is to say: were he arbitrarily arrested, ripped from his family, stuffed on a train heading to an unknown destination, forced to break rocks or gut fish for the economic benefit of the very system that imprisoned him, and then released as suddenly as he was arrested. But why did this constitute reality? Is what we call real nothing more than the con-firmation of ourselves and our expectations by the visible world? And more important: had he brought his voice recorder? He had.

"Do you mind if I use this?" Jim asked Balderis, knowing what the answer would be. Shrug. "Understood. Good. Now, can I ask you: were you in a labor camp on the Solovetsky islands?"

Balderis pressed his lips together in a pained imitation of a smile. "Labor? Is that what it was? Yes, I was in Solovetsky."

"Can you tell me when you were there?"

"From March of 1955 until the winter solstice of 1961. Almost seven years." He knocked a bookend to the ground, causing the two on either side to fall as well. His fist clenched, his face contorted in a mask of fury, and he had even drawn his leg back to kick the table before he got control of himself. He apologized to Jim after two deep breaths. "I don't like talking about this. I'm sorry." He pulled out a pack of cigarettes (Belomorsk: a cigarette brand named for the putatively heroic undertaking of Soviet labor that nearly killed Balderis, and thousands of other lucky near misses like him. A cancerous irony in almost every way) and lit one. The Winstons, apparently, didn't make the cut: too mild.

"Can I ask why you were sent there?"

He took a deep breath, exhaling dragon cones of smoke through his nose as he tilted his chin up and pressed his lips together. "Spying," he said at last. "I was sent to the camps as an enemy of the Soviet people."

"Who did you . . ."

"I didn't. I went to a neighbor's house for dinner, and he had a German father. A Russian mother, of course, but a German father. My neighbor never knew his father. He went back to Germany after the war. The mother had no pictures, no souvenirs, not even an address. All he left was his German last name."

Jim waited for Balderis to continue, but that was the end of the story. A young man lost seven years of his life because of a neighbor's ancestry.

"Where was this?" Jim asked.

"Kaliningrad. You know where this is?" Jim nodded: a little chunk of territory wedged between Lithuania and Poland that remained a noncontiguous piece of Russia after the Soviet Union collapsed. "So you must know, too, that it was also called Konigsberg? And that it used to be German?" Balderis's arms went rigid by his sides and his voice grew louder and faster. He was yelling at someone else, fifty years ago. "And that we Latvians, along with Poles, Lithuanians, and Germans, were there long before the Russians? And that . . ." He cut himself off, turned his back to Jim, and raised the back of his hand to his face. Jim kept quiet. After half a fresh cigarette he collected himself and turned around.

"Do you know why I work here?"

"At Izmailovsky?"

"No. I work at Izmailovsky because I have the right connections and it pays well enough. I mean over here, in this part."

Jim shook his head.

"Then I shall tell you," he said, smiling bitterly. "And I will speak clearly, into your recorder, so you know what it means to be haunted. I used to have a stall inside. Not a shitty pair of tables like this, that you have to fight to set up in the mornings and carry away at night, but a stall that was mine, where I could lock up my goods every night and return to find them in the morning. For eight years I had it. From 1992 to 1999, when the place expanded. You understand?"

"How did you get it?" Jim asked quickly, in a fit of bravery. "At first, I mean. To make the story complete. How did you get it? Does it have any connection . . ."

"Everything has a connection," Balderis said sadly, definitively. "Nothing before, and everything after. The official in charge of giving out permits in the early 1990s, Yasha Luzhin, his uncle and I go back. He sold me the right to stand here. I was good enough at it that when after he got hit and the Bibirevo Boys took over, I could afford to buy the permit again. So. To return to what I was saying: I had a stall inside, where I sold, sometimes, some more expensive items. Harder to find. You understand?"

"Like what?"

"Like more expensive," Balderis said, a steel blade in his voice. "And also harder to find. Clear?"

"As water." Stolen items sometimes turned up at the market, not so much at the stalls as under them or behind them, available to those who knew how to ask.

"But what happened was this: when they expanded, next to my stall they put a beer kiosk. And with the beer kiosk, of course, came tables, and with the tables, in summer, came the fish girls. You understand? Salted, dried fish to go with beer. Understand? You've tasted?"

"I do. I have."

He nodded grimly. "So. They would come around in the summer, and people would buy. Or not. But even if not the girls would take their breaks on a bench behind my stall. With their fish. And the smell, when the sun would heat the fish and the wind would blow it toward me, the smell would remind me of the cannery at Solovetsky. I would close my eyes and I could hear the commander. I could feel the sting on my hands where the salt got into my cuts. It took me right back to those years, those seven negative years in the middle of my life."

He looked right at Jim, tears in his eyes, his lips clenched tight, fists balled, one foot back and the other forward, knees bent in a boxing stance. "And do you say that makes me less of a man? That I ran from a smell, or that I cry, without even drinking, to remember it? Do you say that?"

"No," Jim said. "No, of course not. I don't know what I would have done, what I would have become, if I had been you, and gone through what you did."

"That's right. You don't know. You don't know what they did to Latvians, to their Baltic socialist brothers there. If you were never there, you will never know. And I am one of the healthy ones, one of the better ones. I could show you some men, you couldn't even say they were men anymore. Do you want to see one of them? Is that what you want? Would that make you happy, asking about the past, which should be past and gone?" He balled his fists up again. Jim couldn't follow his chain of hurt and assumptions.

"Can I ask . . ."

"Not now," he said firmly but quietly. He finished arranging his goods on the table, tucked the boxes underneath, and lit another cigarette. "I am sorry. I have no more energy for this. If you want to see what the camps can do, don't talk to me. I work. I don't drink more than I should. I am healthy enough to thank God, and I even have a wife. My story is not the real story. You should talk to Dato."

"Where can I find him?" Jim asked, guilty that he was even asking.

"He only ever goes to one place. I don't even know where he lives anymore. Maybe on the street. Maybe, if he has children, with them. The only place you are one hundred percent guaranteed to see him is at the Super Slots, up by the university. The game room by the station. He's there every day until they carry him out."

"Is Dato his family name or his first name?"

"His first. He's Georgian. Tsepereli is his family."

"How does he get money?"

"People give it to him. I used to. I could never help myself; I knew what he had gone through."

"He'll be there today?"

"Every day. Every morning, every afternoon. Playing the kopeck machines. But look"—Balderis pointed over Jim's head toward the main market. A few intrepid shoppers were milling around: they were open for business. "It's time. I'm sorry if I was rude to you."

"You weren't. I'm sorry if I upset you asking about such things."

"You did. But being upset is not always bad. Lancing a wound hurts more than letting it fester, but it's better for the body." With that, he turned and walked back to his stall. His plume of cigarette smoke waved good-bye to Jim before evanescing.

## 10

JIM STEPPED OUT of the Universitet Metro station just after one p.m.: already shadows were lengthening; the air was getting colder and somehow closer; the day was calling it a day. The otherworldly, star-topped, crenellated skyscraper of Moscow State University loomed. He raised the hood of his coat: the air up in the hills was noticeably colder and cleaner than in central Moscow. It smelled of imminent snow rather than exhaust.

Around the Metro, Jim noticed a near-total absence of anyone recognizable, to an American eye, as a student. Certainly, there were people of student age—he spotted a girl about his height, with white-blond hair and almond-shaped blue eyes, who stared at him with disconcerting directness as she rounded the corner of Lomonosovsky Prospect toward the station—but no name-brand backpacks, baseball caps, MGU sweatshirts or starter jackets, no fraternity regalia or Frisbees. Here, as elsewhere in Moscow, people carried around them an air of mystery and intrigue, purpose and inscrutability, their emotions unreadable. Smiles here had reasons; conversations were personal; voices didn't carry. The students who passed him either walked alone or in groups of no more than three, talking quietly and intently to one another, with none of the backslapping or noisy self-veneration of American youth.

Jim had seen a few Super Chicago Slots around Moscow. The signs above them all said *IGORNIY ZAL* ("game room") and *KASINO*—spelled out in Christmas lights, a good third of which were invariably burned out—but really they were double-wide aluminum trailers. They were among the lesser Metro casinos; more prestigious ones—like the Victory, California, and Beverly Hills chains—were located in actual buildings, usually strip kiosks directly outside the Metro entrance. These had actual neon signs, video poker, sometimes even a dice table. Super Chicago Slots trailers were usually behind the Metro, plunked down on a patch of scrub next to the sidewalk, fighting for space with trailers selling bread, medicine, and beer.

Jim found this one stuffed to bursting with rickety one-armed bandits, reeking of sweat and cheap cigarette smoke and spilled beer and sour, unwashed humanity. Men—and only men—sat on patched stools feeding coin after coin into the machines in front of them. The machines pinged, whirred, and clicked, showing far more life than their users.

Jim didn't want to go up to each of them and ask their names: responses would probably fall somewhere on the spectrum between silence and violence. Instead, with trepidation and a strong sense of foreboding, he walked over to the far corner, where a bored-looking woman with too much makeup and hair spray sat smoking and reading a *detektiv* behind a pane of Plexiglas. Not until Jim had stood in front of the glass for a good thirty seconds did she look up.

"Excuse me, please, but do you know a Dato Tsepereli?"

"What?" She smirked, revealing a row of corn-kernel teeth.

"Tse-pe-re-lee," Jim enunciated. "First name Dato. I'm supposed to meet him here."

"You speak such awful Russian I can't understand you." Just then, with surprising alacrity, she pulled down the shade behind her window. "I am no longer at work," she called out. "If you need change use the machine across from this kiosk."

Jim looked behind him. The change machine looked like someone had taken an ax to it. ZAKRITO, the sign above it read. "Closed."

"But the machine . . ."

"I can no longer hear you! Use the machine or don't; I don't care." Jim heard the trailer's back door slam.

When he moved to knock on the kiosk window, a security guard materialized and pulled him back by his collar, gently but firmly.

Jim raised his hands, palms out, and backed away. He tried the name on the guard.

"Dato?" The guard smiled and crossed his long arms over his beefy body. "Sure, everyone here knows Dato."

"Great. Can you tell me where I can find him?"

He made an equivocal side-to-side motion with his head, his smile fixed, then shrugged. "Maybe."

"Maybe? Can you or . . ." Jim sighed and reached into his pocket. He handed the guard two hundred rubles.

"Right there." The guard pointed to a roulette machine in the darkest corner, farthest from the door. A slumped, swarthy, stoop-shouldered old man in a blue cardigan and a black flat-brimmed cap was feeding it coins and working the arm. "Grandfather Dato is spinning his wheel, same as every day." The guard tapped a thumb against the side of his neck (the Russian sign for drinking) and chuckled. "The secret to his long marriage: he never goes home."

Jim squeezed past rows of players—shambolic, wheezing, unshaven, red-eyed scarecrows, the forgotten and the forgetting, the thieves and the stolen-from, men who'd never told or heard an honest statement in their lives, their hope cresting with every pull of the arm before falling inevitably back to nothing.

Tsepereli cradled a bottle in one arm while he reached into his jacket pocket for coins to stuff into the machine with the other. It was a mineral-water bottle, but that proved nothing; plenty of drinkers made their own *samogon* at home and poured it into whatever bottle happened to be at hand.

Jim walked right up next to him, but Tsepereli's attention stayed fixed on the machine. Not until he opened a metal folding chair that emitted a horrible screech did Tsepereli glance in his direction. "Dato Tsepereli?" Jim asked.

He nodded, still staring at the machine, feeding it a steady stream of fifty-kopeck pieces. He worked his lips back and forth against each other. Sweat beaded on his mottled forehead, splatting his brittle white hair out from beneath his cap and plastering it to his forehead. He had hooked his ankles tightly around a bar at the bottom of his chair. Jim smelled no alcohol coming off him, only sweat, unwashed clothes, and old man's body. "You're the American?" he mumbled.

The American? "I am," Jim said cautiously. "How did you know I was coming?" Tsepereli said nothing, just kept feeding the machine.

"Please." His voice barely rose above a whisper.

Jim retrieved his Winstons from his pocket, put two in his mouth and lit them both, then handed one to Tsepereli. They smoked in silence, as Tsepereli fed coin after coin into the machine. The three wheels spun, revealing barrels, wrenches, vodka bottles, flowers, kerchiefed babies, red stars, black clouds, and Mercedes symbols in the tiny windows, but never three in a row. Beneath each window Jim noticed a button marked "STOP," which would have let Tsepereli keep an icon or two for an additional roll, but he never pressed it, not even when two Mercedes ornaments popped up next to each other with a hopeful ding. He just fed coin after coin into the machine as though fated to do so.

With shaking hands he pulled a pack of Russkaya Troika cigarettes out of his shirt pocket. The top third of the cigarette was a hollow cardboard tube; there was a tightly packed plug of black tobacco at the other end. Tsepereli snapped two matches before Jim took the box from him. Jim lit their cigarettes, took a deep drag, and almost fell off his chair coughing.

"Very strong. These have . . . They are . . . old Russia. Nobody . . . It isn't anymore . . ." He stopped talking and returned his attention to the machine.

Jim noted the trembling hands; wide terrified eyes; intense concentration; and Tsepereli's inability to meet his gaze, and he realized Tsepereli was that most fearful species of human being, the sober drunk. He had the shakes, the sweating, the paranoia, the free-floating and omnidirectional terror. If there were a more unnerving place to be than an enclosed, overheated space full of blinking lights, beeps, dings, and whirs, Jim couldn't think of it. Sometime in the next day Dato would have to either start drinking again, switch from booze to Valium, or find a hospital. Jim knew which he'd bet on.

"I am a janitor's son from Sukhumi," he murmured. "I spent twelve years in Solovetsky."

Jim reached into his jacket and switched on the voice recorder, bringing it slowly out of his pocket and setting it on his lap. "I'm sorry," he said, "could you tell me again . . ."

"Janitor, cleaner, yardman. His son," he said with irritation, miming mopping then sweeping. "From Sukhumi, in Georgia. I spent twelve years in Solovetsky."

"Because you were Georgian?"

He shrugged. "Twelve years. A janitor's son. Sukhumi. Solovetsky. In the camp . . . in the cold . . . With only one friend. Only one." He rooted around in his pocket for another coin to feed the machine, but found none. He just sat and stared at it, breathing hard, still clenching and pressing, wiping his sweaty, newly unoccupied hand back and forth, back and forth, back and forth, on his trousers. Jim handed him a one-ruble coin, and he was now shaking so badly he needed both hands to guide it into the slot. When he finished, he leaned back, breathing heavily from the effort, and tried to light another cigarette.

"Who was the friend?" Jim asked, lighting his cigarette. Dato extended the pack toward him. Jim waved them away, but Dato pulled a poisonous brown tube from the pack and shoved it in Jim's mouth. Jim shrugged and lit it. "Can you tell me who your one friend was?"

"Doctor," he wheezed. "Anybody in the camp, he helps. You are bleeding from where the guard hit you, he stitches. You cannot move your hands at night from digging, all day, frozen soil, no shovel, he makes a potion. Sick from camp food, he knows what plants to boil for tea. All for free. No reason. Still for free. Still my doctor."

"Still? Is he here in Moscow?"

Dato nodded, still staring straight ahead, fixedly, as though scared to move his head. The hand that held the cigarette had drifted down to his side, and the cigarette had burned a hole in his coat. Jim reached over, gently, to move his hand, and Dato jumped as though Jim's hand were electrified.

"Faridian!" he yelped. "David Faridian! Moscow Infectious Disease Hospital Number Two. Vodniy Stadion!" He released this information in one breath, eyes wide with terror, hands rigid with the effort, then finally slumped back into his seat, winded. "David was the only one . . . in the cold . . . twelve years . . . nobody else."

Jim wanted to put an arm around the old man, to reassure him, to comfort him. But what did he have aside from platitudes and incomprehension? A dozen years spent in inhuman conditions for no reason: that was a fact that nothing in this world—and certainly nothing in the comfortable, shiny, predictable world Jim came from—could alter. Only one thing could bring the old man comfort. Jim hesitated briefly before offering, but, aside from a reflexive American moral disapproval—an instinct that any real immersion in Russian life quickly quiets—he could think of no reason to forbear. "Dato, can I bring you some vodka? I just don't . . ."

"No!" he shouted. A few wandering eyes looked over, then drifted back to their games. He turned toward Jim with full, watery eyes. "I promised: not today. I cannot until . . . I was a janitor's son. I was first a child and became a man in Sukhumi. I spent twelve years in Solovetsky." He drank deeply and furiously from his bottle of Bonaqua, mineral water running out of the corners of his mouth as tears ran from the corners of his eyes. Suddenly he stood up and bolted for the door.

Jim followed him out the door, oblivious to the scowls of the security guard and kiosk minder, who both glared at him for not having fed the machines his share of rubles, or for having tried to distract a paying customer, or perhaps simply on principle. Tsepereli looked over his shoulder and increased his pace toward the nearest drinks kiosk, where he handed over a mound of greasy coins and received clear liquid in a plastic cup with a foil top: homemade booze, probably some combination of wiper fluid and acetone, which ranged in taste and quality from nearly drinkable to fatal.

Tsepereli held the cup between two shaking hands and sat heavily down on a nearby bench, enveloped in sorrows. Jim advanced toward him but Tsepereli waved him away, and he relented, hands up, walking slowly back to the Metro station.

Just outside the station door, two young city cops were leaning against a florist's shack, smoking and laughing with an older man with a long, pitted, hawkish face. As Jim approached the cops put their cigarettes out and their hats on; Jim didn't notice them until the bigger one planted himself in Jim's path, saluted, and asked for his passport. This wasn't unusual in itself, but as soon as Jim handed over his passport, the policeman passed it to the man in the suit.

"Vee-lah-tseer, See-yah-moos," he muttered as he flipped through the pages. "You speak our language?" he asked quietly, not looking up.

"Of course," Jim replied, trying to keep his tone amicable and compliant but just sharp enough not to look like a sucker.

"This passport was issued eight years ago, I see. And yet it shows only one trip outside the United States. You went to Canada for ten days. No foreign travel since then."

Jim didn't know he was supposed to respond until the policeman lifted his face and trained his cold blue eyes on him. "Correct," Jim said.

"No unregistered foreign travel?" he asked, flipping the passport shut and tapping it against his thumbnail.

"No. None. Of course not." Jim tried a low-level smile but received no thaw in return.

"How did you come to learn our language, then? Where did you receive your training?"

"At my dinner table. My grandparents came from Minsk."

The man raised his eyebrows slightly, and Jim caught a flicker of interest behind his eyes. "But you yourself have never been to Minsk."

"Correct."

"Not using this passport."

"Not using *any* passport."

"What about foreign travel before this passport was issued?"

Jim squinted and cocked his head. The policemen, now flanking him, stepped toward him, stopping just inches away, their hands on their holsters, reminding him who got to ask the questions and who had to answer them. "Twice, to Ireland."

"What was the purpose of your travels in Ireland?"

"Visiting family."

"I thought your family came from Minsk."

"My mother is Irish."

The smaller cop emitted a soft, sneering chuckle. "Russian Irish," he said, shaking his head in either disbelief or contempt. To him the possibility seemed as impossible as human-feline. The man in the suit shot him a minatory look and the laugh died in his throat. He tapped the passport against his thumb, staring into Jim's eyes so intently he seemed to be looking straight through to the back of his skull. Jim held the stare. After almost a minute, the man handed Jim's passport back with a crisp salute.

"And may I see *your* identification?" Jim asked, gathering up his bravery.

The cops looked at the man hungrily, energetically, waiting to be let off the leash. Subtly, he shook his head and took a leather-covered interior passport from his pocket. He flipped it open inches from Jim's face. Patrushin, Viktor. Special investigator, Interior Ministry.

When he decided Jim had seen it long enough, he flipped it shut, slid it back into his pocket, and cocked his head at Jim. "Satisfied, Vee-lah-tseer See-yah-moos? We are finished with you. Now walk away. You don't want to miss your train."

JIM GOT BACK to the office just past four p.m.: nighttime. For the second time today he tried calling Kaisa and got her voice mail. He left no message.

"Dzheem," called a voice from the kitchen as he hung up his coat. To the left of the front door the office spread out; to the right were the kitchen and the bathroom. Professional needs, human needs: come in and choose which you wanted. Yuri waved him in. He and Fyodor sat across from each other at the round table by the window. A cup of tea and an orange sat in front of each man. Yuri had peeled his in one strip and daintily pulled it into sections, laying them all out in front of him. Fyodor's orange looked like it had been peeled with a shotgun, and he was sucking a meaty hunk of rind. When Jim came into the kitchen he spat it, in a perfect arc, toward a trash can fifteen feet away and grabbed another.

"Tea?" Fyodor asked as Jim sat down.

"Sure, I can get it. Do you want some?" Jim stood up; Fyodor pushed him back down with one of his great paws.

"Here, you are the guest," he said. "You are the guest. You are the guest," he repeated absently as he filled the kettle from the tap and pulled down a mug and a bag of black tea. He opened the refrigerator. "I think . . . yes. Here. With the tea. For the afternoon. Lyudmila made it last night. She worries both of you are too skinny." Jim and Yuri both leaned back and patted their stomachs, Jim with a regretful shake of the head, Yuri with pride. Fyodor sliced his wife's *kholodets*, dabbed some horseradish over the top, brought it to the table with black bread, and stood nervously by the table until both Jim and Yuri not only ate but smacked their lips with obvious signs of relish. Jim's parents put *kholodets* on their menu every so often—whenever Sam prevailed on Rosie **or** Rosie went away for the weekend—but jellied calves' **feet went over** poorly in the American suburbs.

"How were things at Izmailovsky?" Yuri asked. "Anya's brother helped you?"

"He did. My second interview in two days. Now I don't have to feel so guilty about taking the Foundation's money for sitting around the office."

"You should not feel guilty about it anyway. It was never your fault. Sometimes people have a string of bad luck, and then things turn around. It's normal."

"Guilt is weakness," Fyodor grumbled. "It does nobody any good. How much did you pay for taxis today?"

"I took the Metro, actually."

Fyodor gave a distinctly Russian exhalation of disdain. "You must tell me before you go next. I can drive you. Why would you take the Metro and walk, like a student?"

Jim knew any reason he gave—he hated sitting in traffic; he liked getting to know the city; he needed the exercise—would seem silly, trivial, American, effete. Foreigners paid Russians to drive them; foreigners could insulate themselves from Moscow, and Russians could take their money: it was symbiotic, natural, sensible. "I'm sorry," Jim said. "Next time I will call you."

Fyodor nodded approvingly. "Just to drive." He raised a minatory finger. "Not to talk. I'm not a translator."

"I know. I don't need . . ."

"And I don't want to listen to such stories. For me, no. Too much."

"But you have two interviews to process?" Yuri asked Jim, loudly and quickly. Jim had the impression of intruding on a long-standing argument between the two men that Yuri was trying to forestall.

"Three, actually. With a fourth tomorrow, I hope."

"Well done, Jim," Yuri said, leaning back in his chair. He removed his glasses and set about polishing them neatly, almost ritualistically, dipping a corner of his handkerchief into the tea and wiping it vigorously over the lenses and the frames. "Against bacteria," he explained. "On your glasses just like in your throat. But really, you must tell me: how did you manage that?"

"I didn't actually do anything," Jim said, holding his hands up.

"You are much too modest," Fyodor said, a silver-toothed smile creasing his leathery face. He grabbed Jim's hand in both of his and squeezed, testing his strength. "Tell us, what did you use: American money or the lead pipe?"

"Come on, stop that," said Yuri, laughing along with Fyodor despite himself. "Jim has a trustworthy face. An open face. Not a Russian face. People talk to him. Isn't that right?"

Jim shook his head and leaned back from the table. "One person led to another. That's it."

"That's normal," Fyodor said, more seriously this time. "You must get inside first. You must not come as a stranger. That's how things work."

Yuri nodded his agreement.

"So you don't find it strange?" Jim asked.

"What?"

"Nothing for five months, then four in three days."

"What is strange? Fyodor is right: this is how it goes. You need to find just one person to talk to first, and that is luck. Or in your case, charm and alcohol and luck. And then after that, that person can guide you. You spoke to his friends, right?"

"Well, yes. To one friend, then another, then another."

"But a personal connection each time. It's normal. You are one of those people who only believe in bad luck. True? When your life is going well, you hold your breath. You can't enjoy it. Only when you're sick or broke or lonely can you function. True?"

"Is that a problem?"

Both men laughed. "Not for us," Fyodor said.

"Yes," Yuri seconded. "No wonder you feel so at home here."

"What's the joke today, guys?" asked Dave in English, striding into the kitchen with his arms over his head and his hands on his elbows.

Fyodor and Yuri shared a dubious, pitying look across the table; Dave missed it, but Jim caught it. They stood up to leave.

"Is nothing," said Fyodor, scraping the few remaining slices of *kholo-dets* back into its plastic container. Dave couldn't quite keep a look of disgust from appearing on his face. He reached into the refrigerator for a bottle of organic Turkish kefir. "Is only Dzheem crazy."

"I'll stop by before I leave," said Jim to Yuri, less to set a date than to differentiate himself from Dave by speaking Russian.

"As you like," Yuri replied. "You probably have a lot of transcribing to do." He clapped Fyodor on the shoulder as both men left the kitchen and headed in opposite directions.

"Dave, is that normal? Three interviews, one on the back of the next?"

"Normal? Look, Jimmy, these talks really run the gamut, you know? Sometimes we can't get people to stop talking. Others walk away when they see us coming. Some people invite us over and change their minds when we're at the door. Three in one day is great; besides, who's to say the next ones won't be marathons. Outstanding. Congratulations. You'll transcribe them tonight, or is it too much?"

Jim checked the clock—4:15. Kaisa wasn't answering. He didn't want to go home to an empty apartment. The interviews were short; he figured he could transcribe them and be done by nine o'clock. "I'll do them tonight so you can take a look and Yuri can listen tomorrow." Dave read the transcripts and listened to the interviews with an editorial eye: he would decide how to punctuate, title, and summarize each interview. Yuri listened to them with an ear for history, for what new ground each interview broke and what it could be linked with. Together the men would hash out how the interviews would be grouped on publication, a relationship made difficult by Dave's abysmal conversational Russian, Yuri's lack of conversational English, and their mutual suspicion. Both men wanted to be intellectual alphas; Yuri thought Dave's Russian disqualified him (despite Dave's ability to read and write it fluently); Dave thought Yuri's lack of advanced degrees disqualified him (despite Yuri's agile mind and breadth of knowledge). The men would circle each other warily, each shooting down the other's suggestions, until an exhausted consensus emerged.

"So why's Jim crazy?" Dave asked.

"It's not craziness, all right? I just can't shake this feeling that something about this whole thing is strange. Yuri disagrees; he was trying to reassure me."

"Strange how?"

"Like people are actually talking to me is how. Look, what do we do? What is our job?"

"I sense a rhetorical question."

"What we do is, we beg Vassily to take us to pore over some declassified KGB files; he begs the guards to let us in; we find some names, hope they're alive and we can trace them, and we beg them to talk. Every so often someone does. Occasionally. Right?"

"I'm with you so far."

"I mean, this isn't Germany; nobody's up for confronting the past. History fucked everybody; now it's time to move on. Right? You know, the first guy I talked to, Grigory Naumenko, he was as jolly as could be. No sadness, totally matter of fact, happy demeanor. He corrected me when he thought I said something too critical of Stalin."

"Well, you need to consider alternative historical narratives. Stalin turned a poor, agricultural country into an industrial powerhouse." Jim started to object; Dave held a hand up. He was in full academic flow. "That happens not to be the narrative I personally endorse. But I would argue very strongly for the necessary recognition of counternarratives. But you need to be aware that the Western villainization and *otherification*, shall we say, of Stalin is not a universal narrative."

"I understand that," said Jim, using an acid tone to cut through the rich grease of Dave's professorial babble. "Of course. All I'm saying is we found one survivor who defends his jailer, and a chain of survivors who suddenly can't shut up. That's what feels odd to me."

"What do you mean they can't shut up?" Dave smiled and hopped up from the table. Bracing himself against the windowsill, he stretched into an arch and held it for three breaths. He resumed his seat as though doing yoga in the middle of a conversation were perfectly normal. "You just said you have three interviews you'll have done in one night. Sounds like three terse people to me."

Jim sighed and rubbed his eyes. Late-afternoon fatigue made its bulk comfortable on his shoulders. "I guess so. Maybe. Also, the cops stopped me outside two of them. And I saw them watching at a third."

"Really?" Dave asked, drawing his eyebrows together. "Why?"

"I have no idea why."

"Well, what did they say?"

"They asked for my papers."

"Anything else?"

"No, but . . ."

"Then they were just doing spot-checks, it sounds like. You had an unlucky run. See"—he smiled—"it all balances out. One lucky run, one unlucky."

Jim grimaced and shook his head. "Nah, it wasn't like that, Dave. These weren't kids in uniform. The cop was older, in plainclothes, and said he was a special investigative liaison."

"Liaison to what?"

"He didn't say."

"Hmm. You weren't hurt, or anything like that, right?"

"No, no. Nothing like that. It was just odd, is all."

"Well, do you want to stop? Farm out the interviews to Birgitta?"

"No fucking way," Jim said vehemently. Not even if he had to dodge bullets to get to every last one of these interviews would he give anything to her. "These are mine."

Dave unfolded his hands in front of him and nodded serenely, as though he had just imparted a great piece of wisdom. "Well, then. There we are. Now you're looking kind of tired. Sara brought some great roasted-barley tea from California a couple weeks ago. What do you say I brew you up a cup?"

"Coffee, please," Jim called to Dave's back as he headed for the stove. "Please, no hot barley. For the love of God, just black coffee, preferably in a bucket."

IT WAS A LITTLE AFTER ten o'clock when Jim stepped from the station onto Mayakovskaya Ploshchad. He turned up the Garden Ring, passing the Skoda dealership, still fully lit and doing a brisk business two hours from midnight on a weekday. Through the window Jim saw a delicate, bespectacled middle-aged woman with the retiring air of a school librarian heft a carpetbag up from below her seat and start pulling out bricks of American cash. Month-to-month financing hadn't yet caught on; in Moscow, a nineteen-thousand-dollar car cost nineteen thousand dollars at the time of purchase.

He smiled to himself as he passed Pizza Pronto, and was already home in his mind, anticipating a cup of tea and a bolt of vodka, when a knock on the window of the Kauboyee Bar y Stayeek Khaus startled him. Just on the other side of the window from him, warm, well fed, and bright-eyed, was Mina Haddad, looking as composed and elegant as ever, smiling and waving him in.

# 11

RULES SURROUNDED AMERICAN RESTAURANTS in Moscow. Visiting businessmen, especially if they came from the Midwest or the South, often ate three meals a day at the Palm or Ruth's Chris: it was just like being at home, only with smaller portions and higher prices. American students nearing the end of their year abroad crammed Pancho's for burritos and enchiladas (on first arriving, of course, they would have been horrified at the thought of sticking so close to home, but seven months of university canteen food could break the culinary will of even the most determined anthropologist).

Only the most homesick, green, or clueless American expats went to the Cowboy. Most of them, instead, frequented the Starlite, a silver boxcar diner plunked down in a square-block park on the other side of Tverskaya, and they went on weekend mornings, when a well-placed backpack full of ball bearings and explosives would have left the city with just a skeleton crew of American diplomats and journalists.

The Cowboy was for middle-class Russian adults, wealthy Russian teens, and the occasional Western European man trying to impress his young Russian date. The reason, of course, was simple: the Starlite sold hamburgers and Western omelets (the only decent specimens of each between Prague and Tokyo); the Cowboy sold America. From the distressed wood front doors to the mounted deer skulls to the neon Schlitz signs and battered license plates, everything about the Cowboy screamed forced fun and focus groups. Seeing Mina waving to him from the other side of the window, a Lone Star longneck and a plate of potato skins full of Day-Glo cheese in front of her, struck Jim as incomprehensible. He telegraphed as much walking toward her.

"Hi, there," she said, standing up and extending a hand. She sat across from a young man with a scrubbed-smooth face, neatly parted brown hair, and an expression of blank earnestness. He wore a blue oxford shirt tucked into neatly pressed, pleated khakis. Had he wrapped an American flag around his narrow undergraduate shoulders his identity would not have been clearer. Jim ignored him and leaned forward to kiss her on the cheek. She stiffened before responding with a chaste pat on his upper back. "You look so surprised."

"I am. What are you doing here?"

"I had a craving for bad fried food. We come every now and then. Usually in a group."

"Don't you guys do everything as a group? The embassy staff roams in packs?"

"Yeah." She laughed nervously. "Yeah, I guess so. Usually we colonize the whole section over here."

"Ah, *colonize*, Meen? Maybe not the best choice of words," the guy said, with the heaviness of someone who wants his sensitivity appreciated.

Mina gave a midlevel laugh and introduced Jim and the other man with elegant, old-fashioned courtesy—an arcing open palm, head inclinations toward each man in turn, the sort of perfectly modulated voice and length of eye contact that come from extensive travel in diplomatic circles. "Ian, I'd like you to meet Jim Vilatzer. He's a friend from home. Jim, this is Ian Tomm. He works in the visa section."

"Oh, hey," said Ian, extending a hand. "You're coming to the old game tomorrow, right? Meen says you're going to take our money." The world had not yet scrubbed the cocky undergraduate sheen off him. Jim recognized the type from the poker table: a self-entitled winner. Someone who blames the cards, the table, or his opponents if he ends the night down, because his losing somehow goes against the natural order of the world. Either the world seasons such people by their late twenties, or they climb their professional mountainside of choice using knives in backs as picks and crampons.

"So much for the better part of valor," said Jim, sitting down next to Mina and clearing space on the table.

"Huh?" Ian asked.

"Nothing. Mina's just seen me on a couple of lucky nights."

"Yeah? Well, I've had a couple of those myself, to tell you the truth," said Ian, trying to lure Jim into a staring contest. He misread the situation, and saw Jim as a rival. In truth, Jim had willed himself to find Mina attractive on several occasions, but it just wasn't taking. She was certainly pretty, with searching, limpid dark eyes; a long neck; a sinuous, lithe body that looked like it could bend in all sorts of wonderful directions; and the sort of jittery, darting energy—always evaluating, always thinking, always trying to take someone's measure—that made Jim wonder what it might take to calm her or see the world as her or pass muster with her. But their relationship remained sparkless: she seemed to him too self-sufficient, too competent; he could never find in her the flaws and cracks essential for attraction; she remained to him too unblemished and perfect.

"I hope we *both* have our share of luck tomorrow."

"That's sweet," said Ian acidly. "You know where it is, right? This place called Nest . . . Nem . . ."

"Neftchilar. Out near Krasnopresnenskaya, Mina said, right?"

"Reservation's for Woods—that's the consular director—at seven. It'll let us eat, drink, then play a little cards."

"Sounds great. Gambling in the restaurant: God bless Russia."

"Obviously we took one of the private cottages out back."

"Oh, obviously. Can I bring anything?"

"Bring anything?" Ian scoffed. "Ah, Jim, it's a restaurant. You know, these people get really insulted if you slight their hospitality."

"Ah. Of course. I'm sorry; I suppose my experience with these people lags far behind yours."

"No, that wasn't what I was . . . You know I didn't mean it like that."

"I know, Ian," said Mina. "I don't think that's what Jim meant. I think I need another drink, though," she said, looking at her empty glass. The pool of viscous, blackish stuff at the bottom (and the dark tinge to her teeth) showed she was drinking either the noxious house red—invariably Moldovan, shipped in metal barrels like beer—or crude oil. She embarked on lengthy preparations to stand up, indicating she had no intention of actually doing so.

"I got it," said Ian, rushing to his feet and actually putting a hand out to indicate that Jim should stay seated. "It usually takes a while back there." The Cowboy featured a bar where diners could fetch their own drinks: it remained an exotic arrangement for Russia, and would have been unthinkably déclassé in any context other than an American-themed restaurant. Unfortunately for Ian, the bar was not at the center of the restaurant, but at the back. The concept of lining up had never really made it over here, either, especially where alcohol was concerned. Ian took Jim's order (a large Sibirskaya Corona and a shot of Beam, winning him a dubious look from Mina), squared his shoulders, and headed off into the throng.

"Does he make it back intact?" Jim asked.

"He's a nice kid," Mina pleaded. "Very earnest. Still wants to spend his weekends in the office just in case somebody sees him."

"*Kid* is right."

Mina sighed with comic heaviness and fixed her gaze on Jim. "Are you saying you were never like that?"

"Never what? Had a crush on an older woman?" Mina smiled and looked away, blushing in red fingers running down her long neck. "Sure, I did. Of course. I never spent weekends in the office, though. And I don't think I was ever quite so . . ."

"Yes, you were. He just thinks he's being gallant."

"I'm sure he does."

"What about you? Are you being gallant with anyone these days?"

"Me?" He looked over at her, surprised and a little uncomfortable. They had never talked about anything so personal before; their conversations were limited to observations about Moscow, Rockville, and Washington. "Not really."

"No? Nobody at all?" She had a look on her face that Jim hadn't seen before: a coquettish little smile pasted on beneath sharp, searching eyes.

"There was something brief, you know, but that's it."

"Ooh." She sat forward and cupped her chin in her hand: another incongruous pose, like an older woman in too much makeup and fishnet stockings. "Who was it? What happened?"

"Meen, I never knew you were such a gossip. Nothing really happened. I think she's just busy."

"Oh. She's American?"

"Finnish, actually. She's an actress. I guess she keeps odd hours. So what about you?" Jim asked quickly. Mina's expression returned to normal: polite smile; slightly raised chin; watchful, flickering eyes.

"Nothing, really. I just had dinner with a couple of friends last night. That was my most exciting evening in weeks."

"Yeah? Embassy guys? 'Guys' in the fullest, implication-free sense, of course."

"Gee, thanks. God shield me from implication. No, just a couple of people I met at a party a few weeks back. Rodion Lisitsov and Matvei Yagachin." Again, she looked at Jim expectantly, measuring him, but said nothing. "You don't know them, by any chance, do you?" she asked after a few seconds.

"I don't, actually. Who are they? Why would I?"

"Art dealers. They have a gallery together. Rodion's a sort of impresario, goes everywhere, knows everyone, very flamboyant. Matvei runs the business side."

"Are they . . ."

"I think so. Nobody asks."

"Openly? In Moscow?"

"Sure. Like I said, as long as nobody asks. Rodion mounts a few openings a year in New York. I got to know him and like him. Sure you've never run across them at all? They've been trying to open a gallary in the States for years; they really try to cultivate Americans."

"You flatter me, Meen. The only people I've met through my job work in my office, and even them I don't know terribly well."

"Is that right?" Jim couldn't tell if she was just making conversation or if she wanted to know if that was, in fact, right. Her gaze had grown wide and hungry. "They might come tomorrow. To the game."

"Great. The more fat wallets the better." Mina smiled noncommittally. "Actually, I wanted to ask you a question. A favor. I guess it's a question and a favor, really."

"Oh. Oh, sure, Jim. What can I do for you?" She smoothed her hair back and laid her hands on the table in front of her, in ready position.

"It's a license-plate question. I'm not sure if you can answer it, but I also couldn't think of anyone else to ask."

She raised her chin inquisitively. "Don't tell me you're thinking of buying a car. Because we just did a study on road safety in Moscow, and I can tell you . . ."

"No, no. Not mine. Driving in Moscow, are you kidding? No, it's a Russian government plate. At least I think it is." He slid the piece of paper with the plate number from last night over to Mina. They were still sitting quite close to each other, even though nobody was across from them. "I just want to know whose it is. Or at least what department or ministry it belongs to."

Mina took the paper gingerly. "Is this a joke?"

"No." Jim smiled as disarmingly as he could. "No, no. No. I know it seems like it must be, but I promise, I'm totally serious."

"You know, Jim, I'm not above helping an inquisitive soul every now and then, but I always get something in return. What are you selling today?"

"Peace on earth, goodwill toward men?"

Mina gave a tight, indulgent smile. "You should have gone for hometown connections."

"Would that have worked?"

She slipped the paper into her pocket. "Let me see what I can do. I'll let you know tomorrow night one way or the other. But you have to tell me why you're asking."

He told her about the unusual police stops after each of his last three interviews, and about seeing the car. She listened intently, but with an almost blank expression. When he finished, she nodded. "Good. Is that all?"

"It is. I know, it's probably nothing, but . . ."

"Well, if it's just coincidental, then it's harmless enough, right? Here come the drinks," she said quickly, looking down and away from the advancing Ian. "We'll keep this between ourselves."

"There you are," Mina said brightly as Ian set down the five glasses (he had, of course, ordered the same thing as Jim, but with a double shot instead of just a single). "Jim was just telling me about his exciting life. Apparently he's dating an actress."

"Really?" asked Ian, his eyes wide with relief. He handed Jim the drinks, clinked glasses, and even smiled.

"Yeah, well. We'll see. I think I am. Long story." Ian leaned in closer to Mina but kept his eyes on Jim, who feared he was about to ask him to tell the story, at length. He spoke up quickly. "Ian, what about you? What do you do for the motherland?"

"Ian is taking GOV again," Mina said, her eyes twinkling. Jim looked at him quizzically.

"I'm doing protocol for an American Chamber of Commerce dinner we're hosting. I'm researching who can and can't sit next to whom." He gave an embarrassed little grin. Now that Jim was no longer a rival, he almost let himself turn human. "I call it GOV as a mnemonic. Golovna, Orsonov, Vorov. The three people being honored."

"Honored for what?"

" 'Honored for their contributions in fostering Russian-American business relations and for drawing our two cultures ever closer through commerce,' " Ian quoted. "At least that's what the invitations say."

"Natalya Golovna is a famous dancer," Mina said, in a reverent tone that made Jim think he should have heard of her. "I'm not sure about the other two, but she's wonderful. Even if she mostly does movie stuff now."

"You want me to get you an autograph?" Ian asked seriously. Mina giggled, deflating him.

"Vitaly Orsonov franchises Lukoil in Southern California," he explained to Jim. The dancer was for Mina; the business world was for men. "Anatoly Vorov is an economics professor. One of those market-cures-all guys. The president loves free marketeers with foreign accents," he said breezily, as though deeply familiar with all of the president's likes and dislikes. "The Commerce secretary's coming over from Washington for the dinner.

"Listen, don't tell anyone this," Ian said, leaning over the table and lowering his voice. He seemed to think every Russian computer programmer and sales rep in the restaurant was desperate for Washington gossip. "The rumor is it's all a big precampaign campaign dinner for the ComSec." He was the sort of person who would never use a familiar term when an opaque acronym would do. He would go far in Washington. "He's from California, and supposedly he's thinking of running for governor. He wants to make friends with the Russian community out there. They're buying up a lot of San Francisco. California's the new London."

Suddenly Jim felt old, tired, fuzzy. He couldn't remember feeling as certain about anything ever as this kid felt about something he knew nothing about. He leaned back, exhaled deeply, and felt all of his years settle on his shoulders. Questions at the beginning of the day and competition at the end of it. He was done. Mumbling a quick apology, he stood up, dumped the whiskey into the beer, drained the whole glass in a gulp, and went home to sleep.

## 12

JUNIOR YEAR OF HIGH SCHOOL, after returning from a spring break spent with his cousins in Jackson Heights, Vivek started referring to D.C.'s subway as "the Nerf metro." "Look at this," he said, half sneering and half laughing, as they boarded at Twinbrook on Friday evening, against the commute, on their way down to see a show at Fort Reno. "Yellow foam seats, these padded handles, carpet even my parents would be embarrassed to put in their home. Buck Rogers stations. You know how silly this shit'll look in another ten, twenty years? Be like one of those Flash Gordon shows where you can see the strings on the flying saucers."

The conversation stuck with Jim because it was right—nothing dates faster than visions of the future—and because the Moscow Metro, which he was now riding to Vodniy Stadion, on Moscow's scrubby northern outskirts, was the anti-Nerf Metro: hard wooden seats, black metal floors, heavy steel doors that slammed shut so hard they seemed angry, and the military, hortatory voice that addressed commuters as "Respected passengers!" The system covers only slightly less ground than New York's subway, but has far fewer stations; with barely three minutes passing between trains, they hurtle through tunnels fast enough to press forward-facing passengers back into their seats.

The old stations are majestic stone palaces festooned with stained-glass, Social Realist mosaics, or busts of Soviet heroes; the newer ones are bleak, weeping-walled caves with the sort of lighting that makes everyone appear on the brink of vomiting. Armies of stern babushki keep the stations in relative order; they sweep the broad gray staircases, brush the escalators' wide wooden teeth with bunched branches, give the evil eye to everyone who passes them, and sit purposefully but with no evident function in glass booths at the bottoms of escalators. All of this conspires to make Moscow's Metro seem more an ecosystem or a natural phenomenon than a commuter rail network.

Vodniy Stadion station has never quite shaken off its Brezhnevian gloom and grime: the station is long, purgatorial, and fluorescently lit. Jim alighted just in front of a dapper-looking older man in a goatee, a burgundy suit, and a New York Knicks wool and leather coat carrying a stack of records bound in twine. The top record showed a slender silhouette in glasses playing a saxophone against a blue background— Sonny Rollins, *Saxophone Colossus*, which Jim had discovered with Vivek that same year of high school.

Jim walked out of the station just behind a beefy, flat-headed guy who looked like he had been winched into his expensive suit and leather jacket. He wore an expression of utter neutrality, and his rhomboid head sat neckless atop a barrel-chested, boxer-gone-to-seed body. As Jim followed behind him to the staircase, a shambolic little drunk approached them from a bench in front of them, his greasy black hands forming a cup and his stubbly face imploring and streaked with tears. The drunk wobbled his way directly in their path, mumbling with his hands out. The heavy, not even breaking stride, snapped his arm up and out from his side, delivering a quick but effective uppercut right to the drunk's jaw. He reeled backward, spitting rotten teeth, blood, and phlegm. Instinctively Jim slowed and turned toward the drunk, beginning a crouch, when the jazz fan, also without breaking stride, caught his arm and pulled him along, giving a subtle but steady warning shake of the head. "It's over. Leave him be. Better him alone than him and you."

When they got out of the station, the heavy climbed into the passenger seat of a souped-up black Jeep with tinted windows. "See," said the man, transferring the records beneath his arm. "Those types will shoot you as soon as look at you."

The jazz buff gave a Moscow farewell—a nod of the head inextinguishable in time or intensity from an involuntary tic—and trudged off in the opposite direction. This was the welcome counterpoint to Moscow's lawlessness: the readiness—the necessity—of its citizens to look out for one another in endlessly surprising ways. And as much as Jim could boast to himself about liking the danger, the unpredictability, and the toughness of the city, he also loved these unexpected, genuine moments of kindness, too. American life, especially the suburban American life into which Jim was born, tends to flatten out the extreme—one can go years seeing no infraction more serious than running a stop sign, but receiving from strangers nothing friendlier than a professional, tight-lipped grin in a store. Here, though, if you occasionally saw a thug send a beggar sprawling, you also had strangers who pulled you out of harm's way. And, in truth, while events of the former class make better stories, those in the latter are more common.

IF CENTRAL MOSCOW projects state power, limitless and brutal, and impresses on its denizens just how small they are in comparison to this power, Vodniy Stadion is where the state's power ends and nature's begins. The area felt unfinished, vast, with a few industrial sites, a weighing station for trucks, and the usual array of game rooms, portable toilets, and food carts smacked haphazardly in the middle of scrub fields and some low-slung, half-finished or half-started cinder-block buildings in irregular rows a few hundred yards back from the streets. Unimpeded views down a few long streets showed threatening vistas of forest to the east, as if the trees were massing at the edges of this temporary encampment, waiting for the right moment to take back what they had lost.

The Moscow Infectious Disease Hospital Number 2 sat a few hundred yards back from Semyonovskaya Proezd, a good mile's hike from the station. A driveway lined on both sides by decapitated pine trees wended its way up to the bleak, gray building. By the front doors, which flopped loosely in their frames, a quartet of haggard, hollow-cheeked men in slippers and tattered bathrobes smoked and shivered. As Jim walked past them, one bent double with a spoons-on-washboard cough and hacked up a quivering, reddish-yellow lump that landed on the threshold.

He started to walk through an immense entry foyer into the hospital when a guard—really just a tired, rheumy old man in a sweater with epaulets—whistled from a desk in the corner and beckoned him over. "Passport." Jim complied.

"American," he said, with bemused interest. "What is an American doing at this particular hospital on this particular morning?"

"I'm looking for Dr. David Faridian."

"Faridian?" he asked, his eyes widening and cheeks puffing out. "Are you sick?"

"No, no, I'm just . . . I just would like to speak with him."

"He's expecting you?"

"Of course," Jim said confidently. "I am here to discuss his purchase of some specialized medical equipment."

"A capitalist in our hospital." He chuckled. "And meeting with Faridian. Good luck to you. The doctor will probably be upstairs."

"Excuse me, I don't understand. Where upstairs?"

"Young man, how do you expect me to know where the doctor is at all times? He works in the surgery unit. The surgery unit is upstairs. Therefore, as I have just told you, you will find him upstairs. Straight down the long hall and up one story."

"Thank you."

The guard raised his eyebrows and pulled the corners of his mouth down, nodding, a Russian "You're welcome," an expression that said you received only what you asked for, and casting doubt on the wisdom of asking for it in the first place.

The hallway's pale yellow walls looked less like the product of institutional paint than like some sort of architectural decay. Fewer than half of the fluorescent bulbs worked, and some of those flickered; patients in various states of distress lolled in the beds that lined the hallway. Some milky winter light trickled in through the hallway's high windows. A powerful smell of ether, blood, and shit pervaded the hospital. In a small room off the hallway Jim saw two nurses cooking something in an old rusty pot that jittered away atop an electric coil. When he looked closer, and saw that they were dropping metal implements—forceps, scalpels, retractors, specula—into the pot, he realized they were not cooking but sterilizing. As he turned his attention from that scene he accidentally banged his foot into the post of a bed occupied by a mottled, wrinkled, slack-jawed, drooling, glassy-eyed shell of a woman poking spookily out of a yellowed housedress stained with urine and vomit. Only the faintest whimper of protest signified she remained among the living.

At the top of the stairs, Jim passed another room that seemed to be given over to sterilization: a few dozen rusty pots, each the size that Vilatzer's used for stock, sat steaming away on electric hot plates on the floor. All the hot plates were plugged precariously into four jerry-rigged surge protectors in the middle of the room. As Jim looked in, he was shoved from behind; he stepped aside for a battle-ax of a nurse lugging another pot of water, with which she replaced one of the boiling ones.

When Jim walked in she looked up at him almost sweetly. Her blond hair was tucked into a sensible bun beneath her hat, and she had a patient, warm, matter-of-fact expression.

"I'm looking for Dr. Faridian. Can you tell me where I can find him?"

"He is probably upstairs, in surgery. The doctor is very busy today. Come, I will take you," she said, smiling as she hefted a pot of hot water.

"I can take that," Jim said. She shook her head, smiling at him through a wreath of steam.

"Please follow me," she said. "I cannot vouch for the doctor's mood, as usual, but perhaps you already know what to expect. You may need to wait a few moments."

They walked down a hallway just as grim, purgatorial, and crowded as the one below. It was quieter, though: fewer moans and screams. Most of the patients were sleeping, sedated, or unconscious. The nurse turned left off the hallway, and when Jim peered around the door frame he saw an operating theater, of sorts: the patient was splayed naked on a wooden table, with a gas mask strapped to his face. He had no IV, but a drop of blood from an injection trickled down his forearm, which hung off the table. Light came from two halogen lamps, one in each corner.

The doctor, a tall, ropy man with salt-and-pepper hair, slightly tinted glasses, and the sort of tan that comes from working outdoors in one's youth, stood grimly over the patient. He glanced up at Jim then turned his attention back to the patient.

"This procedure is closed," the doctor said. "What do you want?"

"Dr. Faridian?" Jim asked hesitantly.

"Perhaps."

"I should probably come back later, when . . ."

"I can give you five minutes," the doctor said, wiping his hands on his corduroy pants as he advanced. "The patient is healthy and well prepared; he can stand a few more moments under the gas. Masha, do you agree?"

The nurse nodded amicably, and put the pot onto another hot plate. "Of course, Doctor. The instruments are here when you need them."

"You see who holds the real power in a Russian hospital," the doctor said with a tight smile.

"Dato Tsepereli suggested I speak with you. I work for the Memory Foundation. It's a group that records the histories of political prisoners in Eastern Europe."

"A group that records the histories of political prisoners in Eastern Europe," he parroted drily. "How interesting. In what condition, may I ask, did you find Dato?"

"Sober," Jim said plainly. "Terrified. Shaking. But sober."

"Your visit must have been important, then. May I see your passport, please?"

Jim had stopped remarking, even internally, on the Russian fetishization of official documents. Instead he just handed the passport over. "You are Dr. David Faridian?"

He nodded. "Vee-la-tzeer. American. You have been here only six months, and you are on a business visa." He handed Jim his passport and looked at him skeptically. "How does someone like you meet someone like Dato Tsepereli?"

"I was sent to him by Vilis Balderis." Jim didn't explain the name, hoping Faridian would pick up on it. No such luck. "As I said, I work for the Memory Foundation." He pulled a card out of his wallet and held it out. Faridian kept his arms crossed. "We record the testimony of gulag survivors. Like Vilis. And Dato. And you, I understand."

"You understand, do you?" he asked sardonically, leaning over to check the patient's pulse. "I asked you. I want to know: do you understand?"

Jim remained still. He could not say yes, of course, because after a suburban American life how could he? He did not want to say no, because he worried Faridian would take that as a triumph and evict him. Instead, he went for empathy. "I have tried to. I think Vilis and Dato and Grigory Naumenko have helped me, but I would also like to hear your story."

Faridian nodded with satisfaction and turned his attention back to Jim.

"He's well?" Jim asked.

"Well? Is he *well*?" Faridian rose, his deep-set eyes alive with indignation. "You can see his condition for yourself. He is unconscious in an infectious diseases hospital, about to have his chest cut open with instruments that were boiled in tap water. You judge for yourself: is that well?"

Unprepared for such a reaction, Jim stammered, "I just meant . . . the gas . . ."

"Ah, the gas, yes, of course. Among the many things we lack is an adequate supply of Sodium Pentothal, so we must supplement it with nitrous oxide. After we finish our little chat, I must rush to find the nurse—or any nurse; we have too few—to see if she will assist me. If we finish quickly, he will be fine; if not, well, I shall have to revive him and perform the operation tomorrow. And I *will* perform it. Many of my colleagues would not, since, as you can see, this particular patient is indigent, without money for the many 'fees' doctors now require. But assuming he lives until tomorrow, yes, he will be perfectly *well*."

"What sort of operation does he need?"

"He needs a tracheotomy. He has diphtheria."

"Diphtheria?"

"Yes, diphtheria, a disease against which you and I have been vaccinated. Most Russians were, up until the collapse. Do you know how many cases of diphtheria existed in *your* country last year? Five. In mine? About a quarter million. Really he needs an antitoxin, but, of course, we have none. To get that you have to go to a private hospital. And he's immunosuppressed, which means the simple act of cutting into him could well give him an infection that will kill him.

"Moscow's water, as you might know, flows through pipes that adjoin sewage pipes. Over time lesions form in certain places on each pipe, and they leak into each other. For most of us, we run our drinking water through a filter, no problem. But this gentleman on the table is not most of us, and our hospital's filtering system is partly broken, partly stolen. You see," Faridian spat, "how we live today. Have you been healthy since your arrival in Russia?"

"I have. I've been lucky."

Faridian snorted. "Lucky, yes. You people always are. And if your luck stopped, you would not have to rely on us—on me—to restore it. So no, you do not *understand*. You cannot understand. And I am disinclined to pour my memory out into your tape recorder. It happened. Errors were made, perhaps. In judgment, in severity, in procedure, in ideology. And? What then? What nation has never made mistakes? Who benefits when we debase ourselves in the pages of history? Whose plan is it for us to be dragged back rather than forging forward?"

"There's no plan, Doctor. We just think it's important to hear your stories."

"And what if I don't want to tell them?" he asked, glaring at Jim and pounding a fist on the table. Jim held his gaze, trying to look neither confrontational nor weak. Faridian ran a hand over his face, took a deep breath, and began speaking in a quiet, even voice.

"I am a doctor, the son and grandson of village doctors in Gyumri, Armenia. My class background was suspect. I was seized on the orders of a coward, a time-serving army captain who wanted me gone so he could have his way with the woman who became my wife. From a land of bounty and perpetual sun I traveled by cattle train to one of isolation and perpetual cold. That first winter the prisoners trapped fox using contraband barbed wire and bricks smuggled out of the factory. Not for fur, but for food. Some were so hungry they didn't bother to cook it. It became their last meal. Do you think, with a blue passport like yours, that you can 'understand' such stories? Do you think you can convince me you care?"

"Doctor, I'm trying to. What impresses me, though, is how much you care. Dato said you looked after people in the camp. You must have known many others?"

"I knew few other people. I knew as many as I cared to know."

"So you don't remember the names of the people you helped?"

Faridian rose to his full height. In another life he might have been a cowboy; he had that lean, self-sufficient, whipcord look to him.

"In a previous life, *Meester* Vilatzer," he hissed in sardonic English, "I ran an emergency room in a provincial hospital in Tomsk. One night, I failed to save the lives of two women who were brought in with multiple stab wounds. One of them, the older one, was literally holding her windpipe as they brought her through the doors. The younger one had effectively been flayed from the neck up. They were the wife and daughter of a survivor, you see. Apparently they tried to take away his bowl of soup before he finished." Gently but firmly, he started shoving Jim out of the operating room. "One thing I resolved when I returned to society

is that I would never again face another interrogation. I have fond rec-
ollections of only one person from those days. Dato I feel pity for, of
course, not fondness. But every so often I drink with Rukhmanov. He
is a butcher at Tenth Planet. Now, I have no wish to rake myself and my
country over the coals to help the career of a member of the twice-
chosen people. I must go find a nurse willing to help me. Otherwise this
piece-of-shit patient, this man who someone such as you would step
over to get a sushi or a cappuccino, will die. I don't expect you to care,
but I do expect you to leave."

# 13

NEFTCHILAR WAS BUILT AND DECORATED like a country house owned by an Azerbaijani lightbulb magnate who wanted to show off his wares. A stable door encircled with white forty-watt bulbs fronted the street, with the restaurant's name spelled out in small but piercing hundred-watt blue, red, and green bulbs (the colors of the Azerbaijani flag) in Cyrillic, Latin, and Arabic letters. A hallway lined with mellow white Christmas tree lights led to a long, low, carpet-strewn dining room with wooden tables and vine-wound beams designed to look like tree trunks (the cigarette burns and graffiti on the trunks ruined the illusion). Strings of multicolored teardrop lights ran along the tops of the restaurant's walls and up the rough wooden beams and pillars. The maître d' who greeted Jim had a sad-cowboy horseshoe mustache and wore a Russian translation of Caucasian "native garb" that made him look like a cross between a gaucho, a 1970s lounge singer, and a pincushion. He asked Jim if he had a reservation.

"Woods."

"What?"

"Woods?"

"No."

*"Vooods. Vooods."*

"Through that door." He pointed toward the rear of the restaurant. "Farthest on the right."

Jim left the main room, crossed a cobblestone courtyard artfully strewn with hay, and went into one of the five little stone cottages at the back. He thought his arrival, at 7:30 for a 7:00 reservation, bordered on unadvisedly early, but when he walked in he found dinner in full swing. Five people sat around a low wooden table festooned with colorful overlapping cloths, helping themselves from plates of grilled meats, pickled vegetables, and flatbreads. A brazier smoked merrily away in the corner; the room smelled of grilled meat, winter air, and wood-smoke.

"Jim, hi." Mina came toward him and kissed him on each cheek self-consciously, standing ramrod straight, laying one hand on his shoulder like a plank, and bending forward awkwardly from her waist. Even to a poker game she wore a sensible pantsuit. "We didn't want to start without you, you know, but as soon as they showed us back here dinner was already on the table, and we just couldn't wait. Come in and meet everybody. Everybody, this is Jim Vilatzer, who I told you about. He works for the Memory Foundation." It really was an American party: name followed by employer. Get your class background out in the open as soon as possible.

"Okay," said Mina, taking Jim by the hand and turning him to face the crowd, "so starting here, you must remember Ian from last night, right?"

"Of course. Good to see you," Jim said, not even pretending to mean it. Ian seemed to give his hand an unnecessarily hard warning squeeze, but two and a half decades of kitchen work let Jim hold his own: Ian winced first.

"And this is Tim Weber. He's the other foreigner tonight."

A reedy, chinless, balding man in a tan poplin suit gave Jim a dead-fish handshake and a queasy, dying quail smile.

"Foreigner?" Jim asked. "Where are you from?"

"Plano, more or less."

Jim looked quizzically at Mina. "It just means nonembassy staff. You and Tim. This is Harrison Tunney, in the corner, one of our Defense attachés." A craggy man in a leather jacket and black jeans, with deep crow's-feet extending out from coal-black eyes, Tunney nodded silently without standing.

"And Mr. Woods couldn't come tonight, so this is his secretary, Trudy Wurtzel."

"Hi, Jim." Trudy giggled, pumping his hand amicably. She looked like one of the suburban office-tower lunchers he had spent his life serving: frizzy blond hair; agreeably nondescript clothes, face, and body; and an eager, goofy smile much too broad for the occasion. "Mina told us you're, like, really, really good, and I've never played before? So I just wanted to say, you know, you might need, like, a little patience with me?"

"I'm sure you'll do fine. Nice to meet you."

"Oh, you, too, Jim. You, too! Why don't you sit down here and eat something. We were just trying to think of a nickname for Moscow."

Jim took a seat between Mina and Tunney, and across from Trudy, and helped himself to two long skewers stacked with alternating cubes of lamb ribs, lamb fat, and onion chunks. "A nickname? Like what?"

"Oh, you know. Like the Big Apple, or the Windy City," said Mina.

"What about the Big Smoke?" Trudy yelped, raising her hand eagerly. "'Cause it always smells so smoky!"

"That's London," Tunney said, firmly but quietly. Trudy and Tim began tossing other possibilities around, and Jim tuned out.

"No Rodion?" Jim asked Mina.

"No, no," Mina said, unusually quietly. "He couldn't come."

"So, Jimmy," Tim called out, his Adam's apple bobbing in time with his head. He was seated at the opposite corner from Jim, and shouted across the table. "So Mina said you live here 'cause you want to. That makes one of us, right?" He turned to the room, awaiting approbation.

"You were posted here?"

"Yeah, you know. Got sent over for a six-month thing. Might stay for more, though, if the pay's right. Met Tomm over there at a buddy's Super Bowl party."

"What do you do?"

"I'm a sales rep for Frito-Lay. We're trying to open the market over here for some of our exotics. Focus groups show the domestic market has really matured, really come a long way, snackwise, from just vodka and bread, you know?"

"Yeah, if there's one thing Moscow really could use, it's a decent Dorito, and maybe a Funyun or two."

"Exactly!" Weber chirped happily just as Mina nudged Jim under the table. "So you just came over 'cause . . ."

"It's a long story, really. Some family connections, some wanderlust, some inducement."

"But you like it?"

"I do."

Jim expected Weber to ask him what Vivek and his friends back home asked, what he sometimes asked himself whenever a policeman hassled him on suspicion of being Chechen, or a store clerk made his life a little more difficult just because she could, or he felt a draft of freezing air slither through his poorly fitted window, or he passed a thug kicking a frostbitten *bomzh* caked in his own vomit for no reason: Why? And he had the reasons ready, too: the extremes of brutality and warmth, which played out on every level, from the sneering clerk and the office manager who made sure you wore comfortable slippers to the savage apartment blocks and fairy-tale churches; the way the city and its people nurtured their scars; the salutary effects of difference, of being forced to figure out and improvise rather than taking life and its patterns for granted; the lusts unleashed after decades of repression; the honest vibrancy. There were more. In truth, though, falling in love with a city is like falling in love with a person: explicable only up to a certain point. After that other people just have to take your feelings on faith.

As it turned out, though, Weber didn't ask why: he just launched into an extended whine about how he missed the Cotton Bowl because his corporate apartment's manager couldn't find the right satellite channel.

After his second skewer of meat and his third bottle of water (Azerbaijani food tended to be salty, all the better, supposedly, to encourage the consumption of vodka. A night of hydrating with vodka, however, tended to make a person feel the next morning like an anchovy, which in turn encouraged vodka drinking to get over the pain. Lather, rinse, repeat), Tunney, who sat across from Jim and had so far been eating in silence, leaned over the table. "Your job, Jim, allows you to see parts of Russia, and meet Russians, that most Westerners never see or meet. Is that accurate?" He spoke evenly, quietly, his crow's eyes boring into Jim's so intently that Jim had to force himself not to look away.

"I guess so. More than some people, anyway."

"You mean Weber," Tunney said flatly, decisively. "I doubt he's met a Russian since he moved here. And except for the secretaries that work in his office, he probably won't. Why would he? He has no use for them, no feeling for them. But you do."

"I don't know about that," Jim said, trying to extricate himself from the conversation as politely as possible. "I'm really just a researcher."

"Do you have a researcher's certificate?"

"Sure." The Memory Foundation, like every other employer in Moscow, issued identification cards with a picture, seals, stamps, and several signatures. The more complicated the document, the less important the job.

"One of the things you learn, Jim, in a position such as mine, is that we're really only as secure as our citizens allow us to be."

Jim was puzzling through this oracular, if slightly nonsensical, pronouncement when he felt something slide beneath his hand. Tunney had slipped him a business card.

"We have to depend on other people's eyes. If you ever see anything you think we might like to know about, give me a call on that number. Day or night."

"Oh. Thank you. Thanks very much, I think. . . . You might be over-estimating me, you know, but . . ."

"No, I don't think I am. Keep it; you might find it useful sometime."

"Jim?" Mina piped up, saving him. "Do you want to help me clear this and set up the table?"

"Sure. Thanks," he whispered. They started moving the empty grease-stained, bone-strewn plates from the main table over to a pair of round plastic trays in the corner. Nobody else made a move to help.

"Does he always talk like that?"

"Always. We call him 'Spooky.' You know, not like Scooby-Doo spooky, but like a *spook* spooky. I think he likes it."

"Is he?"

"Is he what?"

"A spook?"

She shrugged. "How would I know that? He acts like one. He likes to think he is. But nobody tells me anything. Hey," she said, raising her voice and hefting a tray, "Ian, if you want to get the table set up, Jim and I can bring these over to the kitchen."

"Now you have a servant? You're torturing the poor kid?" Jim asked quietly, when they were clear of the door and a few steps into the courtyard.

"Only a little. No more than he wants to be," she said with a co-quettish, knowing smile. He had always thought of her as somewhat gender-neutral, blessed with gifts she wasn't entirely aware of; it was heartening to see that she could use them. "So the thing you asked about? The license plate? We think it's from the Interior Ministry."

"We *think*?"

"Jim, I just told you: I'm the last to know. I'm not exactly on the Kremlinology e-mail list."

"So how'd you get it?"

"I wore the right clothes and asked the right man." She flashed a quietly confident smile, and Jim returned it. "I didn't give up anything more than a smile and the implied promise of future smiles. Just put that down here," she said, pointing to the back door of the kitchen.

The doorway of the kitchen opened, and two sweaty cooks stepped out to have a smoke. The smaller one said something to Mina in a bouncy, jostling language. Jim could infer the general content from the way he eyed her up and down and looked immediately to his larger colleague for approval. When she responded in kind, however, his face went red, and the big man laughed at him and said something to Mina that raised a smile. He waved at her fondly, paternally, as she and Jim headed back across the courtyard.

"But of course: Mina Haddad speaks Azeri. I would have expected nothing less."

"You know a little Turkish, you know a little Arabic, then you can get by in Azeri."

"What did he say?"

"The little one? Like you can't guess. Like you've never said anything like . . ."

"I haven't," Jim protested earnestly.

"Of course not. It had to do with the cut of my suit being too long. I think the bigger one said, 'A woman who is allowed to talk outside of the house sings her worth from the mountains.' It's a double-edged proverb: on the one hand, we love a strong, smart woman; on the other, those are the only ones we'll let speak outside the house. I have to tell you, I think it's about as good as I'll get in Central Asia. Anyway, he meant well. Hang on a minute. Do you have a cigarette?"

Jim's estimation of Mina rose yet again as he shook two Winstons from a battered pack. "I had no idea."

"It's a useful habit." She put fire first to Jim's smoke then to hers.

"Oh, yeah?"

She nodded. "It gives you time. It breaks the ice. It takes a few cells, of course, as you know, and I wouldn't want to do it forever, but you'd be surprised how much you can learn about somebody by smoking with them." Mina held her cigarette between two fingers, her palm down and her arm extended rigidly downward. "Can you tell me again, just for curiosity's sake, where you saw these plates?" Her voice rose at the end, but it wasn't really a question.

"After a couple of interviews I did. One at Izmailovsky Market and one at a casino by Universitet."

"A casino? Up there?"

"Not a real casino; a trailer full of slot machines. Nasty place."

"And you're sure these cars were there for you. Watching you."

"Not one hundred percent. I mean, I didn't ask anybody. But yes, I got the distinct feeling that they were."

"And who were you interviewing? Survivors, I know, but specifically."

"Specifically? A stallholder at Izmailovsky Market named Vilis Balderis and a drunk named Dato Tsepereli. Why?"

"Just curious," she said, holding up her cigarette hand. She tried but failed to be disarming; again, she had that blank, hungry, calculating look that made Jim feel totally transparent. "You ask me for a favor, I get to ask you for information. Fair?"

"Of course. No problem."

"Do you guys do your interviews alone?"

"Yes. For archival research we need to take a fixer, but when we're actually speaking with someone we go alone. It's easier to talk one-on-one than two- or three-on-one. Especially for someone who's been through what they have."

"So you did these interviews by yourself."

"I did. Why so many questions? And why *after* you helped me instead of when you were deciding whether to help?"

"Because you just told an embassy official you're being trailed by the Interior Ministry," she said sharply. "Because I would like to know why. And how. And who."

"I don't know who. That's why I asked you."

"Jim, in my experience, people know far more than they think they know. They just have to be asked properly."

"I thought your experience was processing."

Mina shot Jim a pitying look, crushed her cigarette underfoot, and pulled the door open for him, forestalling the chance for more questions. As he passed, he caught a scent of lilac and Mina, and let his hand drop to her hip, not quite on purpose, but not by accident either.

"Oh, there they are," cooed Trudy. "Just one hand. Don't worry; we didn't start without you. I just wanted to see, since I hadn't gone yet, what it would look like. I thought I had a flush." She giggled the hand's name like it was funny. "But it was just all black."

"Yeah," Ian said, trying but not really trying to stifle a grin. "I told her it doesn't really quite add up to, you know, a *whole* hand. Now that you guys are here, though—you know, especially you, Jim, since Mina says you're, like, *The Man*—we can start. We got the chips, so we'll do one hundred dollars buy-in? We'll see how everything goes, then we can maybe buy in again later."

Jim rolled his eyes, perhaps more obviously than he intended, because Ian, pleased at the reaction he induced, smirked. Jim preferred being underestimated to being feared, well reputed, or ever taken at face value, but at this point—with Ian smirking and Tunney squinting and Mina with her hand, gently but noticeably, guiding him to his seat and Trudy beaming like a happy cow heading for the blades—that wasn't going to happen.

The cards hadn't even been dealt before Jim realized he was in trouble. Ian badly wanted to beat him; all he had to do was lose a couple of dumb early hands to get Ian's confidence up, then take him late. Mina would break if he so much as looked at her harshly, but he didn't have the heart to do it. Tunney was inscrutable, but perhaps insane, or, better still, all front.

Trudy, unfortunately, messed everything up, because as a beginner and an apparently guileless literalist, she was exactly as good as her cards, no better or worse. This was the rookie problem: you can't bluff them; you can't play them; you can just get out of their way when they go in and hope for a minimum of anomalies. With Trudy out of the way, he could play his opponents; if everyone were like her, he could play the cards, but with a mix, all he could do was batten down the hatches and hope for the best.

As it turned out, his best wasn't so good: Jim hailed a gypsy cab home with thirty-five dollars in his pocket (they played, of course, with American green as table currency). The only saving grace was that Ian lost everything, and he bought in three times. Tunney had the misfortune of squinting intimidatingly around the table at his opponents whenever he bluffed, and the Frito-Lay guy proved himself a rare and powerful species of moron. Mina acquitted herself honorably, breaking more or less even, but Trudy made out best—Jim would have put money on beginner's luck at the beginning of the night—taking home a little over seven hundred dollars. She took most of Jim's money on a hand where he held a queen-high straight. She scrunched up her face and revealed jacks and eights, until Jim pointed out, reluctantly but hoping that heaven existed, that she had in fact made a flush draw on the river that she didn't even know she had.

There was nothing to do but laugh. Spit at fate, it spits back; laugh at its jokes and you'll have a brother. This was one of the first Russian phrases he knew, courtesy of his grandfather, an elementary school janitor with a ringing tenor voice, a teetering gait, and a perpetual crinkle-eyed half smile, like he heard music nobody else could hear. He had a million unfulfilled schemes to make enough money to buy a house in Wyoming—for some reason when he saw money he saw Wyoming, but could never imagine just moving out there without striking it rich.

The game broke up in good spirits: Trudy was over the moon but felt guilty. She was even trying to give money back to the people she'd taken it from. Jim was rueful but probability owed him one: a bad night now meant a good one a few months down the line. Tunney and Tim at least got a night out in good company; the business cards they exchanged flashed white on the deserted, sodium-lit street. Only Ian stepped onto Povarskaya down in the mouth: didn't the cards and his opponents know he was *supposed* to win? He paced back and forth outside the locked restaurant, his head down, seemingly absorbed in thought, but not entirely oblivious: his pacing just happened to lead him around to Mina's side.

"Which direction are you going?" Tunney asked. His walk, apparently, was as dulcet, eerie, and modulated as his voice: Jim hadn't heard him approaching.

"Straight down Krasnaya Presnya to the Garden Ring. Not too far, but the opposite direction from you guys. Right?"

He shrugged. "I could offer you a ride, if you'd like to continue our conversation, or hear a bit more about what I do."

"No. Thanks, but I can hail a cab across the street. When a night treats me this badly, I usually like to just get out of its way."

"Don't be insulted, Tunney," Mina said, sliding an arm under his. Ian had her other arm. She was smiling too broadly, speaking too loudly, and her cheeks had a merry flush to them. He was glad to see she was a happy drunk; it spoke well of her. "Jim probably has someone waiting up for him back home."

"Again she starts with the flattery. The only thing waiting for me in my apartment is roaches and dust."

"No actress?" she teased. "Early rehearsal?"

"Something like that, I guess. I think rumors of our involvement were greatly exaggerated." Then, just to twist the knife back, he kissed her on the cheek, winked at Ian, and, as he raised his hand to hail a gypsy cab, told them to "get each other home safe and warm."


HE AWOKE NINE HOURS LATER to something tapping him on the head. "Jim. Jim, come on. Wake up." *Tap tap tap.*

"Mmph. What time is it?"

"It's just after noon. Come on, time to get up." *Tap tap.*

Jim realized he had no idea who was talking to him. He sat bolt upright in bed. It was Mina, holding a ballpoint pen and preparing to do another paradiddle on his crown. He would not have been more shocked if it was his own mother.

"How did you . . ."

She held up an instrument that looked like one of the picks dentists use to scrape plaque.

"What is that?"

She gestured with it toward the hallway. "That triple-bolted steel door you have is heavy, and I'm sure it makes you feel secure, but it doesn't do any good when it's open. You have a pretty basic wafer-tumbler lock system."

"You pick locks?" Jim moved into a seated position, his blankets still pulled around him. She smiled.

"Come on." She tapped him on the calf with her lock pick. "Put some pants on. Crow wants to see you."

"Crow? 'Crow' wants to see me? Come on, give me a break. Let me make us some coffee and wake up."

Mina stood up and smoothed out her skirt, then handed Jim his jeans and a sweater. "Jim, I don't know what kind of friends you have at home, but mine? When they come over for coffee and a chat, they call first. Then they ring the doorbell and I let them in. They don't show up unannounced and pick the locks. Let's go; this isn't a social call. I'm here because Crow thought you'd come if I asked, but if you'd rather stay, I have two friends in the car downstairs who aren't much for asking."

"You're not kidding."

She shook her head.

"Well, who's the Crow?"

"Crow. I told you: Crow's the one who wants to see you."

"Yeah, but . . ."

"If you ask the same question you'll get the same answer."

"It's okay. I have a good idea who he is anyway."

"Congratulations." She didn't even raise an eyebrow.

"Well, can you at least wait outside while I get dressed?"

"I'm sorry." She shook her head and held up a hand to forestall Jim's objections. Even to a Sunday afternoon kidnapping, she wore a slender gold bracelet and a long gold pendant with a single pearl at the end. "It's actually against protocol to leave you alone."

"Whose protocol? What the fuck is going on? What are you doing in my house?" Jim slipped into his sweater, but kept his lower half beneath the blankets.

"All in good time. Look, I understand this must seem . . . a little disconcerting, I guess."

"Disconcerting, Mina, is a polite word for what it is."

"If it makes you happy I'll look the other way."

"It makes me exuberant, Mina. Thanks."

Mina turned back toward Jim after she heard the zipper. "Good. Now, let's go."

"Can I just . . ."

"No. Look, let's make this as friendly as we can, shall we? Let's just go downstairs and get in the car. We need to have a talk."

"Who's 'we'?"

"The home team." She walked out of his bedroom and into the hallway with a sort of swagger he'd never seen before. "Come on," she said, holding open the front door and dangling the pick tauntingly between her thumb and forefinger. "You first. I'll lock up."

She led him out of the courtyard through a back exit, across the street, through another apartment's archway, and into one of those haphazardly placed and sized asphalt patches that serve as Moscow's de facto parking spaces, parking lots, kiosk habitations, drinking spots, and trash dumps. A black GMC with a blue light on top sat idling. The blue light indicated not police status but sufficient privilege or money to buy police status: private citizens who could afford it bought blue police lights, which entitled them to flout any and all traffic laws.

"Right here. Would you mind getting in the back, please?" Her usually businesslike tone had a steeliness to it that made the final question mark a pure formality.

As Jim reached for the back door it popped open. Inside sat two hulking blond men, whom Jim recognized immediately, and with no small amount of relief, as American: something about the way they carried themselves gave them away—smirking rather than grimacing, with the sculpted muscles and soft hands of the weight room rather than the meat hooks and bulk of the brawler. Also, the one who got out to let him sit in the middle wore a University of Illinois sweatshirt.

"You play offensive or defensive line for the Illini?" Jim asked.

"If you could just climb in, sir," he grunted.

"Jim, I'm sorry about this," Mina said from the front seat as they turned onto the Garden Road. She addressed the rearview mirror; however sorry she was, it wasn't enough to turn around and face him. "We just needed to make sure we got you. If it's any comfort, your seatmates, Gramm and Joseph, were supposed to come up to your apartment with me."

"No problem. I don't have much food at my place anyway."

The bruiser on his left grunted something close to a laugh and shifted in his seat, driving an elbow into Jim's ribs.

"So can I presume you're taking me to the embassy?"

Nobody answered. They stayed straight on Novinsky Bulvar, but when they reached the American embassy they passed it, then the driver—sunglasses, dark sweater, utterly silent—took them into a thicket of Khamovniki side streets. They headed up Ulitsa Lev Tolstovo, past the author's beautifully preserved gold and green estate, and past Moscow's most beautiful church, the Church of St. Nicholas of the Weavers, with its scalloped, Christmas-colored, pagoda dome.

They turned left at an *optika* into the parking lot of a trio of apartment buildings doing the Moscow upgrade shuffle: one was naked cinder block; one had an Italianate umber façade with Florentine detailing around all the double-glazed windows; one was somewhere in between, with the façade abruptly stopping around the fifth floor.

Mina hopped out, at speed, and pulled open the back door. Gramm hustled Jim out. He turned toward the closest entry door, but Gramm grabbed his shoulders and pushed him into a narrow alleyway running between the finished and half-finished buildings. They crossed Let Oktyabrya, with the stark white walls of Novodevichy promising a quieter

188 | JON FASMAN

and holier world just up the street, then turned toward Sportivnaya. Neither breaking stride nor looking around, Mina led them into a shuttered confectionery shop.

Gramm shoved him through the door, into a completely bare room with a concrete floor, cinder-block walls, and three bare lightbulbs hanging from the ceiling. A few cans of paint, brushes, a ladder, and scaffolding stood near the front door, but Jim neither smelled paint nor saw any evidence of its use. As soon as Joseph came through the door he locked it, pulled down the shutters, and set the alarm.

Mina was nowhere in sight. Jim's heart flopped into his throat for a moment, thinking she had left him in this anonymous, empty storefront with two enormous, probably armed strangers.

Then she emerged, frosted in fluorescent light, from a door at the back of the shop. "Jim," she called. "If you could just come this way."

"You want me to just . . ."

"What we want," called a familiar voice from the back room, "is to know just what the fuck it is you think you're doing."

## 14

"TRUDY?" JIM ASKED STUPIDLY, refusing to credit his eyes. Staring evenly from the doorway at the back of the empty room was indeed the wide-eyed, bubbly, lucky secretary from the previous night's game. All traces of last night's wide-eyed bubbliness had vanished, replaced by hooded eyes, a triumphant smirk, and an impatient demeanor. Jim realized, of course, that she had not been a victim of beginner's luck.

"Thanks for coming."

"I wasn't aware you had extended the option of not coming."

She smiled thinly, a small change of expression that evoked the idea of sympathy without extending any actual sympathy. "Just come on back here and have a seat."

Jim looked behind him, saw Gramm and Joseph standing between him and the door.

"I assume he's been searched?" Trudy called over his head.

"He's not carrying," said the one who had jammed an elbow into his gut on the ride over.

Jim stood his ground in the center of the room.

"At this very moment," Trudy said sharply, "right now, you are, I would estimate, about twenty minutes away from being charged with espionage. Do you understand me? Now, please, come back here and have a seat and we'll see whether we can't work something out."

"Espionage?" Jim asked incredulously, his voice cracking and a wave of flop sweat prickling him from head to toe. "Are you joking? Who am I spying for?"

"Well, why don't you come on back and have a seat so we can talk about it." Trudy nodded toward her office, keeping her arms crossed and her expression neutral. Her cocky stillness indicated a predetermined outcome, and her folksy invitations to dialogue were backed with a threat that she made sure Jim felt.

She watched how he walked toward her: not with the solemn, resigned trudge of the condemned, but quickly, with long strides, his eyes alive and his teeth clenched with anxiety, and she knew then that he was there to be used, not arrested.

"Crow?" he asked dubiously as he sat down. Mina followed him in and took a seat behind him, shutting the door.

Trudy nodded. The room was vast and stark, with gunmetal filing cabinets lining the back wall, a bare steel desk with a cheap swivel chair behind it and two metal folding chairs in front. The cinderblock walls had no windows; there was no phone on the desk, no fax or copier, or even, as Jim's eyes scanned the walls, any electrical outlets at all.

The bare cement floor sloped downward toward a drain between the desk, where Trudy settled in, and the chair where she installed Jim. A pair of long brown hairs trailed pleadingly from the drain toward Jim. Next to the drain was a single handcuff attached by a chain to a ringbolt in the floor. When Jim sat down, he started to slide forward on the chair. After righting himself, he did it again. Then he noticed the chair's two front legs were about an inch shorter than its back legs: it was designed to keep the sitter ill at ease. Jim sat forward on the seat with his weight on his legs.

"I was expecting Tunney, actually."

"Were you, now?"

"I guess I was supposed to, right? That's why he was invited last night?"

"Whatever do you mean? He's a regular; I'm not. I was the one who had to waylay Mr. Woods for a space at the table."

"And why did you do that?"

"Well, I wanted to meet you, Seamus. It's an odd name, if you don't mind my saying."

"I mind, actually."

"Let's not start snapping at each other just yet, shall we? We're just here to talk."

"Tunney made me the same offer, you know."

"Oh? And what offer is that?"

"To talk. He gave me his card," Jim said, reaching into his wallet and handing it to Trudy, "and said he paid for information."

Trudy took the card by the corner and, with a cackle, dropped it onto her desk as if it were a dead mouse. "That brooding fuck. Strictly freelance, I'm afraid. Nothing to do with us. Mina, I thought we were going to do something about that." She sighed. "Prick thinks because he's been here forever he knows everything and always has to show it," she said over Jim's head to Mina. "Listen, Jim," she turned her attention back to him. "I'm sorry about all this. You understand we had to do it this way. We couldn't just tell you to meet us here, and hope you'd show up and not tell anyone. Especially given the company you've been keeping."

"What company?"

"Well, we're going to discuss that, too."

"And where is 'here'?"

"Jim, this is what we call a safe house. I imagine you're familiar with the term?"

"I've heard it, sure."

"You were probably expecting something a bit more glamorous."

"I never really thought about what to expect, to tell you the truth. It never even crossed my mind that I'd see the inside of a safe house."

"Well, that's good. That's a good sign, Jim. I'd like to believe it's also true. Do you know why you're here today?"

"I wish I did, Trudy. Crow."

"For our purposes, here, today, Seamus, 'Trudy' will be just fine. 'Crow' is a family nickname. I assume Mina used it?"

Jim nodded. "You're related, are you? The white-bread Minnesota branch of the Haddads?"

"Wrong family, Seamus." She drummed a pen on her desk, then signaled over his head. A shadow moved across his face; instinctively, he winced, but it was just Mina passing Trudy a file. "I'm glad to see we've got your attention. Why don't you tell me how you came to be here. In Moscow, I mean; I know this particular 'here' we're responsible for."

"I was hired by the Memory Foundation."

"Before you left? You arrived here with a job?"

"Not exactly. I had a preliminary couple of interviews back home, but I wasn't officially offered the job until I arrived here."

"And home is where?"

"Washington, D.C."

"The city itself?"

"Don't you know all of this already?"

"I'd rather hear it from you. What we know we know from a variety of sources; when we have the horse we like to make him use his mouth."

"I see. Then, no: the interviews were in the city, but home is Rock-ville, just outside."

"How did you hear about the job? Did they contact you?"

"No, I reached out to them. A friend of a friend profiled the Foun-dation's founder for the *Post*. I was hired through him."

"So you came here without a job."

"Technically, yes. But it seemed likely, after the two interviews back home and a couple of conversations with Dave Willow, who runs the Foundation, over the phone, that they were going to hire me."

"Still, it's quite a risk you took. What motivated you to come here?"

"I speak the language. My father is Russian. And I wanted to live abroad for a while."

"Just wanderlust, pure and simple?" Jim shifted in his seat and nodded weakly. Trudy pounced gently. "Nothing else? I mean, Jim, forgive my pointing this out, but you're not twenty-two. You're not even twenty-five."

"Or twenty-six. Or even twenty-seven. Or twenty-seven and a half."

"I'm glad you can joke, but it's a serious question. I'm asking if anything else prompted you to leave."

"Debts," Jim said quickly, cutting his eyes away from Trudy. He felt her stare. He felt Mina's, too, and his parents', and their parents', and Vivek, and everyone else he had ever met who had done better, or who knew he was supposed to do better. He felt all of them, and his face burned out to his ears, and the back of his neck prickled. When he turned back to Trudy, he saw her face soften: just a slight relaxation around the corners of her mouth, a pulling back of the gaze, and he knew she already knew. He knew he had gambled correctly.

"To whom?"

"A bookie. A couple of them, actually: two brothers who ran a card game and sports book out in Maryland."

"How much?"

"Twenty-four."

"Thousand?"

"No, dollars. Yes, of course thousand. Actually, a little less now: I gave them a down payment, about seven thousand, through a lawyer—the same guy who helped me find this job—and left to try to make back the rest."

"So by your own admission you're over here to make money, right? Don't look at me like that. We're all Americans here, right, and none of us works for free. Tell me you're here for cultural reasons or to 'get in touch with your roots' or something like that, you'll make me retch. It's a bullshit allergy I have. Much more suspicious. Money we can all understand. So. Is that accurate?"

"Sure."

"Have you done anything else for money since you've been here?"

"Like what?"

"Like you tell me. Bartending? Teaching English? Freelance research of any kind?"

"No, nothing."

"So you would be prepared to swear, under oath, to a polygraph, that your only source of income has been from the Memory Foundation. And if necessary, you would permit us to check your bank accounts to verify that statement?" She drummed her pen against her desk while Jim pretended to think, but really just stalled. Then it clicked.

"You've already done that, haven't you? You wouldn't ask if you hadn't."

Trudy pointed over Jim's head with the pen. "Your friend's a bright one, Mina. Paranoid, maybe, but I like him. Yes, Jim, we have." She pulled a sheet of paper from her file. "A paycheck every two weeks. About twenty-seven hundred. Not bad, for Moscow. And you live pretty frugally. In fact, unless you have absolutely no social life at all, I'd say it's almost unbelievably frugally. It almost makes us wonder whether you aren't using the First National Bank of Moscow."

She waited for Jim to get the joke—or, better still, to acknowledge that she made a joke beyond his understanding. He didn't want to give her the satisfaction. Finally, just to get her to start talking again, he gave in and shook his head. "That's cash under the mattress, Seamus. Or in the toilet tank. Or the freezer. Where else, Mina? What else have we seen?"

"Under the oven."

"That's right, that's right. Mina here is a little squeamish, is why she remembers that. Someone—doesn't matter who: an American who was poking around where he shouldn't have been—sealed his payoffs in layers of plastic and shoved them under his oven, where they built up a nice layer of cooking oil and cockroaches. Made sure nobody who didn't really have a good reason to reach down there ever did. Almost eighty grand, he had. You have any special hiding places yourself?"

"You didn't check there, too?"

"Mina?"

"No," she said quietly. Jim thought—hoped—he could hear a touch of shame in her voice. "You're a light sleeper. You were starting to move around; I thought I'd woken you."

He turned to look at her and shook his head with disgust. "No. No special hiding places. No cash at home. And no social life."

"So you're just frugal."

"Cheap, I think I've been called. I prefer cheap. Frugal implies something a little too noble. I'm just cheap."

"I like a man who hates euphemism, I'll tell you that. You don't meet too many of those where I work. Let me try a different question, then: do you know Rodion Lisitsov?"

"Mina asked me that, too. My answer's the same: no, I don't know him."

"Do you know *of* him? Have you heard of him?"

"Again, just what Mina told me."

"Which is?"

"He's an art dealer? Right?" He turned to look at Mina for support but she had her gaze fixed firmly on her shoes. "A gay art dealer? Travels back and forth between Russia and the States a lot?"

Trudy chuckled and shook her head. "For someone who hates lying, she sure is inventive. Do you know his granddaughter?"

"Of course. I was over last Sunday; met the whole family. No, I just told you: I don't know him; I had never heard of him before yesterday; I've never met anyone named Lisitsov, Rodion or otherwise."

Trudy leaned across her desk and handed Jim a picture, facedown. He turned it faceup.

"Fuck you both." He scaled the picture across the desk, baseball-card-style, skillfully enough to hit Trudy in the face. He tried to stand up, but a quick jolt—an electric shock—to the back of his neck made him see white, clamp down hard enough on his tongue to draw blood, and snap forward in his seat. A broad hand pulled him upright and steadied him.

"Thank you, Mr. Gramm, I think that's all. Is that all, Jim, or do you want to throw another tantrum?"

Jim turned around, still angry, and saw Gramm with a sadistic little grin, holding what looked like barber's clippers with a thin bolt of electricity snapping and worming between two poles. Mina was slunk back in the corner, a hand over her mouth, again staring down, unable to meet Jim's gaze. He held up his hands in resignation, but offered no apology.

"You're not the first. People don't like knowing they've been spied on, especially by their own country. You might be the most accurate, though. Nice throw. Gramm, I really think you can go."

He nodded, but before leaving he thrust the Taser at Jim, stopping just short of his face. Jim didn't flinch. Gramm huffed out, dejected at missing his fun. From the back he looked like a walking refrigerator with a crew cut.

"You didn't need to do that, you know. You could have just asked me to sit back down."

Trudy lowered her eyes slightly and nodded. "Maybe you're right. Sometimes people do turn violent, Jim. I'm glad to see you're an exception, and I'm sorry if I skipped a step. Now, will you please tell me about that picture?"

"Will you please tell me why you took it? Why you're following me? Why any of this . . ."

"Yes. Yes, Jim, I will, but you first."

Jim sighed, then spat some blood from his tongue toward Trudy. There was nothing else he could do. "What do you want to know?"

"Who's the girl, Jim? Who is she and who is she to you?"

"Her name is Kaisa Harmaja. She's an actress I met. Just before this picture was taken, it looks like." It showed Jim and Kaisa, their arms around each other, both smiling and looking down the street in front of The Chinese Pilot, presumably to hail a cab. "We were on our way to my apartment."

"How did you meet her?"

"At the bar. This bar, that night."

"You don't mind me saying, Jim, she's awfully pretty for you."

"Fuck you again."

"You're an item, now, are you?"

"No."

"Mina told me you told her you were dating a Finnish actress. Present tense. Now, you might have the strangest and most specific fetish in history, but I assumed you were talking about the woman in the picture. Is this the wrong actress?"

"I seem to have misunderstood the nature of our relationship, Trudy. I thought I would see her again. I wanted to see her again. I've called her a few times. Nothing. I guess you could call what I told Mina aspirational. Hopeful. A positive spin on an ambiguous situation. If you don't mind my asking, why are you so interested in my romantic life?"

"Or sudden lack thereof. It concerns us, Jim, because the woman in this picture, while she may be an actress, is not Finnish. Her name is not Kaisa Harmaja. She's Russian. Her name is Katerina Lisitsova, and she is the granddaughter of Rodion Lisitsov."

Jim clenched his fists in his lap and pressed his teeth together behind his lips to keep himself from saying anything. Nothing good can come from talking when confused. Trudy took comfort from his silence, figuring that if he had actually known who Lisitsov was, he would immediately have denied it, loudly. Besides, she had seen wounded male pride before; she could recognize a man-sulk as well as any thrice-divorced professional observer.

"Would you like to know who her grandfather is?"

Jim shrugged. "If you want to tell me."

"Rodion Lisitsov, just so you know, ran Biopreparat, the main Soviet bioweapons facility, for almost a quarter century. And when I say ran, I don't mean he was the name above the door; I mean he was the real power. The head bureaucrat. Less fame, fewer perks, but more power, and in Soviet times, less danger of being toppled. He wasn't just in charge of security or staffing or acquisitions or anything like that. He's the real thing, and he's a total mystery to us. First Gulf War, when his buddies decided it was time for a little sun and sand in Cairo, Tunis, Casablanca, and places thereabouts, you know where he was?"

"Baghdad?"

"In his apartment. Early 1990s, they pass Nunn-Lugar to keep the nukes and germs where they should be. Every weapons facility, every scientist, every drunken drooling Russian who ever guarded anything with gunpowder just signs on the dotted line for their cash, you know where he was?"

Jim shook his head.

"In his little apartment in Novokuznetskaya. Doesn't even want our cash. We don't think he's still churning out the creepy-crawlies; it wouldn't have cost him anything to just take a little something for under the tree, but he stays home. Yeltsin leaves, the FSB state arrives, Putin starts droning on again about reconstituting Russia's greatness, you know where he goes?"

"Let me guess."

"That's right: in his apartment. At home. Living off his pension. You know how many times we tried to buy this guy? Directly, but also through our Russian agents, Brits, EU, fake Arabs? Not interested. Never has been. Not for anyone. Doesn't have money; doesn't want it. What do you *do* with a guy like that?"

"Forgive me for asking, but how does that hurt you?"

Trudy looked at him with an arch grumpiness.

"Sorry: hurt *us*, I meant, of course." Her expression eased. "If he's happy living as he is, doing what he's doing, why not just let him stay there?"

"Because we prefer *making* people happy to *finding* people who already *are* happy. Unfortunately, we don't know what would make Colonel Lisitsov happy. If it really is living his nice cozy life with his nice cozy family, then God bless him. But he won't even *talk* to us about it." Trudy looked perplexed at the thought that someone wouldn't want to wrap their lips around America's golden tit.

"Why aren't the Russians keeping him happy?"

"They are, apparently. He probably gets a good pension, but not much more. When the military downsized after the collapse, it left hundreds of guys like him out in the cold. The newer generation of weapons are all geared toward assassination, not battlefield use, and they're targeted, usually radiological or chemical, not biological. Guys like Lisitsov are out of fashion, nationally, but they still know their stuff, and there are a lot of actors willing to pay a lot of money to have him design a little something to set off on the Metro or in a shopping mall.

"Look, it isn't the weapons that worries us. Or it isn't the weapons we know about. Those we can track. Those we can prepare for. Sure, nobody wants a suitcase nuke to go off in the Metro, but we know where they are. What worries us more is someone designing new ones, ones we haven't seen, we don't know about. Weapons we can trace. Weapons we can seize. Knowledge and imagination are trickier to lock down. Everyone who ever tightened a bolt or signed a purchase order has had offers. We're not too worried about them; if some schmo who worked on the line at the Kalashnikov factory has figured out a way to bilk the North Koreans, God bless him. It's practically state law over here. Every commander, every general, has a sideline selling equipment. And not just to Russians, but to anyone: Chechen fighters have been killing Russian soldiers with Russian weapons for years now. But the scientists—the real scientists, not the politicians—haven't budged until now."

"What do you mean 'until now'?"

"Matvei Yagachin," Mina piped up from behind Jim. "He was another scientist in Moscow we were monitoring."

"Was?"

"He disappeared. Got into a government car and drove away. Left his wife behind; she doesn't know where he went, but all of a sudden she's got a private doctor and a round-the-clock guard. That's how all of this started. On the same day you met Katerina, which is why we took this picture." Mina looked down at Jim warmly, pleadingly, hoping for a reprieve. "We weren't following you at all, Jim. Not until we saw this. We were watching Lisitsov and his family."

"Who is 'we'? Who's actually doing the watching?"

"That I don't think you need to know," said Trudy, shifting uneasily in her seat. "Neither of us, if that's what you're wondering. But it shouldn't come as any real surprise to you to hear that we sometimes check in with people like Yagachin and Lisitsov. We're getting reports from out east that another one . . . What's her name?"

"Svetlana Rybovna," Mina said. "She went to visit her daughter in Perm and never came home."

Mina handed a file over Jim's head to Trudy. "You see how good she is?" Trudy asked Jim, winking then looking down at the file. "The secret to a successful career: hire good people and take credit for everything they do. She's going to get me out of this hellhole, and she'll run it herself." She snapped the file shut and looked up. "That's three scientists in about as many days. You can see why we're worried. Most scientists of this stature, believe it or not, have turned down all offers. They're Soviet down to their cold Commie bones. They don't want Nunn-Lugar, and they don't want any dinars. Suddenly they start running, we need to know who's chasing them."

"Do you know?"

"At the moment, Jim, we have precisely one connection to any of them."

"Who's that?"

Trudy pointed across her desk at Jim.

"Me? I told you: I had no idea who she was. Is."

"Be that as it may, Jim, she still approached you. She still lied to you. You're still the only person we know to have spoken with her. You've also had some pretty interesting contacts over the past few days. Tell me if you recognize these men."

She handed Jim three black-and-white pictures. One showed a young man in military dress, alarmingly thin, hollow-cheeked and grim, staring at the camera with a Soviet passport face. It was posed, and looked official. The second also showed a young soldier, but this one was ruddy, healthy, and smiling, standing outside against a fence aiming a machine gun at the photographer and laughing uproariously. Jim shook his head. The last showed a man in a white coat, also swarthy, standing over an empty examination table with a look of utter seriousness. It was also clearly posed, and with that picture Jim got it. "Are these . . . I know these men. That last one I just talked to yesterday. Faridian. He's a doctor. And the first one sells junk at Izmailovsky. Balderis, his name was. This second one, my God. He can barely stand up. He's a drunk. But why are they in uniform? They're all survivors."

"Survivors?" Trudy echoed, leaning across her desk. "Survivors of what?"

"Of Solovetsky. The camps."

"Yeah? Did they tell you that, or did you actually see documentation?"

"Documentation? No, no . . . I just . . . I interviewed them; they told me. There was another, too, Grigory Naumenko." He heard Mina writing furiously behind him.

"I find it hard to believe these men were actually in the camps, Jim."

"No, they were. They absolutely were. They said . . ."

"All three retired from the army, Jim," Mina said. "At rank. Colonel or higher."

"What? Why would they lie about that?"

"We don't know. How did you find them?"

"Well, through each other. Each one told me about the next one. All personal connections."

"And the first?"

"Naumenko was . . ." Jim didn't finish the sentence. He let his hand, which he had been using to gesticulate, drop to his lap as his stomach leaped up into his throat. What had he done? "Kaisa—Katerina—said he was her grandfather." He pressed his fingers into his eyes, and let his head fall forward.

"Jim," Trudy said quietly. He didn't move. "Jim. Jim! You can see why we need your help."

He shook his head, defeated, angry, exhausted, ashamed. "What do you want me to do? You know who she is. I don't, apparently. I never did."

"What do you want us to do, Jim: kidnap a Russian national on Russian soil? We can't even talk to her without either asking permission or upsetting our hosts. You can. We'll even tell you where she lives."

"Look, I really need to just think about . . ."

"I'm sorry, you do not have time. We don't. We cannot have the architects of the biggest, most ambitious, and most dangerous weapons programs in history disappearing without us knowing why. Now, I'd appeal to your patriotism or your sense of survival, but like I said before, I like being the one to alleviate unhappiness. You know the saying: Give a man a fish, and he'll come back for more; teach a man to fish, and you're fucked. He's gone. Now, let me have your passport."

"My pass . . . No."

Trudy sighed heavily. "I'm tired. I'd like the rest of my evening to start now. Gentlemen?"

Before Jim could even turn around, one of the linemen had winched his arms painfully behind him while driving a knee into the small of his back while the other searched his pockets. Jim had plenty of time to regret putting his passport in the rather baggy front pocket of these particular jeans. The searcher tossed the passport across the desk to Trudy, who put it in the top drawer and threw another one to Jim.

"This is the same one," he said, finding his name, picture, birth date, on the photo page.

"Almost. If you try to scan the bar code it'll say you're wanted for questioning by the FSB in regard to a series of rapes. Underage Russian girls. We made sure to pick little blondies. A cop stopping you on the street won't care, but if you try to leave the country with that, you'll probably die on the way from the airport to the police station. If you're lucky."

A thousand murderous thoughts raced through Jim's mind, but, feebly, all he could manage was a halfhearted swear.

Trudy widened her eyes and stood up. "Listen, Jim, I do not care about you one way or the other, do you understand? We need your help, and, unfortunately, long experience has taught me that threats succeed where pleading fails. You help us, and you'll find me a very different person in a few days' time, okay? You don't, and it won't just be you that goes to jail. Do you know how many restaurants survive a thorough audit? Do you know Montgomery County just strengthened the penalties for tax evasion?"

Jim snatched up his passport and walked out. Gramm stood in the doorway, blocking Jim's way and sneering confidently. Jim clenched his fist and pivoted his chest back like he was about to punch him, but when Gramm raised his hands to block, Jim drove his knee into Gramm's groin as hard as he could, and the big man fell to his knees, moaning and turning a satisfying purplish color. Joseph advanced toward him, but Trudy called him off, as Jim knew she would. Today he'd have to satisfy himself with being right only in the smallest things.

## 15

"Jim. Jim! Wait a minute," Mina called after him as he charged down Archiviy Pereulok toward Rolshaya Piragovskaya, shoulders forward, teeth clenched. He was so angry his skin was tingling and he exhaled little flecks of foam. Like anyone who spends too much time around a poker table, Jim prided himself on his self-control; like anyone who prides himself on self-control, he had a ferocious temper, once uncorked. Finally he heard her footsteps gather speed and weight as she broke into a run, skirting around before stopping directly in front of him.

"Just hang on, okay? Give me one minute." Jim was breathing hard from speed walking half a kilometer, but Mina wasn't even winded. She put her hands on his shoulders and brought him to a stop, staring right into his eyes. "Just take a deep breath and calm down."

"I just lost it when she threatened my parents," he explained. "I'm sorry."

"I know you are. And I might have reacted the same way. But you need to understand: nobody wants them dragged into this. Nobody, not Trudy and certainly not me, likes that part of the job. We just need to be as sure as we can that you're going to help us, and unfortunately that includes finding leverage as well as asking politely. Nobody wants to put you in jail, either. But we do need you to help us, and we need to use whatever leverage we can." Jim bucked. Mina tightened her grip.

"Look, at the risk of sounding like a cliché, we're the good guys. That doesn't mean everything we do is sweetness and light, and it doesn't mean our methods are always nicer than theirs, but at the end of the season, when all the balances are checked, better us than them."

"That speech was part of your training, was it?"

Mina tried to manage a reassuring smile, but it didn't take. Jim could see she didn't quite have the stomach for her work. Not yet, anyway. "It doesn't mean I don't believe it," she said quietly.

"And better I go to jail?"

"Jim, what did I just say? Nobody wants that, and unless you go off bloody-eyed like this, that won't happen. All we want is your help, and to tell you the truth"—she lowered her voice to a whisper and leaned her head closer to his—"if we didn't think you were capable of it, or inclined to do it—if we thought, in other words, and if you repeat this I'll deny it, but if we thought you had actually committed espionage, instead of just taking a job and not asking too many questions—you'd already be indicted." Her eyes, this close, had beautiful little flecks of green, and a strand of her loosely ringleted hair had fallen out of its band on either side, framing her Modigliani face.

Jim stared as intently as possible. He told himself he was trying to make her feel uncomfortable, but in fact he was just taking her measure, drinking her in, considering what had not yet been considered. He waited for her to look away. She didn't.

"You need to appreciate her"—Mina jerked her head toward the safe house—"for what she is."

"What's that?"

"A politician who wants a career. I do the work for her, and that's fine with me. That's fine. She appreciates loyalty because she has to. I want to do the work, and she wants to be in the papers. Which means she has to succeed here to get out of here."

"What do you mean?"

"I mean the cold war is over, Jim. Nobody comes here unless they're sent. Ambitious people go to the Middle East, or Central Asia. People with brains but no stomach go to Europe. Here we just get the dregs these days. It drives the Russians insane, being downgraded like this."

"So what are you doing here?"

"I got sent. Your first posting out of school you don't get to choose. They sent me to Kiev. The ambassador, he . . ." She looked down and absently put a strand of hair behind her ear. Her modesty came up at odd moments. "He liked me. It wasn't reciprocated. I wouldn't do that. So he sent me here, figuring I didn't know the language and I'd embarrass myself."

"Did you?"

"What do you think?" she asked, smiling slyly. "I did the work. He got sent home; I'm still here." A grim smile rose on her face. She could tell it was unbecoming; she looked down until she could suppress it. "How could I . . ."

"How could you go home otherwise?" he finished.

"Exactly," she said quietly, tucking her hands into her pockets and starting to walk toward the Metro and away from the safe house. "I couldn't. You know," she stammered, "it had . . ."

"Nothing to do with anyone else. Because you know, in your head, they would crawl over fire for you. But it's something else."

"The grandparents. For me, I mean; I don't know what it is for you. The grandparents, who lived in a little hut carved into a mountain."

"Mine were here. Well, sort of here. Minsk. An apartment. But they always had to keep their heads down, you know? They always had to worry, had to apologize, had to fret and pay people off, and curry favor, and give compliments where they didn't mean it and shut up where they should have talked. My grandmother, she'd have been in front of the Supreme Court if anyone had told her she could have. She'd argue anyone under the table." Tears rose but Jim told himself it was the sun and the wind. "She would have, she'd just lay into them. It's why she came. I mean, Fourth of July, baseball, rock music, all that shit made her sick. For her it was Tolstoy, Rachmaninoff, Yom Kippur. But that's the thing: for her son's wife's mother, it was Joyce, church, and Lent. They loved each other, those two.

"All she wanted was to go someplace where they'd leave her alone. Where she could do what she had to, so her kids could do what they sort of wanted to, so her grandkids could really do what they wanted to. And what does he want to do but bet on football games and throw it all away on cards, and come back here?" He wiped a hand across his eyes. Digging deep, extra deep, in his pockets, he finally pulled out a crumpled but not broken Winston and lit it. "You ought to thank God every night you're not Russian. This place won't give you up."

"No place ever gives you up, Jim. If you have a conscience, it's all carved inside of you. But listen, you haven't told me: what do you want?"

"Look, Meen, I'm just . . ." Jim trailed off. He thought about why he had come here: both the primary reason—the debts—but also the subtler one of trying, finally, to do something right, to stop the drift, to begin to make something of himself other than a gambler whose parents still paid his salary. His grandparents came over from Russia so their descendants could make something of themselves; now not only had he regressed from stagnation to dupe, he'd done it on Russian soil. "I'm embarrassed," he said quietly. "I did this. I got suckered. I just . . . I ran around in circles, I let myself get distracted. Now every time I see something in the news about a suspicious outbreak, I'm going to wonder if it was because of me. Can you understand that?"

"Of course I can," she said calmly. "But what do you want?"

He clenched his teeth, and indolently took her hand, just to see what would happen. She looked at him quizzically: it was the worst possible outcome, and he dropped her hand. "I want to do something right!" he yelled.

"Then come with us."

"What do you need me to do?"

"I told you we don't think you did anything, right?"

"You did."

"Prove it. See what Katerina was up to. Find out what you were really doing. Maybe it's nothing. Maybe we had a bad babysitter, and maybe Lisitsov, and Yagachin, and Rybovna, and whoever else, they're all just visiting friends."

"But maybe not."

"That's right. Maybe not."

"And you'll help me, maybe, if I help you?"

Mina reared her head back slightly, and blinked twice, as though Jim's audacity shocked her. "Help you? What do you mean?"

"Look, I don't mean to be greedy or indelicate, but it sounds like you hand out green and white rectangular portraits of Ben Franklin like business cards."

"Jim, how about we just agree not to send you to jail and not to shut down your parents' restaurant?"

Jim felt red rushing to his face again, but he balled his hands into fists in his pockets, bit down hard on his lower lip, and counted to three. "I'm not asking you to make me rich, Mina. All I want is for you to give me enough to take care of a couple of off-brand, cut-rate Balkans in leather bathrobes. If it's any comfort, you don't even have to give it to me; I have a friend, a lawyer, back home who's helping me with them."

"Fighting bookies with a lawyer. Imaginative. Very American." Mina smiled tautly and clicked her tongue in thought. "How about this," she said. "You give us a hand, and we'll see what we can do to help you and your lawyer."

"That's the best I'm going to get? 'We'll see'?"

Mina put her hands on Jim's shoulders and held him lightly, deniably. "In our sneaky hearts of hearts, Jim, we're just bureaucrats. Armed bureaucrats in comfortable shoes. And the secret to negotiating with a bureaucracy lies in knowing the difference between 'We'll see what we can do' and 'We'll see if there's anything we can do.' And *that* is the best you're going to get. I'm sure a poker player like you understands."

Jim put his hands up and, in spite of himself, almost smiled. "He does." He began walking toward the Metro. Mina followed, with her hands in her pockets, wearing her best serious look.

"Do you know who Robert Hanssen was, Jim?"

"The spy, you mean?"

"Yep. Do you know how he was caught?" She kept strolling even when he stopped and looked at her with a mixture of anger and alarm.

"I told you people . . ."

"Jim, calm down. This is an exercise in theory, not an accusation. Just follow me. Indulge me. Now, do you know how he was caught?"

Jim fell back into place beside her. He shook his head.

"He made his usual drop while he knew he was under surveillance. He taped a trash bag full of classified documents to the bottom of a bridge, just like he had done for years."

"So? He's an idiot. And I'm not a spy."

Mina sighed, and pulled a mock grimace. "I know. On both counts, I know. The point is the dead drop. That's how most spies are caught, you know. Bugging phones and reading e-mails aren't usually conclusive. They just tell you where to go. Dead drops are ancient and low-tech, but you can't eavesdrop or intercept unless you know where to look. Of course, once you know where to look, it's all over. They have to set up a new dead drop; to do that they have to meet, which is exactly what they wanted to avoid doing in the first place. I know, I'm sounding like one of my old professors, but this was one of her favorite problems. What is the most secure way to pass information—cryptography and steganography aside—not how to disguise information but how to pass it between two sources?"

Jim shook his head and started to answer that he didn't know, but apparently the question was rhetorical.

"Imagine a dead drop that moves," Mina said, a finger raised and her voice suddenly sharper, more professorial. "I don't mean one that can be moved, but one that moves of its own accord, and moves between contacts accurately."

"You mean a person."

"Exactly. I mean a person."

"You mean a messenger."

"No. Not at all. A messenger has to know the message. A dead-drop box only has to contain it. I mean a go-between who doesn't know the people he's going between or what he's carrying. I mean a human black box."

"What you mean, Mina, is a sucker."

"Maybe. I'd even say usually. But even suckers get their shots at redemption, Jim. I thought that's what you wanted."

"It is, Mina. I just thought I'd done enough of the 'sucker' part back home."

"Home is home, Jim, and here is here. So what happens after you do an interview?"

"What do you mean?"

"Do you record them?"

"I record them all, then I transcribe them."

"In Russian or English?"

"Russian. Dave translates them later."

"This is David Willow?"

"Right. He and Yuri look over the transcripts. They each make their edits, one in Russian and one in English. We release a report at the end of the year with all the interviews in it, in English, French, and Russian, in conjunction with Memorial, the Russian survivors' group."

"So the transcripts are where now?"

"On the Foundation server."

"Can you access that from home?"

"No, just from the office."

Mina nodded slowly, squinting and looking off into the distance. Jim could almost see the gears turning. "Can you go tonight?" she asked.

"To the office? Sure. I have the door code and the key."

"Will anyone else be there?"

"I don't think so."

"What if someone is?"

"I can always just say I forgot something."

"And your colleagues would believe that?"

"Alas, yes."

"You'd have to leave quickly, you know, if anyone came in."

"I'll keep my shoes on."

"I'm glad you find this funny, Jim, but I'm very serious. I don't want you drawing any suspicion. If you even hear the door rattle, you need to grab what you can and leave."

"Give me a little credit, Mina."

"Fine, but just a little," she said with a mock serious face. "And stay in touch."

"I figured you'd make sure of that, right?"

Mina smirked and shrugged, but she did not deny it. "One more thing: Trudy mentioned that we thought we knew everyone who could do something like this? It worries us that we don't. Almost as much as the kidnapping itself, that worries us. It means we don't know what their aims or capabilities are."

Jim felt a silvery prickle along his sides. "What do you mean?"

"I don't mean anything. Just be quick, and be careful. You keeping in touch with us isn't just for our benefit."


JIM SETTLED BACK in his seat, as best as one could settle against the hard plastic seats of a half-century-old wooden train hurtling at full speed hundreds of meters beneath a frozen city. He tried to spot who-ever Trudy had sent to keep an eye on him, but to no avail. All he did was break the unwritten Metro-passenger rule—the same across the world—forbidding eye contact. His gaze came to rest on a broad-faced old man in a fur hat, his face a magnificent topography of carbuncles, bubukles, jowls, spider veins, and one large wart sprouting wild black hairs just below his left eye. The man sat next to a younger version of himself: no warts, but the same wide, fleshy, blank face, already running to fat and contempt, even in his late teens. Grandfather and grandson, Stalingrad and *mafiya*, burying the czars and resurrecting them, victims of circumstance and each other. When the old man caught Jim staring he made a fig gesture, his hand in a fist and his thumb upraised, shoved between his index and the next three fingers.

If they were his spotters, Mina's outfit had deeper roots than he thought. Jim couldn't help but smile. No other country had the power to infuriate you, break your heart, and raise a smile in the same nanosecond. Nowhere else—Jim remembered the screaming fights of his Vilatzer side, that began and ended in savage and unstable love—went in as deeply and wholly for feeling, for extremes.

Jim registered, as best he could, the faces of everyone in his car, noting who followed him out when he changed trains. He changed trains pointlessly at the Barrikadnaya-Krasnopresnenskaya interchange, stopping once to tie his shoe and once to browse the ticket stalls. After alighting at Teatralnaya he sat down on a bench across the platform, rubbing his eyes and trying to look bleary and confused, like he had spent the day drinking. When the platform emptied, he rode the wooden escalator up into the night air, looking behind him. He had the escalator to himself the entire time, something of an oddity, but under the circumstances a welcome one.

## 16

LARISA HAD LEFT twenty minutes earlier. The office was quiet and still. Dinner smells—onions in butter, roasting meat, simmering cabbage—from the apartments below wafted through the vents. Jim could feel the whole space crouching and quivering. The empty office hummed—refrigerator, computers, printers—and ticked. Jim shook his mouse and sat down to read.

He was still reading an hour later when his phone rang.

"Jim, this is Mina calling," she said in her formal phone voice. "Are you alone?"

"I am."

"Can you talk?"

"I can."

"Good," she said. Her voice grew warmer, calmer.

"I'm in the office, doing exactly what you told me to do."

"What does that mean?"

"I'm reading through the interviews. Reading and reading and re-reading."

"Would you like to talk through it?"

"Talk through what?"

"Jim, I've read enough dull government writing to know that sometimes it helps to talk about what you're reading. Sometimes your gears just end up grinding against each other and you need to look up."

"Mina Haddad, purveyor of driving metaphors. Who would have guessed?"

"That's actually Kamal's. My brother. I hate cars. One of the benefits of foreign postings is that I never have to drive."

"Native servants?"

"Please. Our servants are all imported." She gave an embarrassed little laugh at her own joke. Mina could never allow herself to be carried along in a conversation's flow. She could direct a dialogue fine, when it had an end in mind—witness her talk with Jim on the way to the Metro—but the eddies of amicability always threatened to drag her under. At such times she spoke with the hesitant precision that comes from self-observation. "Now, as long as I'm on the phone, can I hear about your reading material?"

"Sure, sure. We'll begin at the beginning, with the one you didn't know about. Grigory Naumenko." Jim heard the clack of typing on Mina's end. "He came from Tiraspol, where apparently everyone lived like brothers."

"They always do there."

"Where, in Moldova?"

"No, in the past. My parents talk about Lebanon like it was paradise. A Benetton commercial with better music." Jim caught the note of sadness in Mina's voice—the first-generation American's longing for a described but unseen and unfelt homeland—but laughed at the joke anyway.

"He still praised Stalin, if you can believe that. Or at least refused to condemn him. He was a strong leader; it was a difficult time; the country made many advances. The standard Russian defense. He did his military service in Belomorsk as a prison guard. The prisoners—these were criminals, he made sure to say, not political prisoners—were carving a canal between the White and Baltic seas. He used to shout at trees."

"I'm sorry, Jim, did you say he talked to trees?"

"Well, to a house that was supposed to be in the trees. 'Turn your back to the forest and your front to me.' You never heard that? Baba Yaga and her chicken-leg house? The witch in the forest?"

"I'm afraid not? What's the name again?"

"Naumenko."

"No, the Bob-whatever-it-is. The witch."

"Baba, not Bob. Baba Yaga. She flies through the air in a cauldron that she steers with a broom. What else: her fence was made of bones and skulls. No Russian fairy tales for you?"

"No, we had the Khoja."

"The what?"

"Khoja. Nasreddin Khoja, the Turkish wise fool. Every Sufi grandfather's favorite. He was . . ." She was about to get expansive and then cut herself off. "Anyway. Baba Yaga. Shouting at trees. What's next?"

"Next is the bad part," Jim said heavily. Not for the first time this week was he struck by the sense that he really didn't understand the world, that despite all of the platitudes about how all men are brothers and we're all the same under the skin, the gap in life experience between him and a Russian political prisoner who fought in World War II just might be unbridgeable. Jim had never understood this viscerally just how large, hard, and full of possibilities the world was. That was why the prospect that these men were lying to him—lying about something like this, lying and, in effect, desecrating the graves and memories of actual survivors—made him so angry.

"He said he was imprisoned for using his military privileges to get a Finnish family some food. A political rival turned him in, and he spent a few years, he didn't say exactly how many, chopping wood and smoking fish in Solovetsky, in the White Sea."

"My God," Mina said quietly. "Freezing. Starving. I can't imagine years; even a week would be too long. What does he do now?"

"He's a guard at Sporting Palace."

"Oh, I know the Palace. Embassy guys love that place. Apparently they show all three football games on Sundays. So he works there? You saw him?"

"Yeah, that's where I talked to him."

"Interesting. You know that place is army-run, right?"

"Army? Like the Russian army? I figured it was some kind of mafia."

"It is, yes. The army kind of mafia. You can't get a better *krysha*. You don't know how long he's been there, by any chance?"

"He didn't say. Why?"

"Well, then I'd know who hired him. Or at least who signed off on letting him work there. Supposedly General Volkhonsky runs it now."

"Volkhonsky the presidential candidate?"

"And Duma member, and former cabinet member. The very same. It's been his for two years. He turned the place into a laundry for his friends. The fees have made him one of the richest men in Moscow. Anyway. So that's Naumenko. Next was Balderis?"

"Vilis Balderis, right. You need me to spell that?"

"Nope. I have his name and a picture right here, remember? Thank you, though. I never could spell."

"Me neither. So Balderis is the stallholder at Izmailovsky."

"And you found him how?"

"Through Naumenko."

Mina paused, typing away in the background. "So it's a chain, correct? All the way through? Each one sent you to the next one?"

"Right."

"That's interesting, isn't it?"

"What?"

"It's a predetermined course. Let's say, for argument's sake, all four of these men were in the camps together. No, wait . . . let's try something else. Think of a group of friends you have from a specific place. College, let's say."

"I don't have too many of those, I'm afraid."

"Well, high school, then."

"Strike two."

Mina sighed. Reality was interfering with her lesson. "You *do* have friends, though, right?"

Jim puffed out his cheeks and let the air slither out his mouth, think-ing futile and deflating thoughts. "One or two. I guess. On a good day."

"Poor Jim. Cousins?"

"Like you wouldn't believe."

"Okay, good. Say someone asks you about your cousins. A group of you who see each other pretty regularly. You wouldn't give that person one name, right? If you trusted him you'd give him a list; if you didn't you'd tell him to buzz off."

"I'd say 'fuck,' actually. 'Fuck off.'"

"I don't doubt you would, Jim."

"You sound like my mother."

"Can you just not say that again, please? It's the curse of the good girl. Do you understand my point? You were given information in a very directed way. If we assume it's false information, then there's a particu-lar reason you saw these four men in this order. Did you ever mention any of the names out of order?"

"I didn't." He felt a familiar tug of regret. "I probably should have, though. Right?"

"Jim, I'll tell you again: we're past *should*s. Either you did or you didn't. And you didn't. That's fine. Let's hear more about Balderis. Naumenko told you where to find him?"

"Yes. Wait: he told me where he worked, but someone else had to show me the exact stall."

"Who?"

"Sergei was his name. He sells music—sheet music and instruments. And him I found because I had dinner with his sister at Yuri and Kirsten's house. So he showed me . . ."

"I'm sorry: Yuri and Kirsten are who?"

"I work with them. Yuri's a researcher, sort of a staff historian. Kirsten's his wife. She's our grant writer."

"You guys survive on grants? I thought you were fully funded by what's-his-name. The software guy."

"Not really. He gave us the seed money, and he throws us a little more every so often, but most of the operating budget, as far as I understand, we have to scrounge up ourselves."

"Interesting. Do you know where it comes from?"

"I think Kirsten said European governments, mostly. Some American foundations. She was pretty vague. Do you think that matters?"

"Right now, Jim, everything matters and nothing does."

Through his window Jim saw the church door open, and a blade of rich, honeyed candlelight warmed the asphalt. Parishioners—mostly older women, but a smattering of intense, bearded young men and a few families, too—poured forth, everyone turning back toward the church on the threshold and crossing themselves, some three times and some with a bow. They walked away in small groups, talking quietly with one another. The scene reminded him of evening mass at St. Anselm's, his family's church and anchor in Hamden for three generations, and homesickness assaulted him like a kick in the chest. He took a deep drink of water, shook his head vigorously, and turned back to his computer.

"Balderis was tougher and quieter than Naumenko. Came from Kaliningrad. He was a political, sentenced for spying, he said, because he was Latvian and spent a lot of time with a friend who had a German last name. Apparently, neither of those things are unusual there. He was in for seven years. Let's see . . . this stuck with me: his stall was on the outside of the market. Do you know where I mean? Have you been?"

"Once. Buying tacky presents for my family."

"Where'd you buy them from?"

"What do you mean? Let's see . . ." He heard the clicking of pen on teeth. "I came out of the Metro and went into this sort of fake castle. Is that where he works?"

"Almost. You probably didn't see his table, because he was outside the walls. He said he used to have a prime spot inside, but another stall opened next to his, and it sold salted fish. The smell reminded him too much of Solovetsky, where he worked in the canneries, so he gave it up and moved farther out. Probably gave up most of his income doing that."

"Do you know what he did after the camps?"

"Aside from this? I don't."

"Before?"

"Army, I assume."

"He didn't tell you? You didn't ask?"

"No, he was just . . . He seemed unhappy. Like he didn't like to be reminded of it. And I didn't want to intrude."

"So you took a job as an interviewer but you don't like to intrude on people? That doesn't strike you as odd? Contradictory?"

"Look, I . . ." Jim stammered, not because he was trying to evade her question but because she was right and he hadn't thought about it. Not since his engagement to Serena ended had someone spent enough time thinking about him to make an observation like this—and this, he knew, was not especially insightful; it just meant that somebody was looking at him from the outside. "I took the job that was offered because I needed the money, Mina. Contradictory or not." He paused, considering more fully the suspicion behind her statement. "Mina, I'm trying to help you. All of you. I thought you said I wasn't a suspect."

"You aren't *a* suspect, Jim. That doesn't mean you're not suspect at all. And we appreciate your help, we really do, but we need you to be as thorough as you can. Maybe even more thorough than you know you can be. Do you understand?" She didn't wait for an answer. "So next came, let's see, how do you pronounce this . . ."

"Tsepereli. Dato. A real broken-down drunk. I interviewed him at one of those slot-machine trailers. You know the ones I'm talking about: they're silver, outside Metro stations?" Anytime Jim mentioned something seamy to Mina, he felt obliged to provide a translation.

"Yes, Jim. I can't say I'm a connoisseur of such establishments, but I know the ones you're talking about."

"Good. So you understand how sad it is when I tell you Dato seemed to be a regular there. Probably pissed away most of his pension in fifty-kopeck increments. Him I couldn't get anything out of. He was in for a dozen years, though. Long enough to break anybody down. I assume he was a political, and went in for the same. He just kept telling me over and over again that he's a janitor's son from Sukhumi. In for twelve years. And he only had one friend."

"Let me guess: Faridian the doctor?"

"Faridian the doctor it was. He was the angriest. The most composed, the smartest, and the toughest, too, but he was furious. He worked at a hospital up in North Nowhere by Vodniy Stadion. Underequipped, understaffed, undereverything. They sterilized their surgical instruments in boiling water. He went to prison for class background, he said. His father and grandfather were both doctors, and a rival used that to send him away."

"Away from where?"

"Gyumri."

"Armenia?"

"That's right. How did you know that?"

"We have a Gyumri headache. The Russian army has a few divisions down there. For 'keeping Caucasian peace,' it used to be; now it's for 'fighting terrorism.' Convenient. The Armenians want them out, and they want us to help them. The Russians, you can imagine, don't want to go anywhere. And the truth is, we like having them down there; in that part of the world, we're fighting the same people. But we could never say that, of course. So we shuffle around awkwardly and say the right things and hope it all goes away. It's the same thing in Sukhumi, except there it's still 'keeping the peace.'"

"Sukhumi? Doesn't . . ."

"Yes. Yes, he . . . Jesus, Jim! Jim! Listen to this: Gyumri, Sukhumi, Tiraspol, Kaliningrad. Where your four prisoners come from, right?"

"That's right."

"They're *all* the same!" Mina said, now almost shouting with excitement. He heard a bang over the phone. It sounded like a fist coming down on a desk. "All four of them: Russian army bases outside Russian soil!"

"Great. Terrific. So what does that mean?"

Mina sighed, deflated. "I don't know yet. But it's something. One of them, maybe, but all four in a chain? That's not coincidental. Let's first finish up with Faridian. What else is there?"

"Nothing, really. He treated people in the camps for free, stayed in contact with Tsepereli, he said, out of pity. He had a nasty story about fox."

"Fox?"

"Prisoners used to eat it when they were starving."

"Yech. White fox," Mina said absently as she typed.

"Sorry?"

"It's Lisitsov's nickname. His underlings called him 'The White Fox' behind his back. He had a reputation for deviousness, pitting rivals against each other, suddenly bestowing or removing funding: basic office-politics tactics. He went white early, and I guess the fox is supposedly an especially devious creature, at least to Russians."

"Well, and 'Lisitsov,' " Jim said.

"What do you mean?"

"His name sounds like *lisitka*, the Russian word for 'fox.'"

"Huh. You're right. That never occurred to me. You know, that makes it even weirder that Faridian would drop that detail into his conversation. Nothing about the camps, nothing about his experience, nothing about how he feels, just a random little detail about eating fox. Don't you find that bizarre?"

"I guess. Hang on: what did you say the name of the first scientist to disappear was?"

"Matvei Yagachin. Matvei like Matthew, and Yagachin like . . ."

"Like Baba Yaga? Naumenko's incongruous detail?"

"Yes," she cried. "Exactly."

"What else: you said another scientist went missing, you heard."

"Hold on. Jim, this is just . . ." She didn't finish the sentence, but Jim heard the rising excitement, the thrill of outsmarting in her voice. "Rybovna. Svetlana Rybovna."

"*Ryba*. Fish. Balderis's fish seller. Is there a fourth?"

"Ah, that, Jim, I can't tell you yet. We're looking into a few possibilities, but it will take some time, and as long as it's unconfirmed, I can't say one way or the other."

"House rules?"

"I'm afraid so, Jim. Do you have a suggestion?"

"For what Russian scientist could have disappeared?"

"No, Jim. For what names we should be looking for."

"I can't believe none of you speaks Russian. Not a single . . ."

"I speak some, Jim, and I understand plenty, just not as well as you. We have a couple of linguists in-house, Jim, but this is not the time to excoriate us. Anyway, my training was in Turkish and Arabic languages; I'm here for a six-month punishment stint."

"Punishment for what?"

"For saying no to a gropey boss."

"So they put you in charge of weapons scientists?"

"They weren't disappearing at the time, Jim," Mina said exasperatedly. "Now, can you please just help me?"

"Sure. For Dato, obviously, it's his father's job, the janitor, that stands out. So you want something, I don't know, something cleaning related. *Dvornik, uborshik, chistiy, opryatniy.* I don't know, though; there are a lot of possibilities. With something like this it always looks easier from the other side. Narrow to broad. But start with those and see if they work."

"*Chistiy, o-pree-yat-nee,*" she mumbled into the phone as she typed. "Good. Now. I need to see those transcripts."

"Hold on, I'll print them out for you." Jim clicked the printer icon at the top of the screen.

"Could you also e-mail them to me?"

"Sure, I'll do that right now."

"No, wait." He heard clicking as she tapped the pen against her front teeth. "Who's the administrator of your office network?"

"What do you mean?"

"Who maintains it? Who's able to monitor e-mails sent from office computers?"

"Vassily's son. He's fourteen. Knows everything. I don't think we even pay him."

Mina laughed. "Where would we be without unpaid child labor? Don't send them to me. I'd guess it might be weird if you were to e-mail those transcripts to an outside party, right?"

"I can't think of any legitimate reason why I would."

"Right. Now, can you tell who's read them?"

"Anyone could have. I don't know."

"Where are you reading them now?"

"At my desk."

"Printed copies?"

"No, on-screen. They're saved to the server."

"Can you tell who's opened them?"

"I can't. I'm worse than useless with computers, to tell you the truth. Typing, printing, online poker, Redskins scores. That's about it."

"Does your office leave computers on or shut them off for the weekend?"

"Off. Everyone's. By order of Larisa, our PR lady. She thinks leaving computers on in a locked office causes a buildup of harmful electrons."

This was one of many Russian theories on health and the modern world that stayed away from—indeed, actively suspected—scientific evidence. Computers ran on electricity so they gave off electrons; our grandparents didn't use them, and our grandparents were heroes, so they must be bad. Mina gave a frustrated sigh. "All right. So why don't you just bring the reports by this evening, okay? We'll meet at that Cowboy place near your house in half an hour."

"That's fine. See you then." Jim hung up and walked over to the printer. Nothing had come out: the blinking red light told him there was a paper jam. He fixed it and the machine started rolling. He stared out the window at the cut-glass winter night below. The service long since finished, the church had reverted to its secular function: a quartet of drinkers sprawled on the steps, passing a bottle around. The oldest of the group, a toothless, pancake-faced guy in a flat cap and greasy ski parka, leaned across to the others and whispered something. All four broke up laughing: undisguised public happiness in Russia was the exclusive habit of foreigners and drunks.

After the last page rolled out of the printer it seemed to sigh and pant, exhausted. Jim grabbed the transcripts and headed into the kitchen for a plastic bag to carry them in. As he put them in, though, he noticed the top page was not the beginning of his interview with Naumenko, as it should have been. Instead it was the sentence and a half—". . . sushi or a cappuccino, will die. I don't expect you to care, but I do expect you to leave"—with which Faridian had dismissed him. Naumenko began on the next page; this one must have been caught in the paper jam and forgotten. At the bottom of the page, Jim read the user ID of the person who had done the printing and the forgetting.

"Mina. It's Jim. I found . . ."

"One moment, please," she said in a sweet, efficient voice that was not her own. Jim heard a series of mechanical beeps and a click. She rejoined him as herself. "Sorry. It keeps it secure on my end. What happened?"

"Dave Willow. He printed the interviews." Jim told her about the orphaned last page.

"Dave Willow, your boss."

"That's right."

She took a deep, quick breath, then Jim heard the tap-tap-tapping of pen against teeth.

"Do you know him?" Mina asked.

"Of course. I work with him."

"No, socially. Outside of work."

"He had a little party at his house when I first arrived. He and Sara do that for all the new hires. It was like a college student's idea of what a grown-up party is: plates of grocery-store cheese and crackers, bowls of olives and pickles, and a few bottles of warm white wine."

"So you know where they live."

"Sure. A huge *yevro-remont*ed place down in Taganskaya. Out with the dark wood and chipped plastic, in with the chrome and glass. I don't know the address, but you can't miss the building. It's one of those marble spaceships Stalin built for his favorites. Supposedly there's a passage that goes straight from Lubyanka into the building's basement for when the favorites stopped being favored."

"So you can find it? You remember which entrance and everything?"

"Well, no, actually, I don't."

"Fine. Here's what we're going to do. There's a branch of Manhattan Coffee at Taganskaya. Meet me there in half an hour. We'll call Dave and Sara from there and you'll say you were just in the neighborhood. You want to see if they'd like to join you for a drink. You'll offer to stop by if they don't want to go out. You'll make them accept. I'll be with you, and you'll introduce me as your girlfriend."

"What? No. They'd never believe I'd do that, just stop by unannounced late on a Sunday night."

"Well, Jim, then I guess you'd better make them believe it. Besides, it's not late; it's only five thirty. We'll be there by six thirty: perfect time for a predinner cocktail, right?"

"Mina, I'm not . . ."

"Jim, listen. We're not priests, and neither are they. Do you understand me? Nobody is looking inside your soul. Nobody has known you for more than a few months. You're going to do what I told you to do, and you're going to do it convincingly." Even when issuing orders, her voice retained its bell, its inborn courtesy. "If you play poker as well as you say you do, bluffing—lying—shouldn't be difficult. You need to remember, Jim, that it isn't who you are that matters here. It's who you can be. Now, get going: I'll see you there at six."

## 17

MANHATTAN COFFEE OFFERED a distinctly Russian improvement on Starbucks: overstuffed velvet chairs rather than wood; Formica tables in every color of the Day-Glo rainbow; thumping techno Russki-pop rather than bland world music; and, of course, a full menu and full bar, complete with an array of Cuban cigars and—the season's current fad—hookahs with your choice of filter liquid: water, juice, vodka, or red wine. The liquid, of course, had no effect on the tobacco's flavor, nor did it ever get hot enough to even give off intoxicating fumes: the point was to let everybody see not only that you could afford to use a bottle of French wine as, effectively, bong water, but that you were discerning enough to choose a Margaux or a Pomerol. Two men with competitively thick necks and granite-hewn physiques at a corner table puffed cigars only a little smaller than pool cues, as their young, pneumatic, and fully paid-for "dates" shared a Macallan hookah. This marked them as climbers: single malt was last year; this year everyone had switched to Armagnac or Pineau des Charentes.

At 6:45 there was still no sign of Mina, and Jim was starting to draw grumbles and attention sitting alone (nobody came to restaurants alone) and nursing a forty-five-minute cup of coffee (the point of going out to eat was to spend freely, conspicuously, and to gorge). A waitress walked past with a steaming bowl of *pelmeni*, and the smell seemed to carve out a hole inside him: he remembered that he had not yet eaten today. He ordered a *sendvitch filadelfski*—salted salmon, pickled cucumbers, and tomatoes on black bread, topped with sour cream and dill—and a large Sibirskaya Corona.

He had a premonition he might be in for a long night, so he got a pack of Winstons as well. Smoking, while it did eventually kill you, was better than anything ever invented for killing time, for making one feel productive while accomplishing nothing. The ability of cigarettes to ward off boredom with just a match and a few deep breaths was ultimately far more addictive to restless gamblers like Jim than nicotine ever could be.

By seven thirty Jim had finished his sandwich and his second beer. He felt that familiar tug inside pulling him toward ordering a whiskey and settling in for the night. He had noticed, not without a tinge of worry, that he often grew jittery and uneasy when nighttime approached and he hadn't yet taken the edge off the day with a drink. Of equal concern was his propensity to continue once he started, which he would have done tonight, had Mina not chosen that moment to stride through the front door. She had pulled her hair back and put on light makeup, a dress with a plunging neckline, and an elegant long coat. She looked dressed for a night out, but as she approached Jim's table, her clenched jaw and white knuckles where she grabbed her purse showed something was wrong. She looked calm, coiled, purposeful, wonderful, like she might bite and draw blood.

He rose and pulled out a chair for her, and she kissed him on the cheek and ran a hand up and down his arm. "You look great. What was that for?"

"I'm your girlfriend, remember?" she said as she sat down, dropped a hand over his, and flashed an obliging smile across the table. "I dressed up because we're going to meet your boss."

"I guess we are. And I guess you are. Is everything okay? Why were you so late? Do you need anything to eat? Drink? Should we go? I'll just settle up here." He began to raise his arm to signal a waitress when Mina pulled it back down.

"You need to calm down and stop talking, first. Everything is not okay," she said. She clasped her hands in front of her on the table, looked directly at him, and leaned in close. "We have a problem. The Russians know."

Jim felt an icicle drop down his chest. "Know what?"

"About the disappearances. And they know that we know. Apparently one of our monitors was less discreet than he should have been. He broke into the dacha of a scientist who he thought had vanished. It turns out he was just sleeping. And it turns out this particular scientist had a fondness for hunting weapons and really didn't like being woken up by a foreigner with lock picks."

"By one of ours? An American?"

"No. This one had a Belgian passport. It doesn't matter where he's actually from; he's passing himself off as Belgian and Belgian he'll stay. But his consulate didn't know anything about him, and so naturally they wanted to stay as uninvolved as possible. They sent the Russians over to us, which is where they would eventually have come anyway. Why I was late: Trudy had me listening to her meeting with the GRU. It was not a happy one."

"Do they know about me?" Jim hoped his voice didn't rise too much, didn't grow too sharp and anxious at the end of that question.

"If they don't they will soon. If we knew enough to keep an eye on Katerina Lisitsova, it's a better than even guess they did, too. That's assuming she didn't work for them. If she did, then yes, I would imagine they know about you. You do seem to have your lucky socks on, though."

"Lucky? You think I'm a spy; they think I'm a spy: what's lucky?" Over the speakers came a grating techno version of "My Friend Has Left for Magadan," a Vysotsky song about being sent to the gulag. Even the jackhammer beat and the unvarying bass could not entirely obliterate the humanity, warmth, and depth of his voice. Jim failed to appreciate the irony in song choice, though.

"You're here, right?" Mina pointed out.

"Just be happy I'm alive, is that it?"

"No, you're *here*. At the restaurant. The GRU requested an emergency meeting with Trudy right after I hung up. You weren't at the office or at your apartment; you were someplace nobody thought to look."

"Are you saying I can't go home tonight?"

"No, not necessarily. But I'd be careful. Look: if they knew about you, they probably would have gone to your home and office first thing. They didn't, right? So chances are you're still clear. With them."

"Not with you?"

"You're on your way," she said, with a mischievous smile. She brushed her hair back from her face without taking her eyes off him. Only then did two things occur to him: first, that she wielded her power well, which meant that he could trust her. And second, that she liked to look good. "But we need to get you out of Russia, and we need to do it soon."

"Great. I'm ready when you are."

"I said soon, not now. You need to take me over to Dave and Sara Willow's house first."

"You know, it might not mean anything."

"What's that, Jim?"

"His printing out the interviews. Maybe he just wanted to take them home to read."

"Or maybe not. Do you have a better place to start?"

"No, no. I guess I don't. Can I ask you one other thing before we go?"

She nodded and took a compact out of her purse. She looked at herself in the mirror rather than at him.

"I want to find Kaisa—Katerina—whoever. I want to know."

"Know what?"

"Everything. I want to know . . ."

"I understand, Jim, how you feel, but we're past that."

He felt his back and hands tense and his face get hot like it did whenever he grew angry. He wanted to yell something, pound the table and tell her no, she didn't understand how he felt. They wanted two different things. Jim had wanted redemption; he wanted to do something right, to put something right for once, and knowing Kaisa was part of that. Besides, he felt that Mina's suspicions about her were wrong.

"Do you know where she is?"

"Jim, I'm not going to . . ."

"Yes, you are. Or I'm not going to. Look, you can do what you like to me; I haven't done anything wrong, and I'm helping you. Just tell me if you know where she is. I'm not asking you to take me there; I just want to know if she's okay. Or if she's really working for them."

Mina again drew her hair back from her face and tilted her chin upward, considering. Finally she gave a conciliatory nod. "We don't think she's one of theirs. We don't know, of course, but we don't think so."

"Why not?" Jim interrupted. He was trying to take her measure, but something about her demeanor this evening seemed glass-fronted, impossible to grip.

"Because we have no evidence of it." She shrugged. "From what we know of her background, she has no training; from what we know of her family, she's inclined to be skeptical toward her government. Now, none of that argues definitively one way or the other, and we would of course like to talk to her, but we don't know."

"Do you know where she is?"

"She's at home. Or at least she was when I left this evening. She and her mother. Rodion spends religious holidays with a friend of his, a monk of some kind, at Sergiev Posad. He's due back tomorrow. But Katerina is fine. We're watching."

"Another Belgian?"

She shrugged.

"How are you watching? Aren't the Russians watching, too? Wouldn't they see you?"

She shrugged again.

"How do I know you're watching? How do I know she's fine?"

"Because I told you," she said, standing up and dropping a few hundred rubles on the table. "And you can't. Now, let's go. We're late enough."

He helped her into her coat and held the door open for her. Outside she shivered and drew up against him. "If everything goes well," she said quietly, looking down at the icy sidewalk as they walked, "we'll have a quick chat with your friends, and then maybe you'll be home by breakfast. Maybe we'll talk to a few more people tomorrow and you'll be home by dinner. If everything doesn't go well, or if you've been less than honest with us, then, old neighborhood or not, you'll die in Lefortovo. We'll leave you here and give you to them.

"Now, hold on to me like you actually want to," she said with a false sweetness, pulling his arm around her waist. "You never know who's watching; they might be out for a walk, too. But if you move that hand down at all I'll break your wrist."

## 18

"HEY, THERE, JIM," Sara sang down the broad half-staircase from her doorway. Jim and Mina advanced up the five flights of stairs in semidarkness, the only light coming through the windows and from the door that Sara held open. Her voice went down and then up on his name, two notes in a syllable. She thought it sounded coquettish and charming; really it sounded like a mother trying to charm a recalcitrant child into doing something he does not want to do. "We're so glad you called. Sorry we couldn't meet you, but, you know, on a Sunday night . . ."

She let the sentence trail off, and at the doorway she greeted Jim and Mina with the broad but tight smile of the imposed-upon. She was smaller than Mina, with sharp features, honey-blond hair pulled back in a ponytail, and the sinewy, lithe physique of a yoga practitioner. Her eyes were light blue, almost clear; where Mina's reflected curiosity and reserve, Sara's seemed hard and judging, with the stock-taking stoniness of a campus radical or a nineteenth-century preacher.

Dave had his hand on Sara's shoulder, and the four of them just stood staring at one another across the threshold, their chimpanzee grins frozen as each tried to figure out what the other was really doing. Jim was right: they knew he wasn't the type to just drop by unannounced, especially with a girlfriend whom he had never mentioned before ("Mina . . . She works in sales . . . over visiting from home . . ." "Washington not quite cold enough for ya? Ha-ha-ha"). But neither could they turn him away. And Jim could not imagine that these guile-less doofuses in front of him could mastermind anything more compli-cated than how to speak in academic, freedom-for-the-masses jargon while maintaining a two-car garage, ethical-granola lifestyle. Eventu-ally, though, propriety asserted itself: Dave and Sara stood aside and allowed, if not exactly welcomed, Jim and Mina into their apartment, while Mina reached into her purse for a bottle of wine and some care-fully wrapped peonies.

"Well, look at these, Mina!" Sara cooed. "These are lovely, just lovely. 'Just happened to be in the area,' huh? You didn't have to do that."

"Yeah, you bet," chirped Dave. "Always welcome over here. Always good to see someone else from home. Gifts totally unnecessary." He started to lean forward with his big goofy smile, like he was about to hug or collapse into Mina. She even stepped back, but, as usual, he was just stretching: he fell into a bridge against the hallway wall, extending his hamstrings and lower back, grunting with showy exertion. Jim smelled beer on his breath as he exhaled.

"David, stand up," Sara remonstrated, looking at Mina and Jim as she shook her head and laughed at Dave. "Stop doing that. We have guests. You show them in; I'll get some drinks."

"Sorry about that," Dave said, looking genuinely cowed. He stared at the floor, scratching his beard and shuffling his feet back and forth. "Guess it's a habit. So you guys were, what, just out strolling, is that it?"

"Yeah, I just wanted to show Mina a quieter side of Moscow. We had a late lunch at the Starlite, walked down to Red Square and over the river, then just followed the Garden Ring around the city for a while. I guess after three days of nobody but each other, we needed a little humanity break."

"That's a long walk. You guys must be tired. Have a seat over here at the table. I'll get rid of these old plates and we'll see if we can't find something else lying around for you."

Mina jumped up to help. She and Dave carried away the remnants of their dinner: two bowls of cloudy green soup with foamy cubes of something that may have descended from a soybean sitting on the bottom, a salad of pinto beans and raw onions, and two glasses of water. Jim shuddered at the health of it all.

The apartment looked like a Russian translation of Swedish design: blond wood floors and built-ins, brushed chrome cabinets and fittings, track lights running in more or less straight lines across the living room. The Russian translation manifested itself in size: instead of small but powerful lights hanging from the ceiling, Dave and Sara's place practically had klieg lights. Circular burn marks made a halo around each lamp. The space itself was massive in every particular: bookshelves that dwarfed the books, a TV cabinet that would have housed a movie screen, brushed steel doorknobs the size of basketballs. It had an Alice-in-Wonderland quality to it, devoid of any sense of warmth or coziness, made to appeal to a Russian idea of Western tastes. Jim imagined the architect shaking his head in bewilderment at what foreigners called home.

In the kitchen Sara was giving Mina the usual litany of American complaints about Moscow (cold, corrupt, bleak, etc.), and Mina chirped sympathetically with each one. Jim marveled not at how much her personality changed (because, of course, it didn't; she just turned up certain attributes and turned down others) but at how different Sara's and Dave's impression of her must be because of how she acted. She was right: what matters is what you can plausibly be. Nobody is looking within because nobody cares. But of course, she was only as right as she had to be: eventually, you would be left with yourself. Fooling other people—whether as a spy or a poker player—is fine, as long as you don't confuse yourself.

"What do you want to drink, babe?" Mina asked from the kitchen. It took Jim a second to realize she was talking to him; it took a second longer to stifle a laugh.

"Ah, what is there?"

"We have water, filtered or bottled," Sara said. "We have some grapefruit-carrot juice I made this morning. We have the wine you brought. And Dave, don't you have something left from the Cal game?"

"Yup, yup. Got a few bottles of Bud Light, maybe some Cokes at the back of the fridge."

"If they haven't frozen," Sara said sourly. "We also have tea."

"A Coke would be great, actually. I don't think I've had one since I left home."

"Coming right up," Dave called out. Jim heard the familiar *pssht*—after so many years in a restaurant, he could tell by that sound whether it was a Coke, Diet Coke, ginger ale, club soda, domestic or imported beer. The only one that gave him trouble was Sprite; depending on the weather and how long it had been refrigerated it could sound more like Coke or more like ginger ale. He knew, even before they reappeared with drinks and a tray of what looked like crushed acorns, he was getting an actual Coke.

"Thank you," he said, taking the can. "Those look . . ."

"Sara was telling me they're live cookies. Right?"

"Not quite. I can't get cane juice here, so I have to use cane sugar, which means I need to bake them," she said apologetically. "But no processed anything. Try one." Jim did: it had the consistency of wood pulp. He chewed it for about thirty seconds to no discernible effect.

"These are great," said Mina enthusiastically. "I'm always trying to get him to eat healthier."

"I know; they never do." Sara rolled her eyes at Dave, who was drinking a Bud Light and intently trying to peel the clear label off the bottle, then adopted a teacherly expression of stern compassion. "But it's not just about the health of the individual. It's about thinking about the whole planet, and using your choices to educate others. White sugar, you know, it's all they have here? My father had to send my sugar from the Berkeley Bowl, but anytime we have guests over, I make sure to have a bowl on the table. That way people can ask me what it is. I can tell them, and I can tell them to tell their grocery store that they should have it. Not because it tastes good, or because people will buy it, but because it's *right*."

Mina nodded somberly, staring into Sara's eyes like an acolyte. She turned to Dave. "Jim told me what the Foundation does. It's such great work. I think it's, like, so important to know about your past. I mean, memory is everything, right?"

"Well, Jimmy's done some great work for us himself. Especially this past week; he's really been on a roll."

Jim explained the past week's activity to Mina, as though for the first time, being careful to remain as literal as possible. She nodded, wide-eyed and admiringly, every so often interjecting a "wow" or "ooh," every inch the adoring, supportive girlfriend. When he finished, she said, "It's like a secret chain."

Dave, his voice full of beer enthusiasm, concurred. "Yeah, he's done great. Just a few more to go, I guess."

"What do you mean?" Mina asked sweetly. Only because he knew her did Jim notice her eyes grow sharper and her jaw set. "A few more to go before what?"

"Oh, you know. A few more in the chain." There are few spectacles more pathetic than someone trying to shepherd spoken words back into his mouth. For a split second, panic jolted Dave's face: he blinked quickly, he let out a breath and tried to say something, but, like a cartoon character pedaling furiously in midair after going off a cliff, he was lost. "No, well, you know. I just . . . I figured he'd tell . . . The chain would keep going, right? I mean, after Faridian . . ."

"Dave!" Sara shouted. "Honey." She giggled nervously. "Honey, what are you talking about." But she did not sound bewildered; her voice had the telegraphed sharpness of intent.

"Oh, just babbling," he said, still trying. "Got a little ahead of myself, I guess." He grinned, shaking his head at his own idiocy for their benefit. "Just figured it would have had to keep going, you know."

"But why . . ." Jim began.

"These cookies are delicious," Mina interrupted, holding up half of one and chewing with great determination. "Can you give me the recipe sometime?"

"Sure," said Sara. Slowly her nervous glances from Dave to Jim to Mina to the table to the floor to the window subsided. She even managed an indulgent smile. "I'd be happy to. Of course."

"Can I take a couple to go?" Mina asked, standing up. "Jim, honey, we should get going. I've got an early train tomorrow." Jim followed her lead and rose.

"Well, that was fast," chuckled Dave, "but I'm sure glad you stopped by. Where's the train headed?"

"Tallinn. I figure Jim's going to be working, so I might as well take advantage of geography, right? Just a quick trip for a couple days, then I'll finish up the week here before heading home and leaving him behind." She clasped Jim's hand between hers and swung it back and forth.

"Oh, absolutely. Oh, Tallinn's great. Just beautiful. You'll love it."

"I'm sure I will. Thanks for the cookies. I'm sorry to eat and run like this."

"That's okay," Sara said. "Maybe we'll see you again later in the week, if you have a free night?"

"Definitely," Mina said enthusiastically. "Definitely let's do that."


At the third story, Mina dropped Jim's hand and pulled out her phone. Jim started to ask who she was calling, but she shushed him until they were out of the building, around the corner, and in the corner of one of those little children's parks—a slide, a bench, a couple of carved wooden gnomes—that dot inner Moscow.

"They knew," Mina said, flipping open her phone. "Even you must have caught that."

"Sure, I did. So what are you . . ."

She held up a hand. "Yes, I'm trying to reach Velez?" she said brightly.

"Econ Affairs?" After a short pause she resumed speaking in her characteristically businesslike voice. "It's me. Our friends seem interested. You should meet them. Yes. Yes. Tonight. I'm at O'Leary's, that Irish place out by Barrikadnaya. How long? Yes, an hour's perfect. Of course. I'll be there by myself. The usual table at the back. Good. See you there."

She hung up. Before Jim could ask anything, she started walking toward the Metro station. Jim rushed to keep up. "This week we're giving opposites," she said.

"Sorry?"

"Stations. When we're calling in from a mobile phone. Sometimes it's one station east, one west, sometimes it's two north. This week it's opposites. The purple line crosses the circle line twice, once at Taganskaya and once at Barrikadnaya."

"I got that. So where's O'Leary's?"

"At Barrikadnaya, of course. Haven't you been there? They show all the games; I thought it was a rite of passage for all young, single male expats to spend a night puking in their bathrooms."

"I hate to disappoint, Mina, but I've been holding my liquor for almost two decades now. Besides, don't they show soccer and Gaelic football?"

"All the same to me, I'm afraid." They crossed through a churchyard and emerged onto Taganskaya Street itself, which had a fair amount of foot traffic for a Sunday night, including the usual crowd of older, grizzled men gathered around a drinks kiosk. Mina tensed and stutter-stepped when the men turned to stare and catcall at her, but she recovered and just put her head down and walked faster. Attractive, young, dark-complected women are still rare enough to be a treat in Moscow. They followed Mina with their eyes until she and Jim reached the Metro entrance.

"Are we going in?" Jim asked.

Mina held the door open, ushering him into the stuffy, fluorescent-lit cavern. "Usual table in the back," she said quietly. "Means second-to-last car."

She led Jim over to the token machines and fiddled in her purse for change, occasionally glancing over toward the door.

"I've got a pocketful here," Jim said. "What do you need?"

She ignored him. Satisfied that all of the drinkers were, in fact, drinkers—one followed them into the Metro—she fed seventeen rubles into the machine and took her single ticket. They sat vigil on a bench at the far end of the station. Six trains came and went. Each time, a few people got off and headed for the exits; a few straggled on. Nobody looked at the two dark-haired loiterers.

Trudy disembarked from the seventh train at the opposite end of the station. Mina rose when she saw her, but rather than walking toward her she led Jim away, up the staircase and out of the station. They crossed Taganskaya and sat down on a bench outside the church. Trudy followed, sitting on another bench on the other side of the steps until she was satisfied that she had, in fact, come alone. She flicked her head up and Mina started retracing their route toward the Willows'.

Trudy's pace quickened on the side street until she drew even with them. "You know, Seamus, it's not paranoia if you're actually being followed."

"Are we?" he asked.

"Who knows? Mina told you that our inquiry acquired a little urgency this afternoon, didn't she? I'm just being safe. How did he do?" she asked Mina over Jim's head.

"Fine, fine."

"A born follower, is he?" Jim shot her a glare. "Keep your temper in check, darling, and take every opportunity to shut the fuck up, and you just might get home alive. Mina, you have our car here?"

"I do. It's on the other side of Taganskaya."

"Why don't you go get it. Keep it parked and running outside the apartment."

She nodded and turned around.

"And you," Trudy said to Jim, slipping an arm playfully under his, "are going to introduce me to your friends."

"They're not my friends, Trudy."

"Well, I hope not. I hope you convince me they're not. Speaking of people who are not your friends, Gramm has promised to make you spit some teeth the next time he sees you."

"Sensitive, is he?"

"Sucker punch a sucker puncher, you get what's coming."

Jim slowed outside the frosted yellow building. "Is this it?" Trudy asked.

Jim nodded.

"Call and tell them you've left something."

"What did I leave?"

"I don't know, Jim. A book. A scarf. A hat. Your wallet fell out of your pocket when you were sitting down. Just make sure you don't say your phone."

"You know, I think even I could have figured that one out," Jim said darkly. He dialed the Willows. Sara answered.

"Hi, Sara, it's Jim."

"Hi, Jim," she said cautiously.

"Listen, I hate to be a bother this late at night, but I think my wallet fell out of my pocket when I was over at your place."

"Oh, don't worry about that. Dave can bring it to work tomorrow."

"Actually, I need it tonight. I was on my way home when I realized my keys were in it."

"Oh."

"Can I just run up for a second?"

"Run up here?"

"Yeah. We're downstairs; we couldn't get into my apartment."

"You mean downstairs from us? Right now?"

"Right now."

She sighed audibly, looking for an excuse. When she couldn't think of one she sighed again. "Sure. Fine. I'll buzz you in."

The lock clacked open, and Jim held the door for Trudy. "Just remember what I said about not talking," she whispered.

Sara stood in the doorway in her sweats. Her expression changed from annoyed to annoyed and perplexed when she saw Trudy.

"Who's that, Jim? I thought when you said 'we' you meant you'd actually have the same girlfriend you had an hour ago."

"Mrs. Willow, I'm Gertrude Bantz. I work at the United States embassy."

"Here?" Sara asked. "At the embassy here in Moscow?" Dave, in a Berkeley football T-shirt and sweatpants, appeared in the doorway and put his arm awkwardly around his wife. She looked exhausted and angry; he looked exhausted and abashed; they had clearly been fighting.

"I'm afraid so. Can I come in?"

"We were just about to go to sleep," Dave said.

"It's not really a hallway conversation." Trudy put a hand on the door and stepped forward. Dave and Sara retreated.

"Two uninvited guests in one night, Jim," Sara said as Trudy slung her coat over the back of the couch. "I had no idea our place was such a tourist attraction. Can I get you anything?" she asked Trudy.

"Just a few minutes of your time. Please." She gestured to the kitchen table. The four of them sat.

"By the way, Jim, if you'd like to look for your wallet, feel free. Poke around anywhere," Sara said.

"Blame that one on me," Trudy said. "I didn't give him a choice. Can you tell me what Jim has been doing for you?"

"For me?" Dave asked.

"For you, yes. We have a few questions about his recent activity."

Dave shot a hopeful glance at his wife: perhaps this discussion was really about Jim. "He's been recording interviews with former political prisoners. I think this week he did, what, three? Four?"

"Four," Jim said.

"Under your supervision?"

"Well, I guess technically, sure, but really he's been on his own these past few days. We don't 'supervise' our reporters; in the field they're mostly independent."

"So you don't know who Jim's been interviewing."

"No."

"No, you don't, or no, you do."

"I do." Dave giggled nervously. "But only because I've read his interviews. The transcripts, I mean."

"You read all of them?"

"That's right."

"As he does them, or at the end, or when?"

"It depends. Usually at the end of the week I just print out whatever anybody did and take it home to read."

"So you've read the interview with . . . what was the name, Jim?"

"David Faridian," Jim said.

"Yes."

Sara narrowed her eyes and pulled her hair band out. She ran her fingers roughly through her hair. "I'm sorry: what's your name again?"

"Gertrude Bantz."

"Right," said Sara. The name bounced off her; she had forgotten it before Trudy had finished saying it. "We're both pretty tired, so if we could do this in the morning."

"I'm sorry," Trudy said, matching Sara's smile with one of equal frostiness, "but we can't. Now, Mr. Willow, you referred to a continuing chain. 'A few more,' I think you said."

"I don't remember that," Sara interjected.

"I do," said Jim.

Sara just stared.

"My associate does as well," said Trudy. "Ms. Haddad, who was over earlier?"

"You mean Jim's girlfriend?" Sara asked sarcastically.

"She remembers it, too," Trudy repeated. "We'd like to know how you knew. By the way, a butcher from Tenth Planet was taken into custody by the Russian Security Services this evening, about two hours ago. He was charged with corruption and receiving bribes, and is being interrogated at Lubyanka right now. So if there's anything you want to tell me, now would be a good time."

"Hey, look," said Dave, waving his hands and growing agitated. "We didn't steal any property. All we did . . ."

"David!" Sara banged on the table. She looked from her nervous husband to a placid, reassuring, but watchful Trudy staring at her and shook her head. Neither of the Willows had any experience on the wrong side of the law; consequently, when it came for them, Dave caved and Sara treated it like something to be sidestepped, tricked. The law was something to be called upon when needed and demonstrated against when not; until they saw Trudy's expression, they never had any sense that a functioning legal system's principal attribute was neither indifference, brutality, nor corruption, but inexorability.

"Do you ever shut the fuck up?" Sara spat. "They didn't give a name, you imbecile. Just don't say anything else." She looked down at the table, picking at imaginary crumbs. "Stupid, weak, fucking, gutless. I knew you couldn't do this," she muttered.

Dave exhaled roughly, shook his head, put his bottle gently on the table, laid the rolled-up label next to it, leaned over, and backhanded his wife across the mouth. She emitted an almost canine yelp, and an arc of phlegm and blood shot onto the table as she fell backward in her chair and slammed her head against the door frame.

Dave stood up calmly, with a vacant, determined look in his eyes, but as soon as he made a move toward his wife Trudy took her gun—an archaic but reliable snub-nosed Dan Wesson .22—out of her purse and jammed it into Dave's side. He collapsed into the chair with his head in his hands.

"Jim, go get some ice from the freezer and bring it to Sara. There's a towel over the oven rail. You, sit right there and put your hands flat on the table."

By the time Jim had whacked some ice free of the tray and wrapped it up, Sara was next to her husband at the table, her arms crossed and her split lower lip already starting to swell. Neither she nor Dave looked at Jim, Trudy, or each other; Dave stared at the table while Sara, smirking, looked over Jim's head.

"Does she need stitches?" Dave asked, still not looking up.

"No. I don't think so," said Trudy. "Do you?"

Sara shook her head balefully.

"I'm . . . I'm sorry. I've never done anything like that." He spoke just above a whisper and now stared up at Trudy with watery eyes, pleading for her to believe him. "I'm not a wife beater or anything. I just . . . I don't know why I did that."

"I don't care," Trudy said brusquely.

"Of course you don't," Sara snapped. "Nobody cares. There are rivers drying up; have another beer. Wars everywhere; here's another credit card; buy an SUV. Gertrude, I'd love to know: how does it feel to work for war criminals?"

Trudy stayed silent, holding Sara's gaze until she looked away. "Would you like to know who I work for, Sara? Dave? I do IIE on smuggling and white-collar crime. That means Intelligence, Investigation, and Enforcement. It's a quiet division of Homeland Security. And at this moment, I am the nicest person you are ever likely to meet again."

Dave and Sara did not look convinced.

"Now, Dave, you said that Jim was supposed to meet more people. This wasn't just a statement of optimism; you seemed to know, roughly at least, how many more. A few, you said. How did you know?" Dave stayed quiet. She relaxed her posture and smiled. "How did you know? How many people was he supposed to meet?"

Still nothing. "Look, you can talk to me, and I can arrange for you to come home with whatever goodwill you generate here, or you can talk to the Russians. They're curious, too. Sara, you got depressed by life in a remodeled apartment in central Moscow. Can you imagine spending the next five decades in a Russian prison?"

"We didn't do anything wrong," she whined.

"Good," said Trudy brightly. "That's good. Maybe this is just a misunderstanding, then. It wouldn't be the first time. But you need to tell me about it. Dave, how did you know Jim was supposed to meet someone else? How many people was he supposed to see?"

"Eight," said Dave, throwing his head back and staring helplessly up at the ceiling. From the vent running the length of the room there came a hiss, followed by a blast of hot air. For all their fearsome reputation, Moscow winters aren't cold; they're stifling. The heat is still controlled centrally, for the entire city; it is turned on too late in the season (usually after a few little old ladies living alone freeze to death) and is shut off too late (to show how much the mayor cares). "I was told to expect eight interviews."

"Do you mind if I open a window?" Sara asked, not waiting for Trudy's response before she stood up.

Trudy gestured her back into the chair with her gun. "I mind. If you'd like to go outside, I'm happy to take you, but we have to finish here first. Dave?"

He shook his head. Trudy sweetened again. "Come on, Dave. Please. Who do you know in the army?"

"The army? Our neighbors back home have a son in the marines."

"The Russian army, Dave. The one you've sent Jim to talk to."

"Who do I know in the *Russian* army? Nobody. Not a soul."

Trudy let a look of puzzlement float across her face. She gave a half-turn to Jim before thinking better of it. "So who told Jim where to go?"

"The people he met did. I had nothing to do with that."

"You were just supposed to start him."

"Right."

"And collect the transcripts."

"I read all the transcripts as a matter of course, yes."

"You know what I'm asking, and it's tiresome asking the same thing over and over. Like I said before, we have you. I'm sure the Russians would like to chat with you, too, but we'd like to keep you. You can tell me now or tell the Russian investigators in an hour."

"Like there's a fucking difference," Sara mumbled.

"I'm sorry you see it that way." Trudy stood up, the gun still in her hand, neither pointed at nor away from Dave and Sara. With her other hand she took her phone from her purse and was about to start dialing when Dave emitted a long, self-pitying sigh.

"Mr. Vorov," Dave whimpered, sliding down in his chair and letting his head loll off to one side, limp on his neck, looking at nobody. "Anatoly Vorov."

Trudy and Jim looked at each other. Each had heard the name before, but Jim couldn't quite place it. "Anatoly Vorov the economist?" Trudy asked dubiously. That did it: Jim remembered Ian's GOV dinner—Golovna, Orsonov, Vorov.

Dave nodded, his head in his hands. Trudy held the pen above her paper, poised, but wrote nothing. She looked at Dave dubiously.

"You are telling me that Anatoly Vorov, who has visited with the president, who's coming here to receive an award . . . when? . . . this week, the vocal opponent of the Kremlin, told you where to send this kid here?"

Dave nodded again. He was sobbing quietly, soft animal noises that bobbed his head up and down. "Jesus Christ, what did I do? What did I . . ."

"Will you just shut up. For once, just be quiet! Stop whining about everything," Sara shouted at her husband. She turned to Trudy. "Yes, Anatoly Vorov. Your dinner guest, right?"

"That's right. But he's . . ."

"A normal American professor? A writer, a thinker?" Sara interrupted. "Don't insult him. He's not normal; he's better than that. Anatoly Vorov is doing something good for the world. We're helping him. At least he's not shuffling papers at the embassy as part of the war effort."

"He must be very impressive."

"I guess to some people, decency and concern for other people and the world we leave our children is rare enough to be impressive."

"And what you've been doing is decent?"

"What have we been doing?"

Trudy opened her mouth to speak, then closed it again, squinting slightly and saying nothing. She didn't actually know what they had been doing. A triumphant smile quivered around the corners of Sara's mouth. She had been worrying the towel that had once held ice, clenching it in her fist, rolling it back and forth: now it was just a wet rag. Sara let it drop to the ground. The heater stopped hissing, and almost immediately, the temperature dropped. It was eleven p.m. Heat went off between eleven and six the next morning. All decent citizens should be asleep—under the covers—at those hours; unsavory elements who chose to remain awake at their fellow citizens' expense had no right to expect their fellow citizens to keep them comfortable.

"Falsifying research, in the first place," Trudy hazarded.

"I never would have published that," Dave said sternly, wagging his finger.

"No? And what would you have told Jim when he saw that all of this research, that you said was so impressive, that you encouraged him to do, didn't make the final report?"

Neither of them said anything. Dave picked up his beer but Trudy took it out of his hand and set it out of his reach.

"I see," she said quietly. "There wouldn't have been a Jim, would there?"

"How can you ask that?" Dave demanded, slapping the table. "How the hell can you sit here in our house and ask that? Who do you think we are? We're not Russians; we don't just kill people we disagree with."

"Dave, fuck off," Jim said, standing up from the table. "Moral superiority doesn't suit you."

"Okay, let's calm down, both of you." Trudy extended her hands across the table and gestured Jim back into his seat. "Sara? Would there have been a Jim?"

"You don't understand." She shook her head slowly, a superior little smile on her lips as she looked over Trudy's head and out the window. In the apartment across the street a young woman stood at the stove, stirring a pot. She brought the spoon to her mouth, nodded, and brought it off the stove and into the next room, where a man and two boys waited, forks clenched in fists, singing and beating them on the table in unison. The man reached over and bopped the youngest one on the head with the fork, then leaned his head over the table to get the same treatment in return.

"Maybe not. Maybe I don't. But look, I need to write something down for my bosses. Why don't you try to explain it to me?"

Nobody said anything.

"Who was Jim talking to? What was Anatoly Vorov getting from you? What were you getting from him?"

Still nothing.

A curtain dropped over Trudy; her polite demeanor vanished. "Either the two of you start talking, or I'm leaving. Do you understand? The Russians are salivating at the prospect of having two Americans, do-gooders, meddlers, in custody. Is this getting through to either of you, or do you think your noble intentions will protect you? Do you have any idea how much they hate people like Anatoly Vorov, and anyone who works for him? I don't care whether you talk to me or not. Tomorrow I'll still have a job, and I can spend my next holiday out in California. What about you? You know where you'll be? Do you know, Dave, what they do . . ."

"We didn't do anything wrong!" he shouted. "We just . . . we just directed."

"What do you mean by that?" Trudy asked.

"All we did was help people get out. Help people who wanted to leave, leave. That's it."

Trudy shook her head, her expression still stern. "Not good enough, I'm afraid. You tell me everything—and that's start to finish, nothing left out—and we'll do what we can for you. But to do that effectively, we need to know details. Do you understand? We can't get caught stupid. So, if you want to dig your heels in, I'm the wrong person to talk to.

You can try it with the Russians. But if you want to start at the beginning, I am, as they say, all ears."

Dave ran his hands down his face like a Muslim preparing for prayer. He nodded once, twice, to himself, then removed his glasses and pressed his fingers into his eyes. When he put them back on, he stared at Trudy with the lively reddish gaze of a rabbit. "Last week, the whole staff goes to The Pilot. Jim comes in late the next day, not the first time. He comes into my office and says he met this girl. Her grandfather was a survivor; should he talk to him. I say yes. Of course; what else would I say. I go to lunch that day and I get a call from Tolya . . ."

"Who you knew how?"

"We met him back home, maybe five . . . no, seven years ago. There are a few Russian societies in Berkeley and the Bay Area. He was at SF State then; I think he's at Stanford now. Anyway, these societies attract a mixture of grad students, academics, reporters, lonely immigrants. Tolya used to buy us all dinner once every couple of months, whenever he was in town, at Shinok Kabudok, this Ukrainian place on Telegraph Road."

"Just out of the goodness of his heart?"

"Yes, in fact, I think so." Dave's voice took on a wounded cast. "Is that so hard for you to understand? He was a long way from home and he liked speaking his own language." He picked up the label and started folding and unfolding it again.

"So a few weeks ago, I'm on my way to my Armenian vegetable guy, and Tolya calls. He says he's coming over to Moscow; he'd love to see us. We talk about work. He asks how everything's going. I tell him our grant came through and we hired this new guy, a Russian American, speaks well. He's interested: starts asking questions. Is he married? Does he have a lot of friends? Is he social? Political? Quiet? I ask why; he says he's just curious, then he changes the subject.

"Then a week or so later he calls and says he's just heard about Jim. He found a survivor. I ask him how he knows and he doesn't say. Tolya says he'll find more. Be sure you keep him interested, he says. I ask how he knows again. He doesn't say anything. He says he wants to see these interviews when Jim's done. I say no"—Dave wagged his finger again, eager to demonstrate his fealty to principle—"I say, Tolya, that's against rules; we can't have anyone influencing what we write; we are an independent body interested only in the truth.

"He says, well, are you interested in helping people, too? Living people? And I remember this, because he said is it more important to you to help living people who need help, or to write about the dead. I said what do you mean. He says to just give him the transcripts of Jim's interviews. He needs to know what they say. I ask why. He says it will help certain people who need it. Certain older Russians, poor people who can't emigrate under normal channels because they're old and poor, this will help them get out. They'll get medical attention in Europe, be reunited with their families. I'll give them something to live on. But you need to get me those transcripts. And you need to decide what's more important to you: the living or the dead. The living or the dead." Dave sighed and pushed his glasses up on his face. He pulled his lips into a grimace. "The living, of course. Always the living."

Trudy shook her head. "You didn't think . . . Never mind. Who are these people that you helped?"

"They served in the army," Sara said. Dave's head whipped around in shock; clearly, he didn't know that Sara had ever talked to Vorov. "And because of what they know, the Russians won't let them leave. Yes, David, Tolya and I spoke. He was always . . . he was a gentleman. Always." Dave collapsed in his seat as though someone had removed his spine. Sara giggled.

"So that's why you did all of this," Trudy said. "To help people."

"Yes."

"Not for money."

Too quickly, Sara said, "Of course not."

"So you weren't paid at all."

Neither of them said anything. Trudy shook her head, slowly looking from one to the other. "The first thing we're going to do is run a check on every bank account in the United States with the last name Willow on it. We'll run down every family connection you have."

"Be our guest," said Sara.

"Then we'll move to Western Europe. Then we'll try here. And I'm thinking we still won't find anything."

"You won't. Because we weren't paid anything."

"And by then," said Trudy, leaning back in her chair and moving into full-reverie mode, "we'll have given your names and information to the Russians. You'll be safe at home, of course, because I'll have kept my promise to get you there, and you will, of course, have given me your complete and honest testimony. Just to be sure, though, the Russians will start checking into offshore banks. Switzerland, Grand Cayman, Liechtenstein. And you still won't care, right? Because a prominent economist promised you that your money would be safe. Anonymous. Whatever happened—even if the unthinkable happened—your money couldn't be touched or traced, because it went someplace with ironclad bank secrecy. Only here's the thing: there's the kind of information we can legally obtain, and then there's the kind we can just obtain. The Russians are great at that second one, when they need to be. Two decades of capital flight and high-resource prices have given them great influence in tiny little tax havens. You know what would happen if a few select members of the Russian government, or some close businessmen friends of the government, were to ask, say, Bermuda or Panama to either trace all deposits, withdrawals, and transfers to Anatoly Vorov's known ISPs or they'd move their billions somewhere else? Do you know how quickly they'd get that information? The country would deny it, of course, and it wouldn't hold up in court here on its own, but we could work backward easily enough. And if we did, I promise you we'd send you back here. My right hand to God, we'd find someone worthwhile to exchange you for.

"Now, one last time, before you make me find out for myself: were you paid at all?"

"Yes, of course, we were paid. We were paid," Dave called out from way down in his seat.

"How much?"

"Tolya promised us two hundred thousand dollars."

"Promised you? So you haven't been paid anything?"

Sara cut a quick warning glance at Dave. Trudy caught it. "David," Trudy said, "if you make us check, I won't be happy. Have you been paid?"

"He gave us twenty thousand dollars."

"When were you supposed to get the rest?"

"When he got home."

"What bank?"

"First National of Montserrat."

"Wow. You guys made out well."

"We fucking deserved it," Sara said indignantly. "You can't say we didn't. Dave gave up a chair at Berkeley to come here. I gave up my family. We gave our lives for this shithole."

"So why didn't you go back? If you hated it so much, why didn't you just go home?"

"And say what? Say we made a mistake?" Sara's voice rose and grew shriller; her hand gestures became more violent and her eyes widened as she considered the prospect of social and professional stagnation, ostracism, error. "And tell people what? Let's go back where we were, with our hats in our hands, please please please take us back? No, thank you. We took this job because we thought it would move us forward. We got here and found out everyone forgot about us. We had to get *something* out of it." She licked her finger and rubbed hard at a spot on the table. "That money was ours," she said quietly, certainly. "We worked for it. We deserved it. So it's 'illegal.' " She made finger quotes in the air and rolled her eyes. "Everything else here is, too. If they won't care—if nobody cares—why should we?"

"Do you mind if I interrupt?" Jim asked. "There's something I don't understand."

"Now, Jim?" Trudy asked.

"Not you. Them." He pointed to the Willows. Trudy looked dubious but nodded warily. "Why me? I mean, why did you have to send me out at all? Why didn't Vorov just tell you where to go? Why didn't he go himself?"

"Vorov couldn't go," Trudy said dismissively, writing in her notebook and not even looking up. "He's the front, right? The straight man. We love him; we're giving him rubber chicken in library paste at an embassy dinner. So the Russians hate him. He starts snooping around himself, the whole thing collapses. Right?"

Dave and Sara sat at the table, across from each other but looking off in opposite directions. Neither of them acknowledged the question.

"Right," Trudy answered. "But I am curious: why Jim? Why didn't one of you just go?"

They remained silent.

"I'll tell you one more time: answer for me or answer for them."

Dave lifted his head, stared off into the distance, and scratched his beard, but still said nothing. It was Sara who broke the silence with a sharp, vicious chuckle.

"Tell them, honey." Dave slammed the table with his fist and looked like he was about to jump across the table until Trudy leveled the gun at him. Sara shook her head, cutting Dave a look that expressed a degree of contempt produced only by long, unwilling, dysfunctional familiarity.

"He just couldn't do it," she hissed. "He was scared." Then she started laughing—not contemptuously like before, but with real venom and vigor. Jim looked at her with alarm, and even Trudy appeared nervous. Her cackle sounded like it had been building for a long time. That, combined with Dave's punch earlier, made him feel almost sorry for her. Almost.

"He told Tolya he would do it, but he can't lie; he can't talk to anyone who doesn't have at least a master's. Except me, of course, who he made drop out to work while he finished his doctorate. He told Tolya he would do it. Dave *begged* Tolya to let him go. You might not think it to look at him, but he takes his manliness seriously. He has to run things.

"So Tolya tested him one day. He sent him out to Yugo-Zapadnaya—you don't mind if I tell this, do you, honey?—on a fake interview, and paid a few low-level cops to scare him a little. Not to arrest him or shoot him or anything like that: just to intimidate him, so Tolya could see whether Dave could handle it."

"And?" Trudy asked.

"He couldn't. Dave cried when one of them pushed him down. *Cried.* I was in the car with Tolya, watching. Dave didn't know that until now, did you? I had to come, to persuade him: he had to be the one inside the office in contact with Tolya. We told Grynshtein we needed to hire someone else—someone fluent, this time; not another library-carrel Russian, but someone who could actually talk." By this time, tears were streaming down her face, though you would not say she was crying, really—there was no grief, only release and anger.

"Why not use someone already in the office?" Trudy asked. She kept her voice calm and her hand near, but not on, the gun.

"Yuri's too smart and Birgitta's too dumb," Dave said softly. "We needed someone new; someone who wouldn't get too used to life here, who didn't have too many connections. We actually interviewed a couple dozen people before we hired Jim. Good language skills, eager to please, not too many friends, unmarried. He was perfect."

"And after he had finished?" Trudy asked.

Dave opened his hands, palms up: what would you expect us to do with him? "I'm sorry," he mumbled.

Jim shook his head and walked over to the window. Let Trudy shoot him; he didn't care. He wrenched the window open and let the Moscow night air, moonlit, smoky, and clean, wash over him.

"So are you coming?" Trudy asked, standing up. She put the pad and paper in her purse but kept the gun in her hand. You can join me now or take your chances with them later. Your choice, but you need to decide right now."

Both of them stood up slowly, as though pulled, and in the mixture of disbelief and contempt on Sara's face Jim saw them for what they were: not criminals or spies, but monsters, people who believed their intentions could justify anything, were all that mattered. Sara didn't say they did nothing wrong to make Trudy leave or mitigate punishment; she said it because she believed it. She was the sort of person who, in building a fire, could accidentally burn a house down and walk away pleased with herself at the warmth she had provided her neighbors.

"Good choice," Trudy said.

THE QUARTET WALKED from the apartment two by two, Dave and Sara in front, Trudy and Jim behind. A light snow—a fine silver dust that sparkled like cut diamonds in the yellow glow of the streetlamps—had started to fall. This late on a Sunday night they passed no pedestrians; even cars were infrequent in the little tangle of side streets that led from the apartment to Mina's car, a black Volga (no diplomatic plates, nothing at all identifying it as embassy-owned).

Trudy put a hand on Jim's chest as Mina held the back door open for Dave and Sara. "Listen, Jim, you did great up there. You have a real gift for silence."

"Thank you."

"Shut up. We're taking them in, and quickly, too. What you're going to do is go back to your apartment and pack your things. Also quickly."

"No escort?"

"No, Jim. No escort." She darted her eyes up and down the street, and for a moment something akin to sympathy flickered across her face. "I'm sorry, Jim. I don't like it either, but we came lean and quietly, and we're leaving that way, too. They go in first, then you. I figure they don't want to come with me but you need to. Less risk of an escape that way. We'll drive you home, but if I send Gramm or Joseph upstairs with you you'll be worse off than if you went alone, right? Just relax, and be efficient. You know the saying 'Go slowly; we're in a hurry?' No? Good. Then you're going to come to the embassy, ring the bell around back, and we're going to get you home. We should have a temporary diplomatic passport waiting for you back at the embassy."

She held open the front door and gestured for him to climb in. She opened the back door for the Willows and watched them slide all the way over. When she was satisfied, she glanced up and down the empty street, got in, and told Mina to go.

"Be quick and careful inside," Trudy said. "No more than fifteen minutes at home. And I don't want you hailing cabs, either: you take the Metro and keep your wits about you. Ninety minutes is plenty of time."

"What if it isn't?"

"I wouldn't worry about that, Jim." Trudy sensed Jim's nerves, and gave something very close to a gallows laugh. Jim couldn't help noticing how hard she swallowed. "If something happens to you between the time you leave this car and the time you reach your building, it'll happen to us, too."

## 19

## RODION LISITSOV

HE JUMPED WHEN SHE KNOCKED on the door. He had told her repeatedly to knock gently if the door was closed: it meant he was working, and his work was often delicate, requiring calm and precision. If a loud noise—like one of her knocks, for instance: seven sharp raps in machine-gun succession on the thin, hollow door—made him jump, everything would be ruined. What he did not tell her was that he had developed safety measures: using two hands, one to steady the other, for the most precise parts of the job. What he did not tell himself, even in private, even in his own mind, was that he had developed this habit not just as a guard against sudden noises but to protect against the old man's palsy—intention tremors, his doctor called them, though there was nothing intentional about them—that had started to wrack his hands and lips. Consequently, when she knocked this time he gave a start but his hands remained steady.

"Yes!" he barked.

She opened the door, peering around the frame with that indulgent look he had come to loathe: it implied the vast distance between what he used to be and what he had become. "I am going to the market," she said. "Will you be home this evening for dinner?"

"What is the date?" he asked, not looking up from his work.

"The date? February thirteenth, is it not?"

He sighed heavily, glaring up at her from beneath a glowering front. "It is indeed," he growled. "Two days before the feast of the Meeting of our Lord."

"Ah. So you are leaving tonight, are you?"

He nodded.

"You need something to eat on the journey."

"This is a meatless week."

"Understood." She looked at him steadily, admiringly. He felt her eyes on him. He tried to keep his expression fixed, but it didn't work: a reluctant smile broke through and his eyes softened.

"Nearly finished," he said proudly.

"What is it?"

"Ach. What kind of daughter have I raised? She does not know the holy feast days, she does not respect a father's wishes for calm and privacy, and she cannot even recognize the instruments that protected her country and her freedom."

She walked over to his desk just as he finished affixing the top of the conning tower. "It looks like a big boat to me," she said with a mischievous smile, kissing him on the top of his head.

He shooed her away with operatic, pop-eyed, exaggerated exasperation. "This is a *ship*, not a *boat*. The *Voroshilov*. It was the second *Kirov* class cruiser we built, and it defended Sebastopol. If it were not for this ship, your mother would have fallen into the hands of the Germans. Then where would you have been?"

"Mother was from Kherson, not Crimea."

"Don't you think I know where your mother was from? Do you ever think I will be so old to forget that? She was in Kherson: correct. The Germans were in Odessa, and if it were not for this *boat*, as you call it, they would have taken Crimea. Kherson was between the two. It was undefended. So."

"The boat goes with the rest of them?"

"It will. On the top." He gestured to a display case filled with model ships that lined the entire wall of the room. There was only one empty space where the *Voroshilov* could go. "Next to the *Molotov*."

"And then you're finished. So sad."

"Finished with our navy, yes. Then comes the British, the Germans, and the Americans."

"Another ten years?"

"At least. Probably twenty." He winked as he rose and wiped his hands on a towel. "I must pack. You can make something for me before you go?"

"Of course." She hesitated meaningfully, one hand on the doorway and her mouth partly open, a gesture she took from her mother: it meant she had something to say but did not know how to begin.

"Masha, what is it?"

"There was someone outside again when I came home."

"So?"

"He asked for you."

"Uniform or suit?"

"Suit."

"Russian?"

"Yes."

"What did he want?"

"To speak to you. I told him you were not at home. He pressed. I told him you were receiving no visitors."

"Yes, of course he pressed," he said quietly. He unlocked the display case and began buffing the shelf where the ship would sit. "He said it would be to my advantage—no, one moment: my *material* advantage— or in keeping with my familial duty, my duty as a man, to talk to him. They always say it would be either my duty or to my advantage. How do they know what my advantage is?"

"Not yours," she said, a frayed edge of worry in her voice. "This time he said it was for Katya."

"What for Katya?"

"A job reading the news, a salary of two million rubles, a car, a driver, an apartment in . . ."

"Enough!" His voice sharpened, but remained quiet. He retrieved the ship from the desk and laid it gently next to the *Kirov*. Enough already. I don't want to hear any more."

"But should you not just talk with him, for her sake now, not for yours? He said all you had to do was talk, and she would have the job."

"And you believe him? You believe any of these people? They are salesmen; they are not honest." He crossed the room and put his small, delicate hands on his daughter's shoulders, looking into her eyes evenly. "I am finished. Do you understand? My work is done. Now, if you would, please, make me a small something for the train, without meat. I leave in twenty-seven minutes."


HE HAD GROWN used to them, and consequently brushed them away with neither pity nor hope. Only recently had they started to approach Masha, though. She was born later and, because of his work, always had a comfortable life, which she missed and wanted back. Materially, of course, not only were they not worse off, they were better: they retained their apartment, and now had two televisions (both color), a personal computer (Katya could spend hours reading foreign newspapers), a (Korean, shiny) stereo system, and all the food and clothes they needed. True, they lost their driver and had to trade down dachas; they vacationed in Sochi every other year rather than Tallinn or Bulgaria every summer; but plenty of people had fallen further. Between what Masha made as a doctor's receptionist, Katya's occasional supplements from acting jobs, his pension, and the occasional loan or favor, they got by. What they no longer had—what Masha wanted and could not admit she wanted—was the comparative advantage: she did not want to be rich; she wanted to be richer, if not in money than in status. Far from considering the solicitations a nuisance, she liked them: she liked being asked for things; she hated doing the asking.

The pride of a cosseted childhood: it never faded. Katya barely remembered, of course, and even if she did, well, not everyone had that nature. It was well known that goodness skipped a generation: darling sweet Katya reminded him of his wife, while ambitious and impatient Masha, alas, reminded him only of himself. He kissed her good-bye anyway, then crossed the apartment's threshold, turned to face the icon, crossed himself three times (with three fingers, of course), then put his hat on and set off for the train.

He picked them out across the courtyard. They sat in one of those new, tanklike cars that suddenly were everywhere; the one in the back put on his hat at a smart angle and prepared to open the door. He suddenly turned around and went through the back entrance.

He neither knew nor wanted to know who they were. They and their kind had been after him for a decade, ever since Biopreparat had closed—or transformed, or gone under, or expanded, or done whatever it did: ever since *his* Biopreparat had closed. At first he listened to their offers and took the time to explain to each one of them: he worked for one country, one cause, and now that was gone. He was done. Did he feel sad? Did he feel betrayed? Did he feel angry? Of course: so did millions of his countrymen. Was he not proud of his work? Again, of course: so was his neighbor, a pipe fitter and a Hero of Soviet Labor. Did he not crave new challenges, new renown? No. He had somehow managed to eke out a living pension from the thieves busy selling their country piece by piece to the highest bidder. That pension somehow continued to be honored, even augmented, however occasionally and irregularly. He had lost a wife; his daughter had lost a husband; he wanted nothing but family, quiet, and the comforts of church—ritual, peace, devotion, brotherhood—like he had out east when he was a boy.

It had long stopped being worth explaining to them. To see the incomprehension in their eyes when he declined promises of wealth and fame saddened him too deeply. True, appealing to Katya, and to him on Katya's behalf, was clever. He won't pretend he didn't feel his heart quiver at the warm breath of temptation. But it was also devious. Katya would have to make her own way, as he had made his and his wife had made hers.

As he walked out of the back archway onto Pyatnitskaya, a sharp-eyed young *muzhik* in a leather jacket whistled, put out his cigarette, and saluted ironically. "How about a lift, Grandfather?" he asked, in a thick, honking Moscow accent. He pointed to a new lime-green Skoda. "Good price, top speed, wherever you like."

He shook his head and headed off in the opposite direction. The pleasure of walking through Novokuznetskaya's tangle of narrow streets on a snowy day: was anything better? He inhaled the city's rough, industrial/piney scent, following the street's curve as it took him past a children's playground dotted with smiling wooden gnomes, past a frosted apartment building the color of beaten eggs, past a courtyard where an auto-repair shop sat between an instrument restorer and the Church of St. Methodius the Revealer, whose roof was a riot of scallops and crenellations, icons both hollow-eyed and rejoicing, blood vermilions and spring-forest greens, summer-sun golds and summer-sky blues. Was any city as nakedly human? Did any other city display our capacity for beauty and brutality in such harrowing, thrilling proximity? Someday he knew he would be unable to walk through it, but until then he would never ride. He would fade but it would not; he would be whisked to his grave through a kaleidoscope; as a blind old bedridden man this visible world would disappear, leaving nothing but color, color, color, and the memory of Katya on his lap and snow on his tongue.

HE LEFT HIMSELF ENOUGH TIME for his Belorussky Vokzal ritual. He went around to the back of the station, away from the crowds. By some unspoken urban arrangement, it was understood that this was where they slept it off. Street whores—women, girls, and boys—were on the east side; drugs of unreliable quality you could buy to the west. The front entrance was for straight begging. The back was where they came afterward.

He walked slowly without strolling; he looked over the unconscious masses without staring; he kept his expression unthreatening but not soft. Huddled in a crook between a column and a service door was a grime-streaked old woman, dead to the world, head back, mouth open, body sexless and ruined, face hairy, teeth blackened and mostly gone. Bodily extrusions crusted the edge of her headscarf closest to her mouth. She snored deeply but slept with the coiled rigidity of the street-sleeper.

Silently, he took the herring and beet salad that Masha had made out of his satchel, and leaned down to tuck it into the bend of her arm. He placed it there as securely as he could without waking her. As he straightened up he felt a scratch, then a prick where his trousers rode up, exposing a line of sock above his boots. Three seconds later the world shut on him like an eye: without color.

# 20

JIM TURNED HIS COLLAR UP and walked quickly into his courtyard. It was snowing harder now; by tomorrow morning a few inches
would have piled up. The city looked silent, monochrome, almost neo-
lithic in size and architectural uniformity. The unnatural immensity of
Moscow's apartments, the violent crenellations of the Stalinist sky-
scrapers, and the fairy-tale onions atop gaudily colored churches, all
beneath a thickening blanket of snow, gave Moscow the improvised,
inchoate air of a dream.

Jim's pace across the courtyard quickened as he anticipated a good
half-hand of bourbon—it wouldn't do to leave that behind—to make
the packing easier. Just outside his entryway door, he slid on what he
assumed was a patch of ice. He braced himself against the snowy hand-
rail as his toe snagged on a package on the front step. Looking down,
he saw this wasn't a package: it was a person sprawled facedown in front
of the doorway. Jim thought it might have been a drunk who fell asleep
looking for someplace warm, but then he noticed the person's coat—
a dark wool coat, the same length and color as Jim's—was covered in a
thin layer of snow, as was his hair, and the bluish-gray skin on the back
of his neck. Jim recognized him; he lived in the building, and they knew
each other by sight, just to nod to as they passed in the courtyard. Leading away from his head, like a final, unfinished thought, was a comma
of blood and brain.

Jim staggered back with horror, and immediately slunk into the courtyard's shadows, the sounds of his breathing and his heartbeat pounding, deafening. He shifted positions and the whoosh of his coat against his jeans sounded like a jet soaring across the courtyard. Still, he was alone, thank God. The quartet of drinkers who spent their evenings sitting on the hood of a rusted-out old Lada Samara across the court- yard had gone inside to escape the snow. He looked up at the seven stories of apartment windows that surrounded him and saw lights, drawn curtains, but no faces.

He was about to turn around and head back to the car—there was nothing he really needed anyway—when he heard footsteps trudging through the archway, echoing as they drew closer. He drew farther back into the shadows, flush against the building, crouching behind a hap- hazardly parked blue Peugeot. The archway was the only escape route. He would either have to sprint past whoever was coming or knock him over; opening the apartment door required too much key-fiddling on the steps. He grabbed a jagged-edged length of rebar lying next to him on the asphalt. It already had what looked like dried blood and hair on one end. As the man's shadow fell forward into the courtyard, Jim tensed and prepared to spring.

Whoever it was came into the courtyard and made a hard right, turning in the opposite direction from Jim and his dead doppelgänger. Even from the back, he didn't look like a killer: he wore a long tan over- coat and a fur hat. He had a backpack slung over one shoulder, and he walked with a distracted gait, his head tilted upward, as if contemplat- ing higher things than a corpse in a courtyard. A scientist, Jim guessed, or maybe a music teacher, but hardly an assassin. He entered the build- ing without even a backward glance, and Jim stood up, unclenched his jaw, fists, shoulders, abdomen, thighs, calves, feet, and even his toes.

He had just turned around when the door burst open, sending Jim reeling backward in shock. Again, he tripped over the body, and righted himself into fighting position, when he saw he was preparing to batter Murat's mother, standing in the doorway holding two bags of garbage.

She looked at Jim in a fighting stance and gave the merest hint of an impression that she might have been thinking about smiling. She then looked down at the body, and hunched up her shoulders slightly, then let them drop. Whether that gesture connoted resignation, or indifference, or was a token of respect, Jim had no idea. She nodded at Jim, holding out the two bags of garbage and pointing toward the Dumpster in the center of the courtyard. When Jim hesitated, she clicked her tongue disapprovingly and thrust the bags at him again, this time betraying a hint of a fearsome scowl. He took the bags from her with a respectful nod of the head, which won him the slightest glint of gold tooth and a bemused crinkle at the corners of her eyes. No event in the world held the power to surprise her, or make her more than momentarily happy or glum. Jim thought she would get along swimmingly with Rosie and the Dooley matriarchs.

When he threw the trash into the bin, she clicked her tongue again and beckoned him over. Jim waited for her to speak, but she just stood, still and watchful, giving away absolutely nothing.

"I found him here," Jim finally said.

"You had better come upstairs."

"I think I should just leave."

She gave a short, mirthless laugh and fixed him with her beady black eyes. "Don't be stupid."

"I'm sorry. I don't know . . . I think that was supposed to be me." He pointed to the body.

"If God had willed you to die, you would have." She shrugged. "And if your enemies are mortal, then they are also *our* enemies, and we will fight them together. Come. Upstairs. We can talk there. You will be our guest."

"*DEAD?*" ASKED A SWEATY, balding little man in a suit. Jim sat at Murat's table, in his overheated, overcrowded apartment, as the mother proceeded to bury him beneath mountains of food and Murat tried to drown him in vodka. The room smelled like a Russian apartment on

Sunday night, awash in clouds of garlic, roasted meat, wet coats, tightly packed humanity, and cigarette smoke.

Inside the room sat Murat and eight of his cousins. All except the dapper little man filled the room with a brooding, minatory presence: aside from Murat, who kept Jim company at the small wooden dining table, and the bald little man in the suit, perched on the edge of a wooden chair, the men sat on pillows on the floor and against the wall, smoking, drinking, occasionally breaking the silence with a word or two unintelligible to Jim, and watching the American eat. Murat had introduced none of them to Jim by name, and none of them seemed inclined to introduce themselves.

The dapper little man peeled himself off the wall next to Murat's plasma TV and walked over to the window. As he reached for the curtain, Murat's mother, waddling over from the kitchen to ladle some more stewed rabbit onto Jim's already overflowing plate, hissed and clicked her tongue. Though she kept her head covered and eyes lowered, nobody doubted who ruled the room. She glanced subtly toward the cousin sitting closest to the window. He put a firm hand on the man's shoulders and led him away.

"Our *doctor*," explained Murat, exhaling vodka as his eyes kindled with pride. The doctor returned to his seat on the wooden chair. He appeared discomfited by the idea of a corpse on his aunt's doorstep; the other men in the room retained a lean, regal wildness, and an unsurprised intimacy with how the world ends.

"Really?" asked Jim deferentially, following the little man as he returned to his seat.

He nodded smugly, inclining his head in showy modesty. "Yes. And I shall tell you that by the end of the spring, I may have the honor of becoming the head of veterinary medicine at the Swedish Feline and Canine Clinic. We see to the safety and well-being of pets belonging to all of the most important diplomats and dignitaries resident in Moscow."

"The pervert sticks his fingers up kitten asses!" blurted one of the older cousins from the other end of the couch. He was wreathed in blankets, vodka fumes, and good spirits. Murat hissed for his silence, but he did so with his face turned toward Jim so the cousin couldn't see him smiling.

Once the cousins fell to talking and smoking among themselves, Murat refilled Jim's glass and pushed a plate of what looked like thinly sliced, gray-maroon hockey pucks toward him.

Jim obediently slipped some onto his plate and, under Murat's watchful eye, shoved a piece in his mouth. It tasted strong, gamy, peppery: not disagreeable, but it filmed his mouth unpleasantly as it went down.

"Smoked mare," Murat said proudly. "Made by Fadlan himself."

Jim tried not to blanch as Murat lifted another three slices onto his plate and refilled his glass.

"So," Murat said, leaning in confidentially and breathing horse and booze over Jim's food. "Did you know him?"

"No. I talked with him once. He lived here. I saw him in the courtyard every so often."

"Yes," Murat agreed. From the way he nodded Jim understood he was asking not to find out the answers himself but to see what Jim knew. "He had a wife, and two young children. One of the Old Families."

"Was he? How old?"

Murat poured more vodka and shrugged. "Brezhnev, I would guess. His father's friend lived in this apartment before we *inherited* it," he said, putting a bright-eyed irony on the word. *Inherited*, in this case, likely meant wheedled or connived or won or accepted as payment on a debt. It did not mean bought, because Murat took great pride in telling Jim the price of everything he bought—the higher the better—and it self-evidently did not mean rented or swapped or anything so aboveboard. "His miserable father spat on us. Hated us. Dogs, blackasses, capitalists, he called us. Always wore a Party pin. The son I don't know. He did not seem, and I say *seem*, like his father. And his children were just children. But such people . . ." He exhaled sharply with his teeth set against his lip and waved his hand.

"So." He bore down further on Jim, as behind him two of the cousins took up a game involving playing cards, knives, and a length of muslin. "You *do* know *why* he was killed, Mother said."

Jim saw the knives come out and he swallowed hard. It hadn't occurred to him until now to consider as a whole the mother's calm, her invitation, Murat's intense interest, the cousins unsheathing their knives, the complete absence of anybody else from the courtyard, stairwell, or hallways of the building, and, of course, Murat's reputation. Without meaning to, he flitted his eyes around the room and behind him: Murat's mother blocked the door, and four more of the cousins drew their knives and cloths. For the second time that night, he tensed and prepared to run: he knew his chances were small against eight armed men, but he wouldn't sit still for the slaughter.

Murat must have seen and sized up Jim's reaction: just as he coiled, Murat banged his fist against the table and shouted something to his cousins in an unfamiliar language. They sheathed their knives and looked abashed, shuffling and staring down. "I told them they frightened our guest," Murat said, laying a giant meat-hook hand on Jim's forearm. "And here you are our guest, and I ask you these questions as a guest. Do you understand?"

Jim nodded.

"So. Speak. Fully and freely."

Jim, figuring he was giving either his last words or (he hoped) a plea for help, spoke less than fully and more ardently than freely. He omitted the meeting with Trudy and referred to Mina only as "an American friend," figuring their antistatist paranoia would fill in the rest. When he mentioned the Interior Ministry car, derisive snorts, murmurs, and tongue-clicks echoed around the room.

The youngest of the cousins, with a linty little mustache only accentuating the baby fat still left on his cheeks and chin, pulled his face into an exaggerated scowl and barked something at Murat. When Murat turned to glare at the kid, though, the scowl melted, and he sank back into his seat, his eyes wide and almost liquid, pleading apology.

"Rekhmat said we should kill someone from the ministry in return. And this I would very much wish to do," he said, placing a hand on his heart to express his sincerity, "but this would be no good. We would lose. You, maybe not. You have a passport to America. We do not. You can go home, and *poof!* Nobody bothers you."

Jim laughed along with Murat's teasing, until something struck him. "Anatoly Vorov," he said out loud, silencing their laughter. It was a shot in the dim light, but not entirely dark: both Murat's clan and Vorov appeared to be smugglers in Moscow. It wasn't entirely inconceivable that they knew each other. Murat glanced over Jim at a lean older man propped against the wall. "Do you know Anatoly Vorov?" Jim asked again.

"We know friend Tolya well," Murat said. "He was . . ."

Just then Jim heard a banging across the hall as his cell phone started ringing. He quickly turned it to vibrate and looked through the peephole: Mina was pounding on his door with an open hand. She must have followed him home. Even from this view, he could see her glare, the set of her jaw, her animal tenseness. She stopped pounding and her hand shot up to her face. Was she crying? Jim opened his mouth to say her name as he reached for the doorknob, but something kept him from turning it.

It occurred to him that he was, in this apartment, as safe as he had ever been—and would ever be—in Moscow. Nobody knew where he was. He was the guest of eight armed men who took their hosting responsibilities seriously. He had no doubt that if he asked them to, they would take him to the embassy.

He also—at last and for once—had the opportunity to put things right instead of—again—running away. They knew Anatoly Vorov; he and Mina did not. This was his choice: open the door now and go home, leaving everything he had been chasing unresolved and letting other people clean up after him. This would leave him at their mercy, and, even worse, leave him constantly looking over his shoulder for Vorov, who was on his way to becoming every bit as American as he was.

Or he could talk with Murat and the cousins a little longer, and see if there wasn't something else he could do.

He knew what he wanted to do: he wanted to go home, forget all of this, ask Vivek for money to pay off the Sjindices, and start again. But he also remembered what Rosie's father, Ulm Dooley, a five-foot-three-inch fire hydrant of a man who owned and tended his bar in Hamden for almost fifty years, used to tell him. Ulm lost fights every now and then, but he never ran from them. One afternoon when Jim ran into Vilatzer's full steam because a few kids in his fourth-grade class played "Chase the Commie," Ulm sat him on the stool next to him and asked why he didn't stand up to them. Jim said there were three of them; he didn't think he was that brave. Ulm fixed him with his clear green eyes and drained his glass. "There's no need to *be* a brave man, you know. You only need to act like one."

"I will tell you what I mean," Murat said, pouring Jim more vodka and serving him a long, curved bone of lamb that looked suspiciously like a mandible. "Us, here, in this room, we are a family. We are also in *bizniss*"—he made an ironic face when he used the English word, lest Jim think he was talking about something legitimate—"and of course we work with other people, other people work with us, but everyone knows, because we take care of our family, all of us, that we will take care of them, too. Everything, you understand, is family, and family is every-thing. This is completely normal: you will find it with the Mukhtandov Boys, Baumanskaya Circus, Perekop Industries: all of them have at their center brothers, cousins, fathers, sons. A connection.

"Tolya Vorov, who does he have?" Resting an elbow on the table, Murat held up his hand, fingertips together, then spread them apart in a gesture of release. "Nobody. Money, of course, and with money you can buy what you need. But he has no friends, no allies. And rumor is he can no longer do business in Russia."

"Why not?"

"His *krysha* is no good. This is just what I heard last week. He bought a dacha, we hear, in Zavodsk, south of Donetsk. Very smart."

"Why there? And why smart?"

Murat scratched his beard and tilted his head philosophically. "Zavodsk is a village of coal and shit. But coal is under the ground, and there is less, always less, every year." He moved his hand down closer to the table to illustrate consistently declining coal. A pedagogical streak was emerging, even if Murat commanded attention as much by the presence of knives and guns as by his lecturing skills. "Less coal means more people out of work; more people out of work means more people to employ in other ways. Guards. Couriers. Muscle. This helps a man like Vorov. Also it helps men like us," he said with a wink and a modest incline of the head. "This is normal."

*Normalno:* Normal. Fine. A very Russian answer: the world is irredeemably fallen and the natural tendency of everything is to go wrong, but only a fool ever expects anything else, and I am no fool. In this case it meant Murat had seen this pattern elsewhere: it was the pattern of post-Soviet Russia. Former factory workers who enjoyed good booze and brawl on the weekends became full-time brawlers, and, as often as not, full-time boozers, too. Murat took out his knife and sliced off a tender curve of meat and soft tissue from the bone on Jim's plate, popping it in his mouth with relish.

"More important: Zavodsk is in Ukraine, but not really Ukraine. Most people in east Ukraine speak Russian, are Russian. This means Ukraine's government has no power there, not really. Vorov, we can say, is generous with people in his town. They protect him. Ukraine would have to send in the army, and even then . . ." Murat made a light fist facing down toward the table and sent his fingers outward, mimicking the sounds of explosions as he moved his hands up the table. His eyes glittered with delight, imagining the battles. "Why would they go? As long as Vorov makes no moves against them, why?"

"So why doesn't he just live in Russia?" Jim asked.

"Why should he? There he would always have to worry who to please, who to pay, who has power and who does not. No, from Zavodsk he can fly to Russia whenever he wants, without worrying. And perhaps Russia likes it better, too: if he does something that Europe, or your America, might complain about, they can say he lives in Ukraine. Do you want us to invade Ukraine? No? Then, *pfft*." He raised a fist, a thumb wedged between his index and middle fingers. "You know, two of our security boys used to work for him. Kyrgyz, of course."

"Why 'of course'?"

"He never hires Russians in Russia. They say he hires only Russians in foreign countries, but here? Never. Why? Because we"—with his finger he drew an imaginary circle around the room, ensuring that everyone's eyes were defiantly, proudly on Jim—"we are most expendable. If you have on the one hand a rich, Russian American businessman, and on the other some . . . I don't know . . . some Uzbek thug, or some Bashkir roughneck . . ."

"Or a Tatar warrior!" the young one shouted.

"Yes. Exactly." Murat smiled. "Or a Tatar warrior. Who will be helped? In this society, if protecting him he has his friends in the Interior Ministry, he will always win. And of course, if he makes his price right, we will always go along. He does—you must excuse me for saying this, because I mean no offense to you or your family—but he lives like an American. He smiles too much, he throws out too much money, he takes what he wants to take, he makes the price whatever he wants. With foreigners—*dark* foreigners, *low* foreigners, not Europeans—he can do this."

Murat's mother waddled in from the kitchen with yet another plate: a bowl of chopped eggplant, tomatoes, and what smelled like several heads of garlic. "A man without a family," she croaked, clicking her tongue disapprovingly as she walked back into the kitchen.

Lost neither on Jim nor, he feared, on anyone else in the room was Jim's own lack of a family. In most parts of the world, he would have been a father for well over a decade by now, but here he was, rattling around the planet alone like a marble in a kettle drum. Just as the lethal combination of vodka and self-pity threatened to overwhelm him, his phone vibrated in his pocket. He figured Mina was trying to find him, and he took the phone out intending to send her to voice mail again.

It wasn't Mina, though. It was in fact someone he had given up for gone.

"Hi there."

Jim heard outdoor sounds—cars, wind, maybe a train—in the background, but no voice. Then he heard crying. "Jim," said Katya between sobs. "Is it you?"

"Yes, it's me. It's me. What's wrong?" He suddenly was wide awake, reaching for his shoes.

"Grandfather never came home," she wept. "I've been waiting for his train for six hours, and he never came. Nobody knows where he is."

21

"I NEED TO GO," Jim said, after he hung up the phone.

"Go?" asked Murat, looking both dubious and amused. "Where will you go? Where can you go now?"

"Kaisa—Katerina, the one I told you about. Her grandfather is missing. She's at the train station."

"And you will just walk there? Yourself? With that—with him—downstairs?"

"Listen, I can't ask . . ." Jim cut himself off and thought better of his refusal. "I would be honored and pleased for any help you and your family would give me. If you will let me, can I hire you? As bodyguards?"

Murat translated for the family, who erupted in laughter. His mother hobbled out of the kitchen, her face mock-fierce, making a machine gun out of a rolling pin and mowing down her nephews. Murat clapped Jim on the back hard enough to make him cough, and poured him another drink.

"We are not for hiring," he said, laughing. "We are not that sort of family. We are only for ourselves and our friends. Do you understand? We are not Russians. They are our enemy, and they now are *your* enemy, too, so you are our friend. Besides"—his smile broadened and he pointed to the flat-screen TV and his DVDs—"we love your America."

The room broke out in shouts of "Skarfess!" and "El Kaponov!" and "Mek my day!" Not exactly Jim's America, but he wasn't about to break a favorable spell.

"If I cannot hire you, will you accept a gift? For your mother, and for your cousins' children."

Murat considered, stroking his beard, then nodded and slapped a fist on the table. He poured healthy measures of vodka all around and raised his glass. "To our children! To the future! And"—he looked at Jim significantly—"to the girls of California, who maybe one day, with the help of our American friend, I will make very, very happy! Death to the enemy!" A chorus all around: Death to the enemy! They drank.

WHEN THEY WALKED OUT the front door and into the courtyard, they had to step over the man's body. It hadn't been moved or disturbed; the snow lay a bit thicker over and around it. If it kept snowing, by morning it—he, Jim reminded himself: he—would hardly be noticeable until someone tripped over him. Fadlan grabbed Murat and Jim and stood a moment over the body. He lowered his head, ran his hands over his face and arms, then cupped his hands in front of his face and recited a prayer.

"He didn't deserve it," said Jim to both and neither of them when Fadlan finished.

"Perhaps not. But it was his time. Death is waiting for us everywhere; you cannot say 'I will go here, or here' to avoid it. Death is more clever than we are. Here, if you are tired, chew this."

He pulled out a glassine bag containing something that looked like wet mulch, and handed Jim a pinch. Jim started to hand it back; he preferred his drugs to start as corn or barley and end up as brown liquid. Murat pushed Jim's hand back toward him. "This is a gift. You must stay awake, so you will take it. Besides, I know you are not stupid enough to become addicted, and I will never give you any more after today, even if you ask. You put it here"—he opened his mouth and pointed to the inside of his cheek, behind what was left of his molars—"and you chew, chew, chew, and spit. If you swallow you will throw up, and if you throw up in Fadlan's car, maybe he will shoot you."

Murat laughed and clapped his hands together; Fadlan's expression remained as still as a statue's. Jim shrugged and put the mulch in his mouth. It tasted like tea, tobacco, and dust. "What is this?" Jim winced.

"A local herb, prepared by our doctor. Come."

"Murat, my debt . . ."

Murat hissed him into silence, and stood tall and severe. "We do not speak of such things. I said tonight you are our guest, and we are responsible for your safety. Besides," he whispered, a naughty glint in his eye, "anything we can do to fuck the Russians, we will do."

Fadlan pulled a pistol from his waistband and handed it to Jim with a wave of his hand. It had a rosewood-plated handle with an aluminum steel slide and frame; having never held a gun before, Jim was surprised at how heavy, smooth, and elegant it was.

"Sig P220," Murat said, wedging himself into his seat and locking the door behind him. Fadlan drove; Murat directed Jim into the backseat. "Nothing on top, you see, so it won't catch on anything. The best. Small and light, made for carrying inside your coat. You must take it. You can use it? Yes, of course you can: you're from America! Everybody has a gun!"

"I appreciate it, but I think we'd be better off if Fadlan or you held the gun."

Murat grinned and lifted his sweater. A larger model was tucked into his trousers. "I carry a .45 here," he said, then lifted his trouser leg to reveal an ankle holster. "And a .223 here."

He said something to Fadlan, who pulled open his long overcoat to reveal a submachine gun strapped tightly against his side.

Jim bobbed his head resignedly, and placed the gun as delicately as possible into the inside pocket of his jacket.

After about five minutes of chewing Murat's gift, whatever it was, kicked in: Jim could neither sit still nor stop grinding his teeth, and he experienced a wonderfully intense clearheadedness and a burst of energy. By the time they pulled into the vaguely pagodalike Yaroslavl Station, with its chameleonic green-brown-taupe-drab bricks and the temple roof above one door and church spire over another, the fatigue had fled from Jim's limbs. He got out to look for Katya, stopping to drool out a good mouthful of mulchy brown goo onto the snow at his feet.

Above the doors and beneath a huge gold hammer and sickle set into ornate black grillwork, a clock said 3:12 a.m. Raggedy survivors in various states of inebriation and chemical joy littered the parking lot and station entrance.

Katya appeared suddenly and from nowhere, laying a hand on his arm and whispering his name. Jim jumped three feet. Her face was tear-streaked, puffy, wracked, but as soon as Jim turned toward her a smile broke it, and she giggled.

"What's wrong with you?" she asked. "You look disgusting. Why are your teeth black?"

"Sorry," he said, wiping his mouth with his sleeve. "It's a sleep aid. Or a no-sleep aid, really. Are you all right? Where were you?"

"Between those parked cars." She pointed toward the center of the parking lot. "It was safer than the waiting room. And I had nobody to wait for." The tears came again.

"Okay, okay," Jim murmured, wrapping her up in his arms and walking her over to the car. "Okay, okay. What happened? Can you just tell me what happened? How long have you been here? Are you cold?"

"I am not cold. I have been pacing for six hours to keep warm. He was supposed to be here at eleven o'clock tonight, and he never came home. He was not on the train, so I . . ." A violent sob cut off the rest of the sentence. "I'm so sorry, Jim."

"For what?"

She threw her arms in circles. It was a desperate gesture, but, with her hands tucked into her long red parka and her carefully wrapped scarf losing its moorings and coming undone, also attractive, adorable enough so Jim had to fight the urge to take her in his arms and laugh. What was she sorry for? For all of it? For the train station? For Moscow? For Russia? For the whole broken world? "I made all of this happen. They said if I didn't they would take Grandfather, and if I did then they wouldn't, but I did and they still took him. They still took him."

"If you didn't do what? What did you do?"

"Find you. Send you to the man."

"What man?"

"Naumenko. The Sporting Palace man."

"Who is he?"

She shrugged. "How should I know? I never saw him."

"Wait: let's go back. Who wanted me to meet him? Who told you to do all of this?"

"I don't know. Some man in a suit. A rich man, he looked like, with blond hair like a movie star and a government pin on his jacket. In my acting class one day, my teacher keeps me after. My teacher is very famous, very respected, so of course, he wants to see me alone, I said yes." She must have caught Jim's dubious expression, because she smiled ruefully through her tears, shaking her head. "It isn't what you think. If I was a boy, then yes, but not me. He brings me into his office and says to this man, here is the one I told you about. He says to me I must listen to this man and do what he says, and then next season I will have a role onstage, featured, at Moscow Art Theatre. Then he leaves.

"The man says to me he hears I can speak English. Yes. He hears I can speak with accents. Also yes. And he hears also I can improvise, so I am the perfect person. And he smiles, but such a smile that you would see on a wolf. The smile makes me shiver, and I think I will leave, but he says he knows my grandfather. Before I ask how, he shows me pictures. Five people, from their passports. He says you must meet each of them, as if by accident. Try to get them interested, to get them to do what you want. I say this is not acting, really, and he says if you do it, no harm will come to your grandfather and you will be onstage next season."

"And if you don't?"

"This, Jim, he did not have to say. The opposite would be true."

"Who were the five people?"

"You were one. The others, to tell you the truth, I do not remember their names. Also Western, also single, also working at sort of small jobs."

"Hey, thanks."

She looked up at him from under hooded lids, daring him to protest that in fact his job was not small; it was important, satisfying, with a future. He could say nothing. "You know what I mean. Small like not for a corporation or a government. Newspaper, radio, that kind of thing. Jobs where they can move around. Each one I was supposed to make interested in seeing Naumenko. I would say to one that he has information on criminal ownership of Sporting Palace. It would all be lies, of course. Another that he has a strange sickness that affects old people who were in Afghanistan. For you, that he survived the camps."

"And each time he would send them on to someone else, and then to someone else after that?"

"Maybe yes. I don't know. My job was just to get the person to talk to Naumenko."

"And nobody else did? Nobody but me?"

"A German says there are no diseases in Afghanistan, and then starts telling me why everything Russians believe about health and everything else is wrong. This man who works for French radio says he will talk to Naumenko only if I sleep with him. Nobody can stand being told what to do by a Russian, especially by a Russian *girl*. We are here for amusement and lecturing and then, *pfft*." She crumpled an imaginary piece of paper and threw it over her shoulder. "Only you listened. Only you cared."

"And it was only me . . ." Jim inclined his head toward her, hoping his meaning would be clear.

"Yes. Only with you. That was not part of my job."

"Why didn't you ever call me back? I missed you."

"The job was done. It was a conversation, plus one very nice night, and that was it."

"So why did you call now?"

"Because they promised this would not happen. I am angry, and I want to know what happened after we left so I can get Grandfather to come home. Who else can I talk to? My teacher was paid, I'm sure; he won't help. My mother will just be worried. And my friends? They will say talk to the police, talk to his friends, or they will say he will come home in a few days. Disappearing, you know, is not unusual for Russian men. They will say he will come home drunk, sleep for a day, and I should not worry. But he does not drink, and I know—*I know*—that he disappeared because of me. Or you. Or something we did. I thought maybe you would help me." She sniffled, thrust her chin up, then looked away. "Or maybe not." Even now, in her condition, her thespian instincts were solid: she projected wounded pride, dignity, acceptance of anticipated rejection, all on an aquiline, elegant face that remained noble, beautiful, with a profile suited for stamping on a coin, when tear-streaked at three thirty a.m.

"Of course I'll help," Jim said automatically. Only when the words were out did Mina's uncertainty about Katya echo in his mind. If he were smart, he would have excused himself somehow—say he had to use the bathroom in the station; he'd have been right back—cross over to the other side of the station, called Mina to apologize, hailed a gypsy cab to the embassy, and left everyone else to their own problems. Maybe Katya was clean and maybe she wasn't; maybe Murat and Fadlan just happened to know Vorov through smugglers' ties and maybe they knew him for a reason. His instincts told him all three were clean; they *felt* clean, but, then again, his instincts had failed him in his interviews. Had they, though? Something felt strange about the whole thing from the beginning, but he allowed himself to be talked into pursuing it. Tonight he decided he'd listen.

"Of course I'll help," he told Katya. He put an arm around her and led her toward the car where Murat and Fadlan waited. She stiffened slightly when he opened the door and introduced her to the two imposing, heavily armed Tatars who had adopted him. To her credit, though, she did not flinch or look askance when Jim asked them if they would mind taking a slight detour to Zavodsk.

## 22

"I WOULDN'T ASK IF I could travel on my own," Jim said, leaning against the front of the car with Murat and chewing more mulch. The clock had just struck four; the morning's first commuters—old ladies from the far suburbs, mostly, who had things to sell and wanted to get a good position in the underpasses—had just started oozing with morning sluggishness out of the station. "My passport doesn't work."

He explained Trudy's trick. Murat nodded knowingly. "Governments," he spat.

"I can pay you. Not right now, but when this is over." He winced internally to hear himself say this, thinking how many times and to how many people he had promised the same. "I will pay you. No matter what I have to do."

Murat looked at him with a mixture of warmth and menace. "I told you," he said quietly. "No payment. Not between us. You are under our protection. It's normal. Besides, you are giving Fadlan the chance to fight the Russians. He hates his government as much as you hate yours. He will thank you."

"The Russian government?" Jim asked. "I thought we were going to find one person."

Murat grinned wickedly and made a clicking sound as he opened his door and motioned for him to do the same. Katya was asleep against the window, a peaceful little drool running down the side of her face. She awoke when they shut the doors.

"So? You're feeling better?" Murat asked Katya. "You're ready to go home?"

"I am coming with you," she said firmly.

Murat shook his head definitively. "No. No, she will go home. We're going to fight," he explained, rubbing his hands together as his smile broadened and his eyes glowed with the thrill of promised violence. "This is no place for a woman. You can see Dzheem after."

Katya looked at all three of the men with contempt and disbelief. Before she could start to protest, Jim held up his hands and smiled as disarmingly as he could.

"Look," he said in English, "maybe it would be better if you stayed here. I don't like their reasoning either." He jerked a thumb toward the front seats and lowered his voice confidentially. "They're more comfortable with you at home, and I need them to get to your grandfather. And I will, I promise. I'll get to him and bring him home to you. But if I don't . . . If something happens and you don't hear from me, say, by tomorrow morning, you need to call Amina Haddad at the American embassy. Here's her card."

Katya kept her hands in her pockets. "Why do I need to call her?"

"Why? I . . . if I can't find him, or something happens, she knows about him. And about me, and Anatoly Vorov, and even you."

"Yes, I'm sure she does. But what will she do for me?"

"She knows all about him," Jim said, knowing as soon as he said it how weak it sounded. His calculus said that Mina represented American officialdom, therefore she was helpful; shamefully, he had never considered what she might want from Katya.

"I don't want to get my grandfather back just to give him away to the Americans. To *anybody*. Do you understand? You do know who he is." It fell between a statement and a question.

Jim nodded.

"Your friend from the embassy told you?"

He nodded again.

"She spies on my family, and you want me to run to her, begging for help? No. Thank you, Jim; I know you mean the best for me and my family, but no. I cannot. Afterward, Grandfather turned down everybody, every request, money, gifts, cars, apartments, travel, all, all, all, everything. All just to be himself. To try to be free, and not free like *you* said we would be free, but free as a person. As a man. Do you understand? Now, you think perhaps your embassy friend will help me find him, only to return him to where he was? No, of course you don't. You are not so naïve; you know what she would want."

"I just thought she could help you. Maybe give you some options."

"You mean help me to get out of Russia, is that what you thought? I should tell you that the smiling wolf man offered this, too. If I help him, he will give me a visa to go wherever I want to go. Everybody thinks we all always are for sale, and we all would do anything just to go out from Russia. But this is my home. Whatever happens, I am Russian." She glared at Jim defiantly, tears welling in her eyes as she pressed a clenched fist to her chest. "I am part of everything here and it is part of me. Would *you* want to leave your home so easily? If you did not absolutely have to?"

"No," he agreed automatically. And then he thought of his parents, his father pottering and bent as he cleaned up the dinner dishes and his mother sitting at the kitchen table with a mug of tea, going over the books. He thought of them with a clarity and intensity that nearly poleaxed him, almost knocked him to the ground in homesick wonder and pain. The only one who could give the restaurant a future was freezing to death outside a train station in Moscow, new tears gluing his eyelashes together but too proud to cry properly. "No, I wouldn't," he said again, this time meaning it.

Katya nodded; she saw something in his eyes forbidding conversation.

"If she is who you think would help me, then I will come with you. I will not have my grandfather left to governments. Not yours and not ours and not anybody's." She stared levelly at Jim, challenging him to challenge her. Kaisa never would have done that.

She looked past Jim to Murat in the driver's seat, and strapped herself in. To certain Russian drivers, buckling a seat belt constituted a grave insult, implying one does not trust the driver with his life; fortunately, Murat seemed to take it in stride. He looked at Jim with a resigned twist of the mouth, but his eyes twinkled and he cracked an imaginary whip.

Fadlan brought his open palm slowly, tenderly toward the side of Katya's face, as his own characteristically grave expression melted into a tender smile, a benediction from some forgotten god spending the last ember of his power. In a tear-tightened voice he spoke to Murat in their own language, touched the corners of his eyes with his fingertips, licked them, and returned to his silent watching.

"His daughter," Murat explained, cutting a glance at Fadlan to see if he objected. "She was a doctor in Kazan in 1991. He was outside the hospital, on the main square, throwing stones at soldiers, yelling, shouting. No guns." He raised a finger in the air and stared at Katya and Jim until each of them nodded their understanding. "No guns. We are warriors, but this was a peaceful demonstration. We all agreed to leave our guns at home. The soldiers, the Russians, they shot anyway. In the air, just to frighten us, they said. They meant to hurt no one, they said. It was our fault, they said. One shot in the air went through a hospital window." Katya gasped and took Fadlan's weathered, scarred old hand in hers. "One shot. I have been shot six times—six!—and still walk the earth. But just one. In the throat, straight through. Her life bled from her in her own operating room. There was no trial. Afterward. Nothing. They told him it was his fault for shouting. *Shouting* at tanks and pimply little *pizda* soldiers with guns. *His* fault."

Fadlan patted Katya's hand four times, then four times, then four times again, replaying in his mind the one-loaf-two-loaves-three-loaves-eat! game he played with his daughter when she was a girl. Then with a last mournful sigh he released her hand and returned to the world.

"FOURTEEN HOURS," Murat said jubilantly, smacking the steering wheel as they drove out of the station, turning south on Leningradsky Prospekt. "We will stay off main roads where we can, so perhaps longer. But we will be there tonight."

A troubling thought occurred to Jim: he would have to cross an international border with a passport that said he was a pedophile rapist. His stomach flopped into his throat. "I have a problem with my passport," he said to Murat.

Murat laughed uproariously, then translated Jim's comments into Tatar for Fadlan, who smiled sadly and shook his head. "Nobody will see your passport," Murat said, smiling at Jim in the rearview mirror as he maneuvered between two army trucks, one loaded with fresh-faced recruits whose faces betrayed assumed confidence and real terror, the other with barrels emblazoned with biohazard symbols.

"You have money?" Murat asked. "How much?" Jim held up a fan of American hundreds, fifties, and twenties ($580) and a small brick of rubles. "Fine. At each crossing we will give the guards a present. They will have a good evening out with their wives, and we can cross while they tie their shoes. Maybe a little beer money for any policeman who stops us. Of course, your passport will remain in your pocket."

The road out of the city was pleasantly empty, while traffic backed up for miles in the other direction. Moscow's rush hours lasted from about seven a.m. until noon and again from four until ten in the evening; between the two, the lunch crowds clogged the city center's roads. Past the Garden Ring, Ryazansky Prospekt grew increasingly bleak, as the late-nineteenth-century broad granite buildings gave way to naked cinder-block towers that wept puffy caulk around each window and sat haphazardly in scrub fields like sandcastles on a deserted beach. The twisted hulk of a car burned black and furious in front of one building as a half dozen teenage boys in tracksuits cackled maniacally and threw bottles at passing cars. At first Jim felt they were leaving the twentieth century the farther they got from Moscow's center, but now he saw they were leaving something more elemental behind. This area had an apocalyptic wildness that made even Fadlan's jaw clench and his eyes dart. The only signs of commerce were vodka kiosks and squatter stands: tables covered with plastic sheeting holding off-brand Chinese cigarettes, single socks, copper wire, and flimsy household goods (soft aluminum screwdrivers and hammers, electric kettles bound to short or explode within a week, plastic plates with bluebirds frolicking in sunshine).

A few miles farther, though, and the city fell away entirely. A few American-style suburban developments—ersatz brick houses, bland and identical, clustered around a single roadway and blocked by a guardhouse watching over a two-story-high steel gate—made only the most perfunctory incisions in the thick pine forest encroaching on the roadway. Eventually even those disappeared: who would want to live in such places, anyway? Europeans would have looked on them with aesthetic disdain; most Americans to whom they would appeal—corporate-suburban types—would probably be too scared to bring their families over in the first place. And as for Russians, why pay all that money to live where nobody can see you paying all that money? The *exclusivniy* places were mostly in central Moscow; villages were for dachas and grandparents.

Outside Moscow's orbit, entire towns looked deserted. They drove through countless villages consisting of a single main street with a crumbling hotel, a dilapidated food store, a traffic circle with a patch of trees, and a statue of Lenin, and just off that main drag, streets of *izbas*—pre-Soviet wooden houses—without windows or doors, with hunks of wood missing, either sold or burned. Whenever they slowed in a town they attracted hostile stares: two swarthy, thuggish men in the front seats; a swarthy bespectacled one in the back, next to a beautiful, blond Russian. Everyone knew she was kidnapped, or a whore, or they had hooked her on drugs, or she liked mingling with blackasses, in which case she deserved what she got. Nothing good could have produced that configuration of people.

They stopped to stretch and eat at a ramshackle collection of tin-roofed stalls just outside Tula. Fadlan and Katya were both snoring heavily; Jim could neither sleep nor unclench his jaw. He and Murat got out of the car, shutting their doors gently behind them. Jim bought a couple of sausages and a sack of hard rolls; Murat hitched up his trousers and swaggered over to the largest, farther stall, whose owner he seemed to know and which sold a baffling array of stuffed animals, homemade pies, and used-car parts. The owner, a middle-aged woman with oversized glasses, a wiry perm, and pursed lips who would not have looked out of place at a university library, embraced Murat heartily, shoving a glass of tea and a cigarette into his hands. Jim ambled down toward the toilets, his hands in his pockets.

When he cleared sight of the car he pulled out his phone and called Mina's cell number.

"Haddad," she mumbled sleepily, "consular."

"Mina, it's me," Jim whispered.

Her voice sparked to life. "Jim! Where are you! What happened! I thought . . . My God, Jim, are you calling from custody? Have you been charged? Do you need a Russian lawyer?"

"I'm not in custody, Mina, I'm fine. I'm sorry I didn't come out of the apartment, but I'm fine."

"You weren't in your apartment. I checked."

Jim skirted the implied question. He figured it was better she not know about Murat and his family unless she had to. "Why did you think I was in custody? Whose custody?"

"After the shooting the police went door-to-door in the building. They searched every apartment. I thought they must have found you."

"You saw the body when you came in?"

"Of course I did. At first I thought it was you. Why do you think I pounded so hard? God, Jim, you . . . you at least could have let me know. Even if you didn't want to come in, you could have said something so I would have known you weren't dead."

"Or worse."

"Exactly. Or worse."

"Did they take anyone else?"

"From the apartment search? Like who?"

"Come on, Mina. Stop." He could feel her searchlight turned on, even now, probing him to see who in the building he was concerned about, who he knew. "Did they or didn't they?"

"Not that I know of, no. We had a peeper sent out. He said there was no neighborhood canvas."

"Is that normal?"

"When they're looking for the person who was supposed to be shot instead of the shooter it is. This morning I heard the investigation was put under the direct supervision of someone at the Interior Ministry rather than the city police or the prosecutor's office. You've made some powerful enemies. And I'm not even talking about Trudy, who's ready to release your passport details."

"At least I'm doing something right."

"You know, your need to set things right is going to get you hurt. It was an extraviolent search. Doors were kicked in, noses were broken. Especially on the sixth floor. Not a door left intact. Come to think of it, that's your old floor, isn't it? You should have come in. Where are you?"

Jim took a deep breath and looked around. A crumbling, minor Russian road; rows of stunted trees that waved feebly, like broken hands, at passing cars; a dozen dilapidated stalls selling beer, canned meat, cigarettes, electrical goods, deflated and probably spoiled homemade baked goods under plastic tarps; a toilet that was little more than a roof over an open ditch. He was further from his world than he had ever been. He had no idea where he was. He was nowhere. "I'm nowhere," he said. "I'll tell you later."

"Later?" Mina repeated, her voice honed to scalpel sharpness. "Have you lost your mind? As we speak, probably, they're sending the tax police over to the Memory Foundation. The prosecutor is also probably at work right now, revoking the Foundation's charter. By this afternoon, tomorrow if the courts are busy, everyone who works there will have their visas revoked. At best, that is; they'll probably also see the inside of a Russian interrogation chamber. I hope you didn't have any friends there, because you certainly don't now. Want to hear more?"

"Always."

"The four men you spoke to? The survivors? They've all been arrested on corruption charges."

"Corruption?" Jim asked. "How can anyone . . ."

"They took bribes, probably. Either from the wrong donor, or they refused to share the wealth. Given their age, we're guessing the former—keeping it all for yourself is a young man's habit. You have to think you're immortal. We're not sure who paid them off yet, but we're still digging. They're all four retired army, but apparently they all did some investigative work for the Interior Ministry."

"Investigating what? What does that mean?"

"Well, it doesn't mean what you think it means. No way they were actual detectives. An investigator's license opens a few doors, makes travel easier, forestalls questions, especially around military installations. Someone trusted them with something. We think they're smuggling, but we don't know what."

"Do people count as contraband?"

"What do you mean?"

"You figure it out. You're the one who mentioned the black box. What about the Willows?"

"They're here. The Russians want them. They want you, too, and they think we've got you. By this afternoon you'll be on RTR. Name and picture. An American spy loose in Russia. Still want to tell me you're nowhere?"

RTR was the most popular of an ever-growing number of government-run television stations: if Jim's name and picture were going out on their afternoon news, his passport's validity would be the least of his problems.

"Can't you stop them?" he asked, more urgently than he wanted to.

"If you come in now, before the Willows give them Anatoly Vorov's name, then yes. Probably. The Russians know the Willows didn't think of this on their own, but they don't know who hired them. Yet. They're going crazy trying to find out who the inside man is: someone in the government must have helped Vorov. My guess is Interior, given what happened with your investigation, but I don't know for sure. But that's who they want: they want their own. There's room for negotiation, but Jim—I cannot stress this enough—we need you here, in the flesh, in the room. You'll be debriefed by the Russians, but then you can go home. Probably. If they find you, it won't be so easy."

"Mina, let me ask you something: how can you promise that if I come in they'll just let me go?"

He heard the click of the pen against her teeth.

"Are you there?"

"Yes, Jim, I'm here."

"Did you hear my question?"

"I did."

"You didn't answer because you can't, right?"

"Jim, I want you to listen to me. The Willows told us where Anatoly Vorov lives." Jim's heart sank: it was the one thing he hoped he'd be able to trade for safe passage home. "He has a house in Peredelkino, just outside Moscow. We are going to trade that information to the Russians for whoever is in the room at the time. If you want to take advantage of that largesse, you must get here, and get here soon. If you aren't here by the time they come to meet with Trudy, you will find yourself very alone. Am I clear?"

Jim figured that with traffic, he was four, maybe five, hours away from Moscow: too far away to get back in time. And either he knew something Mina didn't—Vorov's real location—that he would be able to trade for consideration in a few hours, or he was fleeing the country on a doctored passport and was about to be a notorious rapist and spy. What he felt now was not desperation or fear, but the energizing, spark-in-the-heart rush that accompanies kickoff or shuffle. He had never played for stakes this high before, but he had played enough to know that it was all—everything, always—a game. "Clear, Mina."

"So I can expect you within the hour?"

"Can you trace this phone?"

"Excuse me? Jim, what does that have to . . ."

"Can you or can't you?"

"Yes, Jim. We can. We can trace phones."

"Good. I'm turning it off now, but I'll call you later. Be sure you can trace, on a map, where I'm calling from."

She was still talking when he snapped the phone shut.

## 23

THREE HOURS LATER, just across the Don from Voronezh, they stopped at a roadside restaurant—little more than an oil drum converted into a barbecue with a few tables underneath a canvas tarp strung up like a tent—that appeared to be owned by yet another cousin, an affable, peppery little man with curly black hair, a weathered face, and a mouthful of gold teeth. He hailed Murat and Fadlan even before they got out of the car. He took Katya's hand in both of his and kissed it with an elaborate show of courtesy. When he saw Jim, however, his thick, expressive eyebrows shot up with alarm, and he started gesticulating and shouting volubly in staccato Tatar. Three times he pointed to Jim and pointed to the television, which was currently showing a Mexican soap opera. A fat man with a huge mustache was getting oiled up poolside by two nubile young women in bikinis. Jim had never felt any urge to grow a mustache or surrender to middle-aged spread, but he would have given a lot to change positions with that man just now.

Murat tried to calm him, waving his hands, palms toward the ground, but the man still chattered and fretted like a bird. Without breaking conversation, he yanked Jim over toward him by the arm, and displayed him, asking what sounded like pointed questions as he yanked Jim's coat, flicked his glasses, kicked his shoes, and patted his sides roughly, presumably demonstrating the lack of a weapon. Jim could imagine what he was saying: "This? *This* is the killer American spy? *This* is the man who eluded every policeman in Moscow?" Murat gestured to Katya also, then back at Jim, and he put his index fingers next to each other and nodded.

Not really, Jim thought, but I appreciate the implication.

Only after Murat agreed that they would eat in his house, rather than in view of the public, did the man relent, whereupon he brought them enough food to last them two weeks.

"My grandfather would have loved this," Katya said quietly. She and Jim sat next to each other at the low, round, carpet-strewn table, trying to work their way through yet another massive pile of lamb. Jim imagined that by now every flock of sheep between Estonia and Japan had probably been conditioned to run at top speed when they saw a Tatar coming.

The three cousins were catching up on family gossip: from the way Murat described a sphere in front of his torso with his hands, then adopted a furious expression and a backhand slap, it seemed that someone had become undesirably pregnant.

"His Soviet brothers, he would have called them," said Katya, smiling gently at the memory. "Except he would have meant it. 'The Soviet Union has 130 nationalities, and none are more important than any other,' he used to say. And unlike most Russians, he meant it."

"A true believer, was he?"

"The *most* true believer. He really did think they were remaking humanity. He believed in it."

"But did he excuse . . ."

"He did not *excuse*, as you say, anything. He said you love your country like you love your family, with its flaws. And that just because an ideal has failed in practice, at one time by one group of people, does not mean we should throw it away."

"What would he say if he saw you with an American?"

"Worse"—she giggled—"an American grandson of Soviet refuseniks." She turned serious again. "He would say nothing. He was a true believer, yes, but he is not a person who hates. He worked for his country, and then his country fell apart. Now he works for himself. He is the kind of man who can talk to anybody, listen to anybody." Katya had started crying again. No sobs this time; now tears ran down her face as she spoke, as though crying had become for her a complement to breathing. "This is how I started acting: by imitating Grandfather's friends for him. He taught me how to hear and see."

Jim reached across to comfort her, but the host hissed ("He's very traditional," Murat explained, "and I told him you were not married"). After the ritual protestations that end any hosted meal in Russia—if the diner fails to eat until his stomach actually and visibly explodes, the host must pretend to be insulted until he receives adequate compliments— they rose from the table. At Murat's insistence, this was an alcohol-free meal, but the host insisted on taking down his bottle of clear, lethal *samogon* and toasting, just once, the victory of the people over governments everywhere.

"CHOOSING WHERE TO CROSS the border is a science," Murat explained. He alone had not slept all day, and appeared no worse for it. After Voronezh the landscape had become pitted, boggy, lunar: endless flat plains had given way to endless swampy plains. Sunflower and wheat fields became rice paddies and barley fields, and even in winter the air smelled fetid and heavy. Murat had circumnavigated the main crossings, and had headed south into the Rostov region, where the Don river delta met the Sea of Azov. "Busy crossings are no good," he explained to his three exhausted passengers, "because there they send the best guards. Too sleepy, also no good: there the guards are maybe bored, and so will spend time searching when others might just look away. Sneaking through the woods is good, although if they hear noise they sometimes will shoot before they talk. With four of us, one woman and one American, at night . . ." He gave them a dubious look followed by a reassuring wink in the rearview mirror.

"So we will go not to Novocherkassk, or to Taganrog, but to Malaya Supinkha, along the river. Thirty minutes on. First, though"—he slowed the car and pulled off the road and into a thicket of trees, then climbed out and opened the trunk—"Jim, you will climb into the trunk."

"The trunk?" Jim called out through his window. "No, thank you."

"Come." Murat opened his door and pulled him out by the collar. "You are a spy, and an American, and, worse, on the news. Can we bribe them not to look at a passport? Perhaps. Can we bribe them not to look in a trunk? Again, yes. We hope. Can we bribe them to ignore that they are seeing an American spy rapist sitting in the car staring at them? Catching him would mean promotion, rewards, respect, fame. No, for this, no bribe is enough. In."

His tone would brook no argument. Jim kissed Katya on the cheek and tried to smile. She returned the gesture, then motioned with her head for him to get out. Murat stood smiling over the open trunk. Jim was about to climb in when he saw what he would be lying on: two canvas sacks, stamped sequentially (KΛ-35679 and KΛ-35680). One held a dozen assault rifles, their barrels poking out of the top like gunmetal roses; the other held shotguns. Wedged behind them were boxes of shells and bullets.

"Just move them," Murat said nonchalantly. "From this morning; I will sell them later this week."

"This morning? From the sweet old lady who sold pastries?"

"Yes. Sofia. That woman. Her husband is a quartermaster, and always drunk. He never thinks to ask why his brigade lacks weapons, and why they have a new home and drive a Mercedes. But she is very sharp in *bizniz*. No, wait. A better idea."

Murat lifted them out of the trunk and dropped them on the ground. Once Jim was fetal, he put the sacks on top of him, arranging them so if a guard should happen to look in the trunk, he would see only guns (Murat would insist he help himself to one of each) rather than a person.

This had the effect of sandwiching Jim between a thin layer of rusted-out steel, open around the wheel wells to the road, so he felt the occasional sting of frozen pebbles flying onto his ankles, and a couple of hundred pounds of pointed, lethal metal resting on his side and thighs. The boxes of cartridges were pillows. To complete the effect, Murat laid a thick military tarp over the guns and Jim, leaving him just enough room to breathe at the back of the trunk.

Jim knew they were approaching the border when he heard the squeals of other poorly maintained brakes on either side of them. The red of the brake lights turned his hand bloody, embarrassed. His breath turned jagged and labored; his hands and legs shook beneath his steel blankets. He heard two sets of steady clops, one on either side of the car.

"Good evening," the driver's-side guard said in a slurred, starchy, smoke-cured baritone. "Three people? Your documents?"

"Hello, cutie," said the other guard, who sounded younger, keener, meaner. "Are they bothering you?"

"No," Katya said strongly.

"Are they paying you well?"

She said nothing.

"They do pay you, right?"

"Lyosha," the driver's-side guard warned. "Enough."

"Don't you ever want to get fucked by a man instead of by monkeys?"

Jim held his breath. He assumed Murat had killed people before; he knew Murat had a temper, and took his honor seriously. Jim kept his lips pressed together, but against them, inside his closed mouth, he repeated, "Calm, calm, calm, calm," and clenched his eyes shut.

"Not as much as you do," Katya said.

The older guard gave an explosive, rough, bullhorn laugh, like it was the funniest thing he'd heard in years. "Oh, Lyosha. That should teach you! 'Not as much as you do'! Oh, darling, that's Russian wit! Russian spirit. Lyosha, why don't you go ahead." To the retreating footsteps he shouted, "And don't forget to call your wife! Now," he said more quietly, in his regular tone, "I apologize for my Ukrainian partner. The high spirits of the young. Let me take a peek inside your trunk, and you'll be on your way. I'll bring him the documents so he doesn't have to come back."

"Sir, have you checked the back page of my passport? You should find a permit that will answer any questions you might have."

"Permit, permit," he grumbled, as though the word were foreign. "Ah, a registration! I see, I see. The problem is, my partner might need a similar registration. For Ukraine, you understand."

"Check my cousin's passport, sir. You will find one there, too."

"Ah, there it is. There it is. Let me just take this over to him. A word of advice: this registration stamp works better crossing this way, out of Russia. Coming in, you might need to renew it."

ANOTHER THIRTY MINUTES past the checkpoint, they did the trunk process in reverse. Jim clambered out, stretched, and took a deep breath, inhaling the scents of the industrial Ukrainian seaside: silt, gasoline, machine oil, old fish, marine rot. They had pulled off behind a disused service station on the far side of Zavodsk, by the sea. A pump dangled, forlorn and vestigial, from a rusted iron pipe that rose from a bed of concrete. The windowless concrete cube that once held the station's offices stood mute: an entrance to purgatory.

Jim had never seen as many stars as the sky held that night: it was Russian-winter clear, and they were far enough from any major city that nothing impeded their visibility. They were at the bottom of a hill; the town loomed above them. What little of it Jim could see from here looked like the bottom half of a Chagall painting: asymmetrical wooden houses fronting small tilled patches of black earth, and makeshift storage sheds against which stood scythes, shears, rakes, hoes. Outside the four houses across from them stood not a single piece of electrical equipment, nor any light other than the flicker of a candle in the one-room house farthest from them. These were farmers' houses, and farmers went to bed when the sun did. A fourteen-hour drive had brought them back two centuries.

Finally, Jim spoke. "Do we know where he lives?"

Murat looked at Fadlan, who shook his head gravely and said something in Tatar.

"He said he made a delivery to one of Vorov's clubs here, never to his house."

Fadlan spoke again, this time sweeping away the wax paper he had used for a plate and using his fingers to diagram something.

"He says the club is east, along this road, at the edge of the city. He does not know how many people will be there, but he remembers only two doors. Two of us outside each door, we should be able to . . ."

"One moment," Katya interrupted. She looked as uncomfortable as Jim felt with the idea of staging a raid armed with the contents of Murat's trunk. "Is the club protected? I mean by the police?"

Fadlan nodded.

"I have an idea."


KLUB KALIFORNYA, like the ancient service station, lacked windows. An ocean scene—palm trees, sand, clouds, girls in bikinis—covered its cinder-block exterior, and what struck Jim about the scene was not its incongruity (sunny California in a barely electrified Ukrainian village) but its expertise: the five women and three men were all individuals rather than types, their bodies in motion and their sun-kissed faces radiant, joyful, insouciant, healthy. The shading on the palm trees made it look like they were swaying in a gentle breeze. Jim thought of Yuri and his plays, Kirsten and her choreography, Vassily and his photographs: this was a world of secret passions and talents. Circumstance compelled people to become jacks-of-all-trades: car mechanics with concert-hall baritones, secretaries whose watercolors hung in their bosses' offices, janitors who could hold their own in a Talmudic discussion with every rabbi between Krakow and Vladivostok. Kalifornya's exterior might have been painted by a twelve-year-old girl or an eighty-five-year-old man, but it was almost certainly done by a proud and careful amateur, not by a professional.

Even through those painted walls, in the car, which was parked a quarter mile down the road and around a bend, they could hear the thumping Russkipop. Two policemen—one just inside the main door and one just outside, both armed with Kalashnikovs—stood guard. Only two people had entered during the half hour that the four of them spent surveying the place: it was still early, just past nine p.m., and most Russian clubs, even in the provinces, didn't start drawing a crowd until eleven or twelve.

Katya, Murat, and Fadlan all stepped out of the car quietly. Katya began walking toward the club; Murat and Fadlan followed her halfway there, then ducked down in a ditch. She had made herself up as heavily as possible and exchanged her sweater and parka for Fadlan's button-down shirt. She'd left the shirt unbuttoned halfway down her chest, exposing her white skin and tank top, which she had torn strategically. She had daubed extra powder on her cheeks, smeared her eyeliner, and unzipped her purse, making sure to trail some wads of Kleenex: she was a working junkie in the middle of her shift.

As soon as they cleared the car, Jim crouched down farther in his seat and took out his phone to call Mina.

"I'm still alive," he whispered when she answered.

"Jim, where are you? I'm tired of this." She sounded it. "So is Trudy. So is our press secretary. We've been dodging calls from reporters about you all day, and our flack is getting tired of saying 'no comment.' Trudy wants to change it to 'rogue operative' and pledge full cooperation with the Russians."

"What if I can tell you where to find Rodion Lisitsov?"

She sighed and clicked the pen against her front teeth. "How do you know that?"

"I want you to guarantee that I can go home. Without charges from you or them."

He watched Katya approach the door. Her transformation, even from behind as she walked away, was remarkable. She had the tired, stuttering walk; she clasped her purse tightly to her body with one arm while holding the other straight down, defensive and indignant, rigid at the elbow, by her side; she scratched her head twitchily, nesting up her hair. When Katya told them her plan, Jim asked if it would work, and Murat said a lone prostitute, unprotected and unknown, would be "like buttered sprats to a cat." So it appeared now: the policeman flicked the safety on his gun, moved it around from his front to his back, and dropped his hands to his front, hitching his thumbs around his belt.

"I can't give you that kind of guarantee, Jim. This morning I could have, but it's not up to me anymore." Jim started to protest, and she interrupted. "Look: tell me where you are and what you know, and I promise to do what I can for you. Okay? If you're honest with yourself, you know that's as good as you'll get. Your name and face are known, Jim," she pleaded harshly. "I don't know how you're still alive and free right now, but it won't last long. Now, where . . ."

"Zavodsk. Ukraine."

"Ukraine?" she screeched. "You crossed a border? How . . . No, don't tell me now. Look, just keep your phone on, will you? I won't hang up; you don't either. We'll find you."

"Who's 'we'?"

"All of us, Jim. Home and away teams."

Jim did as requested, and put the phone, still active, in his jacket pocket. Had he kept listening, he would have heard Mina relay their conversation to Trudy. He would have heard a male Russian grumbling in the background, eventually acceding to allow Mina and Trudy to accompany them as observers only, strictly as a courtesy, no weapons. He would have heard that same man order two helicopters for immediate departure south.

By the time Katya reached the club's front door, she was shivering and clutching a cheap brown cigarette between shaking fingers. She dropped her purse, then bent down slowly to pick it up: a nice little extra touch.

"Hey, where's your *mammotchka*?" the guard asked, leering. Katya shot him a bored look, but made sure to include the hint of a smile at the end. She turned around and started walking away, but he called out to her again. "When I ask you a question, you answer, understand? Now walk your narrow ass over here and show me your fucking papers."

"My papers?" she mocked. "That's all your tiny little prick can handle, isn't it?"

The guard grabbed his gun, and for a minute Jim worried he would shoot, or at least hold her at gunpoint, which would have ruined everything. Instead he threw it onto the ground behind him, undid his belt, and started following her back toward the car.

The guard, incensed by a lethal combination of lust, rage, and status insecurity, did not notice how her gait quickened and sharpened as she rounded a bend in the road and moved out of sight behind a tree, nor did he think to remove his eyes from her. If he did he would have seen the two figures crouching in the ditch, and he might have been able to fend them off or at least make a sound before the slender one grabbed him by the throat and mouth and the large one lifted him off the ground as easily as his father did when he was a boy and stuffed him into the trunk, which the smart-mouthed, teetering junkie had suddenly had the presence of mind to open.

They drove east, farther away from Zavodsk and the club, pulling off the road where scrub turned to woods. One thing Russia had in abundance: empty space. Murat and Fadlan pulled the guard out of the trunk and thrust him into the driver's seat. Katya and Jim stood aside, their fingers brushing against each other.

The cop cringed as best he could with his hands bound and splayed on the steering wheel. He had the sort of lean, bland, thin-lipped, Ichabod Crane face that could easily waver between cruelty and servility. It settled on the latter now, as he leaned his head back and down, turning his long chin into his shoulder as best he could. "Are you going to kill me?" he whimpered. "Then just kill me. I know, and the world knows, for you people it is a plus with God to shed Christian blood."

Murat ran the back of the knife blade lovingly across the exposed back of the policeman's neck. He jerked back at the touch, sending the tip of the knife plunging into the wattle of skin just below his hairline. "Why should I kill you when you can do it yourself?" Murat laughed. "But since you know so much about us, you must know that we like to take our time with our prey, and here there is no reason to hurry. You must be aware, too, that sometimes we allow our prey to ransom themselves, and because there's a woman present, I will give you that chance. Are you ready? Do you want to live to daybreak?"

The policeman nodded avidly, though his eyes were still clenched shut and his head was turned away from Murat.

"Good. Now, a man's hands can be cut and jointed into forty-two separate pieces." Murat counted one to six as he tapped, in turn, the knuckles of the policeman's forefinger from top to bottom, then his thumb. The rope holding him to the wheel had been tied in such a way that as he struggled to pull away, the bonds grew tighter, until eventually his hands were almost purple, and bound completely in place. "Did you know that? No? It's true. Now, I want you to tell us where Anatoly Vorov lives."

"Who is that person, please?" he asked.

Murat raised the knife over his head and brought it down swiftly, with a whistle. At first it appeared to have just been an intimidating feint, but a slash opened across the back of the policeman's left hand from his index finger's bottom knuckle to his wrist bone.

304 | JON FASMAN

"I am a Ukrainian policeman, you blackass son of a whore! You will be . . ."

"That one will heal. The next one will disable your shooting hand forever. Now, where . . ."

"We are in front of it, you idiot. These are his woods."

"No," Murat said, laughing with disbelief as he raised the knife again.

"I swear! By Holy Mother Russia I swear! Shine a light on the ground, you'll see!"

Murat shone the light low and into the forest. A thin wire, three inches off the ground, caught the light, then another one just behind it, a few inches higher, and behind that a third, a fourth, a fifth. So much for sneaking in through the woods.

Murat gave a low whistle. "Where is the entrance?" he asked the policeman evenly, holding the knife at eye level.

"Closed to such people as you," he sneered. "Whores and black-asses."

Murat raised the knife and the policeman twisted his head away. "Two versts east on this road. Please, do not! Two versts up, you will see."

Murat brought the knife down. The policeman was too scared to scream; he made a metallic, wheezing sound instead as the knife sliced cleanly through the ropes that held him to the steering wheel. Murat spat on him as he stared at his newly free hands. "We do not stain our knives with the blood of girls. You know our friend Tolya?"

He nodded, still in subdued shock.

"Then come," he said, sliding into the driver's seat behind him as Fadlan climbed in the other side. "Tonight we will be your guests."

MURAT REACHED UNDER the driver's seat and came up with a bottle of vodka, steering the wheel momentarily with his knees. They drove slowly, quietly, with the lights off, along the far side of the road rather than in the middle. "I hope you don't embarrass yourself," Katya said to Murat reproachfully, with a look of disgust.

"With this?" He laughed. He unscrewed the top and poured the contents over the policeman's injured hand. The cop grimaced, inhaling loudly through clenched teeth. "To keep out infection. You see," he said, smacking the cop in the back of the head, "we treat defeated enemies well."

To Jim and Katya in the rearview he said, "This is not vodka. Not even *samogon*." He waved the bottle behind him, under Jim's nose; it triggered an instant memory of late afternoons cleaning the kitchen after all the customers had gone home. He shut his eyes for a moment and saw his father at the counter, working a rag, while he scrubbed the day's grease from the grill. It wasn't soap, and it wasn't detergent; he couldn't quite place the smell. "For cleaning glass. This is only for selling, not for drinking."

"You give people Windex to drink?" Jim asked. "Doesn't that kill them?"

"Don't be such a baby," Katya said. "You throw up first."

"Yes. Also, you can get used to it. Some uncultured people sell methylated spirits, and *these*, no question, will kill you."

"And they sell it only to kiosks for drunks, you know, who probably drink worse every day."

"Actually, we did one time sell to Stockmann's." Murat had a warm, predatory glow at the memory. "Only one time. The second time, we tried again, and they said they would kill us if we returned. You wouldn't expect that from a Swede; Swedes are supposed to be very peaceful. But they had a better *krysha* than us, so we could never try again. But yes: this kind of ethanol is also good for healing and cleaning."

As they rounded a bend a brick wall fronting the street began. It stood about fifteen feet high and a good half mile long, and was topped every twenty feet with carved concrete spheres atop spikes. Murat cut the engine, and they coasted to a stop just before an imposing wrought-iron gate set into the wall, with a camera and a buzzer on the right side. "You have been here before?" he asked the cop, who still gripped his hand.

The cop nodded.

"How many times? Don't think, just tell. One? Five? Every weekend?"

"Every night I work at Kalifornya. After it closes, Mr. Vorov likes us to bring him the night's money in cash, in a box, so he has it counted by breakfast."

"So you've been in the house."

"Yes. Well, no. A private guard drives up to the gate, here, and takes it from me. Only very senior people are allowed into the house. I hear it is a palace, modeled on Alexander Palace. They say you can have anything . . ."

"Yes, yes, yes. Your face is known but not well known; that is all I wanted to know. Go, make them open the door."

Fear and confusion contorted the cop's mashed-potato face: fear not at what Vorov or Murat might do to him but the sort of indolent, hatred-based fear that comes when a person without imagination breaks his routine. His life was watching Kalifornya's door, taking and giving bribes when appropriate, drinking with his colleagues, complaining about his wife, putting the occasional shovel in the ground. He could not fit this action into his hierarchy of actions; he was baffled. Only when Murat stepped out of the car, trailing his knife against the side of the cop's face, did he spring back to life.

"Do you think a man such as Anatoly Vorov will just open the door for anybody? What: I will press the button, and like an elevator it springs open."

Murat nodded slowly, as though considering the point. He scratched his head with the tip of his knife, then he sheathed it. "You're right," he told the cop, who nodded gravely, the corners of his mouth turned down in pompous self-satisfaction. He was about to break into a smile when Murat punched him hard, twice, once in the corner of the mouth, splitting his lip, and once in the eye, knocking it shut. Before he could completely collapse Murat caught him by the collar, pulled him upright, and slapped him back to attention.

"The Kalifornya is being robbed. You escaped out the back. Eight armed men. Rostov accents. Go: tell him now." Murat pushed him toward the bell, moving quickly, before his terror-induced obedience faded. He joined Jim, Fadlan, and Katya, who stood flush against the brick wall, directly to the right of the camera, and therefore out of its range.

When he pressed the button, a red activity light and a harsh white activating light switched on, and the camera came to life, bathing the policeman in the sole cone of light visible anywhere. From behind its Plexiglas covering, the camera took in the policeman's battered face, his gashed hand, his disheveled appearance, and his lack of a weapon. "Yes," a voice barked through the intercom.

"It's Volodya. The Kalifornya is being robbed. I snuck out the back to let you know."

"You told them who they were robbing?"

"Yes."

"How many?"

"Eight. I saw eight."

"Locals?"

"The ones who spoke had Rostov accents."

"Are they still there?"

"I don't know."

The box clicked off but the light remained on, as if considering. Finally the box squawked back to life. "Stay there. Remain in front of the camera. We're coming."

Murat tapped Jim in the chest: his motions had become coiled, purposeful. "You have your gun?" he whispered.

Jim tapped his jacket pocket: he could not believe it, but he was, in fact, carrying a gun. Somewhere in the distance, two engines started.

"The trucks will not stop," Murat said. "They will not stop for our friend the policeman." The cop glared at him, insulted. "He is their doorman; to stop a robbery they will send the real fighters, which is good for us. You will take him and the woman up the path to the front door. Remain visible. Walk in front of the camera. We will duck under in front of you and go around back."

"Why?" Jim felt at a distinct operational disadvantage without Murat and Fadlan. It wasn't just that they were two more people, or even that they were two more armed people. It was more that, unlike Jim and Katya, they appeared to have some idea of what they were doing. The engines grew louder, and the cop tried to smooth out his uniform and stand straighter: they were close.

"Because he will not just shoot an American and a woman. But he will shoot two Tatars as soon as he would look at them."

"And after that?"

"After that it will be in God's hands. Death meets you where he wishes; you cannot hide here, or travel there."

"Then why not walk up to the front with us?"

"Please." Murat chuckled. "Just because Death meets you at his convenience does not mean you must invite Him."

"You already invited Him," the cop hissed. "You were dead as soon as I rang that bell."

With an initial clank and a smooth, mechanized hum, the gates swung open. True to Murat's prediction, the two black Hummers, both with tinted windows, did not stop, and if they gave any indication that they saw in their rearview mirrors four people standing against the wall in the dark, they didn't show it. They roared toward the Kalifornya in a chaos of revving engines and dust.

As the gates started to swing shut, the cop began walking forward; as soon as he was out of the camera's view, Murat brought the butt end of his gun down hard on the back of his head. He fell as though his spine were pulled out.

"Dead?" Katya asked, peering fearfully at what she thought was a corpse.

Murat shook his head. "Resting. For a long time." Jim and Katya walked in front of the camera, staring into its eye with their hands visible. Beneath them, crouching, scampered Murat and Fadlan. Once all five were inside, Murat and Fadlan melted into the woods lining the drive, while Jim and Katya walked up its center.

The birch-lined drive followed a gentle westward curve, which, even if it had been light, would have obscured the house at the top. Knee-high garden lamps lined the path; Jim was careful to stay in their pools. Assuming he was being watched, the last thing he wanted to do was give them any reason to chase after him in the dark.

"Jim," Katya whispered, squeezing his free hand.

"Yes?"

"I always knew we would make it here. I always knew we would get in. What I don't know is how we'll leave. Why would he ever let us go?" Jim swallowed hard. He had thought the same thing, but hearing it out loud made his fears that much more real.

"He's a businessman," Jim said, pretending a confidence he did not feel. "All we want is your grandfather, right? No crusades, nothing else? We promise our silence in exchange for him."

Katya started to speak, but just then they rounded the bend, and the house came into view a few hundred feet up the path.

Jim had been expecting something grand, palatial, Russian: like the cop said, it was modeled on Alexander Palace, where Nicholas II had lived. The cop appeared to have received some bad information, for they did not stand in front of a palace, nor of a new Russian dacha in the fashionable Scandinavian blond-wood-and-diagonal-window style, nor even of a Soviet-style monolith. Instead they stared at an enormous, symmetrical, prefabricated Colonial-style house that would not have looked out of place in a wealthy American suburb. It was a McMansion. Grander than most, sure, with a six-car garage rather than a three, and Jim figured it had some add-ons, especially in the area of security, that its American counterparts lacked, but fundamentally it looked like home, right down to the blue-painted shutters and the carved stone path: no less incongruous than if a Russian turned a corner in Rockville and came upon a replica of St. Basil's Cathedral wedged into a suburban street. It was so strange that Jim laughed and shook his head, while Katya looked on with disgust.

As they continued toward the house, the front door—a thick, sturdy-looking wood model with a black handle and knocker, a peephole, and, lit up next to it with the faint orange glow of home, a doorbell—swung open. Jim held his hands out from his body, palms forward: not raised in surrender, but clearly showing he was no threat. He pushed Katya behind him. He figured it was better to be prepared if Murat's assumption was wrong, and Vorov had no problem eliminating problems, whatever their gender or nationality.

Emerging from the doorway was a chubby, impish, balding little man smiling blandly and peering around with an expression of bemused, benevolent interest. It was difficult to tell whether his suit fit poorly or whether his dumpling-shaped body, high forehead surrounded by tight black curls, and tiny little kumquat-fingered hands would have made any piece of clothing look ridiculous. He could be my uncle, Jim thought: he had Sam's small stature and delicate features, but he appeared more used to smiling, more open, than Jim's father.

"Welcome, welcome. Mr. Vilatzer, is it? Ms. Lisitsova? I am Anatoly

Vorov," the little man said in fluent English that sounded like it was caught in a mid-Atlantic eddy. It had the bite of a Russian accent and the rounded vowels of a longtime English speaker. He looked from person to person with a touch of clinical pride to see what effect his name had on them. "I assume that you have come to see me." He shrugged pleasantly, diffidently, then let his arms go slack at his sides. He looked like an orthodontist, or an ineffectual bachelor relative who makes his living fiddling with numbers. "Here I am. Please, come in, come in. What would you like to talk about?"

"We'd like to see Rodion Lisitsov," Jim said in Russian.

Vorov turned his gaze toward Jim, sharpening it and letting some of the benevolence burn off. "You speak Russian with both an American and a slight Belarusian accent, if I'm not mistaken. Did your parents come from Minsk?"

"My grandparents, actually. Impressive."

Again, the self-effacing shrug and the mild smile. "In my business, it helps to know as much as you can about someone before you have to open your mouth. You learn from small clues and from cultivating your ear. That's all. A useful skill. A learned skill. Little more than a parlor trick, really. I could easily teach you, if we had the time. You also are a Jew."

"Less impressive, that one. Russians seem to have a unique ability to sniff out a Jew at fifty paces. Well honed over the centuries, I guess."

Vorov looked down at the ground and smiled ruefully, embarrassed at having expended his capital on such an obvious guess. "Yes, yes. It really isn't that difficult once you know what you're looking for. And I hope I cause *you* no offense if I say the obvious: it's the complexion, dark, plus the prominent nose, and the shape of your ears. Our Komsomol leader in university used to say that a Jew's ears stick out from his head so that when anybody in his city complains about scarcity, the Jew can hear, and rush in to sell. He said this, of course, as an insult, but I have spent my career trying to cultivate such ears. I have always wanted a pair of sharp Jew ears."

Jim felt his ears go red. Vorov noticed, and smiled: advantage him. The nose Jim was used to—he'd heard the slurs before, especially in his mother's old Hamden stomping grounds—but the ear comment was new.

"I won't insist on practicing my English any further tonight, though I am a bit rusty. Do you have a gun, Mr. Vilatzer? I am afraid that too much time spent living in Nancy Pelosi's district seems to have wiped away my military training and given me rather a horror of guns. I must insist that if you are to be my guest you leave your weapon outside. You may leave it here"—he gestured to a small alcove beneath a row of windows, adjacent to the doorway. "I promise nobody will take it. You may reclaim it when you leave. Are we expecting anyone else this evening?"

"No. We came alone."

"Did you? I am amazed you could find my house. Then again, you certainly have shown yourself to be resourceful. Perhaps I should not underestimate you anymore. Come in, please."

He stood aside, and Jim and Katya found themselves in a two-story entry foyer with a hanging chandelier, hardwood floors, and stairs with a runner carpet and a wooden banister winding their way up. A distant rumbling shook the chandelier, which sent out a pleasant tinkling, and was silent again.

Jim shook his head at how familiar it seemed: the place looked like something a successful athlete would buy—prefabricated in construction and taste. Vorov read his reaction well. "It must seem a bit like home to you."

"Not exactly," Jim said. "Our house is much smaller."

Vorov chuckled politely, his face alive with interest and sympathy. "Is it? You should have seen the hovel where I began. I made this all on my own. A bootstrapper, I suppose. Not unlike you, Seamus. Or your parents." His smile remained fixed, glittering; his eyes stayed on Jim like a snake's.

"What do you know about my parents?"

"Nothing, nothing at all. I've never even been to Rockville, and on those occasions when I do find myself in Washington, I eat downtown, where my business is. I couldn't say I know them at all." He glanced over at Jim to see how accurately the arrow struck. From somewhere in the house came the low clatter of forks against plates, glasses against the table, but no conversation. "I know the type, though, Seamus"—he paused for effect—"or Jim, as you seem to prefer, that was my point: so many of my countrymen see how I live and think where has his taste gone? Why doesn't he live like Berezovsky or Abramovich or Gusinsky? The truth is I keep a Russian home in Pacific Heights and an American one here. When I'm abroad I like to remind myself of my native land, and when I'm here I like to pay tribute to the country that has taught me so much. I'm sure at least you understand, even if your lovely companion looks less convinced." Katya stood against the front door with her arms crossed. She looked not disagreeable or disapproving, but anxious, straining, like she was listening for her grandfather's voice, breathing, presence.

Just then a swinging door at the back of the foyer opened, and a tall, blond man in a suit strode confidently through, his ID flipped open before him and an oily, disarming grin tacked to the bottom of his face.

"That's him," Katya hissed in Jim's ear. "The wolf man."

"I am Nikolai Skrupshin, deputy junior minister of the Interior. Your papers, please. And your mobile telephones."

When neither of them moved he broadened the smile. "Please, for matters of security you are required to hand over your mobile telephones. If you wish to check, you will see that you cannot make or receive calls here, so they are quite useless, and any objection would be simple vanity. I assure you I will return them to you myself, personally, after our business is concluded."

Jim reached into his pocket, flipping the phone shut as he handed it to Skrupshin along with his passport. "Vilatzer, See-ya-moos. No patronymic. No father, perhaps? A bastard?" He held his hand out to Katya without looking up. "Ah. You, I remember. Lisitsova, Katerina Georgovna. And your phones I shall keep here." He dropped them clattering to the ground and stomped them into smithereens. "I promised you could have them back. I made no guarantees as to their condition." The joke pleased him enough to raise a laugh and a nasty curl of his lip. He bowed, first to Vorov and then to Jim and Katya, and retreated back through the swinging door.

"I'm afraid Nikolai does like his theatricality." Vorov sighed. "I'm sorry about that. Please, if you would, let's come out of the hallway."

He led them down a narrow hallway off the right of the foyer, into a small, comfortable room furnished with a long wooden desk, a leather couch, two plush upholstered chairs, and cabinets of books along the walls. He ushered them into the chairs and took his place across from them behind his desk. "Please, sit down. Can I get you anything to drink? Water? Wine? Brandy? Don't tell me you've started drinking vodka, Jim." Vorov laughed and shook his head, kindly crinkles at the corners of his eyes.

"Nothing, thank you," Katya said icily, her hands balled into fists in her lap. "Where did you take my grandfather? When can I see him?"

"Take?" He looked hurt at the implication. "I did not *take* him anywhere. I am not in the business of *taking* people, ever. I promise you, any guests I am currently entertaining have all come completely voluntarily."

"So you admit he's here."

"I do."

"Is he here alone? Are there others with him?" Katya asked. Jim put a hand out to forestall that line of questioning: he thought they had agreed to take Lisitsov and go. Unless the cavalry showed up—and without his phone, at this late hour—that seemed unlikely, Jim wanted to keep things as simple as possible. Vorov, however, caught his gesture and noted it with a narrowing of his eyes, a filing-away expression.

"There are, certainly there are," Vorov said. "Again, I don't see why my houseguests are any of your concern."

"I want to see him," Katya said, her voice rising with fury.

"He's sleeping, I'm afraid. He is the oldest of my guests, and, as you well know, he likes his nights to end early. But, I'll tell you what: come this way. I'll introduce you to some of his friends."

He led them back down the hallway, and then through a kitchen, where six men—expressionless, dead-eyed, thick-necked, leather-jacketed: guards, obviously—sat playing *durak* at a round table. In one corner was a stove, recently used and strewn with pots. Carrot, celery, and onion detritus littered the counter, and a bottle of red wine stood open by the pot. Just behind the table were two sliding glass doors: the same kind that opened, in fact, from the tiny kitchen onto the postage-stamp yard at Jim's parents' house. The men nodded solemnly to Vorov as he passed, but their eyes followed Jim and Katya.

Through another swinging door they entered a long, low dining room, where three people—a man and two women—sat finishing a meal at a table far too long for them. They sat together in a far corner, as though huddling for warmth. When Vorov came in with his broad host's smile, they seemed to retreat slightly into their chairs, hooding their smiles and sharpening their eyes in fear.

"You see?" he said. "They're finishing their dinner; they are about to retire for an after-dinner drink, perhaps a bit of music. There are no guards here. There is no compulsion here. Just three friends enjoying my hospitality. Isn't that right? Svetlana? Matvei? Isn't that true?"

The three nodded in unison as though controlled by strings. Jim read fear and truculence, but Vorov was a far more skilled reader of people than he was, and, still smiling, he snapped his fingers and beckoned them back into the kitchen.

"I enjoy the company of intelligent, serious people," he said over his shoulder, as he gestured for them to sit down at a round wooden table in the corner of the room set with a bottle of Saint-Estèphe and a platter of smoked fish, black bread, and pickles. "I have a university post in California, you see, but here in Ukraine I prefer to cultivate a more in-formal salon. They are my guests for the week."

"And after this week they return home?" Jim asked.

Vorov just smiled and ambled over to the table with three wine-glasses. "Why don't you open the bottle, Mr. Vilatzer." He handed Jim a corkscrew. "And please: help yourselves if you're hungry. Nikolai," he called out. "Nikolai, would you come down here, please. Esteemed Lisitsov's granddaughter wishes to see him."

They entered the kitchen from one end as Skrupshin came in from the other. They hovered by the door, while Skrupshin stood by the table. The guards all had their eyes on Vorov. "Nikolai, could you: as we discussed earlier?"

"Of course."

From behind the house Jim heard two quick pops, followed by a burst of machine-gun fire. "What was that?" he asked.

Vorov, still serene, said, "I think your friends might have just met mine. I enjoy entertaining, Mr. Vilatzer, as you can see, but I prefer my guests invited."

"I don't . . ." Jim stammered. "What are you talking about?" Katya reached for his hand, and he squeezed back.

"Earlier, at the door I asked you if you were alone. You said you were. I believe you were not. Tell me, please: were you alone? Does anyone know you are here?"

"We came alone," Jim said. He tried to speak evenly, but he could hear and feel the terrified tremolo in his voice. "We came because we know you are a businessman, and we thought . . ."

Another bang, this one impossibly loud, made Jim jump and Katya scream. Skrupshin held a Makarov in front of him. It was still smoking. The card game was short a player: the guard closest to Skrupshin was slumped over the table, a sticky, baseball-sized maroon-and-gray concavity in the back of his head.

"That is what we do, Mr. Vilatzer, to spies. His cousin, Nikolai just discovered, is FSB. Who knows how much they know." Vorov's affability had gone, and in its place was a horrible, hard, acquisitive emptiness, a blankness without a bottom. "I saw two shadows duck into the forest when you entered. I will ask you one last time: who else knows you're here?"

"Okay," Jim pleaded. "Okay, okay." Skrupshin advanced toward him with the gun. "Before I came . . ."

Jim's answer was cut off by a loud crash and a riot of shouting as a horde of soldiers in balaclavas, blue uniforms, and OMON badges, their weapons raised, kicked in the back doors. As Skrupshin turned toward the door, the lead soldier—an enormous mountain of a man whose blond beard protruded, hedgehoglike, from beneath his mask—aimed a chunky plastic black-and-yellow gun at Skrupshin. When he pulled the trigger, instead of a bang there was a whistling, whiplike sound as a wire shot from the gun into Skrupshin. He fell over twitching as a wet spot spread across the front of his trousers.

Katya screamed, released Jim's hand, and disappeared through the dining room door. The three living guards dropped their cards and put their hands on their heads, but a group of soldiers started beating them with their gun butts until they collapsed to the floor, their hands still around their heads as the soldiers began kicking them where they writhed.

An immense soldier, with a beard that protruded past the bottom of his ski mask, caught Vorov in the gut with a knee, grabbing him as he fell. He had just turned his attention to Jim when a shrill "Don't move!" in English and in a woman's voice, stopped the room cold.

Mina stood in the doorway in Kevlar and a raised ski mask. She aimed a Glock toward Jim and the soldier. "This is a Russian operation!" the soldier shouted. "You have no jurisdiction."

Jim heard the gunshot, but only for the briefest moment. The bullet caught him in his forehead, just above the eye, and sent him reeling. A warm, wet, red cloud veiled his vision, and then nothing, nothing at all.

## 25

First it was undifferentiated, eye-stabbing white. Then the room went Rothko; brighter and darker whites bled into each other, surrounding the looming blobs. A few more seconds later the blobs started to thin out and take shape. Then words returned and the world clicked back into place: wall, window, arm, pain.

Now I am lying on a bed, Jim thought, in a white room with white curtains and a bare tree beckoning through the window with spindly fingers. Why did Bubby Millie put that tree there? Who sent the window through the fault-line center? Whose fault is it? The restaurant sounds empty; why am I lying on a table in the middle of the lunch rush?

Jim tried to get up to give his father a hand behind the counter, but he nearly threw up from the effort; instead he passed out for another two hours.

Jim's mother woke him up for school the way she always did: by standing over his bed and repeating his name at the same volume over and over until he finally heard. Except it wasn't his mother; it wasn't his bed; and when he finally shoved his mind through the ether-cotton, he realized he probably didn't have to go to school, either.

"Are you awake? Jim, can you hear me? Can he hear me? He looks a little green; is he all right?"

"He's fine. It's completely normal," another voice said. "Sometimes they feel a little sick when they wake up. It's the medicine for sleeping that takes a nasty bite, and he's been out for a few days now. But you've got a strong man here. He'll come round in no time."

Jim tried to ask what happened, but he emitted only a slight croak, and even that made him want to go back to sleep. He shut his eyes again, and felt someone shake him by the hand.

"Sir? Young man? Time to get up now, you hear? You hear me? I know you're hearing me. Darling, just move your head a little back and forth if you hear."

With great effort, Jim moved his head back and forth, knocking away some more clouds.

"There we go," said the voice, now happier and louder. "Maybe you'll just lift your head a bit for me?"

Jim opened his eyes, looked up at her, and, with great effort, said, "Mom?" This provoked a warm ripple of laughter from her: with her healthy round face, broad and beautiful smile, tight braids hanging down to her shoulder blades, a sunny Caribbean accent, and flawless skin the color of strong tea, she could not possibly have looked less like Jim's mother.

Still, she represented home just as surely as Rosie did: except for the occasional student, Jim had not seen a black person's face since moving to Moscow, and, of course, no Russian would ever consent to being cared for by a nurse of any ethnicity other than Russian. (Ukrainian in a pinch, but only if absolutely necessary.) West Indian nurses did not exist in Russia; he was being looked after by a West Indian nurse; therefore, he could not be in Russia.

Jim mustered up the effort to smile at her and tighten his grip, provoking a derisive nasal exhalation from the other side of his bed.

"At least we know you're back in action from the waist down." It was a woman's voice, tough and sharp.

He tried to turn toward the second voice, but first an IV cord and then a wall of pain in his head stopped him. He yelped, and the voice on the other side of the bed exhaled again, this time almost sympathetically.

"You'll be tender for a few days yet. I'll come over there. Nurse, would you give us a minute, please?"

The nurse nodded courteously and left. She was replaced, in Jim's field of vision, by a familiar-looking middle-aged white woman. She flipped on a wide, placating smile a moment too late; the expression didn't suit her at all.

"Trudy?"

"I'm glad to finally see you awake, Jim."

"Where am I?"

"You tell me," she said, reaching down by the side of Jim's bed for a control panel. "Stop me if this hurts."

She pressed a button and the bed whirred him into a semiupright, La-Z-Boy position. Of course it hurt; of course Jim said nothing. Trudy maneuvered the bed to give him a view out the window. He saw a park, the deciduous trees dead in winter, nothing but skeletons manning the rolling hills. A street separated the hospital from the park. It had four lanes, two in either direction. Cars—shiny new jelly bean cars in vibrant reds and blues rather than dusty silver and purple models—rolled obediently along in their appropriate lanes, motoring calmly rather than playing a Hobbesian game of chicken. Even from here, three stories up, he could see the traffic lights were black.

"It's Rock Creek Park," he croaked.

"Welcome home."

Jim tried to adjust his position without raising the bed. The pain wasn't as bad as the first time, but he heard a clanking sound from around his feet: a leg restraint bound him to the bed frame by his left ankle. "I guess I'm not quite home yet, am I? My folks haven't chained me to the bed since I was thirty."

The joke elicited a tight, appreciative smile and a curt nod. "Yes, well, we still have to clear up a couple of things. I didn't want you to leave before we had a chance to talk. Technically, I should have welcomed you to Walter Reed."

"Walter Reed? Don't I have to be in the army?"

"Not if we say you don't, you don't. We needed somewhere secure."

"A military hospital and leg irons for someone who can't even sit up?"

"It's for your own protection," Trudy said mechanically. Her face had an odd absence of expression and a chilly, owlish watchfulness. Jim could imagine her slipping a little something extra into his drip, not out of malice, but just to see what its effects would be. He didn't dislike her, really; he just felt uncomfortably at her mercy, somewhere between a prisoner and a specimen.

"Are you going to tell me what happened?"

"Well, yes. I am. You were shot in the head, and rather than risk treatment in a Russian hospital, we airlifted you back home."

"In the head? And I'm still . . ."

"Plastic bullet. A knockout round. It pierced the skin, and it left a nasty bruise, but that's it. You've been out for three days straight."

"Three days?" Jim asked incredulously. "How did that happen?"

"Notice your headache?"

Jim put a hand to his head. It wasn't so much an ache as a feeling that his head had been hollowed out and stuffed with Silly Putty.

"You were in a coma."

"For a bruise?" Jim asked dubiously. He felt more groggy than pained, and looking down at his body, saw just a bandage only around his shoulder.

"Pentobarbital. It was *our* coma. Officially, we didn't want to risk any nerve damage. Walter Reed has an excellent battlefield surgery unit. Unofficially, we didn't want to leave you to be examined by Russian military doctors. You're welcome."

"I've had surgery?"

"Not yet."

"So I'm going to?"

"Actually, Jim, that's the good news: the doctors don't think it's necessary. As I said, we just wanted to be sure. You have, however, been repatriated. Officially. And, for your own good, probably permanently."

Mina walked in with a floppy leather briefcase and the tense, apprehensive look of a healthy person during visiting hours: too-wide smile, worried eyes, clenched jaw.

"Jim," she gushed, with obvious relief, pulling up a chair next to Trudy, a little closer to Jim. "It's so good to see you. I'm really just . . ." She ran a soft hand down his face and kissed him on the forehead and choked back a sob.

"Mina?" Jim had never seen her this emotional before, about anything. "I'm fine. Have a seat: Trudy was just about to tell me why she induced a coma and chained me to a bed in a military hospital."

"Mina's not authorized to speak," Trudy said decisively. "Jim, before I tell you any of that, I'm going to have to ask you to sign this. It's just a formality, really: a confidentiality agreement."

Without taking her eyes off Jim, she held out her hand, and Mina gave her a sheaf of papers. After flipping through them, stopping twice to scrutinize—once on the third page and one on the next to last—she handed them and a pen to Jim. "Just initial at the bottom of each page and sign at the end, okay? Like I said, it's standard practice. Initial and signature."

Jim took the papers and started reading them, his eyes glazing over at the legalese, the *whereas*es and *hereby*s and "nothing shall be construed in any way other than as its original intent as set forth by the signer and witness."

Trudy cleared her throat. "Jim, I know you're convalescing here, but Mina and I are on a schedule, so if you could just initial and sign, that would be great. Just boilerplate stuff, really."

Jim bit his tongue to keep himself from lashing out at Trudy. That's the problem with smooth, glassy, powerfully backed façades: when you hit them, you end up hurting your own hand, and all it does is slide harmlessly down the target. Instead he turned to page three, found what he was looking for, then turned to the penultimate page and did the same. He tore them both out and handed the agreement back to Trudy.

She gave an acid smile and looked over Jim at Mina. "You can say you told me so, you know. I probably won't fire you for it."

Mina kept her hands in her pockets and didn't lift her gaze from the ground.

"Oh, go ahead already," Trudy sneered. "He's *your* problem. Tell him whatever he wants to know."

Mina pulled up a chair, a subtle triumph glowing in her eyes as she shot a look at Trudy. She tucked an invisible strand of hair behind her ears, and laid her gold cross on the outside of her white button-down shirt. She clasped and unclasped her hands. She was so determined not to look at her boss that all her attention drifted, despite herself, in that direction anyway. "Right. Okay. Right, well, I guess the first thing I have to ask you is who were the two men who accompanied you to Anatoly Vorov's residence?"

"Why?"

"Because one of them is dead, Jim. He didn't make it."

"Only one? I thought they were both shot."

"No."

"Vorov said—I remember this—Vorov said his friends met my friends. He said he saw them sneak into the bushes and shot them both."

"As with many things, Jim," said Trudy, "what Vorov said and what happened were two entirely different topics. His usual contingent of armed guards were dispatched to prevent a robbery. The only retinue left were at the table when Mina entered. Is that right?"

"It is," said Mina, cutting her eyes toward Jim with unease.

"But I heard two shots. Before you . . . I see. You mean you killed him."

"No, Jim. No. Not me. The Russian troops saw two armed men by the back door. They yelled for them to put their weapons down; one of them didn't, and, well . . ." Her voice trailed off. "He had a mustache, but no beard."

"Fadlan." As sad as he felt, he knew also that Fadlan went out as he would have wanted to: armed against Russian soldiers. How many people actually receive their chosen death? "His name was Fadlan."

"He shot at the soldiers, Jim. Even though there were more of them, and they gave him a chance to lay his weapon down, he kept shooting. The other one, the bearded one, he just shouted and kept his hands raised."

"Murat."

"And where is he?

Again, Mina fiddled with her hair. She smoothed an invisible crease out of her trousers and looked down. "Ah, well, Jim, to tell you the truth, we're not entirely sure. He wasn't the main objective for us, so . . ."

"So you let him be taken." Jim felt his color rise and the blood whoosh into his ears. He was angry enough that he ignored the wave of nausea that broke across him when he raised his head. "That's what you're telling me, isn't it?"

"I understand it must be hard for you," Mina said professionally.

"For me? Did you talk to his mother? Did anybody? Of course not. Unbelievable. I'm so glad I'm not you."

"Don't rant," said Trudy from the corner. "Don't you still have something to answer for?"

"Do I? And what's that?"

"Rodion Lisitsov."

"What about him?"

"We'd like to know where he is."

"How should I know? You didn't catch him and Katya at Vorov's house?"

Trudy grimaced and looked down at her shoes. With her eyebrows she signaled for Mina to speak. "Actually, Jim, we didn't. You see, we were technically adjuncts on this particular operation, just seconded as observers to the Russian operation because of the involvement of an American, and so we had no say in the setup. It was just the two of us, plus three unofficial friendlies. I don't remember seeing her with you in the house."

"No," said Jim, remembering that she had run away right when the shooting started. "You're right. I don't know why I thought she was there."

"You don't know?" said Trudy skeptically.

"I guess a friendly-fire bullet to the head does strange things to the memory, Trudy. What can I tell you?" She raised two hands, palms out, in surrender and he turned back to Mina.

"We came by helicopter when you called. We landed just outside of Zavodsk, where you came from, to prevent retreat, but the approach to Vorov's house was on foot, for reasons of secrecy."

"So *you* let him get away."

Trudy exhaled menacingly. "Everyone let him and no one let him, Jim. Neither we nor the Russians could bring the cavalry into a third country. They brought just enough troops to storm the house and bring everyone home; we brought just enough to sneak in afterward. Nobody thought of securing the area against possible escapees."

"What kind of resources do you think he has?" Jim asked.

"Well, we're monitoring his home and bank account. The mother was questioned; she hasn't heard from him. His granddaughter's also gone. You wouldn't know anything about her, right?"

"No. Nothing at all."

"There's been no activity on her bank account either."

"What about the mother?"

"She says she's paid in cash, Jim. The colonel's savings are in the government bank, and the granddaughter's are in TrustEconomBank. Nothing on either in the past five days. The mother said she hasn't heard from them. Katerina hasn't turned up at acting class. Who knows where they could be?"

"Well, how far can they get with just . . ." Jim trailed off, waiting to see whether they would finish the sentence.

"Not very, we don't think," said Trudy confidently. "But in a country that size 'not very' covers a lot of ground."

"But at least you got him away from Vorov."

"That we did, Jim, that we did. In fact, we got all four scientists away, thanks to you. We found them all in Vorov's house. Rodion Lisitsov, Matvei Yagachin, Svetlana Rybovna, and a fourth named Alla Dvorina. Two bioweapons engineers and two nuclear-weapon engineers. They said they were told they would be taken out of Russia and sent to work, but not killed. As long as they cooperated, of course. Their families were threatened if they balked."

"They told you this?"

"They did. And our friend Skrupshin was quite talkative as well." Trudy flipped over a page in her folder and held up a document with the Russian Interior Ministry seal on it. "Very eager to please, that one."

"Was?"

"He died in custody, unfortunately. After two straight days of questioning, apparently he killed himself by sticking his head between the bars of his cell and breaking his own neck."

"Determined," Jim said.

"Something like that, sure. The new Interior minister told the ambassador yesterday that Skrupshin ran a rogue unit of army personnel and policemen for personal profit. He and Anatoly Vorov had been working together since the early 1990s, smuggling everything that wasn't nailed down. Skrupshin, with his army connections, controlled the transportation through and out of Russia, by way of military installations not on Russian soil. Vorov picked up the goods—guns, cars, metals, or, in this case, people—at the bases and sold them. As a favorite of the former minister, Skrupshin was untouchable in Russia, and Vorov made himself equally so outside the country."

"How?"

"Bribery, usually. Transit points in Gymuri, Tiraspol, Sukhumi, and Kaliningrad aren't terribly secure. And once he got the scientists from there to Zavodsk, he could take them anywhere he wanted. There was a small airstrip and a speedboat dock behind his house."

"Why did . . ."

Trudy held up a hand. "Let me read you something. It's from the middle of the letter. 'The sudden death of Minister Khilov and interne-cine disputes within a criminal network disrupted the transportation pattern previously used by Mr. Vorov and Deputy Skrupshin. They were forced to seek the aid of an American espionage agent of Russian an-cestry, one Seamus Vilatzer, who was given cover by a nongovernmental organization.'"

"What?" Jim yelled. He bolted up; a white wall of pain pressed him back down into the bed. "I was never . . ."

"Take it easy, Jim. Let me finish. 'Retired army officers in the illegal employ of Deputy Skrupshin were given the names of certain scientists whom they were told to forcibly extricate from Russian soil with the illegally coerced or purchased assistance of current army officers acting out of venality or traitorousness. Mr. Vilatzer then passed this informa-tion on, encoded, to Mr. David Willow, his superior, who was in the employ of Anatoly Vorov. Deputy Skrupshin claimed that Mr. Vorov intended to hold the scientists at his residence in Zavodsk, Ukraine, until he received payment from all parties, which included a German national, a Saudi national, an agent of the Pakistani military, and an envoy believed to represent the North Korean government. The intent was to send proof of life to all parties to encourage a bidding war. When the desired price was reached, the scientists would be dispersed on pri-vate, heavily guarded sea or air transport. Essential to this plan was Mr. Vorov's certainty that his estate in Zavodsk was a safe haven. Mr. Skrupshin now believes, with good reason, that this certainty was unfounded, and that Mr. Vorov suffered from excessive confidence in his own safety.' Clear enough for you, Seamus?"

The pain in his head subsided from intolerable to extreme. "That's not right. That makes it sound like I was a participant. A willing par-ticipant."

"All you did was carry messages, right?"

"Listen, Jim," Mina interrupted, clasping her hands together and dropping her voice to Beltway professional level. "I want to say—and I think all of us want to say—how grateful we are to you."

"I *did* say it," muttered Trudy. "I *already* said it."

Jim just shook his head and looked away.

"What's the matter? You should be happy, I would have thought," Mina said. "I mean, your head notwithstanding."

"I got suckered. I got fooled. I was an errand boy for kidnappers and murderers."

"Do you feel worse about your actions, Jim, or your ego?" Trudy asked. "Worse because of what Vorov wanted to do or because of what you did? Now, if it's the former, then you know well enough you're not responsible for that. But if it's the latter, Jim, well, the truth is, we all get taken at one point or another. It's what seasons us. The question is how we come back from it. Do we sulk? Do we admire our opponents, align ourselves with them? Do we try to obtain a measure of revenge? Most people fall into one of those categories. You didn't. Your repentance more than erases your sins, Jim. You should have a clean conscience."

Her face had softened into something almost human. "You should also sign that form," she said quietly. "All of it. For your own good."

"Is that a threat?"

"Jim, no," Mina interrupted. "It's an offer."

"An offer?" Jim asked incredulously. He held up the two sheets he had torn out of the confidentiality agreement. "On this page, you have me admitting to espionage. 'Signatory Vilatzer did act on behalf of foreign agents who, in contravention of Russian law and American interests, did conspire to remove the aforementioned scientists from Russian territory, where they were known to American observers, and spirit them to points unknown for purposes unknown, but presumed to be nefarious.' I'm not signing that without your signed and notarized promise not to prosecute. And here, on this page," he said, holding up the other one, "it says 'Signatory Vilatzer agrees to hold no agent in the direct or indirect service of the American government responsible for his injury, or for any consequences arising thereof.' You really want me to sign this?"

"We do," said Trudy, her arms crossed in front of her, peering coolly at Jim.

"Mina?"

She couldn't meet his gaze. She stared at the floor, her shoes, out the window; the muscles at the base of her jaw worked and rippled as she ground her teeth. It takes a lot to completely beat the instincts out of a good and honest person. Though she had been trained well enough to shoot a friend, she still couldn't lie about it. Mina hung her head lower and emitted a wet sniffle.

"It was the only way to get you out," she whispered. "Please don't be upset." She looked up at Jim with fierce, imploring eyes, the tears setting them aswim like coals in rain. "It was the only thing I could do."

Jim let out a brief, mirthless laugh: he was just vain enough so the thrill of being right, of seeing an assumption confirmed, of playing a hand correctly, just began to compensate for hearing a friend admit to deliberately shooting him.

"She's right, for what it's worth," said Trudy, sitting back in her seat and watching the drama before her unfold. "If we hadn't taken you out of the country then, when they were still worried about Skrupshin, you would never have gotten out. Do you know why I'm holding this letter? Why they told me all of this? Because they want you back. You and Vorov both."

"Where's Vorov?"

"Believe it or not, at the moment he's in our embassy in Moscow. At least for now, he's an American citizen. We're trying to strip him, but that might take a while. He's also Russian, though, so someplace way above our heads, they're talking about whether to extradite him."

"Why wouldn't you?"

"Precedent."

"And me?" Jim asked nervously.

Trudy did not so much smile as somehow let a bit of warmth into her face. "Don't worry. Nobody's sending you anywhere. They don't really want you, anyway; they want Vorov, and they want to be sure that Lisitsov isn't in the States, and they need to be sure we're going to keep this quiet. They certainly don't want it happening again. Everybody just wants to get their story down first. Don't you understand that by now? We know and you know and they know there was a plot to smuggle scientists—Russian scientists, Soviet scientists—out of the country. It shouldn't have happened but it did. They were embarrassed. Now, the best of all possible ways to spin this, for the Russians, is an American plot they nipped in the bud. Organized by an American journalist— a Jewish-Catholic American journalist no less. They could direct popular anger at a couple of good old foes and crack down on the press even more in the aftermath. A distant second best would be a rogue Russian official in the pocket of foreigners. But for that they need a foreigner."

She cocked her head philosophically, and took a deep breath. "Or maybe they don't. Maybe there's always a foreigner to blame. Russians love an enemy; they love to feel besieged. Probably nobody would have cared. Anyway. Third best is silence: it never happened. Rumors might swirl, of course, but rumors are rumors and nothing more. And however they swirl, they can always be organized into a plausible story. American lies to embarrass Russia; European nervous Nellies condescend to Russia, or don't take them seriously; Chechen bandits who want to find more effective ways to carry out God's bloody will. I'd bet the house, the car keys, *and* the farm that we never even hear a peep from Vorov again. Too many friends, too embarrassing a prosecution. He had his Icarus moment; either they'll clip his wings or let him fall."

"And this form . . ."

Trudy inclined her head toward Mina. "Career insurance for your friend. In case you find yourself in a vindictive sort of mood."

Jim smiled, extending a hand as best he could toward Mina. She grabbed it gratefully in both of hers. "I'm disinclined to sue my friends," Jim said. "But I never turn down a gift, either: what did you mean by 'an offer'?"

Mina reached into her briefcase and pulled out a manila envelope with three thick packets of stapled paper. She handed them to Jim. "Predrag and Dragan Sjindic were arrested last night on state and federal gambling charges. This is the Maryland state troopers' report; this one is from the FBI. It was a joint raid. Their arrest meant they violated their visas. This third set of papers here is from the INS requesting expedited deportation."

"It means Mina made sure they'll be back in Belgrade by the end of the week," Trudy said. "That's what she meant by 'an offer.'"

"No, it isn't," said Mina. "This is done. Whether or not you sign, it's done."

"God," said Jim, handing the papers back. "If only I'd known it was that easy. Here I was, trying to get a job and pay down my debt, when all I really had to do was go to Russia, break up a smuggling ring, and get shot by the CIA."

Mina laughed with the relief of someone let off the hook.

"I just need one more thing," Jim said, taking advantage of their moods. Murat was too proud to ask for a favor, but Jim remembered that his toast to "the girls of California" had the undertone of a request to it. Besides, after what Fadlan did, Murat would never be safe over there anyway. He doubted the Russians would release him, but it was worth a shot anyway.

"The restaurant could use another body in the back." The thought of irrepressible, raucous, immense Murat sharing space with Jean-Yves—small, fastidious, in almost every way the opposite—brought a smile, a genuine I'm-finally-home smile, to his face. "We're short a dishwasher."

# 26

AND SO, NOT QUITE eight hours later, just in time for dinner, he found himself standing in front of the burgundy front door to his parents' modest, siding-sided Craftsman house. During the last decade's D.C. real estate boom, these had become "starter homes" for young families eager to give their children the best public education money could buy. They would stay for a few years, and then trade up to a more suburban suburb, one where they could be grander and more isolated, could see even less of their neighbors and spend more time in their cars, but feel just that much better about themselves every time they wrote their fashionable 20852 zip code on their return address.

Yet when Rosie and Sam bought the house almost thirty-five years ago, they had no thought of leaving: they had finally arrived. When they had their children, each could have his own room (and if, as happened, only one came along, they could have a library and a guest room, too); they had a patch of yard out front and a garden out back; they had their own garage and their own driveway and their own walkway leading to their own front door. Rose no longer had to live with three brothers and two sisters in three rooms above a bar and grill, perpetually slick and meaty with hamburger grease and ripe with beer vapors that floated up through the bathroom, so you stepped out of the shower smelling like the bottom of a pint glass. Sam didn't have to traverse a maze of fabric, cloth, half-made dresses, and piles of cleaning just to wait outside the bathroom in the middle of the night while his mother took her time, only to be rewarded with half a double bed and a fragrant view of his brother's feet.

For the rest of her life, whenever she told Jim and his cousins the story of their first night in the new house she would say, "At last, we'd live like Americans," and then proceed to recall that every creak and whisper terrified her, the house's empty space pressing in on her like an unwelcome harbinger of purgatory, and they ended up squeezed back in the Hamden apartment with the rest of the Dooleys for the next six days, until Sam finally and for the last time put his size 6 foot down. "He wanted someplace of his own," she'd say with a shrug. "Of *our* own," he'd correct. It was a polished routine; it was a happy marriage; and almost all of it had taken place within these walls and those of the restaurant not two miles away.

Jim put his bags (one satchel, and one cheap Chinese suitcase—bought at the chintziest of outdoor markets on the way, no doubt from Jim's apartment to the airport—that Mina had filled with as much as she could from his apartment) down to the side of the walkway—he didn't want to make his mother step over luggage when she gave him a frantic hug. As he leaned forward to knock on the door, he noticed a thin cardboard envelope propped against the house in the shadow of the eaves. It didn't look like it had been there for long—no water stains, no fraying of the brown paper wrapping—and his parents used the garage door: they wouldn't have even seen it. Jim picked it up, and saw that it was addressed to him. The blocky, unsteady lettering of the non-native writer of roman letters couldn't quite disguise the elegance of the writing. It was addressed only to "VILATZER SEAMUS, VILATZER HOME NOT RESTAURANT, WASHINGTON DC." Jim smiled: a few courier services had their regional sorting services behind the tracks at Twinbrook, and the restaurant always had done well with those employees.

It bulged slightly, and bore no return address, stamps, postage, or evidence of customs inspection; a sticker on the top bore the name "Zachistki International Courier Company, Bayonne, New Jersey."

Jim sat down on the stoop to open it. From beneath the door an evening at home wafted: the smells of frying onions, roasting meat, and cigar smoke; the faint sounds of his mother singing in the den as she folded laundry, and his father opening and closing cabinets in the kitchen. Home. He used his key to tear through the tape, then reached into the envelope. He felt nothing. He turned it upside down and shook it. A postcard fluttered down. The picture showed the tracks of a busy train station early in the morning, the sun rising over two long trains, whose blocky, military-green cars, black and red engine, odd aerial attachments hooking on to the wires over the tracks, and general look of sturdy implacability would have marked them as Russian even without the Cyrillic lettering on the front, without the identifying name—SLYUDYANKA STATION—printed on the border beneath the picture.

He turned the postcard over. In the bottom right corner was an outline map of Russia with a dot showing the position of Slyudyanka: on the southern tip of Lake Baikal, by the Mongolian border. In the opposite corner: his name, in ballpoint pen, swooping handwriting, and Cyrillic letters:

*Dzheem:*

*My grandfather the scientist believes that you are in superposition as I write these words: like Schrodinger's cat, you are neither alive nor dead, because I am not there to take your measure. But I know this is not true. I know you are alive. I know it. I do not know how, but I know it. Perhaps I think that by saying it over and over again, I can make it true.*

*It is a grave sin to depart from someone dear without saying good-bye, and I write hoping, believing, that you can forgive me for it. You see, my grandfather has lived like a prisoner for so many years. He is not jailed, of course, but neither is he free: always watched, always asked, always hounded. He retired and thought he would be free to do as he wished, go where he wished, but his old life has followed him like a shadow, and living always in someone else's eye—someone other than your beloved, of course—is no kind of life. In the confusion at Zavodsk, I saw my only chance to make him free. He has given everything to his country, his family, his work, and he has never asked for anything in return. He deserves to live what remains of his life on his own terms.*

*To tell you the truth, I never thought we would make it as far as we have. I thought we would be caught as we snuck through the woods behind Vorov's house, but the soldiers had more important prisoners to worry about. I expected we would be taken at the train station, then on the train itself, but Grandfather's Hero of War card melted doors before us. Not until we boarded a commuter train here at Slyudyanka and disappeared into the immeasurable space where the tracks give up that I finally realized we might have escaped.*

*I had an inkling something like this might happen—not an escape east, of course, but something world-changing—when Grandfather disappeared, so I have been traveling with all the money I have. It isn't much (to an American!), but it was enough to get us here.*

*But we will not be here for long. To many people—to you, perhaps, and also to us Siberia stands for cruelty, prison, exile, but in truth it has always offered another bargain: freedom in exchange for isolation. Siberia has always been Siberia, never quite Russia, and as I write this looking out the window at the black pines, white sky, and brown soil, I cannot quite decide if it is not of this world or if it is the world distilled. It will, anyway, allow us to live, and pray, and sing, and tell old tales, and laugh at gilded butterflies. I always did like Lear, but I think my days onstage have passed.*

*I am running out of space, but do not think of this as an ending. As surely as I feel you are alive, I feel sure I will see you once again. Until then, I hope you will think of me, too, in superposition, even as you know and feel that I am, in fact, not.*

He ran a finger delicately over the letters, feeling the slight impression, as close as he would ever come in this life to touching her again, and put the card in his pocket. She would be there for a day, maybe a week, and then disappear, like so many others, into Siberia's wild anonymity.

Siberia. In his mind an image flashed as though transmitted: thickets of birch and pine, dense, balsa-scented forests abutting a deep blue lake, tiny villages of wooden houses, smoke curling from their chimneys. Siberia has always offered freedom as much as exile, safety as much as punishment. Jim's grandparents went west for their new world; Katya headed east.

And Jim? As he thought about what he would say to her, to his parents, to Vivek—as he thought about translating experience from feeling and memory into language—he felt the images start to stiffen, go word-brittle and necrotic.

He looked around at the place he had so desperately wanted to flee, and he felt Moscow recede into his past, become swallowed up by everything that he had been and would be here. He refused to allow that. Life's sharp immediacy, the acceptance of risk as a necessary condition of existence rather than—per the American suburbs—as something to downplay or run from: these things he would keep with him here. He wasn't sure how, but he knew that returning home meant more than just sliding back into old patterns, old selves, old expectations. He was himself now, more than he had ever been before.

Jim stood up, brushed himself off, and tried the door. The handle moved smoothly: the Vilatzers were the last couple in suburbia to leave their doors unlocked. Before pushing the door open, Jim took a deep breath, partly to ready himself for the stories and the explanation, but mostly just inhaling the warmth, savor, and welcome of home.

## ACKNOWLEDGMENTS

I suppose anyone fortunate enough to know his grandparents feels they come from a vanished world, which of course is right. Time progresses. The world into which we are born is not the world in which we live; the world that formed people fifty or sixty years our senior must be all the more distant.

But I wonder if this feeling isn't accentuated for the children and grandchildren of immigrants. It isn't just the time but also the place that created our ancestors which vanished—often literally. Where today is the Soviet Union, the Austro-Hungarian Empire, Prussia? Hearing about tenement or shtetl life at a groaning dinner table in a safe, comfortable home in the American suburbs produces an odd feeling: a disconnect, an anomie driven by a combination of gratitude and guilt that can be defeated only by curiosity, which rescues everything and everyone.

This is all by way of saying that just as my protagonist found unexpectedly familiar echoes in Moscow, so did I.

My father's parents, though born in the United States, spoke Yiddish before they spoke English. With a feeling more intense than fondness and more sensual than reverie I remember their brown shag carpet; their kitchen with yellow flowers on its wallpaper and a permanent smell of roasting meat, garlic, dill, and bread; their patio with its multicolored concrete squares; and the faded crescent moon on their doorbell.

They rarely traveled except to see family, rarely ate out except at familiar restaurants, and lived (at least when I knew them) the routine, contented, grateful lives of survivors. It was not until I moved to Russia that I understood just how Russian a home they had.

My grandmother expanded her world through books: she was an English teacher with a particular fondness for English poetry, and could recite Tennyson and Browning as easily as she could swear under her breath in Yiddish. Pinpointing influences is a game best left to barflies, biographers, and blowhards, but there might be something there. Anyway, she was born Lillian Vilatzer. I gave Jim her name.

I plowed, skimmed, and pecked my way through dozens of books on Russia. Of particular help were *Gulag*, by Anne Applebaum; *Siberian Dawn*, by Jeffrey Tayler; *Voices from Chernobyl*, by Svetlana Alexievich and Keith Gessen; and *A Taste of Russia*, by Darra Goldstein.

I was lucky in my acquaintances in Moscow: I am grateful to Jeffrey Tayler and Tatiana Shchukina, and to Andrew Miller and Emma Bell, for their hospitality, warmth, insight, patience, and good humor.

I am also gifted with wonderful colleagues at *The Economist*. Robert Cottrell and Daniel Franklin rescued me from the depths of unemployment and penury. Emily Bobrow, Alex Travelli, Jessica Gallucci, Charlotte Howard, and Roger McShane made coming to work in New York a pleasure; Rachel Horwood, Robert Guest, Adrian Wooldridge, Zanny Minton-Beddoes, Stephen Stromberg, and Brendan Greeley do the same in Washington.

And I would also be remiss if I failed to thank my friend and former colleague Robert Schlesinger for first suggesting the notion—more than ten years ago—of a Jew named Seamus.

My portrait of embassy employees and spies is pure fiction: I met none of either breed in Moscow.

Along those same lines, my novel contains a disproportionate number of nefarious, scheming Russians. I hope it isn't necessary to say that's because it's a novel involving nefarious, scheming people who are also Russian. Ordinary makes bad copy. I trust that behind and beyond all of these obviously fictional characters, readers can see my deep love and respect for the city of Moscow, and for Russia's people, culture, and history (if not for its past or present government).

Rumors of the book editor's demise are greatly exaggerated: Liza Darnton, Randee Marullo, and Eamon Dolan worked wonders with this manuscript, and I'm very grateful for their patience, attention, and sage counsel. I could not hope to work with a better agent and person than Jim Rutman. It's no coincidence that my Russian American protagonist has the same ginned-up first name.

Finally, everyone knows that second-book syndrome is hard on the author, but spare a thought for the author's spouse, too. I just had to live with it; Alissa had to hear about it. She bore the brunt of my moodiness, grumpiness, and persistent doubts throughout this process, and showed more faith in me than I did in myself. On the morning I turned in this manuscript, I promised her three weeks without worries or complaints. I almost made it to lunch.